# A KISS BEYOND THE STARS

"By all the comets, Esme, I am sorry," Raul whispered, shaken. "I did not mean to hurt you. Never . . . never do I want to hurt you."

When Esme at last raised her tear-streaked eyes to look at the hard planes of Raul's face, she saw the obvious distress in his eyes, and got her first glimpse into his mind.

"I . . . I am all right now," she whispered.

Her direct look and the soft touch of her hand on his face tore at Raul's willpower. Though he silently cursed himself a fool for taking the risk, he couldn't help himself. Abruptly, he dipped his head and caught Esme's mouth with his own, intending to take just one chaste kiss to store in his memory.

But as he had feared would happen, the feel of Esme's mouth against his stoked the fire of desire inside him from a simmer to a flame, and he couldn't settle for just a taste of her. The next thing he knew, he was forcing her lips apart and hungrily thrusting his tongue deep inside her warm, sweet-scented cavity. And the more he tasted, the more he wanted.

Cover posed by professional models.

# Dreams of Destiny

## JACKIE CASTO

LEISURE BOOKS   NEW YORK CITY

# DEDICATION

To Holly, Jennifer, Julie, Kay, and Kim, the first readers, thank you for your faith in me and in this book.

To Kim, Howard, Rachel, Jennifer, Karen, Michael, Charlie, and Christina, thank you for your love.

To all who make up my family and friends, thank you for your care and support, in good times and bad.

And, of course, to Charles, who was a giver of many gifts (the best of which was his love) while he was here, and whose absence was the catalyst which spawned another gift, this book, thank you for you.

From and to the Holy Trinity. Amen.

A LEISURE BOOK ®

November 1990

Published by

Dorchester Publishing Co., Inc.
276 Fifth Avenue
New York, NY 10001

Copyright © 1990 by Jackie Casto

All rights reserved. No part of this book may be reproduced or transmitted in any form or by any electronic or mechanical means, including photocopying, recording, or by any information storage and retrieval system, without the written permission of the Publisher, except where permitted by law.

The name "Leisure Books" and the stylized "L" with design are trademarks of Dorchester Publishing Co., Inc.

Printed in the United States of America.

# Dreams of Destiny

# The Master's Prophecy

*T*HUS SAYS THE MASTER. THERE WILL COME A TIME when, because of your disregard for Me and My laws, your hatred of your brothers and sisters, and your misuse and abuse of the Homeland which I gave you, you shall suffer and die in great numbers, and many of you will damage your souls past my recovery.

In the days when your wickedness has reached its peak, the land will be made desolate from your predations, and where once there was plenty for all, there will be sustenance for none. Neither water, nor food, nor peace will you have. Having destroyed your own inheritance, you will then, out of hunger and terror and hardness of heart, turn upon and rend one another, each seeking at the expense of his brothers and sisters to obtain that which is already lost.

Then will I show mercy to those who have sought Me. Into that Valley upon the Homeland which I will keep protected and hidden for the time when it will be needed, will I send a Remnant of My People which I will save for Myself. Male and female, will every race I have created be drawn there, as will those of the lower creatures which My Remnant will need for survival. Their population will not overrun the Valley's resources and among My Remnant will I preserve peace and the knowledge of My truth. And unto the latter days, their awareness of Me and their love for Me and their obedience to Me, will not diminish.

Others will I save also, separate from My Remnant on the Homeland, and these will multiply, fluorish and prosper in the places I will send them. Yet these Others, as did their forefathers and mothers, will come to *follow the enemy. They will make war among themselves, threatening their own survival as well as all that I have given them.*

*Then will I once again show My love and mercy. I will send one of Mine to the scattered, and that one will forge a link which cannot be broken. My two Remnants will then come together—the one to teach My truth, the other to learn it and to protect it . . . against the day of My enemy's wrath.*

# CHAPTER ONE

In front of the entrance to his hillside cave, Malthuzar, high priest of the Remnant of the People, sat bundled against the spring chill before his fire, letting the flames ease the ache that plagued his old bones from dawn to dawn these days. Even in the short snatches of peaceful sleep between the disturbing dreams, it seemed the ache was there, a familiar counterpoint to his rest, a portent that Malthuzar would not live past the next winter's first snow.

Though his creased and veined lids covered his rheumy eyes, making him appear as if he dozed, Malthuzar was deep in thought. He had sent the young seeker who cared for Malthuzar's simple needs to fetch Bazil, and as he awaited the arrival of his protégé and successor, he wondered for perhaps the thousandth time if he were merely a senile old fool, or if something momentous was really going to happen soon.

But the only thing Malthuzar was certain of was that he could not delay any further in seeking an answer to why he had had portentous dreams this past cycle. Whether he would learn that he had been suffering delusions, or that the Prophesy might, in truth, be unfolding after all the centuries of waiting the People had endured, he did not know. But it was time to find out; the time for dreaming and wondering was past.

A deep sigh welled up from Malthuzar's wizened chest as he wished that he could safely leave this for the younger, physically stronger Bazil to handle. The thought of the long, strenuous climb to come made Malthuzar's legs tremble in anticipation. The thought of the biting cold at the top of the Holy Mountain sent an anticipatory shiver quavering through his thin body.

But, pity though it was, the strength of Bazil's body did not seem to be matched by a corresponding depth of character, spirituality, or wisdom for a task of this magnitude. In too many ways, Bazil was a disappointment to the old priest, and there were times when he actively regretted choosing Bazil to carry on the priesthood.

But what choice had there been in these increasingly heretic days when the Prophecy was fading from the minds of the Remnant? Now only a few candidates presented themselves for selection to the priesthood each seventh year. And the year he'd chosen Bazil, there had been only one other seeker, a female of tender years who hadn't come of her own will, but had been pushed forward by her birth mother, the woman

Esther, whom the People feared was a sorceress. Malthuzar had not thought so, but even he could not explain why Esther had been the only one of the People to have such glowing green eyes, nor how she had become with child.

Malthuzar sighed with weariness as he opened his eyes, stretched his palsied hands toward the fire and thought about that long-ago decision that had caused him such uneasy doubts at the time.

Had Esther's little Esme not been cursed with her mother's green eyes, had the child seemed more willing, and had Esther been willing to reveal the name of the child's father, or had the man stepped forward to claim little Esme as his own and thereby stilled the uneasy, nonsensical whispers of some unholy means of conception, then Malthuzar might have chosen Esme and faced down the stir of outrage at his breaking tradition and choosing a female over a male. He'd had the power in those days to make his will prevail. And there had certainly been something behind little Esme's glowing green eyes that hinted of gifts concealed.

But in the end, he'd chosen the easier path, and Bazil, under the guise of relieving an old man of his burdens, had been chipping away at Malthuzar's power and authority ever since the young protégé had completed his instruction and taken on the mantle of priest.

*But he cannot thwart me in the matter of my making a last pilgrimage*, Malthuzar thought with satisfaction, his ancient eyes gleaming with a vestige of the authority that had once been his in abundance.

"Peace to you, Honored Elder."

Startled out of his musings by the smooth voice of

the man in his thoughts, Malthuzar jerked his grizzled head up and peered across the flames at the upright, somewhat arrogant figure of his former student.

"Peace to you, Bazil," Malthuzar responded, lifting the fingers of one hand in an automatic gesture of blessing and invitation.

As Bazil glanced somewhat distastefully at the fraying mat where he would have to sit, then folded himself gracefully into a cross-legged postion upon it, Malthuzar noticed that the younger man was swathed in a new, fancifully decorated, colored robe.

No doubt the robe was a gift from one of the many women anxious to be chosen as mate to the prospective head of the People. Bazil had already made it clear he would not opt for celibacy as Malthuzar had. Indeed, Malthuzar had been troubled lately by rumors that Bazil might be indulging in sexual excess with various women. But the old priest had no proof, and he prayed the rumors were wrong.

"I am here at your command. Let me know your will and it shall be done."

Bazil spoke with his usual smooth courtesy, but Malthuzar thought he detected a hint of impatience in the younger man's tone. Did Bazil now consider himself above being at the beck and call of his mentor?

Yes, of course he did, the old man admitted to himself, and the truth of it had been evident for some time. Malthuzar simply had not had the energy to acknowledge or to challenge that tone when he had heard it before. He acknowledged it now, however, by summoning up a tone of his own—a tone that would brook no breach of the authority he still held.

"I must make a pilgrimage, my son," he said.

Bazil raised his dark, finely arched eyebrows. "*Must?*" he repeated with a hint of distaste in his tone. "Why? You have not been having visions, have you?" Now, there was not only a hint of distaste, but also of disbelief in his arrogant voice. "Or do you simply feel the need to perform the Supreme Duty one last time?"

Bazil's tone troubled Malthuzar deeply, but in obedience to a sudden inner warning a long lifetime of exercising power had taught him to heed, he hid his reaction. Also he decided not to acknowledge that he had indeed been experiencing visions.

"As you know," he dissembled, "poor health increasingly plagues me. I do not think I will be with you past another . . . few cycles. I think it would be wise to go now, while I am still able."

Finding himself misleading Bazil by stretching the time he had left troubled Malthuzar even more. Why was his trust in his protégé suddenly deteriorating to this extent?

Bazil's swarthy expression denoted concern. But Malthuzar doubted the sincerity of that expression, and this further indication that his trust in Bazil was on the wane alarmed him.

"But it is a long, hard journey, Elder," Bazil protested. "What if you do not make it back? The People need you here. Surely—"

"I will go, Bazil," Malthuzar interrupted. "Please do not waste your breath protesting. I shall leave by first light on the morrow."

Bazil's fathomless black eyes immediately sharpened to annoyance over the impatient authority in Malthuzar's voice.

And then it seemed to the old man as though the

annoyance departed in favor of a more calculating look. *Yes,* Malthuzar thought with sad cynicism. *Think about what it will mean for you if such an arduous journey proves to be too much for me, Bazil. You are obviously already impatient to wear my vestments and carry my staff and have the Sacred Pouch upon your belt. And if I do not return from the Holy Mountain, they will be yours all the sooner.*

But then the younger priest's black eyes reflected a new worry, and the old man became aware that Bazil faced another dilemma.

*But you do not want to follow a martyr, do you?* Malthuzar thought with impatient grimness. *Or have your reign subject to a possible revelation if I should come back with the news that I* have *had visions . . . visions that might hamper plans you have already made to change things when you have my power? I wonder.*

There was, of course, a way around both Bazil's concerns and though it nettled Malthuzar to employ it, he wanted no obstructions put in his path. Besides, if his visions were sound, rather than the result of an old priest's hallucinations, forces were going to be set in motion that no mere man, even one with Bazil's ambitious talent, could stop.

"It would be best, I think," Malthuzar said, his dusty voice drier than normal, "if the People do not learn of my departure until after I leave. Let them think I am merely going up to the high pastures to bless the spring foals and kids. Or tell them whatever you think best. I will leave the explanations to you, Bazil. But I must leave with the dawn."

Malthuzar saw the calculating look in Bazil's eyes change into one of relief, and then of feigned concern.

"Well, of course, your wishes are my command, Elder," he said piously. "But I am concerned for your welfare. Why not let Marcus accompany you?"

Bazil was well aware that no one other than a full-fledged priest was permitted on the hallowed slopes of the Holy Mountain, and as Malthuzar immediately reacted to the suggestion with an expression of burgeoning outrage, the younger priest hastened to soothe him.

"Of course, I know the final destination must be reached alone. I was merely suggesting that Marcus go along with you as far as the base of the mountain. You will need help managing a beast-burden, and he could build your night fires and take care of you."

But as it became clear to Malthuzar that Bazil's offer of a companion was merely an excuse to set a spy at his back, the old man straightened his posture and gathered around his frail body every last shred of his powerful aura. His sunken eyes glowed with a fire that had been long absent.

"Be silent, Bazil!" he ordered harshly. "I need no one for anything on a journey to meet my Master for the last time in this tangible form we call a body. I shall go alone. And now leave me! Go!"

Bazil, who had paled under the onslaught of Malthuzar's voice and manner, rose to his feet and hurried away without voicing another word.

As Malthuzar watched the younger priest scurry away, he felt a curious combination of emotions. There was satisfaction, of course, that he could still exercise the power that had made him the head of a people who were dismayingly close to losing the vision that had held them together for centuries past counting. And there was an infusion of energy and urgency into the old man's body and will that he knew would sustain him on the long journey he faced.

But there was also a sense of dismay at how far Malthuzar had let things slide, at how wrong he had been to select a man like Bazil to direct the path of a people who needed more in a leader, especially now, than a cynical, power-hungry priest who seemed to be skirting the edges of apostasy.

"Too late," Malthuzar muttered distractedly. "Oh, Master, what have I done? I have woken to Bazil's deficiencies too late!"

Unless—a comforting thought came to ease the high priest's fear and shame—the visions were true. In that case, Bazil's shortcomings would not matter.

And as Malthuzar turned his rheumy, sunken eyes up toward the Holy Mountain, he prayed that his pilgrimage would prove his magnificent, terrible, confusing visions true to the last jumbled scene allowed him.

In the high meadow, as the shadows of darkness closed in, Esme drew her cloak more tightly around her slim shoulders and arranged her furry burden more comfortably over her crossed bare legs.

As she gazed at the evening sky, she used one hand to stroke the tiny head of the orphaned lamkin she would protect against the predators of the night. With the other, she absently checked to make sure her sling and a sufficient supply of stones lay nearby.

The sling and stones were not necessary, of course. Esme's mind was her chief weapon and always had been. But in the unlikely event another shepherd should happen by her campsite, he would think it strange if she had no weapons to ward off the shaggy wolfhounds that preyed on the flocks.

Soon, without benefit of the flintstone she carried to use when other shepherds were around, she would spark the circle of branches she had set in a well-used depression in front of her into a night fire. But at the moment, Esme was not concerned with anything other than this magical hour when the sun had departed for its nightly rest, and the sky was ablaze with her familiar friends, the evening stars.

One day, according to her dreams, she would be in a strange contraption which she could not name nor clearly describe, in the company of strangers whom she could not identify, and she would sail close to those friends. But she knew not how it was all to come about. When she dreamed, everything was clear. When she awoke, however, the clarity dispersed like the smoke of the fire she would soon kindle.

But while the details of the adventure that awaited her had always been hazy during her waking hours, Esme had never doubted the truth underlying her dreams. From the moment she had lain in her mother's arms, newly born to the People, and watched with eyes and mind more aware than an infant's should have been as the old priest, Malthuzar, had blessed her, Esme had known that her destiny encompassed much that was presently unexplainable, and more than a life among the People. And she had known as well to conceal her thoughts and her unusual gifts, less she be stoned as a sorceress or trapped in the role of priestess.

Esme's mother, Esther, had understood very little. She had been bewildered by the dream that had come upon her one night there on the high meadow, where a man who was not of the People had come to her and left her pregnant with the child, Esme. But Esther had suspected enough to defy, once, the hold Esme kept over her mother's mind. But after that incident, when Malthuzar had denied Esme a place as a seeker, Esther had had to accept her role as outcast and her daughter's future as a lowly shepherdess who would also be shunned by the People.

The bitter loneliness had destroyed Esther. Denied all companionship other than that of her daughter because of the People's fear concerning the mystery of Esme's birth, she had wasted away, and was now enjoying in the spirit more than had been denied her in life.

Esme took comfort from knowing her mother was at peace. And she was also at peace, knowing she would not always be lonely. Whether her future would be easy or hard, she was not sure. But she knew the adventure would be worth any pain that accompanied it, and that her gifts were tools to be used in the fulfillment of her destiny. And lately, she had begun to sense that her destiny was not far off.

"Hallooooo . . . is anyone near?"

Esme started at the familiar call of another shepherd. Hastily, she cast with her mind and discovered the young man was not yet over the crest of the hill, so there was time to light the fire the easy way.

An instant later, the logs were blazing with light and warmth and when young Maza appeared inside the circle of the fire, grinning with anticipation of trying again for the sort of companionship Esme had as yet denied him, Esme smiled at him in welcome.

"Peace to you, Maza," she said. "Sit yourself down and tell me of your fortune this spring. Did your ewes bear well?"

## DREAMS OF DESTINY

Maza promptly squatted as close to Esme as he could without falling in her lap.

"They bore well," he acknowledged cheerfully. "As you would," he added, his dark eyes warm with desire, "if you would ever once let me explore what you have beneath that concealing cloak."

Esme's smile did not falter, but she shrugged her shoulders and casually waved Maza to sit farther away.

"You know well what is under this cloak," she mocked him solemnly. "You have spied on me often enough while I have been at my bathing to know every scar and mole I own."

Maza laughed good-naturedly as he moved to sit beside her. "Do you have scars and moles?" he teased. "If so, I have never spotted them."

"Then perhaps your eyesight is faulty," Esme said, though in truth, she had no moles nor any distinguishing marks on her body. But she knew it would intrigue Maza to think he had missed something during his intent examinations of her, which she had felt from time to time during her ablutions.

Maza's widened his eyes innocently as he inspected her from the top of her head to her sandaled feet. "Show me these beauty marks, then."

"I cannot, Maza," Esme said with an undertone of sobriety beneath her lightly teasing note. "You, nor any other man of the People, will ever see them."

Maza immediately sobered and his fingers were gentle as he touched her cheek and turned head to stare into her green eyes, his own loving.

"This man would long since have taken you proudly as mate, and be damned to the opinion of the People," he said sincerely. "Only say the word, Esme, and you will have my protection from this day forward."

Esme gazed at him with warm affection, and covered his large hand with her own smaller one. Maza, of course, was unaware that she needed no man's protection. Nor did she think she needed any man's love or lust, though once or twice there had been someone in her dreams, someone she could never recall upon waking.

But she was not impervious to love when it was offered, which was a noteworthy experience in her lonely life, nor was she immune to the feeling of gratitude. Maza's offer was exceedingly generous when, had she accepted it, his happiness for the rest of his life would have to come from whatever pleasure he found in their union. For the People would ostracize him should he join his fate with hers.

"If I were supposed to mate with any man of *our* People, Maza," she said gently, "I would accept you. But my fate does not lie here. It will take me in another direction."

She should not have spoken so honestly to him, nor could she say more in explanation, but he deserved what commiseration she could give.

Maza looked downcast, then impatient. "And what direction is that?" he demanded in exasperation. "Who else is there but the People? Where else is there but the Settlement? Yes, the Prophecy indicates there may be others, but where are they? This generation of the Remnant will likely die without the Prophecy unfolding as all the other generations have done. And since that is true, who other than me will give you companionship and love? Do you wish always to be alone? Do you not need anything or anyone other than yourself?"

## DREAMS OF DESTINY

Since Maza's mind was open to her, Esme felt the frustration roiling within him. And for a moment, out of empathy for his pain, she considered allowing him to ease that frustration with her body, if not her future. But an old prohibition, the source of which was not clear, but merely accepted by her, kept her from taking such a step.

Nor did she think it wise to make any further explanation to him, to tell him that one day, he would come looking for her and find her gone. She did not know herself the exact day she would start her adventure, nor the exact path she would take. She merely knew that her destiny seemed to be coming closer.

Since there was nothing she could say, she merely pulled her hand from Maza's grip and stared into the fire, beginning silently to use her mind to ease Maza's frustration.

But then a wolfhound's bay cut the silence of the night and Maza's head jerked up, his thoughts shifting to the protection of the flock.

Esme searched with her mind. "There is only one," she said softly.

Maza darted an impatient glance in her direction. "There is never only one," he disputed as he got to his feet. "Have you your sling?"

Esme sighed. The wolfhound was a young female with a pup, desperate for food, and if Maza had not been there, she would have let it have one of the older ewes who would not last past the next winter anyway.

"I have it," she acknowledged.

"Well, keep it at the ready," he instructed tersely as he set a stone in the one he'd plucked from his belt. "And get that lamkin off your lap. How do you expect to withstand a rush sitting down and handicapped?"

**17**

*There will be no rush*, Esme thought, impatient.

Nevertheless, she went through the motions Maza expected of her. Putting the lamkin aside, she gathered up her sling and a handful of stones. Standing, she charted the wolfhound's course with her mind as it circled the herd, nervously milling around outside the light of the fire.

Maza moved to the other side of the fire and searched the night with his eyes, hoping to spot a tell tale gleam of red reflected from the firelight in the predators' eyes.

Suddenly, Esme was tired of the pantomime. She'd walked a far distance that day and was ready for sleep. The idea of maintaining a long watch for a rush she knew would not come did not appeal to her at all. Nor did the idea of spending the rest of the night monitoring Maza's mind to ease his frustration appeal to her.

Silently, she sent a message to the circling wolfhound, showing the predator where the carcass of a ewe that had died of natural causes was lodged between two boulders a long distance away.

The wolfhound immediately loped away, but Esme stopped it after a few moments and suggested it express its thanks.

Obligingly, an eerie baying sound split the night, but since the sound was obviously farther away than it had been before, Maza relaxed slightly.

"It is leaving," he said in a puzzled tone.

"I would not be too sure," Esme replied, forcing a note of cautious anxiety into her tone. "Perhaps you should track it for a while." And gently, though it was not accepted practice to leave a fire and track a predator in the dark, she pushed the idea into Maza's mind and let it take root alongside his reluctance to

## DREAMS OF DESTINY

display any cowardice in front of her.

"I guess I could," he nodded reluctantly. "But keep at the ready, Esme. You were right. It seems to be alone. But if it is not . . ."

He left the rest unsaid, and Esme obligingly nodded her understanding. But two minutes after Maza had slipped away into the darkness, she had dropped back to the ground, set her sling aside, and positioned the lamkin on her lap again.

Leaning back against a boulder, Esme closed her eyes and composed her mind for sleep, hoping that she would for once be fortunate enough to remember her dreams clearly upon waking. But even if her dreams, as usual, departed like smoke with the morning's dawn, she was eager to begin them this night. For her sense of something momentous waiting just over the horizon was becoming stronger with each passing day, and her impatience for her destiny to begin was rising in exact proportion.

# CHAPTER TWO

"FIRE, YOU SONS OF SAINTS, FIRE!"

As though the roar of their captain's voice was a tangible force, the hands of the two young gunners reacted, convulsing on the firing levers of their weapon computers. Twin blazes of deadly light caught the warship heading straight for them on a suicide run in a pincer of devastation, exploding the ship before it could ram the Condor.

There was no time for either relief or congratulations, however. Again, the captain's voice bounced off the walls of the command cabin like thunder. "Hard to port, Pilot! Gunners, align your weapons and fire at will!"

The thundering voice ceased abruptly as the two young gunners, caught in the frenzy of the battle now, let off simultaneous bursts at the new threat that came into their sights.

As the fight continued, and the Rebels kept throwing ships they could ill afford to lose at his small command, Raul discerned a pattern that made the blue of his eyes turn icy. He was certain they were after him and the Condor specifically. There was no mistaking it. They were ducking his fighter escort more than engaging it, trying to get inside to blast his command ship out of space.

The question was why. Did they know he was in command of this bucket, which was not his regular, readily identifiable ship, the Talon? If they did, it would explain the pattern of the attack, which was completely contrary to their usual style. Considering the amount of damage he'd inflicted on the Rebels so far in their war against the established order of the Empire, killing him would be worth losing a full complement of their fighting ships.

Or did they think he still had the pipsqueak heir on board and wanted to wipe out the high counselor's successor while they had the chance? If that were the case, damned if Raul could understand their reasoning. The boy was so inept as a leader, and especially as a fighter, that the Rebels' cause would be better served waiting for the elderly High Counselor to die and the son to take over than it would be killing the little prig.

Whoever the target was—himself or the heir—there had to have been a leak in very high places or this attack couldn't have been possible. No one other than the High Council had known that Raul had been taken away from his normal battle duties to escort the High Counselor's son to visit his mother on her home planet.

But Raul would deal with finding out who had carelessly talked, or deliberately turned traitor, later.

Right now, if he didn't do something quickly, the Rebels were going to accomplish their obvious goal and blast the Condor out of space.

He waited impatiently for a breathing space, and when it came, he closed the fingers of one huge hand on the collar of the less experienced of the two gunners, jerked him out of his chair, and tossed him aside as easily as though he were throwing a pair of jadene dice in a game of Skol. Then he settled in the gunner's chair and commenced with a cold, relentless eye and a steady hand to reduce the enemy's threat threefold in as many minutes.

It took awhile, and all of the Condor's fighter escort squadron had been destroyed, but finally there were only two Rebel fighters left, and realizing they could not accomplish their goal, they scuttled away with beams of deadly fire from the Condor's weapons systems chasing their tails.

To the accompaniment of cheers from his men, Raul, with a tight, wolfish smile of victory on his rugged face, was lifting himself to his feet when he found out how wrong he'd been in thinking the danger was past.

A slamming shudder traveled through the Condor, knocking Raul back into the chair and then half out of it again, and the damage-alert sirens were screaming in his ear as he hauled himself back into firing position.

But there was nothing to fire at. No enemy ship showed on the weapons panel screen and yet two seconds later, the Condor took another hit.

Even as his ship was still shuddering around him, Raul roared an order only a seasoned war veteran with a well-deserved reputation for courage would have had the guts to issue without fear of being termed a deserter and a coward. But his battle instincts, honed over two-thirds of his life, were telling him to get out of there and fast!

"Jump, Paulo! Now, now, now!"

Raul's pilot, Paulo, had served with Raul long enough to act without even pausing to think, and an instant after his hand had brushed the hyperspace directional control to an unknown bearing, the ship was shuddering into a jump.

For a long, gut-wrenching moment, Raul thought the damage the ship had suffered and the stress of bolting into hyperspace were going to tear the Condor apart, and he and all his crew were going to die an ignominious death, fleeing rather than fighting.

But the metal held, and when the ship dove into clear space again, Paulo thanked his personal ancestral saint for their not landing smack in the middle of a planet or a star. He cut the engines so fast that he knew that if this had been a war game rather than the real thing, he'd have won the pilot's medal hands down.

For a long, tense moment, no one in the ship's command cabin spoke. Then Raul's voice, as soft now as it had been a roaring burst of thunder earlier, filled the silence. "Well done, Paulo."

Paulo's swarthy face split into a relieved grin as he swiveled his head to face his captain. "Aye, and I'll say the same to you, Captain."

Raul smiled sardonically. "We'll see if the admiral feels that way when we get back home."

Rising to his feet, he paced to the navigator's module. "Where are we, Sam'l?" he inquired, his tone calm.

## DREAMS OF DESTINY

Sam'l, his young, intelligent eyes holding a worried expression, shot his captain a rueful look. "I don't know yet, Captain," he admitted. "I think the guidance system is damaged. Give me a minute."

Raul nodded and reached for the communications button. When his engineer answered, he spoke as quietly and calmly as he had to the navigator.

"I want an estimate on damages ASAP, Jase."

"Coming up, Captain," Jase replied in a troubled voice.

Raul's face showed no emotion as he released the button and then turned to face the men in the command cabin. The young gunner he'd relieved of duty was still sitting on the deck, his face in his hands.

Raul crossed to him, squatted beside him, and with a gentleness a mother might have shown to a newborn babe, spoke softly. "No shame to you, son. The situation just called for a little more experienced hand on the trigger. You'll be fine next time."

Slowly, the young man moved his hands from his eyes and looked up, a doubtful, still fearful expression on his unlined face. The fear and doubt began to disappear, however, as Raul, pretending he didn't notice the trace of tears in the lad's eyes, slapped the fellow on the back before getting to his feet to look around the cabin.

Everyone was busy at their various tasks and Raul left them to their jobs and went to check with Jase about the ship's damage.

An hour later, grim-faced, Jase gave his report to Raul, who showed no visible concern over the news, though it was very bad.

"There's no way I can fix the Condor without setting down on land, Captain. The damage is too extensive even to make another jump, so we'll have to find someplace in this solar system where we can repair the ship, or we'll never get home again."

Raul, as if there were no question of their getting home, nodded. "I guess we'd better start looking for an oxygen-atmosphere planet then. First priority is getting the navigational system back on line, Jase. We have to have that before we can find our way to whatever planet in this little corner of the universe might meet our needs."

It took two days of drifting-engineless, in order to save stress on the hull before Jase got the navigational computer fixed. Shortly thereafter, Sam'l announced, in a tone of noticeable relief, that he had found a planet that would support life, and with a judicious use of the engines, they could reach it in approximately two months.

After that, Raul occupied himself in the time-honored fashion of all captains who had the morale of a crew of combatants to consider. Every reachable surface of the ship was cleaned and polished. And his men hadn't trained as hard in simulated battles in war school as they did on their limping journey to a planet they immediately dubbed Hell.

Esme strode with unflagging energy at the head of her straggling flock of ewes, rams, and lamkins toward a pasture where she would find the sweet grass and even sweeter water the animals craved. She topped a hill and paused to survey the gently undulating land before her and the mountains surrounding the whole valley.

It was getting toward evening, and the towering spire of the Holy Mountain was swathed in purple shadows. The snow-clad peaks of the Sheltering Mountains to the north sparkled in a few last rays of sunlight, and the flaming red crags of the Barrier Mountains to the west and the south looked as deadly and lifeless as the desert they barred from entering the Valley of the People.

As Esme stared at the Master's mountain, which was taboo for all but the high priest and his minions to step upon, something made her kneel down and direct her mind toward its base. As her mind soared closer, she saw a tiny shadow, limned by the dying rays of the son, heading upwards, but Esme could not yet tell who or what had the audacity to venture on those hallowed slopes.

Probably it was just an antlop. But normally, even the wild creatures stayed away from that particular mountain, though its slopes were carpeted with a succulent form of vegetation not to be found elsewhere.

And then Esme caught a glimpse of another shadow, well behind the first one, and her curiosity was aroused, so that she sped her mind faster and focused it on the scene before her.

As was usual for her in this sort of endeavor, she felt a soaring sensation of flight, as though her mind and spirit had left her body, and then came a gentle suspension in the air over the target of her search. But when she knew whom she'd found, her spirit almost returned with a whomping thud right back into her body. Her will tightened, however, and she forced herself to stay and watch the hunched, shambling figure of Malthuzar as he made his way upwards, tugging the rein of a lightly laden beast-burden behind him.

Esme respected and revered Malthuzar. A lesser priest, one like Bazil, might not have blessed her birth. There had been mutterings enough over Malthuzar's generous benediction to have daunted a priest less sure of his power. But Malthuzar hadn't hesitated, and as a result of that blessing by a priest respected for his purity, Esme had had an easier life among the People. She had been permitted the normal schooling, for instance, if not the normal companionship of other children. Yet everyone had been relieved when she had chosen the life of a shepherdess and was no longer constantly in their midst.

But Esme also feared Malthuzar because the old priest was the only one among the People, besides Esther, of course, who had even half-suspected the truth concerning Esme's mental powers. When Esther had forced Esme to come forward as a seeker for the priesthood, it had taken all of Esme's skill, not so fully developed at the time, to keep Malthuzar from choosing her over Bazil and from knowing why he'd gone against his spiritual instincts in making that choice. While accomplishing this feat, Esme had become aware of the purity of Malthuzar's mind and spirit, and she felt a respectful affection for him, a drawing of her spirit to his.

In her loneliest times, had Esme not feared Malthuzar's spiritual powers, she would have welcomed his friendship and companionship and instruction. But acting upon a strong inner prohibition not to reveal her gifts to anyone, even Malthuzar, she had avoided him. The risk was too great that with close contact, he might become aware of what she could do with her mind, and would have quite naturally pressured her into becoming a priestess. But the

## DREAMS OF DESTINY

priesthood was not where her destiny lay, of that Esme had always been absolutely certain.

Why was Malthuzar visiting the Holy Mountain? she now wondered. And then, as she took note of his withered, weakened body, she knew. He was dying and this was his final pilgrimage. Soon, the People would be left to Bazil's cynical maneuverings, and that false priest would do no one any good—no one but himself, of course.

The thought of Bazil brought a reflexive shudder of revulsion to Esme's spirit. Bazil had hated her and feared her since the time they'd both been candidates for seeker. There was nothing spiritual about him so he had not been alerted to her real power. He'd been simply resentful that she'd had the audacity to present herself as his equal, and jealous that Malthuzar had taken so long considering his choice. And later, when Bazil had grown old enough to taste the delights of his own sensual nature, he'd desired Esme in a lustful, controlling way.

Had Esme given in to Bazil perhaps his resentment would have lessened but she had rejected him, and her rejection had fueled his hatred.

Because of that, Esme knew, as surely as she knew every ripple in the topography of the high pasture, that with Malthuzar's death, her position among the People would become intolerable. If she did not submit to Bazil, he would make it so. And since she had no intention of doing that, her future, should her adventure be delayed much longer, would become hazardous indeed.

But now her mind's eye was filled with compassionate affection as she watched Malthuzar struggle on his way, and she gently sent a soothing touch to his aching joints and muscles.

Immediately, Malthuzar straightened his stooped back, and his step was lighter, more energetic.

Esme started to withdraw to return to her body when Malthuzar paused, stiffened, then looked over his shoulder up into the air where Esme's mind hovered.

Esme felt the contact of his powerful spirit like a bolt of lightning sizzling through the air, and for an instant, she was seized with a sense of panic that threatened to send her scurrying for safety. But she stopped the reaction cold and forced herself to withdraw in a gentle, soothing departure that would leave Malthuzar wondering whether he'd really felt what he thought he had.

She was returning to her body when she remembered the other shadow she'd seen, the one following Malthuzar, and instantly, she veered and swept upon the figure tracing Malthuzar's steps.

Figuratively, her lip curled as she discovered whom she'd found—Marcus, one of Bazil's minions and a fitting one for a man like Bazil. There was no danger of this one sensing her presence. His spirit was too small and shriveled to sense anything other than its own greedy desires.

Esme wondered why Marcus was following Malthuzar for he could not be a threat to the old priest. It was not possible for any one of the People, even one as deficient in character as Marcus, to wish their revered spiritual leader harm.

Therefore, Esme returned to her body. Since it was almost dark, she quickly gathered her straying flock into a tightly knit unit that would move as one to the edge of the bubbling creek where both shepherdess and flock could ease their thirst and spend a peaceful night in harmony around a roaring fire.

By noon of the next day, Malthuzar arrived, panting and trembling with exhaustion, near the summit of the Holy Mountain. Hauling himself onto the Sacred Ledge, he lay sprawled for some time before he drew himself upright and began the ritual which would either prove or disprove his visions.

As the fierce, chilling wind whipped around him, Malthuzar carefully, with infinite reverence, withdrew from the Sacred Pouch at his belt the first of the Sacred Implements.

The ancient Feather, symbolizing the frailty of man's life, its yellow and scarlet flecks on a background of white as brilliant as when it had been gathered centuries before, was placed in a crevice in the rock to his right. The fearsome wind should have torn it from its lodgings but instead, the Feather merely fluttered gently.

The centuries-old Sacred White Candle, symbolizing the only light that mattered, and which never burned down, was placed in another crevice directly in front of Malthuzar. He did not spark its wick with the Sacred Flint. Instead, he placed a tiny clay bowl beside it, which, from a sheepskin pouch, he filled with a few drops of the Water of Life which he had drawn from the Sacred Stream at the base of the mountain and had blessed.

Last, he sprinkled the Holy Powder, which permitted man's mind to obtain access to that of the Master's, into the water.

Then, composing himself into the proper frame of mind, he began the preliminary prayers, which would put him into the state he must obtain before going on to the most important part of the ceremony.

The prayers lasted until dusk, and when Malthuzar's voice was silenced, so too did the wind cease to howl. Encapsulated in an island of both inner and outer peace, Malthuzar opened his eyes, feeling refreshed and ready rather than fatigued or cramped by the position he'd maintained for hours. Indeed, his body, as well as his mind, felt so young and strong and eager, Malthuzar felt he could scramble up the ladder to heaven itself, should the Master care to extend it down for the benefit of his servant.

With the Sacred Flint, he lit the Sacred Candle, which burned bright and strong, its flame providing all the warmth and light Malthuzar could need. Then, after murmuring a prayer that if his spirit was impure then the Sacred Drink would kill him, Malthuzar lifted the bowl of holy water to his lips, careful not to spill a drop, and drained the contents.

Finally, composed and relaxed, Malthuzar sat cross-legged, his eyes fixed intently on the candle flame, and waited.

Gradually, any awareness of his body faded, and as the candle's light grew brighter and brighter in his mind, Malthuzar became all spirit, totally submissive to whatever the Master might reveal.

And what the Master revealed, at last, was far more astounding than Malthuzar's cloudy visions had promised.

"We're about to hit the atmosphere, Captain. Better strap down."

Raul grunted to his pilot and complied, careful not

to reveal by the slightest flicker of expression any doubt that the ship would not withstand the pressure and heat of descent. He always had to display a confidence that would strengthen his men's. And though some in the cabin closed their eyes to pray, he did not. He was not a man who believed in the divinity of the saints and was therefore not in the habit of praying. Instead, as the ship began to buck and heat, he focused the strength of his entire will on holding its fragile shell together.

When the ship was safely down on the sands of a limitless desert, he did not display his considerable relief that they'd actually made it. Instead, he strode purposefully down the ramp to inspect the one small oasis they were fortunate to have found upon a seemingly barren planet. Satisfied that the oasis contained a sufficient supply of potable water to facilitate repairs on the Condor, he spoke to his second-in-command in a calm, emotionless voice.

"All right," he said. "Get the men out and let them have some slack time before we start them on their new careers as mechanical mules. They've done well. They deserve it."

Nodding, the officer strode away while Raul tilted his head back and looked at the brilliant stars in the sky.

"Well, you're a sight prettier at night than I suspect you are in the daytime," he softly addressed his temporary new home. "But I wish, by all the comets that fly, that I knew where we rest in space. Because unless we find out, we can repair the Condor to a state like new, but it won't take us where we need to go."

Shrugging fatalistically, he began to peel off his

plain bodysuit with only the captain's insignia on the breast to show his rank. He wanted to swim off the sweat of his earlier anxiety in the glistening pool of water that called to his body every bit as strongly as his duty to his men and the Empire called to his mind.

In the spirit, Malthuzar watched as a flaming pinpoint of light descended through the heavens and disappeared behind the Barrier Mountains to the west. It looked like a falling star. But Malthuzar knew it was not. It was the beginning of the Prophecy's fulfillment.

Before the Remnant of the People would experience the fullness of the Prophecy, however, Malthuzar knew he would be long dead, and Esme, whom he was somehow not surprised to discover figured prominently in the fulfillment of the Prophecy, would have traveled long distances and experienced many things, and then would have returned home.

Malthuzar knew the past in fuller measure now than he had before, and he also knew the future and he was content with his knowledge.

Then suddenly, whether in the spirit or body he knew not, nor did he worry over it, Malthuzar felt himself being turned and propelled through the supposedly blank rock face behind him, into a place which contained something alien to the world he knew and had always known, but which he gazed upon without perplexity.

The treasure sat, squat and black, in the center of the crest of the Holy Mountain, its eons of activity stilled now.

And Malthuzar, gazing down at it from a railed

## DREAMS OF DESTINY

platform circling the cavern, thanked the Master for the protection of physical isolation it had given his People. The isolation had permitted their spiritual purity to remain undisturbed and uncorrupted from the Master's other Remnant those of the People who left the Homeland to live on other planets and who no longer followed the Master's way. The isolation had also separated them for when they would teach the separate Remnant the Master's way and would need that Remnant's greater numbers and sophisticated technology for physical protection. And then the Prophecy would have come to pass.

This deceptively simple-looking machine, constructed and placed here by those who had served the Master centuries ago, without knowing the reason for their act of service, had kept the truth safe.

Malthuzar did not wonder how the machine had known to turn itself off so that the visitors he had watched arrive that night could land. He simply accepted that all that had happened had been planned. And he also accepted that one day, when the time was right, the treasure would serve another purpose.

Turning once more, Malthuzar found himself back on the Sacred Ledge and still in the spirit, he gazed again at the Sacred Candle's flame. It gleamed just long enough for him to gather the other Sacred Implements and place them back in the Sacred Pouch. Then the flame puffed out as he reached for it, and the wick was cold as he placed the candle in the pouch.

Composing himself, Malthuzar set off on another brief journey of the spirit. When he returned, the Sacred Pouch was no longer with him, and he was suddenly back in his body, feeling as rested as though he had slept this night away rather than used it to the Master's good purpose.

Rising to his feet, his face exultant, Malthuzar set off in the lightening darkness, moving sure-footedly down the Holy Mountain to the place where he would participate in the final act of his earthly destiny.

# CHAPTER THREE

In that silent, expectant time, when the sun's light barely appeared over the eastern horizon, Esme slept fitfully.

"Esme."

The sound of her name spoken in Malthuzar's unmistakable voice brought Esme abruptly awake, then sitting upright, staring in amazed dismay at the old priest, who was seated across the dying embers of the fire from her.

There was something strangely ephemeral about his image, and there was an exultant glow in his deep-set, ancient eyes. Then his expression, initially sober, turned to one of tender amusement over Esme's fearful alarm at finding him there.

"There is no longer any need to fear me, daughter," he said kindly, his voice echoing with a hollowness that sounded strange to Esme's ears. "I now know everything."

Esme's heart contracted with alarmed foreboding. "Everything?" she responded, cautious. "What do you mean, Honored Elder?"

Smiling, he shook his head. "There is no time to discuss what you have kept hidden because of the admonition against revelation the Master planted within you."

Confused and wary, Esme started to say, "I do not understand . . ." But Malthuzar extended his hand toward her, and Esme flinched as she recognized the object he held. No one could fail to recognize it. The mysterious, fading symbols painted on the side of the ancient leather were a high priest's badge of office more so than his vestments or his staff or any other of the priestly accoutrements that had come to Malthuzar and his predecessors.

"Take it, Esme," Malthuzar said, his tone firm. "It is yours now."

Esme tried to back away, but the boulder she'd used as a backrest prevented it. "No!" she protested, shaking her head violently. "It is not mine! I do not want it!"

Malthuzar ignored her protest, and though his tone remained gentle, it contained the note of authority no one of the People, not even Esme, could gainsay.

"It will not serve as a chain to keep you here, Esme. I give it to you because it is yours to have now, but it will not be needed for the purpose it once held until you return. Take it with you on your journey. Keep it safe and bring it back when you come home. You will need it then."

Esme was again in the act of shaking her head when

## DREAMS OF DESTINY

the pouch came sailing across the fire—not as if thrown by Malthuzar, but as though it moved with a power of its own—and landed in her lap. She would have rejected it, but her hands would not obey her will. The pouch lay where it had fallen on her thighs, and the warmth from it was a living, pulsing force—a force which her body would not reject even while her mind wailed a silent wish to be rid of the responsibility she thought it meant she must assume.

But recalling that Malthuzar had said she was to take it with her on her journey, she grew puzzled. Did Malthuzar's giving her the pouch mean she was to succeed him in the priesthood on the Homeland or not?

"Do not speculate," Malthuzar said, though she had not spoken her question aloud. "The Master will reveal your tasks as each one is upon you." And then, as his voice as well as his body were fading, he added, "Come for me on the mountain, Esme. Take me home. And then begin your destiny."

Malthuzar's image abruptly disappeared, leaving Esme awed, confused and apprehensive. But she had no choice other than to obey the high priest's instructions. His word was law.

Therefore, acting against her reluctance to do so, she tucked the Sacred Pouch inside the bodice of her rough singleton. Its warmth had subsided, but it still lay like a tethering stone between her breasts. Then she got to her feet, and keeping firm control of her flock, she marched them quickly on a search for Maza. When she found him, she made the excuse that she needed to go to the Settlement for supplies and left her flock in his care.

Instead of heading for the Settlement however, she

began her journey to the Holy Mountain to find Malthuzar.

"How long?" Raul growled in response to his engineer's explanation that the repairs to the ship were going to take longer than he'd thought.

Squinting up at the blazing sun, Jase shrugged. "This planet's revolution is roughly the same as that of Genesis. A couple of months, I would say barring any problems."

Raul's ice-blue gaze turned grim. "Let us not have any problems, Jase," he said in a deceptively soft tone. "I have about had my bellyful of problems."

Jase shrugged. "I will do my best, Captain. That is all I can do."

Raul hesitated, then sighed with resignation. "I know you will, Jase," he nodded. "My apologies for my impatience, but this place and the inactivity forced upon me here are already getting on my nerves." Then he waved Jase away. "Go on, man," he said. "Do your job. I will leave you to it."

Jase saluted Raul's departing back and returned to his labors.

Raul, feeling like a Gosflag with a sore paw, stomped out across the desert, intending to walk off his foul mood, but the glaring sun drove him back to the ship before he'd gone very far. With a brooding look on his face that made the steward deposit the captain's lunch in his cabin with unusual speed and made him quickly depart to safer climes, Raul sat and drank more wine than was good for him.

Esme found Malthuzar's lifeless body on the narrow track leading down from the summit of the Holy

## DREAMS OF DESTINY

Mountain. He had been crushed by a boulder.

As she squatted in a trance beside the high priest's body, reconstructing from the psychic energy still present at the scene what had happened, tears ran down her face and a rage against Bazil and Marcus grew to epic proporations in her mind and heart.

Esme had seen Marcus scuttling back toward the Settlement as she made her way to the mountain, but she hadn't known why he was in such a hurry. Then, arriving and finding Malthuzar sprawled dead beneath a boulder, she had wailed her grief until she had regained her composure and reconstructed what had happened.

Obviously, wanting to spy on Malthuzar for purposes Esme could not imagine, Bazil had set Marcus on the old high priest's heels with instructions to stay out of sight. So, at spotting Malthuzar returning to the Settlement this morning, Marcus had hidden behind a boulder on an overhead ledge, waiting for the old priest to pass beneath him. But Malthuzar hadn't passed him. Instead, with a stern expression on his elderly face, he'd looked up and said something to Marcus as though he could see him. But Esme knew Malthuzar couldn't have. Marcus was too well-hidden.

While in the trance she used to reconstruct what had happened, Esme couldn't hear what was said. She could only watch, horrified, as Marcus set a boulder rolling down the incline. Even if Malthuzar had tried to get out of the way, there was no place for him to go. It was deliberate murder.

The last thing Esme saw before she came shuddering out of the trance was the smile on Malthuzar's face before the boulder had crushed him—a smile almost of triumph, certainly of joy.

As Esme sat huddled where she was, tears streaming down her face, it didn't matter to her that Malthuzar had met his death without fear or reluctance. What mattered to her was the loss she felt, though there was no logic for her feelings. She'd avoided Malthuzar assiduously from the age of twelve cycles on. And the rage she felt mattered as well. Her rage against Bazil and his murdering little minion, Marcus, was boiling within her, crying out for retribution!

It wasn't the problems that Malthuzar's death would bring her personally that lay behind her grief and rage. It was something deeper. Her grief was that of someone who'd lost a beloved spiritual companion. Her rage was that of an avenging angel bent on righting an outrage against all justice and truth.

But before she could do anything else, Esme had to obey the instructions Malthuzar had given her in his predawn visit.

"Take me home," he'd said. And that was what she would do.

Raising her head to stare with illogical hatred at the boulder, Esme narrowed her eyes and calculated her thrust to a fine beam. Then, not without a fierce feeling of satisfaction at having something upon which to vent her rage, she exerted the full force of her mind and exploded the boulder into minute fragments.

When the last of the chaff had settled to the ground, she felt a little better, and with tender care, she brushed the debris from Malthuzar's crushed chest.

The problem of moving him came next. Though Esme had no difficulty transporting her mind wherever she wished, and using the force of it to move

## DREAMS OF DESTINY

other objects, her powers didn't extend to teleporting her own body.

Remembering the beast-burden Malthuzar had brought with him, Esme sought it with her mind, and found it grazing nearby. Peremptorily, she called it. It resisted, preferring to stay and continue feasting on the unusual vegetation to be found only on these slopes.

Esme gave the animal no choice. She prodded it with a sharpness that made the foolish animal rear up and whinny in surprise, before it obediently, if resentfully, trotted downhill to join her. Esme then gently, reverently, placed Malthuzar across its back and started down the mountain.

As Esme made her way toward the Settlement, she considered just how long to make Bazil and Marcus suffer before she wiped the two of them off the face of the Homeland for good. And if that left the People without a full-fledged priest for a while, so be it. One of the younger seekers must be far enough along in his studies to take over in the interim, and there were plenty of the Sacred Scrolls to guide him to full knowledge. But in any case, the People would be better off with no priest at all rather than be guided by a false one and his murderous helper. And since Esme's desire for revenge would not, in any case, be stayed by any consideration whatsoever, that was just as well.

In the private chamber of his cave, Bazil towered over the creature he considered his personal tool. "You fool!" he spat at the bedraggled and fear-ridden Marcus, who cowered before him. "You have exceeded your instructions once too often!"

"I could not help it," Marcus defended himself. "Something had happened to the old priest. If you could have seen him, you would know what I mean. He must have had a vision. He was walking like a young man, and his face was . . .was *lighted up!*"

Bazil showed his contemptuous disbelief for such superstitious drivel. He did not even believe in the Master, much less in visions.

But Marcus persisted. "And he knew I was there when he could not have known it!"

Marcus's eyes narrowed into an expression of hate and fear and his mouth drew into a line of bitterness. "He told me I was damned for venturing unlawfully onto the slopes of the Holy Mountain. And you know what that means. If I had let him get back here, he would have had me stoned. And he would have had you stoned as well, for setting me on his heels in the first place!" he added with unrepentant self-justification.

Giving a snort of disgusted disbelief, Bazil turned abruptly to go to the table against one wall and pour himself a cup of wine. As he did, he was thinking hard.

He didn't like the idea of the trouble Marcus could cause him if the man ever told all he knew. But on the other hand, Marcus would invite his own death if he ever talked. And he had always been useful and could be so again, especially if there was active opposition to the changes Bazil would make now that he no longer had the old priest looking over his shoulder at every turn. And hadn't things, in any case, worked out to his own advantage?

Murder had never been in Bazil's plan. But he had to admit, it was extremely convenient to have Malthuzar dead, especially if after coming down from

## DREAMS OF DESTINY

the mountain the old man really had been about to spout nonsense of visions and the advent of the long-dead Prophecy Bazil had never believed in in any case. And it was a relief to know he didn't have to wait any longer to assume the mantle and staff of High Priest!

The thought of Malthuzar's mantle and staff, however, brought something else to Bazil's mind. In an abrupt movement, he swung around and fixed Marcus with an intimidating stare.

"What about the pouch?"

"The pouch?" Marcus's expression was blank, uncomprehending.

"The Sacred Pouch, you idiot!" Bazil snarled. "Did you get it? Did you bring it with you?"

But he already knew the answer to that, even before Marcus's guilty expression answered for him.

"You stupid cretin!" he bit out, as he began to pace the chamber.

It wasn't as if Bazil ever intended using the pouch for the purpose it had always served. He had no intention of climbing the so-called Holy Mountain and freezing on a cold ledge swept by hurricane strength winds waiting for visions he knew wouldn't come. He'd done it once, as his final requirement for assuming the mantle of priest, and it had been the most coldly miserable experience of his entire life. Only his fear that Malthuzar, who sometimes had an uncanny ability to sense the truth, might find out he hadn't actually carried out the final duty, had made Bazil go through the motions.

He'd come back down the mountain, frozen and bone-tired, wanting only a hot drink and meal, and a cozy cuddle with one of his female admirers to finish warming him up. But he knew that he had to delay his physical comforts until he'd reported his fictitious "visions" to Malthuzar.

Aided with a thorough knowledge of the Sacred Scrolls, which contained lengthy accounts of the visions of his predecessors, Bazil had reported a few visions of his own, which had been duly recorded in the Scrolls. And though Malthuzar had seemed disappointed that Bazil had nothing really spectacular to report, he'd been satisfied with what he'd heard, thank the stars. Bazil couldn't have faced being sent back up to that freezing ledge for another try.

But the pouch, the one symbol that truly signified the power and authority of a high priest, had to be recovered so that Bazil could wear it on his belt, just as every other high priest had worn it for centuries. Besides, Malthuzar's body had to be brought back for burial.

Bazil didn't trust Marcus to recover the body and pouch with any real degree of efficiency, however, which meant that he would have to go along himself.

*Ah well*, he thought, as he turned back and viewed with disgust the downcast countenance Marcus was affecting for his benefit. *That little chore, too, can be turned to my advantage.*

"Go round up the seekers," he said to Marcus.

Marcus's shaggy head came up, a fearful look on his brutal face.

Bazil snorted his reassurance. "Do not worry. I am not calling them to put you on trial. I want them to think I have been falling prey to a few visions myself, visions concerning the welfare of our dear Malthuzar that worry me enough that you and I are going to set out after him and make sure he is safe and well."

## DREAMS OF DESTINY

Marcus's eyes lit up with appreciation.

"I thought you would like the idea," Bazil drawled. "Now get on with it. I want to be ready to leave within the hour."

"They will be at afternoon prayers," Marcus said as he got up.

Bazil's face reddened with anger over his underling's stupidty. "Of course, they will be praying, you sheepbrain! I am supposed to have been at my own prayers, wherein the *vision* about Malthuzar came to me!"

"Oh." Marcus's tone was sheepish.

Bazil sighed in weary disgust. "Go on. Get out of my sight!" he ordered, waving Marcus away.

A short while later, Bazil, his face suitably expressing his supposed worry, gently addressed the small group of seekers who stood in his outer room, gazing at him expectantly. Their gazes had turned from expectancy to alarm by the time he'd explained his reason for bringing them here.

He gave short shrift to the chorus of predictable offers of assistance.

"No. Marcus and I had better go alone," he said regretfully. "Malthuzar is getting a bit crotchety in his old age, and if it turns out that my forebodings have no basis in reality, he will be very angry at me if he knows I have worried anyone else unnecessarily."

"But . . ." One of the brightest of the seekers, a young man named Baldor—started to protest. He widened his eyes in surprise when Bazil unconsciously glared at him.

Bazil quickly thought better of his reaction, and gave the young man a kindly look of encouragement. "What is it, Baldor?" he inquired gently.

"Well"—Baldor shrugged "I was just thinking that if anything really had happened to our Honored Elder, would not one of the shepherds have reported it? There are so many of them up on that high meadow that surely one of them would have seen him."

"Malthuzar often likes to be alone up there." Bazil smoothly brushed the idea aside. "After all, some of the shepherds are rather—" He broke off and shrugged, but it was clear that the seekers understood his meaning. The shepherds, lowest of the low in the People's heirarchy, were considered crude and dirty. And the one female among them the green-eyed Esme, with her lovely face and body, both of which she kept cleaner than anyone in the Settlement, though not considered crude or dirty, was considered downright dangerous. Some said she used those green eyes and lush body to entrap men and steal their souls.

"Anything else?" Bazil inquired of his listeners with brisk courtesy. When there was no reply, Bazil glanced out the cave opening at the sun's position on the horizon. "Then Marcus and I, with every hope that we are making a wasted journey, will gather a few supplies and be on our way."

An hour later, Bazil and Marcus were out of sight of the Settlement and the sun was directly at their backs when they spotted a small figure leading a beast-burden in the far distance, and Bazil, afraid of what he was going to find, hurried ahead of Marcus toward the oncomer.

Though the sun was in her eyes, Esme didn't need to see to know who was coming toward her. She didn't increase her pace, nor did she seek to avoid the meeting. She kept walking, the green of her eyes glistening with a warning that Bazil clearly saw as he came closer, and which brought him to an abrupt stop.

Esme stopped as well, and for a long moment, the two adversaries merely stood a few paces apart, staring with mutual hatred into one another's eyes.

Neither noticed when Marcus came hurrying up, and with the cunning of his kind, began to sidle to Esme's rear.

"You killed him." Esme spoke softly, but her voice nevertheless cut like a knife through the air between them.

Bazil involuntarily flinched before he recovered himself. "I did not!" he snarled through the air between them.

"And you are going to pay," Esme spoke as though she hadn't heard his denial. "Both before and after you depart this life," she added with such venomous certainty in her voice that Bazil stepped back.

Narrowing her eyes so that the pupils were mere pinpoints in a sea of green, Esme struck out with her mind, not with enough force to kill, but with enough force to make Bazil's mouth open in a silent scream of agony.

Marcus didn't understand what was happening, but he'd heard enough to know what needed to be done. In his hand was a cudgel he'd instinctively withdrawn from the loop in his belt, and he lifted it high above his head.

Esme, in her concentration on Bazil, sensed the danger too late. As she turned to confront the threat from her rear, the cudgel, deflected by her move, bounced off her head. She barely had time to feel the most excrutiating pain she'd ever known before she fell unconscious.

Bazil, holding his head and still gasping with pain, opened his eyes as Esme hit the ground.

Marcus was in the act of lifting the cudgel again, obviously intending to deliver another, fatal blow, when Bazil held out his hand and shouted, "Stop!"

Marcus instinctively deflected the blow, and it landed on the ground beside Esme's head instead of against her skull. Raising his small, beady eyes to Bazil's face, the question in them was clear.

Bazil didn't know himself why he had stopped Marcus. But he thought quickly. "This has to be handled right or it will ruin everything. Tie her up, Marcus. Tightly! While I decide what to do with her."

It was only as Marcus was grudgingly carrying out orders that Bazil realized the bonds cutting into Esme's delicious skin wouldn't confine her mind. And, as incredible as it seemed, it had to have been Esme's mind that had attacked his own earlier!

He couldn't really believe it, but he wasn't so convinced that the idea was as incredible as it seemed that he was going to take any chances.

Fortunately, Bazil carried a drug he'd had occasion to use on certain reluctant females who hadn't realized the honor he was paying them by inviting them to his bed. The drug was relatively harmless. When used sparingly, it merely dispelled inconvenient inhibitions and produced a sleepy, lethargic state without rendering the inbiber unconscious, which wouldn't have suited Bazil at all. He liked his women compliant, not comatose.

Now he wondered what a larger dosage might accomplish on a woman of Esme's unusual abilities. It was worth a try, and if it failed to work on her, he could always let Marcus finish the job he'd started

## DREAMS OF DESTINY

before she could do anything Bazil might regret.

Looking around, Bazil nervously considered their position. They were in the foothills leading to the high pasture, and though it had been years since he'd been this far, he was sure there was a network of caves in a hillside over the next rise.

He gestured at Marcus, who had finished the job of binding Esme's ankles together and her hands tightly behind her back.

"Put her on the beast-burden beside Malthuzar," he instructed tersely. "Quickly before someone comes!"

Marcus bent, picked Esme up and deposited her where he'd been told, then pulled the beast-burden along as he followed Bazil.

Bazil was much relieved when he spotted the caves and was even more relieved when no shepherd appeared to see him, Marcus, and the beast and its burden before they were safely concealed by the walls of one cave with a second chamber extending into the hill.

"Get her down and carry her back here," Bazil instructed Marcus.

"You want Malthuzar down, too?" Marcus inquired on a grunt of exertion as he hefted Esme from the back of the beast burden.

"Of course I do not!" Bazil snarled. "We'll be taking him to the Settlement when I've figured out what to do about Esme, so why would I want him down? Do you want to carry him all that way on your back?"

In response to the question and its tone, Marcus looked sullen, and Bazil clamped down on his rage with the man—at least in his outward expression of it.

"My head aches," he said shortly, by way of apology and explanation. The necessity to provide either grated on him, but it seemed to be getting dangerously easy for Marcus to kill. Who was to say he might not decide to turn on Bazil if Bazil wasn't careful?

At that, Marcus's sullen expression turned curious. "Was that why you looked as though you were in pain before I hit Esme?" he asked.

Bazil bit back another sarcastic retort. "Yes," he nodded. "But never mind that. Carry Esme to the back chamber of the cave. I will sit with her while I try to decide the best thing to do. You stay up here and keep watch in case anyone wanders by."

"Who would wander by?"

Bazil sighed. "A shepherd, Marcus," he said levelly. "A shepherd might wander by."

"Oh."

Later, Bazil sat beside Esme, watching her carefully while his lust grew and his thoughts churned. He'd never seen Esme helpless, and the sight of her lying there, bound and vulnerable, was making him want her more than he ever had. On the other hand, he cautioned himself, he mustn't let himself be distracted and miss when she woke enough to swallow the drug he held.

As he watched her, his eyes darting from the mounds of her unbound breasts under her singlet to the slight vee between her silken thighs and then to her face, Bazil accepted that he really had no choice but to let Marcus kill Esme. The people mistrusted her, and there was a chance that no matter what she said, they wouldn't believe her. But he couldn't take the risk. If even one person suspected the truth of what had happened to Malthuzar, it was one too many. Everything he'd planned for years could be lost—not to mention his very life.

Still, there was no sense in missing the opportunity to have what he'd wanted for so many years and which Esme, the green-eyed witch, had persistently, infuriatingly, denied him.

Bazil moved closer to Esme and lifted his hand to place it on one of her legs. The skin that covered her exquisitely shaped limb was warm and smooth, and as he stroked his hand up toward her thigh, Bazil's excitement grew, and he forgot that he should stay alert for any sign that she was regaining consciousness.

From time to time, Esme's mind would attempt to swim up toward consciousness, but the pain she experienced there was so intense, she would immediately drop back into the comforting blackness that was all too easy to find. Gradually, however, a sense of urgency that persisted against all her efforts to smother it, forced her to endure, little by little, the pain of awakening. But she didn't open her eyes or move.

For a time, she was immersed in trying to deal with the pain that gripped her. But at some point, the realization that she was being handled in a way she found profoundly distasteful distracted her.

In a sudden swoop of clarity that was like being hit over the head again, she abruptly realized what was happening. Without opening her eyes, and controlling her breathing, she tested the reality in which she found herself.

Her wrists and ankles were bound, but that presented no problem. Even as she used her mind to assess Marcus's position, and to control her body's impulse to shudder under Bazil's touch, she was also sparing a tiny portion to unravel the ropes that held her.

Bazil was crouched astride her with his hands under her singlet, searching for her breasts. But when they found what they sought, they also found the Sacred Pouch. He paused, puzzled.

It was time to make her move, and as Esme opened her eyes, she smiled dangerously as she saw the puzzled expression on Bazil's face turn to recognition as he understood what he'd found.

"Malthuzar gave it to me, Bazil," she whispered. "It is mine now."

Bazil's head came up as though jerked by a line, and even as he was opening his mouth to scream for Marcus, Esme struck out with her mind and inflicted a carefully calculated degree of agony upon his brain.

Marcus, growing more curious about what was going on at the back of the cave than he was fearful of Bazil's displeasure, stepped into the chamber just as Bazil, his hands to his head, his mouth open in a silent scream of agony, was falling backward off Esme's body.

For a stupid man, Marcus was remarkably quick to act. He had his cudgel out and was almost upon Esme before she could turn her mind in his direction. And as she had with Bazil, she allowed her desire to draw out Marcus's punishment rather than end his life immediately override logic, so that she tempered the blow she struck at him.

It wasn't enough. Whether Marcus's deficient brain was less susceptible to such an attack or whether he simply had an incredibly high pain threshhold, Esme would never know. At any rate, though he staggered back for a moment, he resumed his attack, and Esme, caught in a well of panic at the thought of enduring another blow from his cudgel, lashed out full force this time, and quite literally exploded Marcus's brain within his skull.

He fell across both her and Bazil, his cudgel clattering harmlessly onto the stone floor.

Shuddering over the sight of his mangled head, Esme reacted blindly, scrambling out from under the both of them, not even bothering to get to her feet at first, but rather scuttling on her hands and feet as far away as she could get.

As she huddled against the fall wall of the chamber, Bazil, sobbing with pain, struggled to push Marcus's weight off him and sit up.

In the next instant, voices sounded from the outer cave. The seekers, after further thought, had realized Malthuzar, crotchety or not, wouldn't really be angry with them for their concern over his welfare, and had followed Bazil's tracks.

At finding Malthuzar's body in the outer cave, there was a sudden silence, followed by a chorus of grief that raised the hair on Esme's neck and brought a momentary confusion to her mind.

Despite his pain, Bazil had never had more reason to think quickly and seize any opportunity offered. Therefore, as Esme sat immobilized for a moment, he screamed at the top of his voice.

"Help! Seize her! She killed the High Priest and Marcus as well!"

And before Esme could react, a dozen seekers had flooded into the chamber and were staring down at Marcus's lifeless body and mangled head. Then they followed with their eyes Bazil's accusing finger pointed in Esme's direction. They saw the huddled figure of the only woman of the People who had a sorceress's green eyes, and whom none of them had trusted since the day they were old enough to listen to and understand the fearful, superstitious mutterings of those of the People whom they had no reason to doubt.

# CHAPTER FOUR

In the hope that Esme's charity would extend further than his own would have under the same circumstances, Bazil screamed out again for the seekers to seize her. And to his immense relief, they not only obeyed, but he found he'd guessed right about Esme's reluctance to harm them. She did not struggle, either mentally or physically, as the seekers surrounded her, pulled her to her feet, and held her tightly.

Esme tried to keep her eye on Bazil but it proved impossible. He was careful to keep one or another of the young seekers between the two of them, and at last she realized he did so because he had guessed she wouldn't harm them. And he obviously presumed she couldn't send her mind around corners either.

She knew she had better show him differently and fast. Otherwise, he might order the seekers he was using as pawns to kill her immediately without giving

57

her a chance to make him confess the truth about what had happened to Malthuzar. Then she would be forced to defend herself by inflicting damage on innocent bystanders.

She sent her mind soaring over her captors and almost gently, as though she were a mountain cat playing with one of its small prey, nudged Bazil's mind with a whispered, *Behave, Bazil.*

Bazil's reaction was a startled scream, and the seekers shifted to look at him in alarm. Their movement caused a clear space to open between Bazil and Esme, and she swooped back to her body, then stared straight into his eyes in a way she knew he would interpret correctly.

"Don't!" Bazil yelped. And then, at seeing the puzzled expressions on the seekers' faces, he held up a hand. "Stay here!" he ordered his youthful followers as he began to back away. "Hold her!" he quickly added. "I—I need to think!"

His trembling legs barely carried him to the outer cave, where he collapsed onto a boulder. With his head in his hands, he tried to sort out how he was going to rid himself of Esme and the danger she represented to his lifelong plan, without giving her an opportunity to kill him first.

Esme left her body and sent her mind to join Bazil.

*Greetings, murderer,* she hissed into his mind.

This time, Bazil didn't scream. But a low, terrified moan issued from his mouth as he jerked his head up. He shook his head violently. "I did not—" he started to say between chattering teeth.

*Hush!* Esme silently, impatiently cut him off. *Just think what you want to say to me, and I will hear you.*

She did not want the seekers to hear their conversation because she was afraid that Bazil would mention her mental abilities. The seekers might then be even more convinced she had had something to do with Malthuzar's murder and might dismiss any confession she wrested from Bazil, preferring to believe she had used a sorceress's powers to make him confess to something he didn't do.

But she couldn't let Bazil know she wanted to keep her powers secret from the seekers, lest he try to blackmail her into going easy on him. Instead, she wanted to make him confess what he had done as quickly as possible, with the seekers as witnesses. Then she would find some way to kill him and make it look accidental. She was afraid if she left his punishment to the People, he would find some way to wriggle out of it.

Bazil's whole body was trembling, sweat was pouring down his face, and his black eyes held a wild expression as though he were going to go over the edge at any moment. Thus, Esme was forced to calm him, though she would much have preferred to rip his mind apart.

Afterwards, Bazil gulped and started shaking his head again. *I . . . I . . . I . . . did not tell Marcus to k-k-kill Malthuzar,* he defended himself mentally, his mind stuttering as badly as his voice would have if Esme had permitted him to use it. *I j-j-just told him to keep an eye on him and let me k-k-know when he was coming back. I wanted t-to k-know—*

*Whether he had had any visions that might interfere with your plans?* Esme interrupted, her rage making the words slash at Bazil's mind. But when he moaned and swayed as though he were going to pass out of consciousness, she calmed him again.

Bazil's terror abated slightly and he sat silently trembling, his eyes wide and flicking all around the cave as though searching for her spirit.

Esme was suddenly distracted when the young seekers holding her body grew restless. She knew they were thinking of sending one or two of their number out to see what Bazil was doing. Esme was forced to withdraw from Bazil briefly and gently scotch such a notion without allowing the young men to know their minds were being tampered with. It turned out to be more difficult than she'd expected to spread herself among so many minds, especially minds that were as skittish as these were.

Unfortunately, the calm she'd given Bazil was enough to allow him to think rationally and he used his brief spell of freedom to search desperately for a solution to his dilemma. He was afraid Esme would kill him soon if he couldn't think of a way to stop her—unless she chose to torture him endlessly instead.

Bazil shuddered as he relived the pain Esme had inflicted upon him earlier. But an instant later, much to his surprise, he realized that that pain, bad as it was, was nothing compared to what he would feel if Esme elected to let him live without the power he'd craved and worked for all of his life. Even death was preferable to such an existence!

And suddenly, Bazil was gasping at a straw, and he desperately tugged at it, trying to make a half thought into a whole one. There was an answer there if he could only. . . . But of course! he thought excitedly. The only weapons he had were Esme's obvious reluctance to hurt the seekers and his own willingness to die!

His mind veered for a second into a rather wondering amazement over his own courage. He felt elated to discover that he was a braver man than he'd realized!

Impatiently, he dragged his mind back to the problem at hand. If he didn't handle things right, his bravery wasn't going to matter. Nothing was going to matter ever again! And suddenly he realized he had another weapon to use against Esme. She wanted no one to know of her powers! Otherwise, why conceal them all these years? And why conceal them now when she might free herself from danger unless she still had strong reasons for keeping them secret?

Bazil didn't know what those reasons might be, but he was determined to act upon what little he did know to save himself.

*I want you dead.* Esme was abruptly back in his mind. *But first, I want you to admit what you did.*

Bazil shuddered, then forced himself to reply. *You know the truth,* he agreed. *Technically, I guess I am responsible for what Marcus did. But,* he quickly added, *I would have stopped him if I had been there, just as I stopped him from murdering you when we met up with you today.*

He felt the contemptuous scepticism in Esme's mind, and it propelled him into the most prodigious juggling of his own thoughts he'd ever had to accomplish. He had to let Esme see the truth of his assertion that he'd stopped Marcus from killing her on the trail, without letting her know that he'd later changed his mind and had been prepared to see her dead—after he'd satisfied his lust, of course.

As it happened, the memory of that lust was what saved him. As Bazil deliberately relived in his head the scene where he'd stopped Marcus from killing her,

Esme saw it clearly herself. And then Bazil quickly skipped to where he'd been exploring her body while he thought she lay unconscious.

Esme was so repulsed by that memory that she gave him the equivalent of a mental slap and quickly shut his memory down.

When Bazil had stopped reeling from the pain in his head, he elected for a tone of humility. *You see?* he said quietly. *I did stop Marcus from—*

*Never mind!* Esme shot back. *That does not excuse you from setting Marcus on Malthuzar's heels in the first place!*

*I know,* Bazil said, with quiet dignity now, and he wisely let the matter rest while he controlled his thoughts.

Esme made a sound of angry impatience. Unwilling to let Bazil escape punishment for what Marcus had done to Malthuzar, she was nevertheless disgusted to find that she was also in Bazil's debt. If he hadn't stopped Marcus, her gifts wouldn't have saved her from lying out on the road with a crushed head.

Then a solution occurred to her. Given Bazil's cleverness, it was a risky solution, but it would satisfy her debt to him, and still result in his just punishment if all went well.

*All right, I will not kill you, Bazil,* she announced grimly. *I will force you to confess and after your trial by the People, they will do it for me.*

She felt Bazil's mind swell with a sudden infusion of mindless fear, and then, strangely, he went completely blank for a moment. Esme was beginning to fear she'd driven him insane when she felt his quiet, absolutely determined answer in her mind.

*No, Esme. I have no intention of going on trial.*

*You have no choice*—she started to say, but he cut her off.

*Yes, I have choices,* he said firmly, and before she could do anything to stop him, he yelled out loud to the seekers in the other chamber, "Bring Esme in here!"

*What do you think you are doing?* she hissed as the young Seekers immediately started dragging her body into the outer cave.

*Showing you your own choices, Esme,* Bazil said, using only his mind to speak again. *These young men are used to obeying me. If I tell them of your mental powers, they will believe me and fear you. And if I tell them it is too dangerous, because of what you might do to their families, to take you back to the Settlement, and that they must therefore kill you here and now, they will obey me. At least, they will attempt to obey me. And you will be forced to defend yourself, will you not?*

The seekers were all in the outer cave now, clustered around Bazil with Esme's body still in their grasp.

"What are we going to do with her?" Baldor asked grimly of Bazil as he stared at Malthuzar's body still lying across the beast-burden near the entrance to the outer cave. "Take her back to the Settlement for trial?"

Bazil looked directly into Esme's eyes, though that was not where her spirit was presently resting. "What shall we do with you, Esme?" he asked aloud. "*Did* you kill Malthuzar?"

Silently, Esme answered. *I do not have to really hurt these young men in order to defend myself, Bazil,* she said grimly. *I can merely . . .*

*. . . let them know that what I say about your mental powers is true,* Bazil finished for her in his mind. *The seekers are waiting for your answer to my question, Esme. You had better give them one.*

Esme had no choice. It would look very strange if she didn't answer. Therefore, in a short, impatient swoop, she returned to her body.

"No, I did not kill Malthuzar!" she grated, startling the young men who were holding her. They'd become accustomed to her quiet, docile manner. Instinctively, they tightened their hold on her arms and several of them muttered angrily over her reply.

Bazil held up his hand and the muttering ceased. "Let me meditate a moment, brothers," he said piously. "It is possible I could have been wrong in accusing her. I want to see if she could be telling the truth."

"She is not!" Baldor declared in a forceful manner.

Bazil, who if he lived through this, suspected he might one day have trouble with this particular young man, fixed Baldor with a stern eye.

"Are you as yet a full-fledged priest, Baldor?" he demanded.

Baldor flushed a little. "No," he responded, "but I have eyes!"

"And I, as far as I know," Bazil responded in his most authoritative voice, "am the only full-fledged priest in this chamber, with a priest's powers of divining truth from lies. Now kindly let me get on with it!"

Baldor flushed again, but he remained silent.

Contrary to Bazil's opinion of Baldor as a trouble-

## DREAMS OF DESTINY

maker, and in spite of Baldor's erroneous conviction of her guilt, Esme found herself in sympathy with the young man. At least, he was intelligent enough to know that Marcus's death was unusual, and his anger and desire to see her punished for Malthuzar's death sprang from a genuine respect and love for the old man and an honest desire to see justice prevail.

Bazil, with his head lowered as though in prayer and his eyes closed, spoke silently to Esme again.

*So what will it be, Esme? Shall I tell these young seekers you are innocent of Malthuzar's death, that he died as the result of an accident. Shall I merely suggest that you suffer exile for Marcus's death because he attacked you in the mistaken belief that you killed Malthuzar?*

Esme gasped at the effrontery of Bazil's suggestion that *she* suffer exile for what *he* had done. True, her destiny seemed to be hard upon her. She had sensed it coming nearer, and Malthuzar had confirmed that she would soon be making a journey, so it seemed likely she would be leaving in any case. But leaving as a result of her destiny being fulfilled was one thing. Being unfairly accused and exiled was quite another!

*Life will become intolerable for you here now in any case,* Bazil interrupted her thoughts. *Even if I convince the seekers you are innocent of Malthuzar's death, they have seen Marcus's body, and they can never forget that. I may not even be able to convince them not to kill you despite declaring you innocent of killing Malthuzar.*

*They will not kill me if I force you to tell them what really happened!* Esme flared. *They will likely kill* you *instead!*

*But I am positive you do not want them to know the whole truth,* Bazil said firmly. *You must have concealed your gifts all this time for fear the People would stone you as a sorceress. And they very well still might, despite learning the truth about Malthuzar's death. At the very least, you will have to be put on trial to determine if you are a sorceress. Can you control the minds of all of the People and make them decide in your favor, Esme? Will their minds stay controlled? And if they do decide in your favor, your obligation to serve the People will then be evident. Do you want to be their high priestess? If so, why have you not already become such?*

Esme was dismayed by Bazil's perspicacity. *I should kill you and be done with it!* she snarled.

Bazil, head still down, eyes still closed, controlled his fear. Quickly, he reminded himself that he would prefer death to the destruction of all his plans.

*If you want to repay me for saving your life by taking mine,* he responded firmly, *I cannot stop you. And you will have to kill me if you decide not to go along with my proposal of exile, Esme. There are ways I can force you to kill me before we leave this cave, perhaps even before you can make me confess the truth. And if you kill me the same way you killed Marcus, that will surely result in convincing these seekers you are a sorceress who has to be killed for the safety of the People. You will then either die yourself or be forced to kill the innocent.*

As Esme, enraged and frustrated, began mulling her options, Bazil saw that the seekers were growing impatient for his decision, and he didn't give her time to think. Instead, he prodded her for a quick decision.

## DREAMS OF DESTINY

*Make up your mind, Esme!* he demanded. *Kill me or leave! Do something quickly or I will!*

Esme's lips twisted in a bitter grimace. There seemed only one decision possible, but she was reluctant to concede anything to a manipulative, amoral scoundrel like Bazil. Still, she was apparently beginning a journey anyway soon, as she had always known she would someday. And it was her own conviction, and Malthuzar had confirmed it, that she would one day return. Therefore, Bazil's seeming victory would be only temporary. However, to ease her frustration and to make him suffer the punishment of always looking over his shoulder, wondering when her revenge and his eventual defeat would be accomplished, she intended to let him know, at the last moment before she was banished, that she would one day be back.

*All right, Bazil,* she said, fury in her tone. *I consent to exile.*

Immediately, the force of his relief came at her in a wave so strong, she actually drew back against the grip of her captor's hands.

*A very wise decision, Esme,* he said, jubilant. *I shall now pronounce you innocent.*

Convinced that speed was of the essence now, Bazil quickly raised his head and fixed the seekers with a look calculated to impress them.

"I now know the truth!" he said in a strong voice containing utter conviction. "Esme is not guilty of Malthuzar's death, and . . ."

But Bazil had to pause because the seekers at once raised their voices in active protest to his conclusion. He acted speedily to crush their rebellious behavior.

Not only did it threaten his very life at the moment, it boded ill for the future if they were allowed to get away with challenging him.

"Silence!" he thundered in a voice that reverberated off the walls of the cave and repeated the order in a series of echoes.

In the silence that followed the last echo, Bazil majestically rose to his feet, and his black eyes fairly blazed at each seeker in turn.

"Who will challenge my seeing?" he roared at them. "Which *priest* among you knows the truth better than I? Step forward, if you dare!"

Not even Baldor was sufficiently self-assured to accept Bazil's challenge. No one said a word.

Esme was cynically impressed with Bazil's performance. *Well done,* she silently congratulated him in a dry, mocking tone.

Though Bazil's expression remained locked in the intimidating aura of power and authority he'd donned like a mask, his mind chuckled back at her. *Yes, was it not? I will make an impressive High Priest. I have been practicing for a long time.*

"As I was about to say," Bazil said aloud, his voice grim, his eyes flashing with furious determination. After all, he was fighting for his very life here. "Esme is innocent of Malthuzar's death. She was merely bringing his body back from the Holy Mountain, where he was killed in an unfortunate accident, and had stopped here to rest when Marcus and I came upon her. Considering her reputation, we jumped to the erroneous conclusion that she had had a hand in his death."

Bazil paused for breath, his eyes searching each

## DREAMS OF DESTINY

young seeker's face for confirmation that they were accepting his words. Though there were still one or two slightly doubtful expressions, Baldor's especially, most everyone hung on his every word, and more important, accepted them.

"I ordered Marcus to seize Esme, intending to take her back to the Settlement for trial," Bazil continued. "But Marcus's grief over our high priest's death was more intense than I realized. Before I knew what he was about, he attacked Esme."

In a glance at Baldor, Bazil was annoyed to see him nodding, as though his reaction would have been the same. If he couldn't learn to take orders, something was going to have to be done about that young man, Bazil decided. That was all there was to it.

"Esme," Bazil went on, hoping against hope there was a rock somewhere in the chamber big enough and close enough to support the lie that had just occured to him, "naturally defended herself."

He paused and closed his eyes, as though grief were overwhelming him for a moment, robbing him of his voice. Actually, he was silently inquiring of Esme if her powers extended to arranging a little convenient evidence in the next chamber.

Esme drily assured him she was quite capable of handling the matter, and as Bazil raised his head, displaying convincing tears in his eyes, Esme sent her mind to arrange things next door.

While she was there, she realized that the damage to Marcus's head was a bit too extensive to be explained away in the manner Bazil intended, and as revolting as the chore was to her, she paused long enough to repair some of the damage she'd inflicted.

Back in her body, she listened with grudging admiration as Bazil described the fictitious struggle that had occurred between herself and Marcus. Her admiration turned to disgust as Bazil explained that he himself had jumped bravely into the midst of the fray, but had been too late to prevent Esme from crushing Marcus's head with the rock.

As Bazil again paused, ostensibly to get his emotions under control, Esme glanced at Baldor and correctly interpreted his expression as disbelief. Quietly, she nudged him to go check the scene of the crime again, and she watched with empathy as Baldor slipped away.

"I realize," Bazil said with a deep sigh, "that Marcus was wrong to attack Esme as he did." Then he raised his eyes, in which the stern expression of a judge had replaced his previous apparent sorrow. "But Esme was wrong as well. She did not have to hit Marcus as hard as she did. I confess, it seems strange to me that a mere woman could inflict as much damage as she did . . . unless . . ."

He let the word hang there for a moment, long enough for the seekers to consider his unspoken meaning and to stir uneasily while they glanced fearfully at Esme out of the corners of their eyes. A glance into their minds showed her, to her disgust, that they were praying for protection against her.

Baldor, a puzzled expression on his youthful face, returned to the outer cave then, and Esme, lightly searching his mind, again felt sympathy for him. She wondered if he would ever resolve the puzzle that plagued him. Lightly, she did what she could, assuring him that he wasn't crazy. It was just that the lighting in the cave was inadequate.

"Now, in my seeking for the truth," Bazil was speaking again, thoughtfully now, "a curious thing happened. I had a vision of Esme leaving us . . ."

An audible sigh of relief echoed around the cave, making Bazil pause a moment to savor his satisfaction over the reaction.

Esme tightened her jaw at the seekers' reaction—and at Bazil's.

Bazil shook his head as though in wonder. "She was striding off into exile. And that," he said gravely, raising his head to stare each of the seekers in the eye, "was so clear that there can be no mistaking its reality. Our Master has spoken. Esme will leave us forever."

A murmur of agreement came too quickly, considering that what they planned violated her right to a trial by a full complement of the People. Esme silently demanded Bazil's attention. He didn't want to give it, but he had no choice.

*Don't count on forever, Bazil,* she uttered in the tone of a promise.

*Can I count on the length of my lifetime, at least?* Bazil responded with brisk dryness. *I like to sleep nights.*

*No, you do not. You like to violate women at night,* Esme responded grimly. *And if I did not have my own plans, believe me, I would—*

Bazil cut her off. "I do not want to be unnecessarily cruel about this, however," he said aloud as he walked quickly toward Esme, withdrawing something out of his belt pouch.

Esme sensed treachery and shrank back, but the grip on her arms was too strong to break without using

71

her mind as a lever.

*Do not fear me, Esme. I am not going to hurt you,* Bazil silently assured her in what was for him, a kindly manner.

Though Esme still mistrusted him profoundly, his tone threw her defences off long enough for Bazil to accomplish his purpose.

With his eyes and a gesture of his head, he instructed those holding her to keep a good grip on their captive. Then, moving with a speed borne of desperation, he slipped an arm around the back of Esme's neck, gripped her nostrils with his fingers, tilted her head back, and closed off her air supply.

Esme struck out at him with her mind, an attack Bazil had expected and had primed himself to bear. The pain immediately caused his brow to break into a sweat and he had to bite his lip to keep his groan of agony inaudible. Then she opened her mouth to breathe and Bazil poured a healthy draught of the drug he'd intended to use on her earlier down her throat.

Choking and sputtering, Esme tried to keep from swallowing the surprisingly pleasant-tasting liquid, but Bazil clamped her mouth shut with his other hand, and since he still held her nostrils together so that she couldn't breathe, the liquid went down.

Esme might have expelled it from her stomach later. But Baldor, who had included ancient disciplines of body control into his training, and who badly needed to satisfy his sense of justice in some manner, no matter how small, put his hand on a nerve at the side of her neck. "Here, let me help," he said with grim satisfaction. As he pressed the nerve, Esme's con-

# DREAMS OF DESTINY

sciousness slid away so quickly and thoroughly, she didn't even feel the bruising fingers that endeavored to keep her from falling.

Bazil's relief at being released from the pain Esme had been inflicting was so great, he couldn't speak for a moment. He merely stood with his head down, panting for breath. Then he raised his head and fixed Baldor with an ambiguous look.

"Thank you, Baldor," he said aloud. But inwardly, he once again promised himself to keep a sharp eye on the independent young seeker. He was too prone to act on his own. Something needed to be done about him—and soon.

Immediately, a plan to at least get Baldor out of the way for the immediate future surfaced in Bazil's mind. The plan had the advantage that Baldor might also indulge his propensity for disobedience in a way that Bazil would approve of.

"Who will volunteer to take Esme across the Barrier Mountains and deposit her in the desert?" he asked, his eyes singling out Baldor.

"The Barrier Mountains!" A horrified murmur arose from the seekers.

"Yes," Bazil said sorrowfully. "That was what the vision showed. I did not want to say it while she was awake for fear she might . . . Well, never mind." He glanced around at the seekers, his gaze resting on Baldor.

"I'll take her," Baldor promptly volunteered.

Bazil eyed the young man in a considering manner. "You will remember that the vision said nothing about killing her," he said in a soft, firm voice. "And I want you to abide by my vision, Baldor," he lied.

## Jackie Casto

Actually, he hoped that Baldor would follow his independent nature and disobey orders.

Baldor gazed back at his superior in a calm way that ruffled Bazil's sense of authority. He didn't want his subjects to cringe from him, but neither did he want them to feel as if they were his equals. Baldor obviously didn't understand that. On the other hand, that rebellious quality in Baldor made him ideal for this delicate mission.

"I will do what is right," Baldor nodded.

He sounded like he meant to follow his own idea of what was right, much to Bazil's relief.

"Very well," Bazil said in his gravest tone. "You may take the beast-burden to carry her to her destination. The rest of us will carry Malthuzar home in our arms, as is fitting for such a beloved leader."

As the seekers were reverently removing Malthuzar's body from the beast-burden and replacing it with Esme's unconscious form, Bazil drew Baldor aside and held out the vial containing the drug he'd used on her.

"You may need this," he said quietly. "I would not allow her to wake until you are well away from where you leave her, if I were you."

Baldor shrugged his muscular shoulders, held up his hand, and flexed his strong fingers. "I do not need that," he said confidently.

Bazil held his temper. "I am sure you do not," he nodded, smiling in a comradely manner, "but take it anyway. When she starts regaining consciousness, give her another dose and administer your touch to her neck. It will save trouble."

But still Baldor hesitated, and Bazil silently fumed

over the reaction. He wanted Baldor to use the drug as he would were he escorting a woman with Esme's powers to the desert. But despite his earlier hints concerning her powers, wherein he'd played on the seekers' fear of her, he didn't really want anyone to know that she had such gifts, nor how powerful they were. They might begin wondering why Bazil himself didn't have such gifts.

Finally, Baldor reluctantly reached for the vial and stuffed it in his belt pouch. Relieved, Bazil quickly set things in motion.

By sundown, the seekers slowly made their way to the Settlement, carrying Malthuzar gently and reverently in their arms, while Bazil marched solemnly at their head.

In another direction, Baldor strode confidently toward the towering Barrier Mountains, pulling the lead rope of a beast-burden behind him.

Her stomach across the beast-burden's back, her legs and arms hanging downward, Esme jounced along unconscious of her uncomfortable position or anything else. Beside her was a packet of food and two pouches of water Baldor would need for his journey. No one had instructed him to leave any supplies with Esme when he abandoned her on the hot sands of the desert, and he had no intention of doing so. If she were truly a sorceress, and if, despite Bazil's so-called vision clearing her of guilt in Malthuzar's death, she was guilty, she didn't deserve such help.

Baldor was not at all convinced that Bazil had actually had a vision clearing Esme of Malthuzar's death. He had, for some time now, doubted Bazil's spirituality. But since Bazil's solution to the problems the green-eyed Esme might make for the People met with Baldor's sense of justice, he was content to follow Bazil's orders—in this case at least. But Baldor had a strong feeling that if during Bazil's reign he turned out to be as unspiritual as Baldor suspected he was, then the two of them would clash.

# CHAPTER FIVE

After a night of checking Esme regularly and administering nerve pressure if she so much as twitched a muscle, Baldor, by the following afternoon, was not only slightly sleepy, but bored. The dry foothills of the Barrier Mountains were desolate and forbidding, without color, vegetation, or wildlife to provide distraction.

Baldor would never neglect his duty out of boredom, but before he climbed the mountain and had to pay more attention to his footing, he wanted something to occupy his mind. Since Esme was unconscious and could not trap him with her sorceress's eyes, he studied her, something he'd never dared do before.

Coldly objective, Baldor scanned the lines of her small, delicately slender body and acknowledged that it was as pleasing to the eye as he'd always heard it was, and smelled like the flowers that grew on the high meadow.

Her silken smooth, cream-colored skin was lovely as well. There were a few others with such coloring among the People. There were also black-skinned People with black eyes and pale-skinned ones with blue, but most were brown-skinned and dark-eyed. Baldor himself had brown skin, while his eyes were a blue and brown mixture.

But none save Esme and her mother, whom Baldor barely remembered, had those large, startling green eyes that seemed to contain an inner glow. And none had copper-tinged hair of such thick softness and length. Nor did any other woman of the People refuse to confine her hair in a neat braid.

His study completed, Baldor had to admit that had Esme not been tainted with the brush of sorcery, she would have made him a fine life companion, and he shook his head in angry regret that it could not be.

But Baldor shook his head again, this time to clear it of such a dangerous thought. He began uneasily to wonder if her powers could ensorcel a man even while she lay unconscious. Why, he would as soon mate with an asp as take a murderess to wife. It would undoubtedly be safer, at least for his soul!

But an instant later, Baldor remembered that Esme was presumably innocent of murder. Bazil had cleared her of guilt concerning Malthuzar's death, and declared she had acted in self-defense in killing Marcus. And perhaps Baldor's suspicion that Bazil hadn't actually had the vision was unfair. Surely, the new high priest, though his spirituality, in Baldor's opinion, could not compare with Malthuzar's, would not lie about such an important matter?

## DREAMS OF DESTINY

Troubled by such thoughts, Baldor nevertheless concluded it was safer all around to cast this woman away. Perhaps they'd never know if she was really a sorceress. Malthuzar hadn't seemed to think so, and Baldor had had a great deal of respect for the high priest's powers of discernment. But if there was even a chance that she might be—and there was certainly that!—then it was best to get rid of her before she harmed someone else besides Marcus.

That night, however, Baldor slept fitfully, and his checks on Esme were more frequent than the previous night. And his hands lingered oftener and longer on her silken skin than was necessary.

In the mid-hours of the night, Esme's consciousness returned enough for her to dream, if not to come fully awake. She recognized the dream and welcomed it. She rode in the craft which took her among the stars, and she enjoyed the companionship of ones who were nothing like the People except in that they were recognizably human. Especially did she enjoy the companionship of a man of power and strength and beauty, who taught her the pleasures of her own body.

In her dream, Esme was immersed in the pleasure this man brought her. On the hard, cold ground where Baldor had tossed her, her body stretched, twisted, and arched in reaction to their joining, while small sounds of exultant joy escaped her lips.

Across the fire, the sounds brought Baldor awake and to his feet. Quickly, he squatted beside Esme, his eyes narrowing as he observed her writhings, the smile on her lovely lips, and the faint flush to her skin.

It was clear to him what she was dreaming. What was not so clear was why he didn't immediately reach down and still her erotic motions with a touch to her neck. Instead, he continued to watch her until his own desire had caught fire, heating his loins and harshening his breathing and sending him dangerously close to doing something unforgivably foolish. But at last, he found the strength to bring his trembling hand down to the pressure point on Esme's neck and send her back into a state of unconsciousness.

When she lay still again, Baldor hung his head and fought for his breath and prayed for the strength to remove his hand from Esme's silken skin. In answer to his prayer, his feelings gradually changed from passion to tenderness as he realized Esme's skin was as warm and smooth and soft as an infant's.

His fingers then drifted to her swollen, slightly parted lips. They were dry and parched, and though Baldor hadn't planned to care for her physical needs on this journey, he now felt a stab of guilt that he hadn't given her any water, though this was the second night of their journey. Rising to his feet, he fetched one of the water pouches, and when he returned to her side, he poured a little over her lips. But her head lay on the ground and the water merely ran over her cheek to soak into the dirt.

Frowning, Baldor wondered if he was a fool even to think of doing what then came into his mind. Were these tender feelings he was having for Esme putting his soul in danger? Was she beguiling him with compassion rather than passion?

Nevertheless, Baldor lifted Esme's head into his lap, and got a few swallows of water down her throat. Afterwards, he felt reluctant to put her away from him and to go back to his sleeping skin. Surely, it must be too cold for her to lie there unprotected?

## DREAMS OF DESTINY

For a few moments, Baldor cradled Esme against his chest as if she were a child he had to tend, and he scowled into the embers of the fire, torn between caution and compassion. But at last he had a thought that cheered him with its practicality. If he held Esme close, then he could sleep peacefully because he would feel her if she started to waken and he wouldn't have to get up to administer the nerve block.

A relieved smile replaced his scowl as Baldor slipped his free arm under Esme's thighs and got to his feet. Across the fire, he put her on the ground, lay down beside her and covered the both of them with his sleeping skin.

The ground was cold, but Esme's body, cuddled close to his, was warm, and her breath against his neck was sweet. And within a very short while, with a peaceful smile on his lips, Baldor was fast asleep.

As was his habit, Raul prowled the corridors of the Condor before retiring for the night. But it was not his habit to do so with a scowl on his rugged features, and when he became aware that his unusual mood was making his men uneasy, he retired to his cabin early.

Raul knew that his reputation among the men of the Space Service was that of a fair, courteous, and even-tempered commander except in the heat of battle, when he occasionally roared in anger. But no one minded Raul's temper or roar in battle; in fact, they found them encouraging.

Therefore, knowing his reputation, Raul also knew his present ill-humor was worrying his men. But, for once in his life, he couldn't seem to control it, and he thought it unwise to explain to anyone the reason for his unusual behavior. His well-honed senses told him that something or someone was out in that vast, desolate desert surrounding his helpless ship. He could feel a presence there. What he didn't know was whether whatever or whoever was out there was friend or foe, and he was not a man to appreciate such uncertainty when his ship was incapacitated.

Shucking his bodysuit for a comfortable Alpan silk robe, he placed a decanter of aspwine by his bed and retired. But he knew he would sleep little more this night than he had the last which was another reason for his short temper. He was physically and mentally weary.

As he lay on his bed in the darkness, he whispered, "Come on, then. Friend or foe, show yourself! Anything is better than this damnable waiting!"

The only answer he got, however, was silence.

Baldor's caution concerning Esme returned when he realized he was reluctant to throw her over the beast-burden's back the next morning. He actually found himself contemplating letting her return to consciousness so she could ride the beast more comfortably. And that idea, if she really was a sorceress, was completely insane!

*Stop this foolishness!* he said grimly to himself. *Get on with your duty!* And he did, though his handling of his prisoner was still a great deal more gentle than it had been.

At last, he reached the summit of the mountain, and Baldor halted the beast and surveyed the vast desert stretching from the base of the mountain as far as his bleak gaze could see. It was an unholy vista, all right, he thought, a fitting abode for a sorceress.

But Baldor had more and more trouble thinking of

## DREAMS OF DESTINY

Esme as a sorceress. He just didn't know if his feelings were based in truth or if Esme had worked her wiles on him even in her unconscious state. And if he wasn't careful, he was afraid he would cease to care.

With a deep sigh, Baldor turned his gaze from the desert and sought an easy path down to it. But there was none apparent, and he realized he would have to search for one. Since the terrain was formidable, he elected to leave Esme and the beast-burden where they were.

He set Esme in a shaded nook carved out of the base of a gigantic boulder, then squatted beside her with a worried look on his face. He had no idea how long it would take him to find a suitable path, and what if she came out of her unnatural sleep while he was gone? What would she do?

That question was the source of his whole mental quandary concerning Esme and if he had an answer then he would be at peace again.

Had his own welfare been the only consideration, Baldor might have left her as she was. But in the end, it was the thought of what she might do if she returned to the Settlement that decided the issue.

With a grimace, he withdrew from his belt pouch the small vial Bazil had given him. Then, with Esme on his lap, he paused. Bazil hadn't told him how much to give her. For all Baldor knew, he might give her so much it would kill her or so little as to be useless.

With another sigh, he prayed the Master would guide his actions in accordance with His will. Then he patiently poured what he assumed was an adequate dose down Esme's throat, followed by a sip of water. Afterward, he sat for a moment gazing down at the exquisite features set in Esme's oval face, and a great sadness came upon him. Before he was aware of what he did, he raised her in his arms, pressed her lips gently with his own, and then he held her fiercely to his breast while his eyes inexplicably filled with tears.

"The Master keep you," he whispered, before he carefully set her aside, got to his feet, and strode rapidly away on his quest for a path.

Even as he disappeared over the crest of the mountain, Esme's eyes, containing a dazed, cloudy expression, fluttered open. She began to drift in and out of consciousness.

She was dozing when Baldor returned, and though she surfaced a little when he placed her over the back of the beast-burden, she was asleep again when he started off. But finally, the jolting, stomach-bruising ride brought her frowning to the surface of consciousness, and with her hands she tried to push away the terrible pressure on her midriff.

Baldor, glancing over his shoulder to check on her, caught the movement of her hands, and froze, bringing the beast-burden to a halt. Stepping quickly to Esme's head, he bent his knees until his head was level with hers, and he put a hand on her cheek, turning her face up to his.

Esme blinked drowsily, and Baldor caught his breath as he caught flashes of green between her heavy lids. Then, for one long moment, Esme's eyes stayed open and she gazed into Baldor's. Her expression was that of a serene, sleepy child. Far from glowing, her green eyes were cloudy and mild. Then she smiled at him, and Baldor's heart leapt in his chest at the sweetness of her smile.

"Peace to you, Baldor," she said in a slurred, indistinct voice. Then her eyes closed and she drifted

## DREAMS OF DESTINY

off to sleep again.

Baldor could have wept. Leaning his head in his hand, he knelt silently, with his eyes closed, as duty and compassion warred within him. He prayed as he never had before and when he at last raised his head, there was an expression of agony on his face.

But he'd had his answer, and there was nothing to do but obey. So Baldor, with parental tenderness, raised his hand and pressed the nerve in Esme's neck, rendering her completely unconscious again. When he was certain she was under, he rose and continued down the forbidding mountain, at the base of which was a sea of lonely, deadly sand.

That night, when at last a series of sand dunes hid the Barrier Mountains from sight, Baldor stopped. He lifted Esme off the back of the beast-burden, wrapped her in his sleeping skin, and lay her in the flat valley of sand on the other side of the dunes.

The moon lit the barren landscape with an eerie white glow, and Baldor knelt beside Esme to pray again for release from this, by now, loathsome task. He shivered as much from a sense of horror inspired by the lifeless landscape as from desert night's chill.

Had the Master said otherwise—or said nothing at all, for that matter—Baldor knew he wouldn't have left Esme here. But each time he prayed, he was left with the implacable feeling that he must do this horrible thing that his growing feeling for Esme, as well as all the humanity within him, cried out against.

This time was no different. And at last, Baldor, feeling exhausted and hopeless, gave up praying and simply looked down at his charge with the agony afflicting his soul reflected in his eyes. Given the sincerity of his piety, and the implacability of the answers to his prayers, there was nothing he could do but obey.

But as he hesitated, trying to gather the strength to get to his feet and leave poor Esme where she lay, he realized that there was at least one thing he could do, as useless as the gesture was.

At this point, given the depth of his depression, Baldor cared little if he made it back to the Settlement alive. But some nagging intimation of an important duty that remained to be performed in his life argued for survival. Since there was no chance of foraging from the countryside for most of the return journey, he went against his inclination to leave Esme everything and removed from the beast-burden's back the barest minimum of water and food he calculated he would need to get home.

Returning to Esme, he knelt beside her and gathered her limp form into his arms. As he held her, he prayed once again for her safety, though it seemed to him futile. Then, after hugging her to his chest, he kissed her dried, cracked lips, and whispered a tearful farewell.

Half an hour later, his expression and bearing reflecting a great deal more maturity than he'd had upon starting this journey—and more grief than he'd ever expected to feel—he topped the first sand dune. Forcing himself not to look back at what he'd done, but knowing he would carry the guilt of it for the rest of his life, Baldor disappeared over the dunes and headed home.

Esme dreamed of bathing naked in the Pool of Stones, of drinking her fill of its clear, cold water, and of eating a thick, succulent mutton steak and a whole round loaf of grain bread, freshly baked and warm.

But in the dream, the heat of her body was not lessened, and neither her thirst nor her hunger was slaked. Frowning in her sleep, she began again. But no matter how many times she repeated her efforts, the result was the same.

At last, her burning skin, her aching, parched throat and her cramping belly brought her partly awake. But immediately upon opening her eyes, the searing light all around her forced her to squeeze them shut again.

Her head swam, and her thoughts, for the most part, were disoriented. But one thought was clear. She must ease her thirst or die.

Through her slitted eyes, she saw a beast-burden standing with its head down nearby. And thank the Master, there was a water pouch on its back!

Esme started to move her arms and legs, only to find they were bound by something hot and heavy which she desperately wanted to cast away from her overheated body. Eventually, she realized a sleeping skin was wrapped around her and little by little, she forced her arms and legs to push it away. Then she lay panting and exhausted for a while before she could sit up and call the beast-burden to her, discovering in the process that her mind power was almost as weak as her body.

When the animal finally came, moving with agonizing slowness across the sand, its head down, its tongue lolling, and stopped beside her, Esme made the beast kneel so that she could untangle the thongs of the water pouch from the rope circling the creature's neck.

Her arms and hands trembled as she wrestled the stopper from the pouch, but at last she raised the object to her lips and let a trickle of water from it flow down her throat. The water was warm, but it was a life-giving, reviving miracle to Esme, and it was the hardest thing she'd ever done to lower the pouch before she'd drained it completely. But some sense of caution ruled her confused mind and she forced herself to put the pouch in her lap.

She sat still with her eyes closed against the glare surrounding her. She licked the drops from her mouth and felt the water slosh in her empty stomach, which she feared, for a few terrifying moments, would reject the needed nourishment. Slightly refreshed, she wondered where she was.

Cautiously opening her eyes to a slit, she let them adjust to the light and then looked around her at the barren, lifeless landscape and a chill of horror traced her back. There was no question of where she was. The question was why?

The shock of finding herself on the desert disoriented her. But after a while, her memory returned and she recalled Malthuzar's death, Bazil's part in it, and her battle with Marcus.

Esme felt bitter self-disgust at having failed to anticipate Bazil's betrayal of their bargain. True, she had anticipated a journey, her destination unknown. But she had never thought she would end up in the western desert. There was nothing here to sustain life for any human, even one with her powers. When Bazil had convinced her to accept exile, it had never occurred to her he would send her in the one direction that was tantamount to a death sentence. Her mistaken trust in Bazil's humanity had put her in mortal danger.

Esme fought her growing panic by concentrating on

## DREAMS OF DESTINY

her immediate needs. She could do nothing to help herself until she gained strength, and with that in mind, she focused on what the beast-burden carried.

The water had strengthened her and she had less trouble retrieving the food packet than she had the water pouch. Unfolding the skin, she was grateful to discover a few sun-dried strips of mutton, three hard cakes of grain bread and a handful of dried redfruit.

This time, her caution in restraining herself from gobbling everything was more the result of clear thinking than instinct. She nibbled half a grain cake and when her stomach accepted the offering without too much protest, she added a couple of the small redfruits. She ignored the mutton for it would create a thirst she could ill-afford to satisfy.

As she ate, Esme became aware that the light was fading and a wind was stirring. Grains of sand began to sting her cheeks, bare arms, and legs. She also was aware that the beast-burden lay with its eyes closed and panted with severe distress.

Esme was immediately torn by a softhearted desire to give the beast some water but the coldly logical part of her brain argued against it. True, if she could revive the beast-burden, she could more rapidly return to the Settlement to extract her revenge for Bazil's treachery before setting off on her real journey. But she didn't think the small amount of water in the pouch would ease the beast's condition enough to make the journey.

Another spate of sand stung her bare skin. Grimacing with discomfort, Esme looked up from the beast and discovered the blazing light of the merciless sun was now almost completely obscured by the clouds of sand beginning to fill the air. Even as she watched, the sandstorm's ferocity doubled, and Esme's heart clutched with fear. She knew her gifts, even had they been at their best, weren't sufficient to control Nature's unbridled force. And her power was so diminished at the moment, she doubted her ability to send her mind ten feet away, much less to somewhere really safe.

In any case, it was her body that was threatened, not her mind, and she quickly looked around her, searching for any form of natural protection, though she didn't remember seeing anything but sand when she'd looked before. Now there was nothing at all to be seen other than swarming clouds of sand that stung her eyes and her skin.

That left the sleeping skin and the beast-burden, and Esme hastily wrapped herself in the skin with the precious water pouch and food packet tucked inside her improvised shelter. Fortunately, since she didn't think the beast could move and her mind couldn't budge it an inch, the wind was coming from the other side of the animal, so she lay full length against its hairy back for protection, then pulled the sleeping skin over her head and body.

She had no sooner taken shelter when the storm escalated to an intensity that frightened Esme as she had never been frightened before. She thanked the Master that the beast, instead of taking fright and struggling, lay quiet. The wind rocked it, but otherwise it didn't move, and Esme couldn't tell if it was still breathing.

On and on, the howling wind raged. Esme felt hot and suffocated, both by the confines of the skin and by her own fear. But she didn't move, except for the trembling of her body which she couldn't control. She merely waited for Nature to vent its wrath.

By the time the wind died down, Esme was exhausted and feared suffocation. She barely had the strength to throw the sleeping skin aside and lay panting for breath, each whiff tainted with a metallic taste and smell.

Finally, she sat up and looked around. Esme wasn't sure if the light was muted by the storm or if it was getting dark. She then glanced at the beast-burden, its head and body almost covered with sand.

Knowing it was dead, at first, Esme was sad for the animal but then she realized she was overlooking how the beast's death might aid her own survival. Though bile rose in her throat, she forced herself to accept that the meat on the beast's bones and the blood in its veins could restore her strength more than the precious small amounts of water and food she'd ingested. Furthermore, she had no idea how far away the Settlement was, but if the distance was long, wisdom argued for saving the remaining water in the pouch and the dried food for the journey. Partaking of the beast-burden's flesh and blood might make the difference in her ability to arrive at all.

Her gruesome decision reluctantly made, it only remained to find some way to butcher the animal. She had no knife.

Managing to stand, she shuffled in a circle, searching for a sharp stone. But there was nothing on the barren ground other than sand, and eventually she returned to the sleeping skin to rest and think. As she sat, she was aware of the grittiness of her skin, and she raised a hand to brush at her arms, then her face and neck. And as she lowered her hand, it brushed her breast and touched the bulk of the Sacred Pouch under her singlet.

Esme went still for a moment, then quickly pulled the thongs over her head and, with her trembling fingers, opened the mouth of the pouch that was rumored to be as old as the People's sojourn in the valley. One by one, she drew out a candle, a feather, a tiny bowl, a smaller pouch containing a powdered substance and a palm-sized, sharp-edged flintstone, thank the Master! For a long moment, she held the objects in her lap and stared at them. There was a subtle aura surrounding them, an aura of power.

Reverently, she put everything back in the Sacred Pouch but the stone, set the Pouch aside, and turned to the dead animal lying beside her to make the first cut.

Darkness had arrived by the time Esme had filled her belly with raw meat and eased her throat with warm blood. Though she'd had to blank her mind during the so-called feast in order to get the bloody meal down, she felt strengthened beyond measure by its sustenance.

She would have liked to sleep again, but a sense of urgency was upon her. Night was the time to travel in the desert, and perhaps, if she walked quickly, she could be at the Barrier Mountains by dawn. And wouldn't Bazil shrivel with fear when she strode into the Settlement like a ghost arisen from the dead! she thought with grim satisfaction. He probably thought that he had got away not only with treachery against Malthuzar, but with her own murder disguised as exile. But she would make him pay in full for his evil deeds, and afterwards, she would start her adventure!

As darkness deepened, Esme stood deciding which direction to take. The Sacred Pouch was again around

## DREAMS OF DESTINY

her neck, as was the water pouch and the scant remainder of its contents. In her hand, she carried the packet of food that had been left for her. Though she had no memory of how she'd reached the desert, she was grateful to whoever it was who had left her these few necessities of life.

Casting with her mind, Esme, for the first time in her life, found nothing to greet it; her mind touched absolutely nothing in this forbidding land. She didn't even sense the stir of any desert creatures.

Whatever tracks might have been left by those who'd brought her there had been erased by the storm, as, indeed, had any sense of their presence at all, so that Esme couldn't follow them either with her naked eye or the seeking of her mind. And there was nothing to be seen in any direction to give her a clue concerning the way to take, not even in the sky. The haze the sandstorm had left in its wake obscured the stars.

She was completely disoriented, and she stood quietly, waiting for her heretofore never failing senses to guide her. At last, it seemed to her they were tugging her in one direction, and with a fatalistic shrug of her shoulders and a prayer on her lips that her instincts were true, she started walking.

Bazil paced his cave, well satisfied with his present position. Even without the Sacred Pouch, which for some unaccountable reason he'd completely forgotten to retrieve from Esme before he'd sent her off with Baldor to her death, the People, after burying Malthuzar, had acclaimed him High Priest.

So why should he envy Esme's formidable gifts? What good had they done her when pitted against his own particular gift, his formidable brain? He had bested her in the end and as a result, his years of hard work and planning were about to pay off. He was safe and more important, he was safe with his power intact.

As Bazil was congratulating himself on his cleverness and his success, Baldor arrived at the entrance to the cave. He appeared to Bazil's startled eyes as though he'd been up to the Holy Mountain and had been granted a vision that rivaled anything Malthuzar had ever seen in all his one hundred cycles.

After one glance at Baldor's haunted expression, Baldor's self-satisfaction swiftly gave way to an unreasoning fear that everything he'd thought was safely in his grasp might instead be once again at risk.

# CHAPTER SIX

ON THE MORNING AFTER HER FIRST NIGHT'S WALK ACROSS the desert, Esme meant to use the sun to verify that she was headed in the right direction. But instead of the sunrise, dawn brought another sandstorm that forced her to take shelter under her sleeping skin for the entire day.

The sweltering heat and lack of air under the skin were almost intolerable. To reduce her awareness of her consuming thirst and the discomfort of her overheated body, Esme put herself into a trance state and lay utterly still, her mind and body equally at rest.

When the wind died down at last, and she came to full awareness again, she pushed the skin violently away. As she lay taking deep, reviving breaths of metal-tasting oxygen into her lungs, she discovered it was almost dark and again, the haze obscured the sky, allowing her no way of knowing the right direction to travel.

Quelling a pang of uneasiness, Esme sat up and reached for the water pouch. Her thirst urged her to raise it quickly to her mouth and drain it dry, but her mind forbade such a foolish act. Trembling in her efforts to keep her body's needs in check, Esme raised the pouch to her lips and took barely a trickle into her parched mouth.

After forcing herself to lower the water pouch and stopper it, she fumbled for a grain cake out of the folds of the packet, and forced the dry crumbs down her protesting throat. After eating, she took only one more drink before stoppering the pouch and slinging its thongs around her neck.

In a short while, after once again consulting her senses as to the correct direction to walk, Esme was on her way again, striding as fast as she dared into the hazy darkness that surrounded her.

Bazil took the time to fetch Baldor a cup of reviving wine before demanding, in a hoarse, strained voice, to know the results of Baldor's mission. But Baldor drank the wine in eager gulps instead of answering immediately, and Bazil couldn't control his impatience.

"Answer me!" he demanded. "Is she gone? Did you leave her on the desert? Is she—dead?"

At last, Baldor lowered the cup and stared at Bazil, who was not reassured by the haunted look in the young man's eyes.

"Yes," Baldor nodded. "I left her on the desert. But as to whether she is dead, only the Master knows."

Bazil was only partly appeased by the reply. He had

## DREAMS OF DESTINY

hoped Baldor would return asking for forgiveness for having allowed his rage against Esme to provoke him into killing her. Bazil, of course, gravely dismayed by Baldor's actions, would then have granted the requested forgiveness while at the same time having a hold over Baldor.

Failing that most fortunate of communications from Baldor however, Bazil was anxious to know if Baldor had allowed Esme to speak to him during their journey and perhaps to raise questions in his mind.

"Did you keep her under all the time?" he asked curtly.

Baldor nodded, much to Bazil's relief. But he did it so absently that Bazil's fears were not completely assuaged.

"Good," he said smoothly. "I am glad you did not give her an opportunity to confuse you."

At that, Baldor eyed his superior in puzzlement. "Confuse me?" he asked. "What do you mean?"

Bazil was encouraged by the question, but he was also still feeling uneasy about Baldor's strange manner. He shrugged. "Esme is very skillful at scrambling men's brains," he said drily. "Surely, you knew that. You have heard the stories."

Frowning a little, Baldor nodded hesitantly. He had thought about those stories he'd heard all his life, trying to pin down even one specific instance where Esme had done anything to harm anyone. And he realized the stories had been bereft of any such details. In truth, they had been warnings rather than stories of things that had actually taken place, consisting of such phrases as, "It is said she can do this or that terrible thing," with no verifying instance whether she'd actually done "this" or "that."

Baldor shook his head as he realized the one real basis for any suspicion about Esme lay in the mysterious circumstances of her conception. No man had ever stepped forward to claim her as his own, and Esther had told some impossible story about a visitation from a stranger on the high pasture. But there were no strangers here.

Had Esther not had those astonishing green eyes, the piercing glance of which never failed to make people uneasy, Baldor doubted if her story would have had any credence at all. And Esme's only sin was the lack of a father and her possession of the same green eyes as her mothers.

"What are you thinking, Baldor?" Bazil asked, impatient. "What is wrong with you? You are acting very oddly, young man, and I am beginning to wonder if you have been lying to me. Are you sure you did not allow Esme to return to consciousness and she then worked her wiles upon you?"

Voicing the half question, half accusation brought back Bazil's fear. What if Baldor hadn't really left Esme in the desert? What if the two of them, Esme and Baldor, had formed a partnership with the object of taking the priesthood for themselves. What if, any moment now . . .

"I did not allow her to wake."

Baldor spoke with such quiet firmness that his tone splintered Bazil's fearful thoughts and brought him back to reality.

"And I did leave her out on the desert," Baldor continued in that same quietly firm tone. "But you are right on one count . . ."

Bazil immediately tensed again, and his dark eyes blazed at Baldor and the young man suddenly knew he must be very careful what he said to Bazil about

## *DREAMS OF DESTINY*

Esme. Otherwise, he might eventually—probably sooner rather than later—find himself accused of some crime meriting death by stoning.

"I think she tried to work her wiles on me, even while asleep," Baldor continued, amending what he'd been about to say, which was that he'd become convinced of Esme's innocence during their journey together.

"Why?" Bazil snapped.

"Because as we got closer to the desert, I began to find myself reluctant to leave her there," Baldor responded truthfully, his blue-brown eyes steady. "However," he added, "I prayed about it, and the Master gave me the strength to do His will."

"Of course, He did," Bazil said in a solemn, high-priestly tone. Coming to Baldor's side, he placed a hand on the young man's shoulder. "You have done well, Baldor," he said with smooth approbation, "and no doubt you will have a reward for your obedience. But now you must get some rest. You look very tired and hungry. So go to the seeker cave, have a hot meal, and get some sleep. We can talk further about this another time. That is," he quickly added, for in truth he had no desire ever to discuss this matter again, "if you feel the need to talk."

Baldor nodded agreement and handing his empty cup to Bazil, he left the new high priest's cave without speaking another word.

But on his way to obtain the meal and the rest he needed, Baldor's thoughts were far away from his physical comfort or lack of it. He was thinking that he'd been right to assure his own safe return to the Settlement. Because as far as he knew, he was the only one of the People who suspected that there was little of the spiritual about their new high priest, and a great deal of the very practical. Practical in the sense that Bazil would most likely place his own interests over that of the People.

It remained to be seen whether Bazil's self-interest would one day lead to actual oppression of the People's rights. But if it did, Baldor intended to do what he could to thwart their new high priest, despite the fact that there had never, in the whole history of the People, been an instance where such action had been necessary.

And Bazil, as he watched Baldor's departure through narrowed eyes, told himself once again that, sooner or later, something would have to be done about that young seeker. For he was as certain that Baldor would one day cause him trouble as he was of his own plans—and that was a great deal of certainty indeed.

On the high meadow, Esme had greeted the arrival of the sun each morning as though it were an old and valued friend. For it had brought welcome light and warmth to humans and animals, as well as stirring the regeneration of the succulent vegetation that fed her flocks as well as the People.

But by the morning of the fourth day of her journey across the desert she hated the glaring light and broiling heat of her former friend with an intensity that she had only felt in connection with Bazil and Marcus. She had also accepted that she'd been going in the wrong direction all along and was now so lost there was no hope of ever finding her way back to the Settlement.

Now, after dully realizing that the red circle on the

## DREAMS OF DESTINY

horizon heralded the approach of her relentless enemy, she used her remaining strength to dig a depression in the hard-packed sand in the hope of finding some coolness, then crawled into it and dragged the sleeping skin over her.

Immediately, she slept, a deep, exhausted sleep that lasted until the smoldering heat of midafternoon threatened to bake her where she lay.

Not fully awake, she gasped for breath as she scrabbled at the sleeping skin and at last pulled it aside to form a small opening. The heat did not lessen, but the air was more breathable, and as her hand fell away from the skin, her lungs expanded, taking in the hot dry air in huge gulps.

She slept more fitfully then, occasionally opening her eyes only for a few moments in which her gaze was clear and her mind cognizant of her hopeless position. She assumed that by the time the sun had set, relieving the unbearable heat of the day and replacing it with the bone-chilling cold of the night, she would already be dead. So she used her moments of clarity to try to make her peace with the Master.

According to Malthuzar, the Master had had a task, or tasks, for her, and the fact that Malthuzar had given her the Sacred Pouch was evidence that he believed she would serve the Master's purposes. And indeed, Esme herself had often sensed the Master's hand in her life. Why else the mystery of her birth, her possession of gifts no one else had, her certainty of not becoming a priestess, and her secrecy about her powers? Why else the dreams that had haunted her sleep for so many years?

But if her destiny had once been meant to encompass something significant, she must somehow have failed the Master along the way, and He had subsequently changed His plan for her. Perhaps it was her rage and thirst for vengeance against Marcus and Bazil that had offended the Master. The Sacred Scrolls said vengeance was His to take and that killing was wrong. But even in her present state, Esme could not feel sorry that she had killed Marcus nor could she find an attitude of forgiveness toward Bazil in her heart. And perhaps her unrepentance might also be offensive to the Master.

Therefore, Esme humbly accepted the Master's right to take her life, apologized for failing Him, requested His mercy for her shortcomings, and once more fell asleep.

When she at last opened her eyes, she discovered she couldn't see and at first assumed she was dying. Then, as she gradually realized that the sun had set, she focused every portion of her will upon crawling out from her shelter. She didn't want to die in a hole in the ground under the stinking, suffocating folds of a sleeping skin she'd grown to hate almost as much as she did the sun.

Somehow, emerging from the skin, she lay beside it and the hole to gather her last few tatters of strength. Finally she lifted herself to her hands and knees, and she began to crawl.

Neither time nor pain existed for her. Her mind was blank, and her limbs moved seemingly of their own will. Indeed, when she crawled into a pool of water, and her limbs recoiled at the touch of the freezing chill, her mind hardly reacted at all. When her trembling, overworked legs, hands, and arms collapsed, she flopped down abruptly onto her stomach with her face in the water. Then her mind roused itself and she drank, though her mouth and throat shook with the effort to suck up the water and swallow it. When her thirst was finally eased, she exerted her very last ounce of strength to flop over on her back so that her face was out of the water and she wouldn't drown. Her consciousness slipped away then, and she lay still as death.

Shortly thereafter, when Jase came to the oasis pool at dawn to swim before starting the day's work, he discovered her sprawled motionless form lying half in the water.

Raul was abruptly awakened from his fitful sleep by Jase's hand shaking his shoulder and Jase's urgent voice calling his name.

"What is it?" he asked, glaring sleepily up at Jase.

"It's a young woman, Captain!" Jase stammered. "Down by the pool! I found her this morning, and by all the saints, it was a shock!"

Raul quickly sat up and reached for his robe. "Just one woman?" he asked tersely.

"Yes. Of course, there must be others somewhere, but she seems to be alone for the present."

Raul got up from the bed and belted his silk robe as he strode toward the door to his quarters. "Show me!" he ordered.

A few moments later, Raul stood gazing down at the burned skin, cracked lips, matted tangle of long copper hair, dirty, broken fingernails, and filthy tattered singlet of a small female who lay unconscious on the couch in sick bay.

He thought she might be pretty when she recovered —if she recovered. She had good bones, but it was hard to tell much of anything about her at the moment, except that she looked utterly defenseless, utterly unthreatening. Though Raul's face showed no expression, he thought that if this small creature, who aroused his pity to an unusual degree, was who he had sensed out on the desert and feared as a threat, then he ought to be shot for cowardice, unless, of course, the rest of her kind were numerous and hostile.

"Can you help her?" he asked his medic, Thorson.

"I think so," Thorson said, shrugging.

"Then do so," Raul ordered, "as quickly as possible. I want to talk to her."

Turning away, Raul headed back to his quarters, instructing Jase to tell Paolo to round up a small party of armed men and have them wait for him at the exit ramp.

Five minutes later, fully dressed and armed with his side laser, Raul joined the men. One look at them told him there was no need to explain anything—the grapevine had already been activated.

"Spread out in a circle around the Condor and walk as far as you can manage in this hellish sun and sand," he ordered. "See if we're going to have any more visitors. Then report back to me. Dismissed."

As the twelve men headed in all directions, Raul strode toward the oasis with Jase.

"She was right here, Captain," Jase informed him, pointing to the edge of the pool. "The back of her head and her shoulders were in the water, which was lucky. If she had been lying on her face, she would have drowned for sure, the shape she was in."

Raul stared down at the crushed grass where Esme had lain. After a moment, he followed a faint trail in the grass to the edge of the oasis. There he found a scuffed trail in the sand.

## DREAMS OF DESTINY

"Looks like she was crawling on her hands and knees," Jase said from beside him, and there was a tinge of awed admiration in his voice.

"I am more interested in where she came from than how she got here," Raul said absently as he raised his head and stared out across the sand.

But there was nothing out there to see other than sand, and more sand, and to the right and the left, the small figures of the men, who were on reconnaisance patrol.

Raul stayed quiet for another few moments, searching his instincts for any sign that there were more people out there waiting to advance on him and his crew. He felt nothing now. The presence he had sensed before was gone but his instincts might be wrong for once, and it was best to play it safe.

"Mount a guard here, Jase," he said, turning to return to the ship.

"Captain?"

Raul paused and looked back over his shoulder.

"Do you think there are more like her coming, Captain?" Jase asked.

Raul's mouth twisted in a faint smile. "Anything is possible, Jase," he shrugged. "But as of right now, no, I think she is all there is."

He strode away then, aware that Jase had looked decidedly relieved by his pronouncement—which Raul had made in good faith—and that his opinion would spread to the men with the speed of light.

But Raul was also aware that any man's instincts could play him false, and the fact that his own never had in the past was no guarantee they weren't wrong now or wouldn't be in the future. He just hoped this wouldn't be the first time he'd made a bad guess—not when they sat here almost as helpless as babes, armed with nothing more than a few hand weapons.

Though the portion of Esme's mind that had faced the spectre of death for the first time in her life lay cowering in some dark, safe haven deep within her skull, another part—the part that transmitted to and received messages from her body—knew she was now safe.

Her throat had noted the delicious trickle of cold water bathing its parched surface and it reported easement, while her stomach cramped because of the water and reported pain. Her skin, immersed in a cool soothing liquid that it embraced with thirsty relief, smoothed itself out into its customary creamy silk, and her cracked lips accepted the balm of some thick, healing grease and began to seal. The scrapes on her tattered palms and knees stung as they regenerated.

So even though her conscious mind wasn't ready to emerge from the sheltering safety of its own darkness, the rest of Esme renewed itself and exulted in its salvation.

As she lay unconscious in the bath he had filled for her, Thorson watched with amazed disbelief as his patient's body seemed to heal at an unheard of speed. Her skin, dehydrated and burned red by the sun, seemed to relax into a satiated smoothness, its redness fading to pink. Her lips, as well, seemed to be healing with remarkable speed under their coating of thick pergrine grease. Such rapid regeneration was decidedly unnatural.

Thorson knew the captain would want to talk to this woman when she regained consciousness and he would not be pleased to be presented with a female

## DREAMS OF DESTINY

whose hair was a ratted, dirty mass of dull, tangled copper. So Thorson leaned forward and gently soaped the long, wet strands that floated around the woman's perfectly shaped body.

As he cupped both hands around the woman's head to dip her hair backward in the tub and rinse away the soap, he felt a sudden jarring shock. Her hands had gripped his forearms so hard, he felt her broken nails digging into his skin.

Thorson quickly glanced down at the woman's face. He saw two large green eyes staring at him with a piercing look that seemed to spear his soul, and he sucked in his breath.

Though he was used to treating warriors, who required little in the way of a pleasing bedside manner, Thorson, from his unused past training, dredged up a soothing, calming tone. "You are going to be all right," he said softly. "I am a medic. I am treating you for exposure and dehydration, and you are going to make it. Your body seems to have...ah... remarkable recuperative powers." *Which is the understatement of my career*, he thought to himself wryly.

Esme was not really fully conscious. Her body had simply reacted to a perceived threat of drowning when Thorson had tilted her head back. But though she didn't understand a single word of the tongue this stranger used, his soothing tone and the lack of animosity in his eyes reassured her.

Slowly, she loosened her grip on his arms, but she didn't let go completely, and she remained staring into the man's face as he at first hesitated, then lowered the back of her head into the water. She hung on a little tighter when he removed one hand from her head to squeeze the suds out of her hair.

## Jackie Casto

When the suds were gone, Thorson, smiling reassuringly, said, "There. We're done. Now . . ."

But as his gaze returned to her face, he saw that her eyes were closed, and she was again asleep. Shrugging, he attached a harness to hold her head up out of the water, then set the control to let the water drain, and got to his feet.

As he dried his hands on the length of cloth he meant to use to dry his patient, he stared down at her beautiful body. It was small, but in perfect proportion, decidedly pleasing.

"No one heals that quickly," he muttered to himself. "It is not possible. And no one has eyes that shade of green," he added. True, it was a beautiful shade of green, just like everything else about her was beautiful, but it was also decidedly unnatural. Despite the rational protest of Thorson's mind at what he saw, he could not dismiss the evidence of his own eyes.

At last, shaking his head and shrugging away his bewilderment, Thorson gently dried Esme's body and hair, then carried her to the couch and covered her with a feather-light Blancspider spread, leaving one arm bare. Then he attached a vein feeder to her arm and regulated the amount of nourishment that would flow through the clear tubing into her body. After, he sat down at his desk nearby and thumbed through his microreader, looking for anything that might explain his patient's rapid regeneration.

Sometime later, he sat back and rubbed his eyes. He hadn't found anything, of course. He'd half known he wouldn't but it had been worth a try. Then his whole body jumped as his patient's voice echoed behind him, speaking in a language he'd never heard before.

## DREAMS OF DESTINY

Esme woke in a calm, accepting state of mind. As she looked around vaguely at an environment totally alien to her, she did not worry or wonder about her surroundings. She merely accepted them in the manner of a child transported with its protecting parents to a rather puzzling new place.

It was all strange, yes. But she remembered that the man sitting at a nearby table had helped her earlier, and brushing his mind now, she sensed no threat, only kindness. Courteously, she waited for him to cease what he was doing, so that she might greet and thank him.

When he sat back and rubbed his eyes, she quickly spoke up. "Peace to you," she said in the formal language of the People. "I thank you for your help."

She was a little startled when the man jerked around in his chair rather violently. Was he frightened of her? she wondered, puzzled. Why should he be? Then, remembering that she had killed Marcus, Esme wondered if this stranger somehow knew what she had done. Did he have powers to read minds as she did? she wondered, half nervously, half excitedly.

"I won't harm *you*," she hastened to reassure him, speaking in a reasonable, soothing tone. "After all, you saved me from—"

But Thorson interrupted her. "Shhh . . ." he said as he got up and came to check her condition.

Esme reluctantly stayed silent as the man briefly examined her. When he finished, she opened her mouth to speak again, but he held up a cautioning finger and after covering her with a sleeping skin that was lighter and finer than anything Esme had ever felt before, he moved away.

Esme watched, frowning with impatience, as he

extracted something from a cupboard that seemed to open magically to his touch. This strengthened Esme's feeling that he had special powers, but she forgot about that when he turned with the thing in his hand.

It had long cords, at the ends of which were little flexible cups. The other ends of the cords disappeared into a small black box with odd-looking knobs.

Esme instinctively shrank back as the man brought the contraption close to her, but he smiled and shook his head. Searching his mind quickly, she realized he meant her no harm, so she allowed him to set the black box on her stomach and place the flexible cups in her ears. Then he gestured at her mouth and said something. Esme understood that at last, he was ready to listen to her words. Thank the Master!

Smiling, she offered him her thanks and told him he had nothing to fear. Her voice trailed away, however, as he didn't look at her, but merely fiddled with the knobs on the black box. He looked up when she fell silent and with strange words and gestures, indicated that he wanted her to go on speaking.

Esme frowned a little. She'd thanked him and reassured him. What else was there to say until he said something? But there was no mistaking what he wanted, so Esme asked him about himself and her rescue. Who was he? Where had he found her? Where were they now? What was this strange cave in which he'd placed her?

Since she received no answer, she eventually fell silent again, staring at the man with puzzlement written clearly in her large green eyes.

He smiled at her and said something. Esme jerked as though she'd been stung by a stingwasp when his voice came through the little cups in her ears and she understood his words!

"You are healing very well. Certainly, with rest and nourishment, you will be all right in a day or so. Now hold still while I give you something you need."

As Thorson turned away, Esme blinked rapidly in amazement and thought hard. She lifted her head to gaze at the little black box on her stomach, but she was still weak, and after only a moment, she let her head drop again, but by then she'd figured out what had happened. The box somehow enabled them to understand one another. Obviously, they had different words for things because she hadn't understood a word the man had said until now.

A movement by her side made her glance up. The man poured something into a pouch that had a long tube which traveled down and into her arm. Esme gasped and tried to pull away, but the man laid a hand on her shoulder and quieted her.

"Do not fear this," he said, and the words tumbled out of the cups in her ears and into her mind. She understood them clearly. As her eyes, still wide, but slightly less alarmed, returned to his face, Thorson smiled. "You need to rest to get stronger," he said soothingly.

Even as the last word entered her mind, Esme grew sleepy. She didn't want to sleep, however, and she struggled against the warm, dark clouds submerging her mind so that she could search the mind of the man standing over her. But she still found nothing to fear there. Though he seemed a little uneasy, she knew he meant her no harm.

With that comforting reassurance, Esme allowed her eyes to close and before another second had elapsed, she was deeply asleep.

Thorson stood frowning down at her, once again troubled by the strange power in her unusual green eyes.

"Well, it is not my worry," he muttered aloud as he removed the earphones of the translator from Esme's ears and set them and the black box aside. "The captain is the one to deal with this female, and that beautiful body and those unusual eyes won't do her any good with him. He is not a man to be swayed by any woman's appeal when he does not yet know whether she is friend or foe."

Thorson then performed the routine task of withdrawing some of his patient's blood and testing it. But when he got the results, he was more bewildered than ever.

# CHAPTER SEVEN

The desert heat drove Raul's reconnaissance patrol back to the ship just before mid-meal. They'd seen nothing other than enough sand to fill a black hole. Raul was not displeased that his instincts had been confirmed, but he couldn't afford to take any chances. Though it would deplete the manpower for Jase's repair work, he ordered the guard doubled on the periphery of the camp for the time being.

Soon afterward, Thorson requested a meeting to report on their strange visitor's condition.

"How does she fare?" Raul inquired as he settled into his chair.

Thorson sat down, sighed, then shrugged. "She fares very well," he said with dry puzzlement. "Too well, if you ask me."

Raul's smile was wry. "That is exactly why you are here, so that I *can* ask you."

113

Thorson absently nodded. "Well, Captain, I have been a medic for a long time, but until I saw this woman, I had never seen anyone heal with a rapidity that takes my breath away."

Raul's gaze sharpened. "Is there any chance she was faking her condition?"

Thorson shook his head. "No, the damage she sustained was real. It's just that her injuries are healing in record time, faster than anything I have ever known to be possible."

Thorson paused and Raul, his interest intense, waited.

"On top of that," Thorson resumed, "every test I have run indicates she has never had an illness of any kind. She has no antibodies at all in her blood. Also, her teeth are perfect, and I would bet she has perfect eyesight."

"So she will be well soon," Raul said with thoughtful satisfaction.

Thorson snorted. "Sooner than anyone who has been through what she has has any right to expect." He nodded then shook his head. "I tell you, Captain, I have never seen anything like it. Nobody, especially someone who has grown up on a hellish planet like this one, in fairly primitive conditions if you go by her clothes and her reaction to modern technology, should be that healthy."

"She finds modern technology foreign?" Raul inquired. "Are you sure? Or could she be merely pretending?"

Thorson hesitated. "Well, of course, I can't be absolutely certain," he admitted. "She didn't understand when I spoke Confed to her, so I put the translator on her and she seemed to have no idea what

## DREAMS OF DESTINY

it was. Also, when she looked around the sick bay everything seemed new to her. But come to think of it," he added thoughtfully, "though she was a little nervous, she was not nearly as frightened of all the strangeness as she should have been if she'd never seen it before."

"Then the matter is in doubt," Raul said drily.

Thorson's brow knitted. "Yes," he agreed. "And there is something else, Captain. When she was afraid, she would look at me, study me really, and then she would relax. It was as if she could read my mind, and whatever she saw there reassured her. So it may well be that she is telepathic. I did not actually *feel* her in my mind, if you know what I mean, but I can do some tests and try to find out if she is."

"But if she can read minds," Raul pointed out, "she will know what the tests are and whether we find out anything will depend on how much she wants us to know, will it not?"

Thorson hesitated, then nodded unhappily.

"If she has no antibodies in her blood, is there any danger one of us may contaminate her, make her ill?" Raul asked.

Thorson lifted his shoulders in an uncertain gesture. "We have all been inoculated against the common illnesses," he said, "but who knows what she might react to. But," he added drily, "considering how she is healing now, I would be very much surprised if she cannot shrug off an internal illness just as effectively as she does external injuries."

"Let us hope so," Raul said wryly. "At any rate, let us hope she stays healthy long enough for us to find out a few things, like where she comes from, and whether there is any likelihood others of her kind will turn up, and whether they will be friendly or hostile."

"There is always the chance she could be a spy for her people," Thorson agreed.

"When will she be able to talk to me?" Raul asked.

"I would say by tonight," Thorson replied. "You will have to use a translator, but—"

"Very well," Raul interrupted. "Bring her here when she is ready. Can she eat yet?"

Thorson said he didn't know and wouldn't until the drug he'd given her wore off and she woke up.

"Well, if she can, please extend a gracious invitation for her to dine at the captain's table," Raul said in a tone of dry mockery. "Otherwise, bring her here after I have eaten."

Thorson nodded. "Certainly, Captain," he said, and after raising his palm in a respectful salute, he went back to his patient.

Raul sat thinking. Contrary to his first impression, it was possible, especially if their very seemingly unthreatening guest was telepathic, that she was dangerous.

He shrugged his wide shoulders. If she was, he'd know by the time their interview was done. Or if she was skillful enough to hide her intentions from him in a face-to-face encounter, he knew a way or two to find out the truth of where she came from and what her people's intentions might be toward him and his men.

This time upon waking, the significance of the presence of the man who was not one of The People and a place which was not the Settlement began to dawn on Esme. She was not only saved from the desert, but must have started her adventure! Praise the Master, he had turned Bazil's treachery to His

## DREAMS OF DESTINY

own ends and led her here!

Her smile upon this realization was radiant, and it faded not at all as the man who was caring for her, noting she was awake, brought the little black box and placed the cups in her ears. He seemed momentarily startled by the intensity of her smile, but after an instant's hesitation, he smiled back.

Esme lightly searched his mind. Again, though there was still a certain wariness there, she sensed no hostility, and she relaxed and watched interestedly as the man attached another set of earphones to the black box and put them in his own ears.

"How are you feeling?" he asked.

"I ache a little," Esme replied politely, "but I think that will fade soon. And I am hungry and thirsty. Otherwise, I feel wonderful."

Her words brought a look into the man's blue eyes that contrasted with the friendliness of his smile. It was a drily cynical look.

"Can you sit up?" he asked.

Esme was delighted to show him she could, indeed, sit up. Her movement disturbed the tether leading into her arm, which stung.

As she glanced impatiently down at the unwelcome impediment to her movement, she realized the feather-light coverlet had fallen down to her waist and that she was naked. Hastily, she pulled it up with her free hand and glanced at the man standing at her side to see his reaction. It was only then that she remembered he'd already seen all of her and hadn't reacted as most men would have.

The man wasn't looking at her body, anyway, but at the tube in her arm. The he glanced at her face and said, "I think we can remove this now."

Esme nodded gratefully and held her arm up to him. It stung a little as he removed something sticky from the crook of her elbow, and then Esme's eyes widened perceptibly as he withdrew something thin, sharp and shiny from the vein in her arm, leaving a little well of blood behind. It looked like a needle, but the needles she had always used were made of bone and didn't shine.

"What is that?" she asked curiously, pointing at the shiny object.

"A needle," the man replied, glancing at her in surprise.

"Oh." But still puzzled, she hastily added, "But why does it shine in the light like that?"

His look became confused as he explained. "It is made of metal. Many metals shine in the light."

Esme looked up at him wide-eyed, suddenly feeling less calmly accepting of her new surroundings than she had earlier. This new place was filled with things she didn't understand, but she must learn, she decided, and quickly, so as not to appear unintelligent.

"Metal," she repeated, implanting the word in her mind. She fell silent and merely watched as Thorson disposed of the needle in a cubicle he opened mysteriously, without using his hands.

Esme wanted to ask him how he did such a thing. Did he create the opening with his mind? But she decided it would be best just to watch and wait for a while rather than to ask him about his mind powers— or lack of them—or to reveal her own. The old prohibition against revelation was still operating strongly within her. If the man didn't have the same powers she did, he might resent and fear her, and she wanted him to accept her as a friend.

He returned to her side. "Do you think you can stand?" he asked.

Nodding, Esme handed him the black box, then swung her legs over the side of the sleeping couch, noticing for the first time that it was made of some soft, flexible substance rather than carved out of rock and covered with skins or feather-stuffed woven cloth. She smiled, thinking this peculiar substance was a great deal more comfortable than a rock covered with the softest of skins.

The man helped her hop down to the floor, which was covered with another strange material that felt cool. Looking down, Esme squinched her toes against the substance.

"That is plasticene," the man volunteered the information.

Esme glanced up at him and nodded, mouthing the word silently.

Thorson, who had never been inclined to feel particularly paternal, was annoyed to find that he was smiling at the small woman's effort to learn, the way he might smile affectionately at a child. Then he realized she might be pretending to be ignorant, and he grimaced instead. But when Esme frowned at his expression, he smoothed it away.

"What is your name?" he asked.

Esme smiled again, and her smile was so radiantly appealing that Thorson's breath caught in his throat.

"Esme," she said firmly, and held her hand out, palm up. "I am Esme."

"Esme," Thorson repeated, hesitantly lifting his own palm.

When Esme realized he didn't know the appropriate gesture, she hugged the coverlet with her elbows to keep it from falling down, then reached with her other hand to take Thorson's and placed it, palm down, on her own outstretched palm.

"Oh," he said, nodding and smiling.

Esme smiled back and removed her palm from under his.

Thorson found the contact much more disturbing to his male equilibrium than examing her naked body had been. He cleared his throat and gestured at the coverlet Esme clutched to her body.

"I guess we had better find you some clothing," he said.

Esme looked around. "Where is my singlet?" she asked. Then, remembering the Sacred Pouch, she quickly raised a hand to her throat. It wasn't there! Had she lost it in the desert? If so, she would never forgive herself. And more importantly, the Master might never forgive her!

"The pouch!" she exclaimed in an alarmed tone. "Where is it?"

Thorson frowned, remembering the leather pouch that had been around Esme's neck. He'd looked through it, but the contents meant nothing to him. The best he could figure was that the artifacts were used in some primitive ceremony.

"I have the pouch," he said soothingly, and he moved to retrieve it from a cupboard. "But your garment . . . What did you call it? A singlet? I'm afraid it was too tattered and dirty to save. You will have to wear one of our bodysuits, though the saints know it will swallow you."

As he withdrew the pouch from the cupboard and turned, he found Esme had moved silently up beside him. She practically snatched the object from his

## DREAMS OF DESTINY

hands, then stood feeling it with her hands. Thorson decided not to tell her he'd already examined the contents. Obviously, she didn't want him to see what was in the pouch and since the objects were harmless, he saw no reason why she couldn't keep them.

Satisfied that everything was still in the Sacred Pouch, Esme drew the thongs over her head, then lifted her long hair, freeing it from the circle around her neck.

Breathing a sigh of relief, she glanced up at Thorson and nodded. "I thank you," she said gravely.

Thorson nodded just as gravely. "You are welcome," he responded. "Wait here," he added. "I will get you something to wear."

After removing his earplugs and setting the black box down on the couch, he went through a sliding door that Esme had had no idea was there. She had even less idea as to its method of operation, but she had no doubt that she would soon learn.

As she waited, she turned her head and inspected everything in the room. Most of the articles were so alien to her that she couldn't even begin to understand their use. But at the same time, there was something vaguely familiar about them. Then, as she realized that the reason for their familiarity was that she had dreamed of them, she smiled radiantly. Truly, her adventure must have begun!

But then she frowned again as she realized how superior everything was to anything the People had and that made her feel uneasy and inadequate. What must these people think of her? And if they also had the same powers she did, or even more impressive ones, what did that signify concerning her status among them?

Before she could dwell on the matter, however, the sliding door whooshed open and the man returned with something in his hands.

He put the earplugs back in his ears, then said, "Here," and held out a garment the same black color as the one he wore.

Esme took it and held it up for inspection. Glancing from the man's clothing to the garment and back, she realized they were exactly the same.

"Do the men and women of your people wear the same clothing?" she asked curiously.

Thorson laughed as he thought about the thin, elegant, whisper-soft, brightly colored gowns Genesian women wore. "No." He shook his head. "But we have no women on board, so this is all that is available for you to wear."

"On board?" Esme asked.

Thorson looked at her thoughtfully. If this woman was pretending ignorance, she was an exceptional actress.

"This," he said, gesturing at the room in which they stood, "is only one chamber of many. All of the chambers together make up what we call a 'ship.'"

"A ship?" Esme was frowning with concentration.

"Yes," Thorson said patiently. "Some ships are earthbound and sail on the seas and oceans. Some, like this one, are not. They sail between the stars."

Esme knew nothing about oceans, but she did know about stars. Still, it took a moment before a piece of her dreams clicked into place and the implications of what she'd heard struck her full force.

Abruptly, the green of her eyes began to glow with such wondrous joy, it seemed to Thorson as if a lamp had suddenly been turned on inside them.

"You sail among the stars," she whispered with such absolute acceptance and satisfaction in her voice that Thorson grew confused. Would a primitive such as she seemed to be accept such a radical concept so readily? On the other hand, if she was more sophisticated than she wanted him to think, would she make the mistake of showing her acceptance?

"We do," he affirmed.

Then, acting with a compulsion she did not understand, Esme quickly stepped forward and lifted a hand to touch Thorson's face. She stared eagerly into his eyes and searched his mind, unaware of exactly what it was she wanted to find there. But after a moment of intense scrutiny, during which Thorson's expression turned to one of bewilderment, she realized whatever it was she sought was not there, and she felt a sense of disappointment so acute that tears sprang to her eyes.

"Esme . . ." he said gently, raising his hands to clasp her shoulders. "What is it? What is wrong?"

Esme knew not what was wrong with her any more than Thorson did. Nor did she know why she then asked, pleaded, "There *are* others of you, are there not?"

"Of course," Thorson nodded. "There are many of us." Again, his suspicions were aroused. Was her question an attempt to find out how large a force was aboard? "In fact," he added, "the chief among us, the man whom we call 'Captain,' has asked you to dine with him." *And I hope he is better at discerning whether you are acting than I am*, Thorson added silently.

The knowledge that there were more of this man's kind on the ship brought a great relief to Esme's heart.

# Jackie Casto

"Oh, that is good," she said, releasing a deep breath. Then she grimaced. "Of course. I should have known. It is just that I could never remember the dreams clearly upon waking, so—" She stopped. The man was looking at her as though he thought her wits were scrambled. And maybe they were. She was confused herself over what had just happened and she burst into giggles.

"I am all right," she chuckled. "I know what I am talking about even if you do not." An instant later, she realized there was still a great deal she didn't know but she was confident the rest would come. Then she realized she did not know her caretaker's name.

"What are you called?" she asked cheerfully. "Do you have a name?"

Relieved that she seemed to be making sense again, Thorson nodded. "My name is Thorson," he said politely. "And I am a . . . a healer." If she really was a primitive, he assumed that term would be more familiar to her than medic, which he had used earlier, not thinking she wouldn't understand. But she looked blank and uncomprehending.

"I heal people who are hurt," he added. "Like you. I . . . ah . . . healed you." But he was uncomfortably aware that he hadn't really. He had merely aided her in healing herself. A sudden question occured to him. "Who heals sick people where you come from? Do you have healers among your own kind?"

Esme thought about the word "sick," but only when she searched Thorson's mind did she understand its meaning. Then she shrugged. "The Master has promised we will not get sick if we love and obey Him. Therefore, we do not get sick inside our bodies. We wear out. And if we get hurt, most of the hurts heal by

## DREAMS OF DESTINY

themselves. But if a bone is broken or a cut is very deep, one of our priests takes care of it."

Thorson wondered who this "Master" was. Some charlatan who practiced mind control over his people? But even if that were true, the medical implications were astounding.

"You say your people wear out," he said. "Do you mean they die?"

Esme's eyes widened, thinking the question incredibly ignorant. "Of course," she said, sounding as puzzled as she felt. "Death is the only way to release one's spirit to join the Master. Flesh and blood cannot inhabit His realm."

She stopped speaking, wondering if these others didn't know about the Master and His eternity. Surely, they must. But though this man Thorson was nodding as though he understood, she had a sense that he didn't really.

In fact, Thorson was more convinced than ever by Esme's explanation, providing she was not lying through her teeth, that she and her people were ruled by some religious cult which practiced mind control.

Esme looked back at the garment she held. "I do not know how to put this on," she said as she held up the bodysuit. "Will you show me?"

"Yes," he agreed, and helped her dress.

Esme was so absorbed in learning the proper way to don and wear the strange garment and how to manage its fastenings that she felt no embarrassment, standing naked before Thorson.

Thorson, though unembarrassed, certainly was aware of her in a way he didn't particularly want to be. There was no point in desiring a woman who might turn out to be an enemy.

In a few moments, Esme stood with her arms out, her feet spread, looking down at herself with distaste.

Thorson thought she looked like a girl-child wearing grown-up clothes. He'd had to roll up the sleeves and legs of the bodysuit several times in order to free her hands and feet from its folds. The crotch almost reached her knees, making it difficult for her to walk.

"I think I would rather wear my singlet," Esme said, looking hopefully at Thorson.

"It is gone." He shook his head firmly, but then he smiled and fetched her sandals from one of his cupboard. "But you still have these, and later I will give you some sewing materials and you can try to turn this into something you like better. Right now, it is time to take you to the captain."

As Esme slipped her feet into her sandals, she was experiencing an excitement tinged with fear. Suddenly, the room around her seemed very familiar and comforting but then she shook the feeling aside. Of course, she must leave this room and meet the rest of Thorson's people. She couldn't stay in these small confines forever. Nor did she want to, she firmly reminded herself. There was much of the dream she still couldn't recall, but she had never once woken from it feeling unhappy. So what was to follow had to be pleasant.

In any case, whatever was to come was her destiny, and one had no choice when destiny called. So she stilled the frantic beating of her heart and slowed her breathing and meekly took Thorson's hand, allowing him to draw her toward the sliding door.

She watched him closely to see if he pushed anything to make the door open, but it seemed the door opened of its own accord, and after they stepped

## DREAMS OF DESTINY

through it, Esme was still not sure whether Thorson had mind powers like hers.

Then, as they entered a corridor, Esme was held spellbound by the strangeness of her surroundings.

She looked up, down and all around, and decided the "ship" was like a cave in a way, but it wasn't made of rock. Perhaps it was more of this "metal" Thorson had mentioned. In any event, she sensed it was a very large "ship", and she must learn her way around it quickly.

After a short walk, they reached a door which slid open, and Thorson pushed Esme ahead of him into a room that was more sumptuous than anything she could ever have imagined. Her green eyes were huge as she looked down at her feet and saw something that looked and almost felt like grass, but couldn't be because it was red.

Raising her head, she stared at a huge raised platform that must be a sleeping couch, but it was like no couch she'd ever seen. It looked softer even than the couch in Thorson's room, and it was covered with a material that was much too thin and beautiful to be a sleeping skin.

Then she heard a deep male voice, and her attention was immediately diverted from the luxurious room to the source of the voice. And what she saw made her breath die in her throat and a sinking, not altogether unpleasant, sensation come into her stomach.

The man who rose from a chair before a round table was huge. Esme thought she could probably step into his body and get lost there. His weight was undoubtedly at least twice hers, but it was distributed very neatly on his large frame, and his muscles bulged beneath the black material of his bodysuit.

One look at the man's rugged face, which was quite beautiful without being the least effeminate, and the expression in his unusually clear blue eyes convinced Esme that this was the powerful one among Thorson's people. While he would have made three of Malthuzar, he had the old high priest's air of authority and surety about him. Besides, she could feel Thorson's respect and deference toward the giant.

He was looking at her and saying something in a deep, rumbling voice that made Esme shiver in a peculiar way, but she didn't understand his words.

Reluctantly, she tore her gaze from the giant and looked up at Thorson, who looked down at her. "The captain says 'Greetings to you,' Esme," Thorson explained. He meant to say something else, but Esme was already looking back at the giant, giving him her brilliant, radiant smile.

In the language of the people, she said, with soft deference in her voice, "Peace to you, High Priest."

Thorson was startled. "Esme, he is not a priest," he explained. "He is the captain of this ship." He then took the plugs out of his ears and walked toward the captain.

Esme, confused over the difference between a priest and a captain, had to follow him because of the cords.

As Thorson held out the earpieces to the captain, Raul continued to stare at Esme, thinking he had been right that she would be pretty once she was cleaned up. But she was more than pretty. Those unusual green eyes gave her an exotic beauty that hadn't been evident when she'd been unconscious.

"She called you High Priest, Captain," Thorson got his attention. "You have been promoted."

## DREAMS OF DESTINY

Raul's mouth twisted into an unamused smile. "It depends upon your viewpoint, does it not?" he responded in a dry tone.

Thorson had forgotten the captain wasn't a religious man. "Yes, sir," he said respectfully. Then he lifted the earplugs again. "You will need these to talk to her, Captain."

Frowning, Raul glanced down at the plugs. He would much have preferred to do without them, but if he was going to interrogate this beautiful little primitive—if she was, indeed, a primitive and not just pretending to be—he supposed he would have to tolerate the ridiculous appendages.

"All right, Thorson," he said quietly, taking the plugs. "You may leave now. I will call you when it is time to come for her."

At that, Thorson hesitated and Raul looked at him inquiringly.

"Well, as to coming back for her, Captain," Thorson said, "she does not need any more medical treatment, and there is no place to put her other than the royal cabin. Is that where you want to quarter her?"

"I will think about it," Raul said calmly. "Good eve, Thorson."

Thorson nodded and turned to leave. Glancing at Esme, he was surprised that he felt a little protective toward her. The captain could intimidate hardened warriors, much less a woman.

But Esme didn't look in the least intimidated, Thorson realized. She looked respectful, but also relaxed and almost radiantly happy.

*So much for your needing protection*, he thought drily.

As he walked to his own quarters, Thorson was surprised and alarmed that his suspicions of Esme had somehow dissipated. And more than that, his sudden lack of importance to her, now that she had met the captain, was sparking a feeling akin to jealousy inside him.

*That cannot be*, he told himself firmly, but he was not reassured as he had to keep repeating that assertion to himself in order to believe it.

# CHAPTER EIGHT

Raul kept his eyes on Esme's face as he inserted the plugs of the translator into his ears. Though he was by no means immune to her exceptional beauty, it was not her considerable feminine appeal that held his attention, but rather her lack of fear and her radiant happiness at meeting him.

Just as Thorson had found her remarkable recuperative powers out of the ordinary, Raul thought it strange that a young primitive should, upon stumbling head-on against some of the most sophisticated equipment and people the Empire boasted, not only take it all in stride, but be so obviously delighted over her circumstances.

She might, of course, be too simple-minded to appreciate the complexity of a civilization which was capable of producing something like the Condor. But the look in those fascinating green eyes was much too intelligent for Raul to risk such a conclusion.

A Space Service telepath had once told Raul that, if he was not a full telepath, he certainly had the potential to become one. But Raul preferred to think of his capacity to anticipate events and read people as instinct, and his instincts were telling him now not to underestimate his guest. Therefore, he took the precaution of raising the mental shield that the Service telepath had taught him so he could hide any knowledge which might be dangerous for this woman to know if she were a telepath herself and had been sent here to spy for her people.

"Greetings, Esme," he said in what he thought was his normal speaking voice. But it must have been too loud because she winced and brought her hands up to her ears.

Though the prospect of having to remember to whisper to his guest irritated him, Raul showed no sign of his feelings. Softening his voice considerably, he apologized. "My pardon. I'm not used to this contraption. Please . . . sit down." He gestured at the chair opposite his at the table. "Are you hungry?" he asked as Esme moved to the other side of the table.

"Yes. I am hungry," Esme answered soberly. She had been too awed by the captain's commanding physical presence and aura to attempt to search his mind until Thorson had left them. But as he'd been donning the earplugs, she'd sent out a very light, very tentative touch, looking for the same thing in this man that she had sought and failed to find in Thorson. But as her mind had sought to enter his, it had a met a barrier, the first she'd ever encountered in a human mind. And before the shock of that experience had

## DREAMS OF DESTINY

faded, he had blasted his greeting into her ears and caused her head to ache. Now, she was not only confused, she felt very uneasy. Why could she not enter this man's mind?

Raul noticed how her smile had abruptly faded and her eyes had widened, and he then heard the change in her voice that signaled her mood had turned from one of open and cheerful anticipation to subdued confusion. He wasn't sure what had happened to cause the change in her, but he meant to find out—just as he meant to find out everything else about her. The safety of his ship and his crew might depend on it.

Esme hesitated by the chair she'd been about to take. Denied her usual method of obtaining information as to how to behave, she had to rely on her normal human instincts. And her instincts were screaming at her to be very careful with this powerful man until she knew more about him. That she had begun her great adventure seemed evident. But whether she would be allowed to continue it most likely lay in the hands of this one man. Therefore, she couldn't afford to offend him in any way.

"This is where you would like me to sit?" she asked quietly, careful to put respect into her tone and her eyes as she raised them to Raul's.

Raul noted Esme's respectful attitude, but he didn't necessarily trust it. He also noted that his reaction to her green eyes, which were undoubtedly the most fascinating orbs he'd ever encountered, was growing too intensely favorable, given the situation. It was far too soon in their acquaintance to trust the seeming candor of her eyes or to fall prey to their beauty. Therefore, he clamped down his male attraction to his guest.

"Yes, that is where I wish you to sit," he nodded as he took his chair.

As Esme sat down, she was dismayed to find that her legs were trembling. The last time that had happened was when her mother had forced her to come forward as a candidate for seeker and she had been terrified that Malthuzar would guess how she was manipulating his mind.

But at least she had had some control of the situation then, unlike now. For when she tried once again, very lightly, to enter the captain's mind, she couldn't. And if she couldn't get into the captain's mind, there was no way she could gently influence him to regard her favorably.

So it wasn't only the power over her the captain held that was making her begin to fear him. It was her own sudden helplessness. And the way his unusual eyes, eyes that resembled the color of sun-sparked ice on a winter pond, studied her so thoroughly made her wonder if the tables had at last been turned on her. Perhaps this man, whose mind was closed to her, could read hers like an open scroll?

As Raul leaned forward and punched a button beside the table, Esme tried to conceal her anxiety. Then, as Raul slouched in his chair and unabashedly studied her face, Esme hastily erased everything from her mind other than offered friendship and appreciation for her rescue. If he could read her mind, she wanted him to see that he had nothing to fear from her.

As far as Raul could tell, Esme showed little ill effect from her sojourn in the desert. Indeed, she seemed a completely different person from the filthy, injured

## DREAMS OF DESTINY

savage he had seen that morning. But it wasn't her recuperative powers that interested him. It was where she had come from and why she was here. However, he observed the amenities.

"It seems Thorson was right about you," he murmured softly.

The softness of his voice made Esme's stomach clench against an unfamiliar sensation that was not unpleasant. Then she realized he didn't seem the type to speak so softly under normal circumstances. In fact, she had the disquieting feeling he might be at his most dangerous when he sounded the most pleasant.

"What do you mean, Honored Sir?" she asked.

"Thorson said you heal very quickly," Raul murmured. He sensed that the softness of his tone made Esme nervous, so he softened it even more. "I see he was right. And there's no need to address me so formally, Esme. You may call me 'Captain,' as everyone else does."

"Captain . . ." Esme tested the word on her tongue, then dared a question. "Is it a form of address, or is it your name?"

To another man, Esme's hesitant, respectful formality, as well as her innocent curiosity, might have been appealing but her manner irritated Raul and made him suspicious. It was too radical a departure from her former cheerful enthusiasm. Besides, on a purely personal level, he preferred the former behavior over the latter.

"It's a form of address," he drawled. "A captain is the head of a ship, and I am the head of this one. My name is Raul. Some call me Captain Raul, and if you would prefer to do so, you may."

Esme, who found the name more pleasing than the title, nodded. "Yes, I prefer Captain Raul," she said, and then answered his first question. "And Thorson is right. I do heal quickly. All of the People do. Do not you and yours?"

"I suppose some of them do," Raul answered absently. He'd lost interest in the subject of healing as soon as she'd mentioned the People. "Is that what you and others like you call yourselves, Esme? The People?" he inquired, displaying only the mildest of interest.

Esme sensed that his interest was not mild at all, but she saw no reason to conceal the truth, so she nodded. "That or . . ." But now she hesitated. She had not had time to think of it before, but she wondered if Thorson and Raul and their people could be the separate Remnant spoken of in the Sacred Scrolls, those whose ancestors had left the Homeland centuries ago. Surely, since the Master was the creator of all humankind, they had to be! But Thorson hadn't seemed to know who she was talking about when she'd mentioned the Master, which confused her.

If these people were the other Remnant, did this meeting with them signify that the Prophecy that the two Remnants would be reunited was to be fulfilled? If so, what was her part in that? She could not accept that she had been chosen to forge a link between the two Remnants, despite the fact that she was so far the only one of the People to meet them. But she was still not certain that these people actually were the other Remnant.

In any case, a long lifetime of being treated as an outcast precluded the idea that she could be of such

## DREAMS OF DESTINY

importance. Therefore, the Master must have some other task in mind for her.

Esme's hesitation in disclosing what her people were called raised Raul's suspicions. Why should she be reluctant to name her people unless she feared he might recognize them as an enemy? Had the Rebels found this planet and established an outpost, and was Esme playing the role of primitive in order to elicit information in preparation for an attack?

"Or?" he prompted softly.

The suspicion in Raul's voice puzzled Esme but there was also a note of command in his tone she could not gainsay.

"The Remnant," Esme said, watching his face closely for some sign of recognition but there was none. Confused further by his lack of recognition, she added, "In the ancient scrolls, we were called both the Remnant and the People. But in latter days, we seldom call ourselves anything other than the People."

Raul did not recognize such a name, and he was about to ask the key questions of where the Remnant or the People, or whatever they deigned to call themselves, were located, and whether they were warlike or peaceful. But before he could, the door tone announced the arrival of the steward. Raul, hiding his annoyance over the interruption, pressed a button that slid the door to the stateroom open.

Esme felt disappointed that the captain seemed not to recognize the designation of "Remnant." And she was more puzzled than ever. If the captain and his people were not the separate Remnant mentioned in the scrolls, who were they?

She was distracted from her thoughts as a slender man wearing an odd white coat came into the room and carried a laden tray to the table.

As the man set the tray down, Raul tilted his head at him. "This is Jaco," he informed Esme.

The man named Jaco kept his expression neutral and merely nodded in a formal manner to Esme.

Esme nodded her own head, and gave the man a faint smile. Then she watched with fascinated interest as he began to remove domed metal covers from the tray, displaying steaming mounds of food beneath them.

Had she been sitting across from Thorson, Esme would immediately have launched an onslaught of questions concerning the repast. But she dared not say an unnecessary word to the captain, not yet anyway. So she sat quietly as Jaco placed empty plates and clear glasses so beautiful and so fragile Esme feared they would shatter at the merest touch in front of the captain and in front of her. Then he straightened and bowed.

"Thank you, Jaco," Raul nodded. "I'll do the serving. You may go."

Jaco bowed again, lifted his hand in a salute, and departed.

Raul was aware of Esme's interest as he picked up the bottle of wine Jaco had left on the table and squeezed the percussion cap. She jumped a little when a loud pop accompanied the release of pressure inside the bottle. Her reaction seemed to favor the idea that she really was a primitive, but he wasn't about to take anything she did or said as truth until he had interrogated her thoroughly.

## DREAMS OF DESTINY

"Do your people drink wine, Esme?" he inquired with a friendly smile.

The question presented Esme with a quandary. Of course, the People drank wine, though it was kept in clay vessels, not in anything which popped when opened. But Esme, finding that the beverage produced a confused and unpleasant whirling inside her head, had long since stuck to water and milk except during the long cold winters, when a steaming cup of caffee warmed her in the mornings. But what if refusing to drink the captain's wine offended him?

She cleared her throat. "Yes," she allowed. "The People drink wine."

"Good. Then I hope you will enjoy this rare vintage. It is from Varius, where the aspfruit grows sweeter than honeil," Raul responded smoothly. He had, of course, detected the note of reservation in Esme's voice, and he hid a satisfied smile as he filled her glass. Perhaps, if she was the type to be affected by strong drink, this interrogation would proceed faster and result in more candid answers.

Esme took the glass from Raul, hoping she masked her reluctance to drink its contents and her plan to drink as little as possible.

As she started to raise the glass to her lips for a tiny sip, Raul held up a hand to stop her. "Shall we have a toast?" he said as he filled his own glass.

"A . . . t-toast?" Esme stumbled over the unfamiliar word.

A tiny gleam appeared in Raul's eyes as he realized she didn't understand his meaning. Or at least, she was pretending not to.

"Yes," he nodded, speaking solemnly. "A toast is a

139

formal ritual we use when two strangers break bread for the first time. It is a sign of friendly intent. The more one drinks, the friendlier the intention."

Esme was dismayed. Of course, she desperately wanted to signify to the captain that her friendship was his to be had. But she dreaded the inevitable result of imbibing such a potent beverage in large quantities.

"To our friendship," Raul said softly, catching and holding Esme's gaze with his own as he held out his glass toward her.

Esme didn't know why he extended his glass toward her if he intended to drink its contents in this toast of his, but she decided the best course was to mimic his actions, so she held her glass out as well. She was nearly startled out of her wits when he banged his glass against hers—why had the fragile cup not broken?—then put the glass to his lips and drained it.

Esme hastily brought her own glass to her lips, and sipped, watching Captain Raul over the rim. She sighed with resignation when she saw that he finished every last drop, and closing her eyes, she forced herself to do the same.

The taste was not unpleasant, but when she opened her eyes and set her glass down on the table, she was dismayed that Raul immediately filled it again, before refilling his own. Did he expect her to drink another glass of the wine now? she wondered unhappily.

She was much relieved when, instead of picking up his glass again, he filled their plates with the steaming food on the table, saying, "I hope our food agrees with you, Esme. The cook had no idea, of course, what you are accustomed to eating."

The food smelled pleasant but it certainly looked unappetizing all piled together the way it was.

"I am used to meat and grainbread and milk mostly," she said in a faint voice. "And the greenleaf that grows around the pools."

Already, Esme could feel the fiery wine in her empty stomach circulating to her brain, producing a confused dizziness she disliked intensely.

"So you are used to a rather simple diet," Raul said encouragingly, while he wondered where on this Hell planet anything could grow.

"Simple . . . yes . . ." Esme said, her voice slurring very slightly.

Raul heard the slur and quickly glanced at her. He hid a smile. Judging by the way Esme's large green eyes were clouding, she apparently had even less capacity for strong drink than he'd suspected. Perhaps it would be wise to revise his plan to ply her liberally with wine. At this rate, even one more glass might send her into a swoon.

"Well, try some of this eggveg," he invited, gesturing at the mound he'd placed on her plate. "I asked the cook to prepare something bland, in case one of our richer dishes might sit ill on your stomach."

Esme tried to smile, but it was a wavering effort at best. Then she brought her hand up to grasp one of the metal utensils beside her plate. To her dismay, the wine had already affected her to the point that she misjudged the utensil's position. But she managed to snatch it up on the second try.

Raul could hardly believe that anyone could be so rapidly affected by one glass of wine. And he was much amused as he watched Esme's struggles. She clutched her spoon the way a child just learning to substitute utensils for fingers might, and as she lowered it to the mound on her plate, her hand wavered very slightly.

Esme somehow managed to get a bite into her mouth, and though she found the taste not especially to her liking, she carefully chewed and swallowed the strange food, hoping it would mitigate the effects of the wine.

Preoccupied with her struggle to fill her stomach, Esme temporarily forgot about Raul, and he, his suspicions muted by his enjoyment of her comic efforts to eat, made no effort to call attention to himself. Indeed, he was so engrossed in trying to keep from laughing at Esme's delightful behavior that he had forgotten that he had no business regarding a possible enemy with such affectionate amusement.

Suddenly, however, he saw Esme's hand pause in mid-air on its way to her mouth. Then he saw her other hand clutch her stomach while she raised her head to look at him. In her eyes was an expression of alarmed misery.

"What is it, Esme?" Raul asked, his amusement fading.

"I think . . . I . . . am going . . . to . . . lose . . ."

The spoon clattered to her plate as Esme clapped her hand over her mouth and began to retch.

Raul, moving quickly, ripped the translator plugs from his ears and went to her. He snatched Esme's plugs away, then lifted her into his arms as easily as though she'd been a child, and hurriedly carried her to his sanitation chamber, reaching it just in time.

He held her head as she lost the wine and the small

## DREAMS OF DESTINY

amount of dinner she'd consumed. Esme, feeling so miserable that she didn't even notice the strange contraption over which it seemed she was spilling every one of her internal organs, was grateful for the support.

Finally, she was done, but she trembled and felt so weak, that she leaned against Raul. He supported her with one arm and bathed her face with a soft wet cloth square, then picked her up in his arms again.

Her eyes were closed as he lay her on his bed and she quickly curled up into a little shaking ball without opening them.

Raul stood beside the bed for a moment, silently cursing his own stupidity in allowing her to drink wine in her condition. He was consumed with anxious concern for her. He was also shaken by the strength of his physical reaction to her when he'd carried her and held her close. The warmth, texture, and smell of her body had lit a fire of desire within him, and he had a feeling his reaction had nothing to do with his long-term celibacy because of his months away from Genesis on battle duty. There was something different about the quality as well as the strength of the lustful desire he'd felt for Esme that he couldn't explain.

As Raul stepped to his communication panel to call Thorson to come and check Esme, he tried to get his emotions and his body under control so he could think clearly. As he waited for Thorson to arrive, he came to a conclusion that explained his unusual reaction to the woman on his bed. The thought brought a grim expression to his face, and sad regret to his heart.

After examining Esme, Thorson voiced the opinion

that it wasn't just the wine that had affected her so badly, but also the impact of solid food on a stomach deprived of nourishment.

"She will be all right," he informed Raul, who stood leaning against the wall with his large, muscled arms folded over his chest and a remote, icy expression in his eyes. "I have injected a sleeping potion, and when she wakes, we will start her on solid food more slowly." He shrugged. "I should have known, but she was doing so well, I assumed she could handle anything."

When Raul didn't respond, Thorson asked if he wanted Esme taken back to sick bay.

Raul looked up from staring at Esme's huddled form, and noting his glacial stare, Thorson was alarmed.

"Leave her where she is," Raul ordered curtly.

"But where will you . . ." He started to ask where Raul would sleep, but Raul's look made Thorson swallow the rest of the question and hastily bend to pick up his medic bag. "Well, if you need me . . ." he started to say, but the unnecessary words trailed away.

A moment later, Thorson stood in the corridor and asked himself worriedly what had caused that icy look in the captain's blue eyes.

He shook his head as he walked toward his own quarters. It must be that he was merely angry that his questioning of Esme was cut short by her illness, he told himself. But he was worried that Esme had somehow aroused the captain's anger. The captain did not lose his temper often, but when he did, saints help the target.

\* \* \*

## DREAMS OF DESTINY

Raul was indeed angry that he had made a mistake that had robbed him, for the time being, of the chance to find out more information from Esme. But there was more to his anger than the delay of his interrogation of her. There was his long-held, violent repugnance for what he realized she might be, and his disappointment in himself for falling prey to what might be her calculated effort to arouse his feelings. And there was also, admittedly, his deep regret that those feelings had to be squashed since they might be extremely dangerous to himself, his ship, and his crew.

Alarm bells sounded in Raul's head that in his position would be fatal to ignore. The personal reaction he had had to Esme was exactly the sort of reaction every Service man was taught accompanied the attentions of a trained enemy seductress. And if this small, copper-haired, green-eyed primitive was a trained seductress, she had most likely been sent here to ensnare his heart, mind, and body as a pre-battle tactic. Possibly other key men in his command were her targets as well. And Thorson's suspicion that Esme was a telepath only added to Raul's suspicions. All trained seductresses were telepathic, at least to some degree.

But Raul was a fair man and he was not as yet absolutely positive that Esme was the vanguard of an assault by her people, nor that her people were in any way connected to the Rebels. He hoped, too strongly for his peace of mind, that she was not, and his hope lay not only in his concern for his men and his ship, but for himself personally. But he dismissed personal considerations. He could not afford them.

Even though the Empire used such women against the Rebels who warred against the Empire's central authority, Raul loathed such tactics so much that if it were up to him, he would abolish their use immediately and forever. So he would much prefer to learn he was wrong in his suspicions about Esme and he would delay taking action against her until he was sure. But he would take no chances either. On the morrow, he intended to question her thoroughly to find out the truth.

Had he not been suspicious of Esme, Raul would have stretched out beside her and slept. But under the circumstances, the wisest course was to keep his distance. Such women as she might be were more dangerous than a division of enemy warriors. Warriors fought in an honest fashion, head to head on the open battlefield. Seductresses could rot an army from within.

Raul, his eyes narrowed, his mouth stretched in a thin line, moved away from the wall where he'd been leaning and fetched his sleeping robe. Then, he switched open the communications line between this cabin and the royal one he meant to use for the night. Without a backward glance, he left his cabin, sealing the door behind him, and made his way to the royal suite where the heir had been quartered on the journey to visit his mother.

Once there, he called the duty officer, and speaking in a voice that brooked no questions, let him know where he could be found should anything require his attention during the night. Then, after fetching a bottle of royal wine from the cupboard where it was kept locked away from mere warriors, he propped

## DREAMS OF DESTINY

himself on the royal bed and prepared to spend another sleepless night.

But this time, Raul wasn't sleepless because he sensed that something was waiting to come to him out of the desert. Though the Condor might indeed have other visitors eventually, he didn't think Esme's people were poised out there, waiting for a signal to attack. It was too soon. If Esme had been sent to soften up their target, they would know she hadn't as yet had an opportunity to do her job thoroughly.

No, Raul would spend this night deciding how to find out what he needed to know from a certain woman who might not only be the advance guard for her people's soldiers, but was the only woman in Raul's memory who had ever made him forget his duty, however briefly.

Esme dreamed, but her familiar dream now contained disturbing, frightening elements that had never been there before.

As usual, she rode the vessel that passed between the stars, and now knew it was the Condor. But the familiar people of her long-time dream—especially that special person who'd been her source of joy and comfort in previous dreams—were no longer her friends. They viewed her as an enemy, and Esme couldn't discern why, nor could she convince them differently.

Esme moaned and twisted in her sleep. Sweat stood out on her forehead, and bitter tears coursed her pale cheeks. She felt hot and sick and desperate to restore the adventure which, in the dream, was threatened beyond all recall.

Suddenly, in her dream, she felt a great threat approaching the Condor, and she cried out a warning, but no one would listen. They turned away from her as if she hadn't said a word. Then the ship was rocked with a blast that threw her off her feet, and as she was trying to get up, another blast came and another and Esme screamed.

"Esme, wake up! For the saints' sake, wake up! You are dreaming!"

Shaking with sobs, Esme felt herself being pulled into an upright position, and though her eyes came open, she didn't actually see Thorson sitting beside her. She did, however, feel him shaking her shoulders.

Her eyes wide, she clutched his arms. "Listen!" she yelled at him. "Listen to me! There is danger! Please listen!"

"Esme, stop it!" Thorson yelled back. "Wake up!"

Neither of them understood a word the other said because Thorson hadn't thought to hook up the translator. Being roused from sleep by a terse call from the captain, who had heard Esme's scream over the intercom, Thorson had rushed in and had found Raul leaning against the wall by the bed, watching Esme with a cold lack of sympathy as she lay writhing and twisting in the grip of a nightmare.

"Do something," Raul had instructed Thorson in a voice Thorson had thought incredibly calm and even slightly cynical.

Finally, after babbling at him a little longer in her language with her eyes streaming tears and her nails digging into the skin of his forearms, Thorson saw Esme's eyes abruptly widen and she bit off whatever she was saying. Then, like a bundle of cloth that had

## DREAMS OF DESTINY

been supported by metal which had been withdrawn, she collapsed in his arms, where she lay quietly weeping against his shoulder.

Thorson looked up at Raul over her head, his expression bewildered. He thought Raul's returning expression hard and unsympathetic, and he felt angry toward the captain. What man with any heart could listen to such weeping and remain unmoved?

Thorson lowered his eyes and, in an unconsciously protective gesture, stroked Esme's hair.

As Raul watched Thorson comfort Esme, he felt jealousy raise its ugly head inside him, and he quickly, coldly, pushed the emotion away. Then a cynical smile curved his lips as he saw how thoroughly Esme was beguiling Thorson into becoming her defender. The medic stroked and patted his patient the way a father might soothe a child—or the way a lover might comfort his beloved? Raul's suspicions concerning Esme abruptly escalated.

Straightening, Raul spoke to Thorson in the tone of a command. "Put her to sleep again."

Thorson jerked his head up, still looking bewildered, but also slightly belligerent. "Captain, I do not know if that is a good—"

But Raul's expression stopped Thorson cold and his voice was very soft as he said, "I did not ask your opinion, Thorson. I gave you an order. Obey it now."

Thorson tightened his jaw in unspoken rebellion, but wasn't so unwise as to challenge Raul's authority.

Esme clung to him as Thorson tried to get up and fetch his bag. He spoke gently to her, knowing she couldn't understand, but hoping his tone would reassure her.

"I am going to give you something to make you feel better, Esme. Let go of me now. I will be right back."

Esme reluctantly released her grip. As Thorson got up from the bed, she curled her fingers into tight fists and wrapped her arms around her tiny waist.

While Thorson fumbled in his bag for a sedative, Esme abruptly sensed another presence in the room. She jerked her head over her shoulder to find Captain Raul standing with his huge hands on his narrow hips, staring at her, which brought a chill to her spine.

For a long moment, the two of them stared at one another without saying a word. Raul's face was cold and set and unyielding. His eyes looked like chips of blue ice.

Esme at first was puzzled by his expression. He'd been very kind when she'd been taken ill earlier. Then, as the barest shards of her dream came back to her, she felt a shaft of emotional pain flare through her mind that stole her breath away for a second. Finally, as Raul continued to gaze at her as though she were an enemy to be viewed without pity, she felt a deep, invasive fear crawl through her senses, so that she had to look away to keep him from detecting her reaction.

"Here, Esme," Thorson said gently as he took hold of her right arm. "This will make you feel better."

Esme trusted Thorson by now. And she didn't move, even when, after he pressed a small black instrument against the crook of her arm, she felt the sting of a needle being pushed into her vein.

Immediately, she became drowsy, and didn't protest as Thorson helped her lie down on the bed again. She lay there with her eyes closed, her body relaxing by degrees, while her mind started to float. Just before

# DREAMS OF DESTINY

she fell asleep, she was aware that Raul and Thorson were speaking to one another, but even if she could have understood the words, she wouldn't have been interested in listening. She felt a great disinterest in everything. She wanted only to sleep deeply, too deeply to dream.

"Captain, I . . ." Thorson was trying to think of some way to have his medical authority prevail over Raul's authority as captain of the ship so that he could get Esme back to sick bay and out of the captain's cold grip of unsympathetic harshness.

Raul held up a hand to silence Thorson as he bent over Esme to make sure she slept. After all, she might have only pretended she couldn't speak Confed in order to gather information. Therefore, he didn't want to say anything until he was certain she couldn't hear.

When he was sure she slept, he straightened and turned to his medic. "Did it ever occur to you, Thorson," he said, speaking very quietly and grimly, "that Esme might be a trained seductress?"

The idea startled Thorson. Of course, he knew such women existed. He'd studied them as part of his preparation for service in the military. They were usually at least slightly telepathic in order to plant suggestions into their victims' minds. They were implanted with pheromones in their skin which worked upon men to attract them sexually, even against their will. They were taught male psychology and were given males, usually men from among their own people who were in trouble with the government and could be disposed of later, to train on. And when one of them got their hooks in a man, the only way to break the bond that had formed on the man's part was to kill the seductress and subject her victim to long-term psychological treatment.

"I—" Thorson stopped, swallowed, and shook his head. "No, Captain. It . . . it had not occurred to me."

Raul smile was faintly sardonic. "Perhaps the reason it did not was that she did not intend for that thought to occur to you," he suggested.

Thorson shook his head again, this time bewildered, as he stared down at Esme. "I . . . I guess it is possible," he said doubtfully. "And of course there is no real way to tell."

"Is there not?" Raul said in a way that brought Thorson's head up.

"Well . . . not medically," he clarified his statement.

Raul nodded. "Perhaps not," he agreed. "But I assure you, there are ways to tell. And I intend to begin finding out tomorrow morning."

Thorson, aware that he felt protective toward Esme again, but now suspicious of his own feelings, eyed the captain uncertainly.

"I just wanted you to be aware of the possibility, Thorson," Raul said, his voice quietly calm. "It is by no means a certainty yet. But," he added, and now his voice held the tone of command no one under his authority would dare challenge, "I do not want any protests from you when I start trying to discover the truth. No matter what I order done, you will accept it and you will do your part. Understand?"

Thorson hesitated, swallowed, then nodded. "Aye, Captain," he said, his tone slightly shamed. It had

## DREAMS OF DESTINY

been his job to bring such a possibility to the captain's attention, not the other way around. And he had failed in his job, which was bad enough. What was even worse was that he still felt reluctant to harm Esme in any way or to let the captain harm her. And that was a very strong indication that the captain might be right about her.

"Very well, Thorson," Raul said coolly. He hadn't missed Thorson's hesitation, and he was aware of what was behind it. "I will be in the royal cabin if you need me. I am leaving the communications channel open in here, so I will hear her if she has any more bad dreams. You are dismissed."

Thorson looked at the captain with shamed understanding in his eyes. Before this conversation, he wouldn't have recognized the danger Esme might represent, and he would have slept peacefully beside her—or perhaps not so peacefully if she turned out to be what he hoped she wasn't.

Not for the first time, Thorson realized why Raul was the captain and not just any captain either. He was considered the best of the best, not only by his men, but by his superiors as well. Even the High Counselor was said to consider Raul the example other commanders should follow, and he had shown his favor by entrusting his son and heir to Raul for safe transport during wartime across an entire galaxy.

"Aye, Captain," Thorson repeated with quiet acceptance, and sketching a salute, he left the cabin.

Raul paused for a moment, gazing down at Esme where she lay sleeping heavily now. She looked like an innocent child, and his instincts told him his tests would fail to convict her of anything more serious than the ignorance of one who'd been born and reared far away from civilized worlds.

But he couldn't trust his instincts in this case. Certainty was mandatory. When dealing with the possibility that a trained seductress had been let loose in the midst of his crew, he couldn't afford to trust anything other than irrefutable facts.

# CHAPTER NINE

Upon awakening, Esme's first concern was her body's discomfort. Her head throbbed, and her tongue was coated with some foul substance that made her grimace the moment she opened her eyes. But her most immediate need was to relieve her full bladder.

Gingerly, she sat up in the bed and looked around the cabin. She was relieved to find she was alone. Captain Raul was not a man she cared to face when she didn't have her full wits about her, and she hoped fervently he wouldn't return before she'd had time to attend to herself.

Scooting on her bottom to the edge of the huge bed, she got to her feet. It was only as she felt the tickle of the strange floor covering that she discovered someone had removed her sandals. She glanced absently down, but the red color of the surface hurt her eyes and made her stomach feel queasy, and she quickly looked up again. The movement sent a shaft of pain knifing through her throbbing brain, and a soft moan escaped her lips as she closed her eyes and lifted her hands to press them hard against her skull.

After a moment spent using her mind to bring the pain into relative submission—a moment she could ill spare from her search for a place to relieve her bladder—she lowered her hands and opened her eyes again. Then she headed for the small, adjoining room where Captain Raul had taken her the night before when she was ill. Inside, she stared around in puzzlement at the totally alien equipment.

Fastening her eyes on the gleaming receptacle which had accepted her stomach's contents, she gave a shrug. If it could dispose of one thing, why not another?

It took her a very uncomfortable few moments to get out of the bodysuit, and when she at last stepped out of it, she impatiently kicked it aside. Then, approaching the receptacle attached to the wall, she straddled it with her legs and sat down on it facing the wall, closing her eyes in blissful relaxation as she began to ease her bladder.

Raul, having slept barely at all and anxious to begin his interrogation of Esme, arose early and went straight to his cabin. He spared the empty bed the barest glance as he headed for the sanitation chamber, but what he saw when he reached the open hatch brought him to an abrupt stop.

The soft carpeting had muffled his steps, and Esme's sensing powers were on hold for the moment as she gave herself up to her body's needs, so that she was unaware there was anyone behind her.

After a moment, Raul, a reluctant smile of amusement at Esme's unorthodox use of the sanitation

## DREAMS OF DESTINY

receptacle pulling at his lips, retreated to wait for her in the outer chamber. Even a potential enemy deserved a modicum of privacy, he thought with self-mocking dryness as he went to the communications console to punch the button that would summon Thorson.

When Thorson appeared in the captain's cabin slightly out of breath from having run from sick bay, Raul forestalled his greeting by putting a finger to his lips and gesturing with his head toward the sanitation chamber.

Esme was just standing up when Thorson appeared in the doorway, and he had his smile under control by the time she turned around. Actually, he thought it intelligent of her to have figured the contraption out at all. She'd been so dehydrated while under his care, she hadn't needed to use the facilities in sick bay.

Esme gave a little jerk of surprise at finding Thorson behind her, and her look conveyed dismay for a second. Though she wasn't all that pleased to see him before she'd had time to attend to her aching head and to find some way to rinse her mouth, she nevertheless smiled wanly and nodded her head at him. "Peace to you, Thorson," she said.

Thorson motioned her to stay where she was and said, "Wait."

Esme understood the gesture, and when he disappeared, she shrugged, then looked around her. The preceding night, Captain Raul had obtained water from some source, but she'd been in no shape to see where he'd gotten it. She spotted the square cloth he'd used to wipe her face, however, and she picked it up and cleaned her thighs.

She finished as Thorson returned with the transla-

157

ter, and Esme, tossing the square of cloth back where she'd found it, resignedly took the two plugs from him and placed them in her ears.

Thorson, remembering Captain Raul's suspicions, determinedly kept his eyes off Esme's naked body as he smiled and greeted her.

Esme responded, using his form of address rather than hers. "Greetings, Thorson," she nodded.

"Do you feel unwell, Esme?" Thorson asked, noting the heavy-lidded look of her eyes and the dark circles under them.

"A little," Esme sighed, pointing to her head. "My body does not tolerate wine easily. Normally, I do not partake."

Thorson smiled a little, and asked, "Then why did you drink it last night?"

Esme gave him a look that made a verbal answer unnecessary. It said quite clearly that one didn't act impolitely and refuse anything offered by a man such as Captain Raul.

Thorson chuckled. "Of course," he nodded. Then he looked at her kindly. "Would you like me to show you how to use all this, Esme?" he asked, gesturing around him at the room.

Esme brightened up immediately. "Yes, please," she nodded.

Thorson set the translator box on the counter, then gently took Esme by the shoulders and guided her back to the receptacle she'd used earlier. When she started to turn around, he held her firmly, and when she glanced up at him inquiringly, he said, "You sit on it this way, Esme," and he pushed her shoulders a little to make her bend her knees.

"Ah!" Esme exclaimed in a pleased fashion. She

## DREAMS OF DESTINY

found this position much more comfortable than the other one.

"And when you are done," Thorson said patiently, "you push this." He guided her hand to a button on the wall behind the receptacle and used her finger to push it. Immediately a brief flush of water descended from the upper edges inside the receptacle and washed down a hole at the bottom of it, nearly startling Esme out of her wits.

"Oh!" she exclaimed as she jumped to her feet. But then she turned and bent cautiously over the receptacle. "Where does it go?"

Thorson thought about the difficulty of explaining the ship's recycling system and found it too daunting. "Never mind," he shook his head. "I will explain that some other time. Come here, Esme," he added, and taking her hand he pulled her to a flat space protruding from one wall, in the middle of which was a bowl that Esme had noted earlier. Above the bowl was a metal spigot and there were two buttons on the wall above it.

"If you want to wash your hands and face," Thorson explained, "you push these." He took her hand again, but Esme pulled it away and eagerly pressed one of the buttons by herself. She was delighted when a gush of water issued from the metal thing, and with a small sound of pleasure, she thrust her cupped hands into the water, intending to get herself a drink.

"Esme, don't . . ." Thorson started to say, but it was too late.

"Yowww!" Esme yelled as she jerked her burned hands from the water.

Thorson sighed and fetched her a small square of

cloth which she quickly seized and used to dry her hands. Then she looked up at him with such a comical expression of betrayal on her face that Thorson issued a grunt of laughter.

"I tried to warn you," he said, shrugging. "Now are you ready to let me show you the proper way?"

Esme nodded.

During the next few moments, Thorson pointed out the basic principles of using the sanitation chamber, including the shower, the air dryer, and the way to get a drink of water, which Esme eagerly gulped down. Neither he nor Esme were aware that Raul stood outside the door and watched the proceedings with a sardonic expression on his rugged face.

His eyes, as he let them wander in a leisurely, cynically appreciative journey from the top of Esme's tousled head to the tips of her small feet, showed no expression. But inwardly, he was fighting his body's inevitable reaction and thinking that if Esme really was a trained seductress, her people had chosen well.

She was small, but everything was in proportion. And every portion of her, especially the firm, creamily smooth and delectably uptilted breasts, was luciously female. Raul particularly liked the way Esme's long copper hair hung down her smooth back to her firm buttocks. A man with a little imagination could find a thousand uses for hair like that.

Esme glanced through the door and saw him staring at her, and her sudden alarmed expression brought Raul's thoughts away from her physical charms and back to what transpired in her clever little mind.

In preparation for his forthcoming interrogation, he deliberately let his glance travel her body in an utterly impassive inspection designed to make her think he found her barely attractive. Then he tilted his head at her in the slightest of greetings before directing his attention to Thorson, who was now looking at him in an uncertain, half-apologetic fashion. It was obvious that Thorson had gotten so caught up in teaching Esme the intricacies of modern plumbing that he'd forgotten the captain was waiting.

"When you are ready, Thorson," Raul said with exaggerated patience, "perhaps you and Esme would join me in a meal. You can choose what is least likely to upset her delicate stomach."

Then he turned away and crossed to the communications console to let the duty officer know his location.

Esme stared after him, wary caution in her eyes.

Thorson privately couldn't blame Esme for feeling wary of the captain. Then he reminded himself that the captain might very well be right about Esme being a trained seductress who was serving as an advance guard for an attack by her people and he decided to keep a watch on his wayward sympathies.

"Dress yourself, Esme," he said, gesturing at the bodysuit in the corner where Esme had kicked it. "The captain is not a patient man."

Esme followed his glance, her expression eloquently expressive of her distaste for the clothing she'd been provided. But she picked the garment up and began to put it on.

In the interest of speed, Thorson helped her close the fastenings and roll up the sleeves and legs, then escorted her to the outer cabin.

Raul was seated at the table, and his face gave nothing away to Esme's hurried glance at him as she took the chair she'd occupied the night before.

## Jackie Casto

Thorson sat between them.

Raul gave her a brief nod, then told Thorson to order a meal. When Thorson had chosen a normal meal for himself and the captain and a small portion of gruel for Esme, Raul turned his cool, light-colored gaze on Esme. Suddenly, a shiver of dread ran through her at the look in his eyes. There was no acceptance of her there this morning. She didn't know what had happened to turn his pleasant civility toward her upon their first meeting to the coldness he'd displayed later the preceding night and was displaying now.

"Give me your plugs, Thorson," Raul said in a quiet, authoritative tone, and Thorson immediately complied.

Esme noted that instant obedience, as well as the way Thorson avoided looking directly at her now, and deduced that she could count on him for no support in whatever was to come. The realization left her bereft.

Returning her gaze to the hard planes of Captain Raul's face, Esme took a deep breath and used the time while he inserted his ear plugs to calm the turmoil that had begun to roil inside her. She was certain that she would need all her wits and all her courage to face whatever the captain had in mind for her.

"After our meal, Esme," Raul's voice echoed softly in her ears, "you and I are going to have a long talk."

Esme blessed the fact that she had used the time allowed her wisely. Her returning gaze, in the face of Raul's intent, probing inspection, displayed a great deal more calmness than she felt.

"My life is in your hands, Captain," she stated the obvious with quiet dignity.

"Aye," Raul agreed, his tone flat. "You would be

## DREAMS OF DESTINY

wise to remember that fact. Also would you be wise to remember that I do not tolerate lies, half-truths or evasions from those whose lives I control. I will have truth from you, Esme, or you will wish you were back in the desert, at the mercy of sun and sand. For your chances there will be better than here, if I find you trying to conceal anything from me that I wish to know."

Esme could tell the captain meant what he said. Her fate would undoubtedly depend on the answers she gave to the questions he would soon pose. And beneath her calm exterior, she struggled with a hard decision.

The inner prohibition she had felt all of her life against disclosing her special powers still operated within her. If these people she found herself among had no such powers of their own, might they not react badly to her? Might they possibly deposit her back in the desert to die, the way Bazil had, or kill her outright?

Yet, the fact that she could not read Captain Raul's mind worried her greatly. She could not fathom how he hid his thoughts from her. She would not know how to conceal her thoughts from invasion if she were confronted with someone who could read minds as she did. She had never had to. So might Captain Raul have powers similar to her own—or even greater ones?

If he did, surely he would know if she concealed her gifts from him and then he might be angry enough to deny her her adventure, or possibly even kill her. But on the other hand, if he didn't have such powers, she might be sealing her death warrant by revealing her own.

Esme didn't know what to do. But for the present, her inner prohibition to conceal her gifts was stronger than her fear of what might happen if she was found out. And in any case, if she was found out, perhaps she would be given time to explain why she had opted for concealment, and perhaps Captain Raul would accept her explanation.

It seemed the wisest course to risk concealment until she knew more. Therefore, Esme silently gathered all the protection her own mind could give her, and all the courage she possessed. It seemed to her as though she would need both to lie convincingly enough to salvage her fate from disaster.

A few hours later, Thorson was long gone from the cabin, but Esme still sat in the same chair, which was turned outward to face the room. Her head rested wearily upon the updrawn knees her arms circled, and her eyes were closed. She fought to cope with the utter exhaustion dragging at her every nerve and cell.

"Once again, Esme," Raul's voice echoed softly in her ears. "I want to hear it again."

Esme didn't immediately answer. Having no experience with modern interrogation methods, she was too wearily incredulous by his asking her to repeat a story she had already told him half a dozen times to respond.

But Raul's voice again echoed in her ears, soft and relentless. "Sit up, Esme. Look at me."

Esme slowly lifted her weary head. When she saw the hard, purposeful expression on Raul's face, she knew her freedom from his relentless questions would be a long time coming. Concealing an exhausted sigh, she obediently put her legs down and sat straight.

## DREAMS OF DESTINY

Another man might have taken pity on a woman whose lids drooped so tiredly over bewildered eyes filled with exhausted pleading for release from questioning and an opportunity to rest. He might have given in to feelings of shame at knowing he was responsible for the dark circles under those eyes.

Raul, however, forced himself to push such emotions aside. Deep within him, in that place that had never failed him before, he knew Esme was holding something back. She was not telling him everything. And since the lives of his men and the safety of the Condor might be at stake, he had no choice but to ignore pity. He had to ignore anything that might hinder him from learning what Esme concealed.

"You say your people distrusted you and your mother," he said, his soft voice tinged with steel. "They thought you were sorceresses." He paused as Esme's head bobbed weakly in an affirmative gesture. "Was it only the color of your eyes that sparked their mistrust, Esme?" he asked. "Or," he added with a casualness that he hoped would lull her into a revealing reaction, "did they sense you were telepathic?"

But Raul's trick failed. Esme's only reaction was the same sort of muted confusion she had shown before when she didn't understand some of the terms he used. However, as he had before, he wondered if she was only pretending to be confused.

Angry over that possibility, and tired from a lack of sleep the night before and the hours of questioning that had fatigued him almost as much as they had Esme, Raul temporarily lost control over the soft, relentless tone he had been using with her since the interrogation began.

"What is the problem now?" he asked, his tone

grimly rasping. "What is it you do not understand *this* time?"

Esme licked her dry lips before answering. She had had no water since the interrogation began, and her pride wouldn't let her ask for any because she feared Raul would reject her request. She had stopped Raul often for explanations of his terms, and though he always provided them without any change in his voice, she had sensed that the interruptions made him impatient. Now, he sounded angry as well, and she did not want to make him angrier by asking for further explanations.

She croaked out, "Nothing. There is no problem."

Raul frowned, positive she was lying. And then as he studied Esme's wan, delicate face, trying to decide if she was lying because she didn't want to answer his question about being a telepath, she ran her small, pink tongue around lips that looked dry and parched. Suddenly, he realized she was extremely thirsty.

Automatically, he turned, intending to get her a drink of water. Then he stopped, realizing that as much as it went against his humanitarian instincts— as well as other uncontrollable instincts that were still operating inside him where Esme was concerned— this was no time to play the gentleman. Too much depended on finding out what she was hiding. He'd gone easy on her long enough. Now, it was time to see what a little cruelty might accomplish.

Pushing his normal inclinations ruthlessly aside, Raul walked to the sanitation chamber, where he drew himself a cup of water. Then he walked back to stand in front of her, and deliberately drank it all.

The coldness in his eyes, the deliberate cruelty of his action, brought a sob of despair welling up into

Esme's throat. Her body was crying for water. But she swallowed the sob, refusing to grant him the satisfaction of knowing that his cruelty had had the desired effect. Her resolve to withhold certain knowledge from him had weakened another notch.

Courage and pride were two qualities Raul admired, and wryly, he offered Esme a silent "Bravo!" in recognition of her performance. But he showed nothing of his admiration. Instead, he bored in on the weakness he perceived developing in Esme.

"If you do not understand any of my terms, say so!" he bit out in a deliberately badgering tone. "Unless you choose to play the primitive to hide the truth? Is that it, Esme?"

An involuntary shudder shivered through Esme's body before she could stop it, making her even more aware that her reserves of strength were waning. She opened her mouth to speak, then closed it, and shook her head.

Raul bent down until his face was only a bare inch from hers. Esme's body tensed, using energy she could ill afford to waste, and she tried instinctively to draw back from the hard purpose in his eyes, the intimidating hugeness of his muscled body. But there was nowhere for her to go. Her back was already against the chair.

"Speak up, Esme!" Raul demanded. "I want an answer!"

Wavering on the edge of panic at the discovery that her strength was failing her when she needed it most, blinking away tears that suddenly stung the backs of her eyelids, Esme acted instinctively. Raising one of her small hands to push against Raul's broad chest, she quavered out an answer to his question, shaking her head as she did so.

"It . . . it makes you angry when I ask," she said, her unshed tears in her voice. "I . . . d–don't want . . . to make you angry."

Esme's tears tore at Raul's heart in a way no woman's tears had ever affected him, and his strong emotional reaction took him completely by surprise. But it was another reaction that made him momentarily freeze into immobility.

He was still wearing his robe and Esme's hand had landed in the gaping opening of it on his bare skin. Instantly, her touch set a fire of desire raging through his body that was so overwhelming, it was all he could do to stop himself from pulling her up from her chair, crushing her in his arms, and plundering her mouth.

But the very strength of his reaction was a warning. For one thing, he had never reacted in such an out-of-control fashion to a woman before. And for another, it was exactly the sort of reaction a trained seductress was able to elicit in a victim.

Breaking that contact was one of the hardest things Raul had ever had to do, and for that reason, his next action was harsh and violent. With a flashing speed and an undercurrent of savagery that terrified Esme, he reached down and flung her hand away from his chest. Then abruptly, he straightened and turned his back to her.

Esme stared at his back, helpless fear and desperation shining from her eyes. She had no idea what she had done to make the captain so angry, and the violent emotions she sensed in him confused and frightened her.

Desperately, she wondered how much longer she could hold out. How long before he got from her the

## DREAMS OF DESTINY

information that she could read other people's minds, minds other than his, and that she had killed a man using only the force of her own mind. And when he knew, would he kill her rather than take the risk of having a force he couldn't control in such close quarters to himself, his men, and his ship? Was there even the slightest chance that he would believe her if she told him she had no intention of using such force against him? That if he wanted, she would use it for him to show her gratitude for her rescue and to obtain her dream?

But Raul's expression when he at last turned around to face her again argued against any such belief on his part. His demeanor was now so menacing that Esme, after one frightened look at his expression, used the last of her depleted strength to shore up her defenses.

"You will not touch me again," he said in a low, dangerous voice that struck terror in Esme's breast. "Do you understand?"

Esme nodded, her head trembling on the slender stalk of her neck.

"I will control my anger," he said in a soft, cold voice, "and you will ask for the definitions you need to answer my questions."

Esme was unable to look away from the fearsome strength and blazing power reflected in Raul's eyes. Quickly, she nodded her agreement.

He nodded back curtly. "Now what words in my last question did you not understand? Tell me!" he ordered.

For an instant, Esme's mind was blank. Then, desperation leant her mind the clarity it needed to answer. "P-p-p-primitive," she stammered out.

Raul was surprised. But his surprise passed quickly

as he sensed an opportunity to widen the crack of Esme's defenses further and get at the truth. Because of what had just happened, he wanted this interrogation over as badly as she did now. But not at the cost of leaving his ship and his men exposed to danger. Therefore, he decided to step up his cruelty to get the answers he needed.

"Primitive," he said coldly and clearly, "means people who are so ignorant they do not even know what a ship is, much less how to construct one. And," he added, forcing a contemptuous tone into his voice, "it means people who have barely invented the wheel for themselves."

He paused as Esme frowned in confusion. He'd used another word she didn't understand—"wheel."

Raul understood her expression and what it meant, and as he stared at her, a rush of frustrated anger shot through him. Could any woman be that good an actress? he wondered grimly.

The safe answer was yes. But for the time being, he had no choice other than to proceed as though she were exactly what she seemed to be—too primitive to understand some of the simplest terms among humankind. Furthermore, he had to continue to speak to her in a manner that aroused self-contempt inside him that he could barely tolerate.

"'Primitive' also means someone who doesn't understand what a sanitation chamber is or how one is used," he said contemptuously.

At his pointed words and his hateful tone, Esme went suddenly unnaturally still. His final jibe brought a clear flash of knowledge to her mind. She now realized that the vast gulf of technological knowledge which separated the two of them aroused Raul's contempt for her and her kind. Therefore, there was little hope of expecting to have her dreams fulfilled by this man upon whom she had unconsciously based all her hope. Obviously, nothing short of exposing her unnatural gifts would gain her any respect from a man such as Captain Raul. And if she exposed her gifts, she might sign her death warrant.

A new strength swelled through her body and mind as Esme understood for the first time the real peril of her position. Perhaps, if she could stay alive long enough to see this ship and its captain leave here, another ship would come to her rescue—the ship of her dreams, the ship which would truly spell the beginning of her adventure. For this must not be the right one. This ship and this man could surely not be the instruments of her freedom to brush the stars.

"Telepathic," she said in a calm, strong voice.

Raul frowned over the new resolve he sensed in her. "What?" he said softly.

"The other word I did not understand," Esme said, her voice quietly calm, utterly unintimidated. "It was 'telepathic.' Nor do I understand the term 'wheel.'"

Raul stared at her, feeling an unwilling admiration for her strength and courage. But so were the Rebels strong and brave—and they were still his enemies. As Esme might be.

Slowly, he raised his hands in front of her eyes and made a circle with his fingers. "This is the shape of a wheel," he said. "When one makes a platform that rests on four such strongly constructed shapes, one can push the platform and transport things more easily than carrying them on one's own back, or upon the back of an animal. And if one has a source of power, such as an engine, to push or pull the platform, one can go very fast and carry a great deal with him."

Esme didn't understand what an engine was, but she understood the general principle of what Raul said. "I see," she nodded.

If Esme was a primitive, Raul could admire her quick grasp of his explanation. But if she was acting, though he admired her thespian talents, which were obviously considerable, he was in no mood to appreciate her efforts at all. In fact, his patience was growing short enough that he decided to add a threat to his next explanation.

"And 'telepathic,'" he said in a grim, rasping voice, "means someone who can read minds."

Esme froze. With her eyes locked on Raul's, she sat as still as though she'd been turned to stone.

"Sometimes," Raul continued, his voice growing harsher, "that ability to invade the minds of others is coupled with an ability to move things without touching them, to hurt people without using any weapon other than the power of the telepath's own mind. In my society, Esme, we train telepaths very carefully and make sure their unusual powers are coupled with ethics. Because if we can't trust them and can't put them to good use for the benefit of the rest of society, they are a danger to everyone. And if such training fails, and if their ethics prove to be deficient, we kill them and save ourselves the trouble such people can cause without even half trying."

As Raul spoke, Esme was aware that her mind shouted a desperate warning. *Close down! Close down!* her mind repeated over and over. But it wasn't until Raul had finished his last sentence that Esme heeded the warning.

As her mind screamed a final "*Close Down!*",

Esme's lids closed over her eyes. Her body tumbled out of the chair, landing in a tight, embryonic ball right at the feet of the man who'd become even more than the desert, the biggest threat to her survival she had ever faced in her life.

Once again, as Thorson rushed into the room, he found Raul leaning against the wall with a tight, controlled expression on his face. Esme lay on the bed where Raul had put her, her body curled into a tight ball.

"What happened?" Thorson exclaimed, his tone unknowingly accusing, as he bent over Esme and tried to straighten her so that he could perform an examination.

Raul's eyes went even colder, and his voice was like ice as he said, very softly, "Your concern may be misplaced, Thorson. Keep in mind what she may be."

That brought Thorson's head up. Then he grimaced. "Aye," he said in a much more subdued tone.

A moment later, as Thorson became aware that he wasn't going to be able to straighten Esme's body, he frowned. "She is catatonic," he said, amazed. "I cannot budge her."

Raul accepted Thorson's verdict. He'd tried himself to straighten Esme's limbs and had finally stopped out of fear of breaking some of her delicate bones.

"What is to be done?" he asked coldly and calmly.

Thorson, still staring at Esme's small, huddled form, shrugged. "The drugs we use to relax men who have become paralyzed with fear in battle should work," he said. "But I am not absolutely positive they will."

"Try." And after voicing that one word, Raul

abruptly turned and left his cabin.

Thorson picked Esme up and carried her to sick bay, where he began administering the drugs he'd seldom used before. And despite the fact that Esme might be an enemy, he couldn't help hoping, for her sake, they would work.

Raul's calm exterior hid a great deal of inner turmoil. Despite his reminder to the medic that his concern for Esme's well-being might be misplaced, Raul himself was far more concerned for her than was wise. Trying to restore his objectivity, he made his rounds.

He checked with Jase and found the repair work progressing as well as could be expected, considering that too many men had been pulled off the job for guard duty. He checked with his navigator and found that Sam'l still hadn't figured out where they were in space.

"We may just have to keep jumping until we find a system we recognize," the navigator shrugged. "As you know, with no coordinates, that is extremely dangerous. We could end up in the middle of a star or a planet. But at this point, that is all I know to do."

Raul nodded, told Sam'l to keep working on it, then left to make a slow tour of the whole ship. By the time he returned to his cabin, he was ready to do some clear, logical thinking, unclouded by emotion.

Obviously, he decided as he leaned back in his chair and stared into space, Esme's reaction to his discussion of telepathy was proof that his instincts about her were correct. She was telepathic herself. The question was, why did she feel it necessary to go to such extreme lengths to hide it?

There were only two possible answers to that question that made any sense to him. One was that the story she'd told him about her background was true, and despite the fact that he had explained that his people, unlike hers, understood telepathy, she was too conditioned by her fear of revelation to trust his assurances. Or else she simply didn't want to bear the responsibilities to society that went along with her gifts, and was unwilling to risk death for selfishly rebelling against those responsibilities.

The other possible answer was, of course, that she was a trained seductress for the Rebels, in which case, she would know Service regulations concerning the disposition of such women caught at their trade during wartime—summary execution. Given that knowledge, she would go to almost any lengths to keep her skills hidden—at least until she had accomplished her objective, after which she would accept death if it couldn't be avoided. Raul might despise trained seductresses on principle, but he accepted their bravery, even though such bravery was mainly instilled by psychological conditioning.

In his position of responsibility for the safety of his ship and crew, and for purely personal reasons as well, Raul fervently hoped the first explanation lay at the core of Esme's reluctance to confess her gifts. And could he have thought of any way to force her to make such a confession short of what standard Service procedure demanded in such cases, he would have employed it the moment she awoke from her catatonic state. But the very fact that she had been desperate enough to put herself into such a state was proof that she was prepared to do anything to keep her secrets hidden.

Therefore, standard Service procedure was the only option left him. His duty was clear. Even if Esme was innocent and it turned out he and his men had never been in any danger, he would face court-martial upon returning to Genesis for disregarding the procedure that had been designed to preclude a commander, for personal or any other reasons, from failing to take proper precautions in such a case.

But his duty also had its price, and closing his eyes and tilting his head back, Raul grimly dealt with his deep regret over what he had to do.

Esme would be in no physical danger, of course. In fact, in addition to the order he intended to issue that she be treated with reasonable care, if she was as talented a telepath as he was convinced she was, she would be able to defend herself better than a hardened warrior deprived of weaponry could. And that was Raul's one consolation in the matter. At least, her life would be spared.

But if she was as determined to keep her gifts hidden as he was sure she was, she would have to temper her defense in a way that would leave her pride and status forever damaged. She would then despise the man who was responsible for her predicament. And Raul, because of the change in her status, would not only be deprived of any chance to act on the feelings she aroused in him, he would also have to suffer her hatred.

Impatient and angry, Raul pushed such considerations aside. With his ship and his crew at risk, any selfish considerations of his own, as well as any consideration for Esme's feelings, had to be dismissed. In any case, whether she was innocent or guilty, her dishonesty was the root cause of what was going to happen to her. It was only just that she bear the consequences for lying about such a serious matter rather than tell the truth and thereby save herself an abundance of grief.

He did not consider it just, however, that she had somehow snared him into a state of mind where he would be forced to share her grief. But there was nothing to be done to change things, so he made up his mind to bear his sorrow with grace.

# CHAPTER TEN

"SHE IS NOT YET CONSCIOUS, BUT HER BODY IS NO LONGer rigid," Thorson said when Raul called him to his cabin to report on Esme's status. "The drugs worked."

"Good," Raul nodded, beckoning Thorson to sit down while he hid his considerable personal relief over his medic's status report. He had no intention of disclosing to Thorson or anyone else how deeply Esme had entangled his emotions. There was no point to such disclosure. "Then she will be ready for what I have in mind soon."

Thorson looked up, curious, and Raul outlined his plan.

Thorson was troubled by Raul's idea. "But if she is an innocent primitive—" he started to say.

"Thorson," Raul interrupted him, "all we really know of Esme's background is what she has told us

179

and what we have *assumed* from her appearance and actions, remember? For all we know, the Rebels could have discovered this planet, and Esme may be one of them and is merely playing a role. We can't trust what she says nor rely on assumptions. We have to know without a doubt that she's told us the truth. And in any case, I have no choice other than to follow regulations. You know the rules as well as I do. Should I risk court-martial for a woman who may be our deadly enemy, simply out of the hope that she might not be?"

Thorson unhappily shook his head. He knew the captain had no choice in the matter.

"By the way," Raul said grimly. "Make a note to stock some truth dope in sick bay if we ever get stuck with royal transport duty again. If we had some now, we wouldn't be faced with this distasteful way of trying to find out the truth about Esme."

Thorson nodded. Like Raul, he also wished fervently that they had some truth dope available. It was a safe, effective means of interrogation, and much preferable to the alternative they were going to be forced to use now. True, if Esme was a talented telepath, she would be in no physical danger but the whole idea left a bad taste in his mouth. And if he was any judge of the captain's mood, Raul felt the same way.

But there was nothing either of them could do about it. If Esme was innocent, they would both heartily regret subjecting her to the test that would take place. But if she was not, a decision to spare her the ordeal would be a fatal mistake.

"All right, Thorson," Raul said heavily, in a tone of dismissal. "We'll go ahead as planned as soon as Esme

## DREAMS OF DESTINY

is physically ready. Just make sure none of the men gets carried away and goes too far regardless of what she turns out to be."

Thorson frowned. As he got up to go, he asked, "You won't be there?"

"No," Raul said, his tone curt. "Dismissed, Thorson."

As Thorson left the cabin, Raul knew his medic was wondering if his captain was too much of a moral coward to witness Esme's testing. But moral cowardice had nothing to do with it. The truth was, Raul didn't trust his emotional control. He was afraid Esme had already seduced his emotions to the point where he might stop the test before it could produce the proof they needed. And if he did that, not only might he put his men in danger, he might end his career for failing to follow standard procedures for no sensible reason.

Feeling so relaxed and mentally quiet that it was an effort just to open her eyes, Esme nevertheless forced them open and saw Thorson leaning over her with the translater plugs in his ears. She became aware, peripherally, that he had placed plugs in her ears as well. She wondered why he seemed so watchful and reserved.

She smiled at him. "Greetings, Thorson," she said, and at hearing how slurred her voice was, her smile broadened. "Have I been drinking wine again?" she asked, her tone languid.

Thorson took a deep breath. "No, Esme," he said quietly. "I had to give you something to bring you out of your self-induced catatonic state. The drug I gave you is making you feel the way you do."

Esme was unconcerned. She felt as light as a cock feather, as carefree as a lambkin. "What is a catatonic state?" she inquired with lazy curiosity.

Thorson told her.

Esme yawned, then shrugged as best she could while lying on her back on the couch. "But why would I . . ." she started to say. But suddenly her mind cleared, and she remembered. Her eyes widened, her body tensed, and the look she gave Thorson contained a secretive terror.

To Thorson, Esme's behavior suggested that the captain's fear that she might be a trained seductress was valid. Though he was still troubled about the method to be used to prove it, her manner gave him the impetus to carry out the captain's instructions.

"Do not put yourself in that state again, Esme," he said, his voice firmly unyielding. "It will do you no good, because I will bring you out of it with the drugs again, and such drugs are dangerous if used too often. They can damage your mind."

That last part was only partly true. It would take a more substantial dosage of the drugs which he had no intention of ever administering in order to induce the damage he'd described. But he hoped there was enough truth in his statement to fool her as the mental shield the captain had taught him wasn't solid. He hadn't had time to practice it much.

The lie worked. Esme was horrified by the idea of having her mind damaged, and her expression disclosed her reaction.

Noting that reaction, Thorson didn't know whether to be discouraged or glad. Was Esme's horror the normal reaction anyone might feel at having such a

## DREAMS OF DESTINY

threat hanging over them? Or did her mind have certain special qualities that made her fear their loss even more than was normal?

"Sit up, Esme," he said quietly. "You have been unconscious for some time. Your body needs use."

That unfortunate phrase his unconscious mind had conjured up almost made Thorson wince. If the captain was right, Esme's body would soon be in use all right, and the morale of the Condor's crew would experience a dramatic upturn as a result. But whether that morale boost would be a one-time experience or a regular occurrence remained to be seen.

Esme shakily obeyed, dismayed to find that she was physically very weak. But it was the foggy state of her mind that really concerned her. If she were going to be subjected to another one of Captain Raul's interrogations—this time without any hope of using the escape she'd discovered at the end of the last one—she would need every weapon she could muster.

"I am thirsty," she said to Thorson, her voice containing a note of desperation. "Please . . . give me some water."

Thorson was puzzled by that note of desperation in her voice, but he filled a cup half-full of water and handed it to her.

Esme looked at the small amount in dismay.

"Your stomach will not tolerate more for the time being," Thorson said firmly. "You can have more later. And do not gulp it," he added hastily when Esme raised the cup to her lips and it was obvious she was prepared to drain every drop as quickly as possible. "Sip slowly," he instructed, placing his hand on hers to make her withdraw the cup from her lips.

Esme glared at him hostilely. She trusted Thorson, but he didn't understand. If she was going to be tossed to Captain Raul's untender mercies again, she wanted to be prepared. But an instant later, she felt her stomach lurch in slight protest over the arrival of the cool liquid she'd drunk, and she realized Thorson was right. Her hostile glare faded and she nodded her agreement to his instructions.

"Good," Thorson nodded. "Now, Esme, let me help you down. I want you to walk a bit."

Whether it was her desperate intention to be at her best when she was thrown to Captain Raul or whether it was her remarkable recuperative powers at work again, even Esme didn't know. But within an hour or so, she was walking unaided, and she was tolerating more water.

Thorson then allowed her a bath, and when she was refreshed, he handed her a robe Raul had provided from his own wardrobe—one such as he had worn during his long interrogation of her.

Esme hesitated, weighing her reluctance to wear something that reminded her of that dreaded interview against the comfort the garment would provide as opposed to her former attire. Comfort won out, and she practically snatched the robe from Thorson's hand and closed her eyes in pleasure as she wrapped it around her damp body.

Thorson eyed her actions with his jaw set. Was the eroticism of that gesture normal? Would his manhood be stirring as much had any other attractive woman taken such obvious pleasure in the feel of silk against her skin? Or was Esme's sensuality, and its undoubted effect on a male viewer, the product of long training?

## DREAMS OF DESTINY

He didn't know. But the question gave him even more incentive to carry out the rest of Captain Raul's instructions.

For the rest of that day, Thorson worked on helping Esme get her strength back. It was a task he found pleasing from a medical standpoint because he could see her vitality picking up almost minute by minute. From a mental standpoint, however, he found it exhausting to maintain the shield Captain Raul had taught him.

By the time they were sharing a last-meal, Esme's body was back to normal. But her nerves were so on edge, she couldn't hold back the question that had been trembling on her lips ever since she'd woken from her self-induced catatonic state and learned she couldn't use it again.

"Now that I am better," she said to Thorson, her tone sober, her eyes wary, "will C–Captain Raul question me again?"

Thorson immediately slammed everything he had into holding his mental shield. "No," he said levelly. "At least not right away."

Though a part of her experienced a tremendous sense of relief over Thorson's answer, another part of Esme couldn't quite believe it. Automatically, she sent a searching touch to Thorson's mind to verify the truth she'd heard in his voice and for the second time in her life, she met a barrier that made her eyes open wide in astonishment.

When Thorson raised his head, she quickly hid her reaction. "Why not?" she ventured hesitantly. Again, she tried to enter Thorson's mind, and again there was a barrier. It wasn't as strong a barrier as the one in

Captain Raul's mind, and Esme thought she could breach it if she pushed hard enough. But she hesitated to exert that much power. If Thorson felt it, he would tell the captain.

There was perspiration breaking out on Thorson's brow now, but his voice was only slightly strained as he answered. "Because he has something else in mind for you, Esme."

"What?" she asked, her fear rising.

"I cannot tell you," Thorson responded, and Esme heard no hope of persuading him otherwise in his voice.

Unconsciously, the need to be prepared spurred Esme into pushing harder against the barrier in Thorson's mind. But when he looked up at her and began rubbing his forehead, a frown of thoughtful wariness on his lips, Esme hastily withdrew from him and lowered her eyes to her plate.

Thorson couldn't be sure, but he suspected the discomfort he'd just felt was a result of a mind probe. And if that was the case, he was both more suspicious that Esme might be a trained seductress than he'd ever been, and yet at the same time relieved. If she wasn't a trained seductress, he wanted her to have the protection of her mind the next day.

"Do not worry, Esme," he said levelly. "If you are what you say you are, you will eventually be all right."

Esme lifted her head and stared at him, her eyes wide with wariness and fear. "Eventually?" she asked, her voice faint.

Thorson nodded. "You are not going to have an easy time of it tomorrow," he said. "Or, at least," he added drily, "that is true if you *are* what you say you

## DREAMS OF DESTINY

are . . . if the story you told the captain was the truth. But if not . . ." Thorson shrugged, and Esme's heart thudded in her breast. "If not," he repeated quietly, "you may just enjoy what is about to happen."

That last sentence brought a beam of hope into Esme's eyes. Thorson saw the reaction, and his hope that Esme was innocent grew fainter. He abruptly pointed at her plate. "Eat!" he ordered. "You are going to need your strength, Esme. Believe me."

Esme did believe him and as a result of that conviction, she obeyed his order, shoveling the bland, nourishing concoction he'd had prepared for her into her mouth without tasting it. When her shrunken stomach had had all it could hold, Thorson administered a very mild sedative and escorted her to his own quarters to sleep, as ordered by Raul.

"Rest, Esme," he said as he paused by the door on his way out. "Gather your strength. As I said, you are going to need it."

But Esme, though she took Thorson at his word and sent her body into the relaxed state that Thorson was so sure she would need, used her mind to good purpose for the rest of the night.

For the first time since her rescue, she was in a position to fully explore the ship that sheltered her and the men who owned it. With that object in mind, she sent her mind soaring past the barrier of the door Thorson had locked behind him on his way out, and down each and every corridor of the Condor until she knew it as well as the Settlement and the high pasture. Along the way, she found minds that held no barriers, minds filled with anticipation over what the next day would bring.

187

As Esme took from those minds a knowledge of the prominent part she was to play in the next day's activities, as well as many other things she had trouble accepting, disbelief, horror, and rage swelled inside her. She could not at first accept that any woman would mate with multiple male partners, none of whom she loved, for something called "money," when the cost of such behavior was a shattering loss of respect in her community.

Yet the minds of these seemingly civilized men not only accepted that such females existed, they enjoyed their use, even while they held them in deep contempt. And Captain Raul intended her to become such a woman herself in order to repay him for her rescue by raising the morale of his crew!

Esme was deeply offended and enraged. Abruptly, the sense of inadequacy she had felt because of this people's technological superiority compared to her own people's disappeared. Their intelligence and cleverness might enable them to create such marvels as the Condor and travel through space, but their morals had not kept pace with their technical achievements. In the matter of true wisdom and decent behavior, it appeared they were seriously deficient.

In the grip of her rage, she went to Raul's cabin, to stare wrathfully down at him where he lay sleeping on the big couch where she had slept twice now. Sleep had erased the barrier that had hitherto kept Esme out of his mind, but he slept so heavily, he had no thoughts for her to read.

As she hovered above him, Esme struggled with conflicting feelings. Part of her wanted to hurt him as badly as he intended for her to be hurt the following

## DREAMS OF DESTINY

day. But having had second thoughts about the wisdom of awaiting a second ship to fulfill her dream, she could not afford to give in to her desire to inflict pain upon him. For what if the coming of a second ship was long delayed? How would she live? There was water nearby, yes. But there was no food. And what if a second ship never came at all? So if there was any way at all that she could salvage her dream by way of the Condor, and galling as it was, its captain, she must not risk destroying her chance in favor of indulging in precipitate revenge.

Surely, she thought as she continued to hover over Raul's nude sprawled body, there had to be a way she could turn things to her advantage without doing what Captain Raul intended, and without disclosing her gifts, which she was now more than ever determined to keep secret. For she had not forgotten his words about ones with her power having to be trained and put to use for the benefit of society and killed if they did not conform.

Such a concept was no different than what she had faced back in the Settlement. And she had no more liking for the idea of her life being controlled in Raul's society than she had had in her own. The Master was the only one who had the right to control her life. Though she did not yet know what He had in mind for her, except for her dreams of sailing among the stars, she was not prepared to give His control over to anyone else.

Though Esme knew she must prevent the Condor's crew using her as a sexual partner, and that her powers must be kept secret, she also knew she must find some way to be of valuable, even if temporary, service to

Captain Raul and his crew. Otherwise, why should they take her with them when they left here? They might instead take her back to the Settlement, or even leave her in the desert to die. And she *must* sail among the stars! That much of her destiny was clear.

An idea started to form in Esme's mind, but before she could consider it in detail, she became uncomfortably aware that staring at the captain's nude body was having a strange effect on her. Swimming softly, at the very bottom of her consciousness, feelings for him that were decidedly improper, and most inappropriate considering that she now considered him her enemy, were struggling to surface.

Confused and dismayed, she tried to crush such feelings down. And then Raul suddenly stirred, and not wanting him to sense her presence, she abruptly returned to her body.

For most of the rest of the night, Esme considered how she would make Captain Raul's plan work to her own advantage instead. And by the time Thorson came to fetch her, she was ready. The expression in her green eyes clear, calm, and determined, if a little sad, she ate, bathed, then dressed again in the silken robe her skin found so agreeable.

The Condor's crew were not told that Esme might be an enemy seductress for fear they would not behave normally with her. And Raul had decreed that neither Esme nor his men would be provided with translators. Trained seductresses could accomplish their purposes without their victims being able to understand the honeyed words that were part of their arsenal of weapons, the tone was enough. Still, as a safeguard,

Raul didn't want Esme to converse with his men.

As a further safeguard, none of his men would be exposed to Esme's talents if she was a trained seductress long enough to suffer permanent risk to their welfare or their loyalties. That would have been not only impractical, considering how many men there were, but criminally foolish.

But Esme didn't necessarily need words to explore the minds of others. Words were only symbols for pictures, after all. And the pictures in the mind of the first man to cross the threshhold into Thorson's cabin, Tomas, roused her temper to the point where, had she not been prepared, she would have slammed Tomas straight back through the hatch.

Instead, as the hatch closed behind him, and Tomas came toward her, she sat waiting cross-legged on Thorson's bunk, her gaze clear and steady, her body relaxed.

He stood over her for a moment, his eyes greedily roving her body, his breath audible. Then, growling something Esme didn't understand in the literal sense, though his mind provided all the information she needed, he reached for her breasts.

Without moving so much as a muscle of her body, Esme stopped his hands a bare inch from their goal. Tomas, an almost comical expression of startled disbelief on his heavy features, looked up at her, his hard eyes wide with surprised dismay.

Esme then deftly locked his mouth, and knocked his legs out from under him. He sprawled with a loud thump on the floor in front of her while she deftly took from his memories the information she needed not only to subvert his present intentions where she was concerned, but also to make him view her with only respect hereafter.

Outside the cabin, Thorson sat listening at the open console panel, and the thump he heard made him frown. The men had been told that no rough handling of Esme would be allowed. However, when Esme made no protest or outcry, Thorson's frown subsided somewhat, and he began to hope he had things the wrong way around. Perhaps it was Esme who was handling Tomas roughly by inflicting pain on him with her mind. But then why had Tomas not cried out in protest?

Thorson wished heartily that the Condor had video equipment so that he could see what was happening inside his cabin. It was difficult to tell anything just from sounds. But of course, when Tomas came out of the cabin, they would have his report. Thorson also wished, resentfully, that the captain was here to oversee the testing instead of being outside the ship inspecting Jase's latest repairs. Thorson was pretty sure the much vaunted courage of the most famous commander in the service of the Empire—a man who had watched men who served under him being blown to bits without faltering—had failed him when it came to turning a woman who might be innocent into a whore for his crew.

But if Esme was a telepath, Thorson reminded himself in order to ease his conscience, she would prevent Tomas from making use of her sexually. Thorson only hoped she didn't hurt him. Tomas was a good warrior, and in any case, it wasn't fair to the man to send him in there expecting pleasure, only to receive pain instead.

Suddenly, moans of pleasure delivered in Tomas's deep voice came over the intercom, and Thorson closed his eyes, sick at heart. Apparently, Esme was, indeed, a trained seductress, and was welcoming Tomas's attentions as only a seductress would do.

Inside the cabin, Esme held Tomas at her feet in his uncomfortable position while she poured scene after distressing scene into his mind. He saw his wife, a woman with a formidable temper, watching him attempt to find pleasure with Esme. And she showed him himself unable to perform. Each time he tried, the member of his body he viewed with inordinate pride shriveled into impotency, and his wife laughed with angry mockery over his wasted efforts.

And while he was not receiving the enjoyment he had expected, Esme forced moans of pleasure from his mouth. The moans finally culminated in a false cry of ecstasy that had no basis at all in truth.

Thorson winced as Tomas's cry of ecstasy echoed through the intercom. There was little doubt about it now. Esme must be the trained seductress he had so badly hoped she was not.

Sadly, he wondered what Raul would do once Esme had finished raising the crew's morale. The regulations were clear. She had to be killed and the thought of killing Esme was upsetting. But first, the captain would want to know the number, battle strength, and location of the soldiers who no doubt waited for her signal to attack. The question was, how would he get such information without the use of truth dope?

Thorson paled as the only answer that seemed likely to work occurred to him. He only hoped the captain would not force him to help use it.

Had wisdom not argued for a certain degree of mercy, Esme would have sent Tomas scurrying out of the cabin looking as wretched as he felt. But she was aware that such behavior would be as revealing to Thorson and Raul as though she'd openly confessed to the powers of her mind.

Therefore, as she gradually eased her hold on Tomas's muscles and he lay panting in an effort to recoup his strength, she carefully smudged the images she had used to bludgeon her visitor, leaving only enough remembrance to create the uneasiness one might feel upon waking from an unpleasant dream.

When she at last allowed Tomas to rise shakily to his feet and to back away from her, Esme waited until the door slid open behind him. As he turned and stepped through it, she added a last little touch of authenticity. She made him appear to be fastening his bodysuit as if he had just donned the garment.

As Tomas entered the room where Thorson sat waiting, Thorson looked at him without enthusiasm. And then he frowned. He was expecting to see a very modified type of the exalted ecstasy common to a man who has just been in the hands of a trained seductress. Instead, Thorson saw an expression of grave thoughtfulness carved on the features of Tomas's rugged face.

Puzzled, Thorson said, "Well, Tomas, how was it?"

Tomas then attempted a jaunty smile, but he wouldn't meet Thorson's eyes.

"Oh . . . ah . . . it was quite an experience, sir."

Tomas did not want to disclose that he had just failed to live up to his lusty reputation. But neither did he want to tell an officer an out-and-out lie. Therefore, pleased to have found an appropriate description of the events that had just occurred, he repeated his words. "Aye, that is what it was . . . an experience."

Something was not quite right about Tomas's manner, and Thorson leaned back in his chair to eye the other man in a thoughtful manner.

"Would you want another experience of the sort you just had, Tomas?" he asked curiously.

For an instant, Thorson was positive he saw a naked look of pure dismay flicker in Tomas's muddy brown eyes before the warrior hid his reaction.

"Ah . . . well . . . as to that, sir," Tomas stumbled for an appropriate reply. "Well, the fact is, I'm feelin' just a tad guilty. I've got a mate back home, you see, and I wouldn't want to do nuthin—"

"*You* are feeling *guilty*, Tomas?" Thorson interrupted in amazement. Tomas's lusty portside adventures of the past were no secret, and no guilt had ever interfered with his activities before.

Now Tomas looked defensive. "Well, I'm gettin' on in years," he attempted to bolster his position. "I'll be retirin' before too much longer and settlin' down with my mate. So I've been thinkin' lately that I oughta' get used to stickin' to my own hearth, so to speak. Understand?"

That last word contained a note that Thorson could only interpret as a plea. But Thorson didn't understand at all. In the first place, Tomas wouldn't be retiring for another seven years. In the second place, even when he did retire, he was not the type of man anyone who knew him would expect to adjust to the constraints of monogamy without complaint. And in the third place, why wasn't Tomas as happy as he should be after having supposedly experienced the type of skilled attentions a trained seductress knew so well?

"Can I go now, sir?" Tomas asked, again in a pleading tone.

Thorson hesitated. But he could tell from Tomas's expression that he wasn't going to get any more of an explanation from him for his unusual behavior. Thorson nodded and dismissed him with a wave of his hand, then watched in amazement as Tomas took his leave with an aura of relief surrounding his large form like a bodyguard.

Thorson sat for a moment longer, trying to figure out what was going on. At last, he got to his feet and went to see Esme, hoping her manner might provide the answer to the questions that had suddenly arisen in his mind.

Among the People, sex was a very private matter, and whenever Esme had encountered sexual thoughts in anyone's mind, she had always been politely punctilious about prying. Since her mother had died when Esme was barely past puberty, she had never explained the facts of life to Esme. Esther, living without a man herself and assuming that Esme was unlikely to be offered the opportunity to mate, had seen no point in such an explanation.

All Esme really knew about sex was what she had taken from the minds of the Condor's crew the preceding night, which was technically explicit, but not detailed, and from the minds of Bazil and Maza, which were also not detailed, and from what she had seen practiced among her flocks, which she did not equate to human mating.

She had never been sexually aroused in her life, nor been in the presence of a male who had just had sex. Therefore, she did not know about the wetness that came with sexual intercourse nor about the barrier inside her that would be breached the first time she was penetrated, which would likely result in bleeding.

Therefore, to convince Thorson she had pleasured Tomas she tore a small rip in the sleeve of her silk robe, but not enough to prevent its further use, tossed the garment to the floor, then disarranged the coverlet on the bunk and huddled in a ball on top of the coverlet while she tried to dredge up tears.

Thorson stepped in the cabin and reluctantly cast a glance in Esme's direction. At seeing the tears in her eyes and her shoulders shaking—a convincing touch Esme had decided to employ at the last moment—he thought he had an explanation for Tomas' strange behavior. Tomas must have been rough with her and had feared punishment. But remembering that he hadn't heard Esme cry out in pain over the intercom, Thorson was again puzzled. Even a trained seductress yelled when she was hurt.

Then, with a suddenness that made him sick at heart, another possibility for what had happened occurred to Thorson—one that neither he nor the captain had thought of. What if Esme was not a trained seductress, and had been too intimidated by her situation to use her telepathic powers to protect herself?

Crossing quickly to her side, he sat down and placed a gentle hand on her quaking shoulder.

"How do you feel, Esme?" he asked with tender

sympathy. "Are you all right?"

Esme opened her eyes wide, and through a mist of tears gave Thorson a look that was filled with a bitter expression of betrayal, a look she hardly had to fake.

"How do you expect me to feel?" she choked out. "Of course I am not all right! No decent woman who has been used by a man for the first time in her life under such loathsome circumstances could possibly be all right! Especially when she cares nothing about the man at all!"

Her own words elicited such an unexpected feeling of self-pity that her next sob was genuine rather than faked.

Thorson went still. "For the first time?" he repeated.

Esme glared at him through her tears. "Of course it was my first time!" she cried out in disgust. "Just because you and your people are morally deficient does not mean that I am! My people wait until they have found their life partner before they mate!"

Frowning in distress, Thorson looked down at Esme's body. If this truly was her first time, then she might be bleeding. Indeed, if Tomas had been too rough, she might even need medical attention.

But Thorson saw no bleeding, and his frown deepened. Was Esme lying? Or had she sustained some injury in the past that had already broken her maidenly barrier?

"Esme, turn over," he said quietly. "I want to examine you."

Esme froze. She did not know what such an examination might reveal but she didn't think it wise to risk it.

"I do not want to be examined," she said on a convincing sob. "I just want all this over with. So if you are going to make me entertain the rest of your men, get on with it! Send in the next of your violators!"

Thorson's thoughts were hidden behind his mental shield, which was fortunate because they were filled with confusion. He knew no more now than he had before Tomas had entered this room, except that his former conviction that Esme was a trained seductress was no longer so certain.

Slowly, he got to his feet. He couldn't stop things now because he was inclined to believe Esme's present convincing performance without any evidence. So there was only one thing to do.

"All right, Esme," he said thoughtfully. "If you are sure you are all right, I will send another man in here."

Esme gave him a look that could have rivaled the scorching heat of the desert. "Yes, you do that!" she said in a scathing tone. And then, as a sudden alarming thought hit her, leaving a surge of panic in its wake, she added, "But when the men have done with me, do not think that I will be amenable should you or Captain Raul want a turn. You can kill me before I will submit to either of you!"

Thorson raised an eyebrow. Esme's statement made no sense if she was a trained seductress. Captain Raul, especially, would be one of her prime targets, but if she was innocent, it made perfect sense. She must now hate the captain for ordering that she be put through this experience, and she must think that he, Thorson, had betrayed her by helping carry things out. It also made sense if Esme was trying to hide her powers. He and the captain were the only two men on the ship she could not fool because she could not get into their minds.

Suddenly, Thorson was feeling a great deal better than he had a few moments earlier. But he was still too uncertain about Esme's innocence to clear her with the captain.

Testing, watching closely for her reaction, he said, "You do not have to worry about that, Esme. It is not the custom for officers to take the crew's leavings."

The insult infuriated Esme to the point where it was all she could do to keep from striking out at Thorson with her mind. But that would have lost her all she was trying to gain, so instead, she said, with haughty pride and deadly hostility, "Thank the Master! The two of you would be too much to bear!"

Esme's reaction brought a feeling of intense relief to lighten Thorson's heart. Now, he could conduct the remainder of the test with the almost certain assurance that Esme would come through it undamaged, except for her status, which at the moment seemed minor compared to the death and torture she would have faced. The men would also be unharmed.

Hiding a smile, he turned and went to the door, then glanced back at Esme over his shoulder. "Prepare yourself, Esme," he said with dry humor. "You are going to have a very busy next few hours."

When the door had closed behind him, Esme let her tense muscles relax, and collapsed against the bunk to rest for a moment before she began the tiresome task of controlling and directing the thoughts of the remaining men.

As she lay there, she became aware of a deep sadness inside her, a sadness Thorson had evoked with his remark concerning her status as the crew's "leavings."

The night before, she had decided that if the only way she would be permitted to remain on the Condor was to pretend to be the men's whore, then she had no choice. She had to accept the insulting, degrading title to be of use to Captain Raul so that he would take her with him when the Condor left the Homeland. But she would not accept the actual role, of course. She had no intention of letting any of the men touch her.

But in her anger, she had glossed over the hurt that acceptance of the title would cause her. She had forgotten in the heat of the moment how much she wanted Thorson's and Captain Raul's respect and friendship. But now, realizing that she would be treated with contempt, she was deeply grieved. But there was nothing to be done about it. She could not enter either of their minds and change their perception of her without risking a life of duty, and perhaps even death.

Furthermore, she realized, frowning with concern, she had perhaps made a mistake in leaving a feeling of respect for her within Tomas's mind. A whore did not command respect from such men. And if she did, the men would most likely not want her, which would end her usefulness to Captain Raul.

A deep sigh of resigned sadness escaped Esme as she realized she must adjust the mental programming she would use on the rest of the crew. It was well that Tomas was the only one she had entertained so far, and at some point she would have to find him and replace the former perception of her with a different one. But she was at least grateful she had discovered her error before Captain Raul and Thorson could detect that none of the men wished to avail themselves of her services on an ongoing basis. Otherwise, her plan might have failed.

# CHAPTER ELEVEN

WHEN THE NEXT MAN EXITED ESME'S LAIR, EXHIBITING more normal reactions than Tomas had, Thorson questioned him closely. "What was it like?"

The man hesitated and scratched his head. "Well . . . all right, I guess."

Thorson couldn't credit such a lack of enthusiasm. The crew had been deprived of women for a long while and for any one of them to react so matter-of-factly, especially to a woman as beautiful as Esme, seemed strange.

"You don't sound enthusiastic, Pack," he commented. "Is Esme not the sort of woman who attracts you?"

The man called Pack smiled ruefully. "Oh, she attracts me all right," he nodded. "In fact, she's one of the most beautiful women I've ever seen. It's just that there was something strange about the whole thing. It all seemed sort of like a dream. I don't know exactly how to explain it, but I don't feel . . . satisfied."

Thorson hid a smile. "But you would go back for more if you had the chance?" he asked.

"Oh, yes," Pack nodded. "Any time."

Thorson dismissed Pack then and went in to check Esme again. She did not cry this time. Instead, she glared and refused to speak to him. And neither did she look like a woman who had just had sex. She was entirely too unruffled.

Thereafter, as man after man went in eagerly and came out looking only vaguely satisfied, Thorson checked. The small room should have begun to reek of sex and Esme should have begun to look decidedly ill-used. But that was not the case, and by the time the last man left the cabin with a vague smile on his face, Thorson was sure of his own conclusions. Nevertheless, there was one last thing he wanted to do before reporting to the captain. Actually, he wished he'd done it long before this. First, however, he must put Esme to sleep.

Gathering up his medic kit, he entered the cabin. Esme was sitting on the bunk, looking somewhat fatigued and decidedly cross. She had a disgruntled scowl on her lovely face. But her physical and emotional states had not deteriorated to the extent they should have had if she really had serviced the men.

"You look tired, Esme," Thorson said with dry and amusedly false sympathy. "I am going to give you something to make you rest for a little while."

"I do not need anything to make me sleep," Esme snapped, glaring at him. "What I need is a meal and some solitude."

"The nap will give you solitude," Thorson said firmly as he got out the sedative. "And after last-meal, you can have the night to yourself. That is," he added, as he approached her with the small needle gun in his hand, "unless the captain wants to talk to you."

Esme stiffened and was sufficiently distracted by the disquieting thought of having to endure another "talk" with the captain, that Thorson was able to administer the sedative without her uttering a word of protest.

Immediately, she felt the effect of the drug, and as her eyelids began to droop and her body to sag toward the bunk, she thought, rather crossly, that if sleep were all she needed, she would have been perfectly satisfied with life on the Condor considering the amount of slumber she'd endured since her rescue.

As consciousness left her, Thorson tossed the needle gun aside and lifted her into his arms to carry her to sick bay, where his examination would be more easily accomplished.

Approximately ten minutes later, he deposited Esme back on the bunk in his quarters, a look of delighted amusement on his face. He would swear in open court that none of the crew had so much as touched her. And yet every man who had visited her believed he had.

"The women on Europa could take some lessons from you, Esme," Thorson commented humorously as he tossed her robe over her sprawled body. "And if the captain agrees to take you along with us when we finally leave this hellhole of a planet, which, I suspect, has been your intention all along, that would be a good place for you to take up residence. But I suspect you will do even more good in the service of the central government, after the psychic boys have evaluated the full scope of your telepathic talents and have decided how you can best be put to good use."

As Raul listened to Thorson's report, he concealed behind an impassive expression his tremendous relief that Esme was not a trained seductress, as well as his deep sense of regret over what his experiment was going to cost her.

"Then there is little doubt that though she is obviously not a trained seductress, she is a telepath," he commented when Thorson finished.

"There is no doubt at all," Thorson shrugged. "Esme's never been with a man. Her maidenhood is intact and yet every man who went in there was positive he had had her. However, they all also reported that the experience was more dreamlike than real. So obviously, she merely manipulated their minds into thinking they had had her."

He paused, then added, "I've been trying to figure out why she didn't just toss them out of the cabin with the power of her mind, instead of pretending she was going along with things. And all I can come up with is either she doesn't have the sort of telepathy that can move objects and inflict pain, but only the kind that permits her to read and to manipulate other minds. Or else she took from the men's minds what was expected of her and was afraid if she didn't go along with it, we wouldn't let her stay on the Condor. At any rate, I'm very glad things turned out as they did."

Raul looked at him curiously and Thorson shrugged. "It is not just that I am glad we are all safe from what she might have been," he explained. "It is that I have grown fond of her, Captain. She is a charming, beautiful, remarkably innocent woman, the kind of woman it is very easy to like."

Thorson shook his head, a smile tugging at his lips. "I don't think she even knows she will most likely bleed when she does have sex for the first time," he said, his tone incredulous. "Nor, apparently, does she know that men leave traces when they have been with a woman, the way she was trying to make me believe our men had been with her."

Thorson took a deep breath and went on. "I also believe her story, Captain. I think she has been exiled from her home by a primitive, superstitious people who do not understand telepathy, at the instigation of a priest who understands it all too well and perceives it as a threat. And it seems to me that leaves us two choices."

Thorson paused, waiting for the captain to react. But Raul merely sat, watching him through half-closed eyes, his expression impassive. So Thorson continued, "Once we get the ship operable, we can either take her back to her home and try somehow to get her people to accept her or we can take her with us, which is what I think she really wants. Trained the way she should be, she could be a valuable asset to the Empire."

Raul got up to pace the cabin, unsure if he could stand much more contact with Esme now that his actions had surely precluded any chance of his being with her the way he wanted to be. Not only did the men think they had had her, which meant Raul could *not* have her and retain their respect, but Esme herself no doubt hated him now.

And even if he could have her, he would have to give her up when they reached Genesis. And though Raul had walked away from many women in the past without regret, he had the uneasy feeling that that might not be possible with Esme. She might be the one woman who could snare his heart as well as his body, and he had no taste for the prospect of enduring love that could never result in a life-mating because of his duty. Esme, too, might have important duties if she was as talented a telepath as he suspected she was, which was another reason they most likely would be kept apart.

Still, he could not send her back to people who might make another attempt to kill her and in any case, if she could be an asset to the Empire, his duty was clear.

He stopped pacing and faced Thorson. "Even if it were our task, which it decidedly is not," he told his medic, "we cannot spare the time to take up her cause. We have been away from the war too long as it is." He paused, then asked, "Are you really so sure she wants to come with us?"

Thorson shrugged. "It is a strong feeling I have and it makes sense. As I said, unless she doesn't have the kind of mental powers that would have allowed her to stop the men today, why else would she go along with what happened except to assure herself a welcome on our ship?"

But then he paused, frowning. "But her eagerness to go with us may also be accompanied now with a certain amount of hostility toward you and me, Captain. I am afraid she is very upset with us."

"I am not interested in her feelings, justified or not," Raul lied. "I had no other choice. If she had admitted her skills, it would not have been necessary.

## DREAMS OF DESTINY

Since she did not..." He shrugged and resumed pacing.

"I imagine she was afraid to admit them to us, Captain," Thorson ventured. "After all, she has been ostracized most of her life for less reason. She obviously had to hide her abilities all that time. Why should she think we would regard them with any more acceptance than her own people would?"

Raul didn't answer as he thought about his own part in instilling such fear of revelation in Esme. He also wondered how she was going to react to having her life taken over by the Empire. If he was right that she was reluctant to be of service, and that was one of the reasons she hadn't wanted him to know about her mind powers, then she might change her mind about wanting to leave on the Condor. But he doubted it. He couldn't imagine that she would want to go back to her own people when they had left her in the desert to die. And he wasn't going to allow her to be put at risk in any case.

He shook his head with regret. Then, realizing once again that his emotional and physical reactions to the little green-eyed seductress—well, "sensualist," at least—were stronger than was good for his peace of mind, he irritably pushed aside personal considerations and focused on what was necessary to do.

"You say she is sleeping?" he inquired, turning to look at Thorson.

Thorson nodded. "Yes, sir."

"Bring her here to dine when she wakes up." Having given his order, Raul made a gesture of dismissal. But Thorson, though he got to his feet, stood, hesitating.

"What is it, Thorson?" Raul asked.

"You will remember she has had a hard day?" Thorson suggested quietly. "And that she has no reason to regard either of us kindly?"

Beseiged with guilt over what Esme had lost as a result of her "hard" day, and an equally strong regret over what he had lost as well, Raul became angry. And he took his mood out on the nearest target—his medic.

"And you will remember, Thorson," he said in a hard voice, "that I have a ship to get repaired and a crew to get home. The repair work has been slowed considerably by Esme's advent into our lives. And though I am now reasonably certain that if I pull the men off guard duty, and put them back to work on the ship, it will not be a mistake but I intend to make *absolutely* sure of that, whether it offends our guest's sensibilities or not! Now get back to that woman and get her ready for last-meal! Immediately!"

Thorson, properly chastened, snapped a salute that was crisper than any he'd delivered in a good many years, turned smartly on his heel, and hastily left the cabin.

When Thorson had departed, Raul returned to his chair and sat staring grimly into space, wondering if it was going to be worth it to the Empire to provide them with a talented telepath when that same telepath had the capacity to induce an officer of Thorson's caliber to forget, even for a moment, where his duty and his loyalties lay.

But the bigger question in Raul's mind was whether he himself was going to get through the trip back home unscathed by Esme's damnable capacity to provoke his lust, his admiration, and his emotions to an extent no other woman ever had before, and which he had never wanted to experience. His life was too unsuited to mating, and he had always treasured his previous emotional autonomy too much for him to welcome his reactions to Esme.

Therefore, Raul told himself, he should be grateful that in the minds of his men, she was a whore, which meant that he would now have to keep his distance from her. A captain who took his men's "leavings" was unworthy of respect and obedience, and without those two attributes, a battle commander might as well hang up his emblems of office and go home to rot.

Yes, that was what he told himself but, to his disgust, he did not entirely believe it.

Esme was not at all happy at learning she was to end her already trying day at the captain's table. The nap had helped, but she had expended so much energy on the crew, she still felt drained, an undesirable state when facing another interview with Captain Raul.

However, Thorson's tone ordering her to bathe and dress and to accompany him to Captain Raul's cabin had brooked no dispute, and Esme hadn't wasted any more of her energy in useless argument.

Neither did she waste her energy on dispelling the scowl that distorted her features when the door to Captain Raul's cabin slid back and Thorson pushed her through it.

Raul, from his position where he was propped against the dining table, thought she resembled a sulky child who'd been deprived of having its own way.

With one hand on Esme's arm, forcing her along with him, Thorson carried the translator to the table and offered the captain one set of plugs. He already wore a set himself, as did Esme.

Both Raul and Esme looked at the plugs with hostile resignation as Raul put them into his ears.

Then Raul nodded at Esme. "Greetings," he said, remembering to keep his voice low. "I trust you are well?"

Esme's eyes flashed fire at him for a moment before she looked away and shrugged one shoulder. "I am well," she said flatly.

Had she been looking at him, she would have seen one corner of Raul's mouth quirk in the beginnings of a wry, fatalistic smile, which he quickly controlled. As he had suspected she would, Esme now seemed to regard him with a great deal more hostility than respect and he couldn't blame her. In fact, he respected her reaction, and was pleased to know that she apparently had a rather formidable temper.

Then his eyes ran over her body, and it was harder to conceal the pleasure he felt at seeing her in one of his silk robes than it had been to conceal the fact that he was pleased that her temper was in good form.

"I am pleased you have deigned to accept my offering of comfort," he said, nodding at the robe she wore.

Esme glanced back at him and caught the end of the gesture. She frowned. "I do not take your meaning, sir," she said.

Raul noted that the "Honorable" she had formerly attached to the "Sir" when addressing him had somehow gotten lost from her vocabulary. He glanced at Thorson, who hastily turned to Esme.

"The robe you wear is from the captain's wardrobe, Esme, as was the one you wore earlier."

Raul watched, his ability to control his amusement stretched to its limits, as Esme's expression conveyed first shock, then resentment, then dismay at the thought that to salvage her pride, she should perhaps decline to accept the captain's generosity.

"It is nothing, Esme," Raul said dismissively as he straightened and turned away to hide his grin. "I have many such robes."

Esme glared at his back. Then upon catching Thorson scowling a warning at her, she resentfully turned the glare into a mere frown.

A knock came at the door, and Raul gestured with his head at Thorson, who reached over the table and pushed a button. Jaco entered bearing a laden tray.

"Be seated, Esme," Raul invited in a casual drawl. "I understand your stomach is better able to tolerate food now. That is good."

Having reluctantly settled into the chair she now hated since it had imprisoned her for hours during Raul's interrogation. Esme looked up, her gaze hostile and purposeful.

"My stomach tolerates food, yes," she agreed shortly. "But I have no tolerance for wine. So if it is your intention, sir, to serve it with this meal, I request permission to decline it."

Raul's gaze turned cool. Though he understood Esme's mood and even respected her for it, it was clear to him that she was feeling her power after her day's work. And though he had no objection to her foregoing the wine, he had no intention of allowing her to believe, now that she disliked him, that she could challenge his authority any time she pleased— not when she might have the power to turn disobedience into disaster.

"If," he said with a soft inflection of authority in his tone that could not be mistaken nor ignored, "I wish you to drink a whole bottle of wine with your meal, you will do so, Esme."

Esme's head tilted back in a gesture that seemed to convey a haughty negation of Raul's authority. But at the same time, he saw her eyes widen with wary shock. She resembled a child who had dared to defy its parents, only to find there was a price to pay for such defiance.

That look in her eyes satisfied Raul that she would not be so foolish as to defy him to the point where she might put the ship, and his authority as its captain, in danger. And as he sat down and leaned back in his chair, his mouth slanted in a smile that was somehow as intimidating as his voice had been. "However, tonight you may have water if you wish it," he added with gracious condescension.

Esme hesitated, knowing what he required of her, but resentful of having to give it. Finally, however, at seeing the look of almost desperate warning in Thorson's eyes, she spoke. "I thank you," she said stiffly.

"You are welcome, Esme," Raul drawled, well aware that her gratitude was seriously deficient.

During the meal, Raul did not speak of how Esme had spent her day, which at first infuriated her. Was what he had put her through so negligible in his eyes that it was not even worth mentioning? But on the other hand, she had no desire to follow up the humiliation she had suffered by discussing it.

In any case, as Raul chatted casually to Thorson of worlds Esme had never dreamed of, she began to forget her personal circumstances in her fascination

## DREAMS OF DESTINY

for what she was hearing, eventually falling a wide-eyed victim to the two men's every word. She had never known anything but the Homeland, and the things Raul and Thorson discussed stretched her imagination to its limits.

By the time the meal was over, it was all she could do to remain silent rather than launch a thousand questions concerning those worlds the two men discussed so casually. Only her feeling that it would be better not to call attention to herself stopped her eager tongue.

At last, Raul pushed his plate away and when he turned his gaze on Thorson, Esme knew from the look in his eyes that the pleasantries were over. Immediately, she grew tense.

"You may go, Thorson," Raul said.

Thorson nodded, and after taking the plugs out of his ears, he got to his feet. "Good eve, Captain," he said formally, bowing to Raul. Turning to Esme, who was looking at him the way a condemned prisoner might view the departure of all hope, he bowed again. "Good eve, Esme," he said, gentling his voice and smiling at her.

Swallowing down a sudden obstruction in her throat, Esme nodded back. "Good eve, Thorson," she said faintly, then watched as he turned and walked across the room. It was only when the door closed behind him that she remembered that Thorson had betrayed her trust, so there was no reason to consider him an ally.

By the time Esme faced Captain Raul again, she had gathered her resources. Since there was no one to help her, she thought she had best stand for her own interests with everything she had.

Raul slouched in his chair, his eyes half-closed, silent and brooding for a moment. Then, softly, he said, "I understand you pleased my men well today, Esme. I am indebted to you for raising my crew's morale."

Esme's returning gaze was bleak. "And I, of course," she said with hollow mockery in her voice, "am so pleased to have been of service to those who rescued me from death."

Though Raul was saddened by the bleakness of her expression, he hid his reaction and merely nodded. "Gratitude is an excellent quality to have, Esme," he said, though in truth he understood perfectly why Esme was not as grateful as she claimed to be. "And I compliment you on possessing such a commendable virtue."

Esme smiled without humor. "Would that I could accept your compliment, Captain. However, as you well know, I had no choice other than to do your will."

"Are you then *un*grateful, Esme?" Raul asked, his cool blue eyes hiding the warmth he felt toward her.

Esme hesitated. "No, Captain," she finally said, the sadness in her eyes and voice stirring Raul in a way he would have given much to have been unable to feel. "I am not ungrateful for my rescue."

She hesitated again, but then, looking straight into his eyes, she spoke with an honest dignity that sat surprisingly well on her, despite her youthful appearance, which Raul could only admire. "But my people do not engage in such activity as you forced upon me today, Captain Raul. Our matings are a result of love between life companions. And since that is the case, I would have much preferred to be of use to you in a different way than you required of me. However, had you *asked* me for repayment in the form you took this day, instead of forcing it upon me unawares, I would have obeyed you no matter what my personal feelings concerning the matter. My debt to you would have required no less."

Raul sat very still, studying her, searching, out of habit, for the truth of her words. But he'd already heard the truth in her tone, and seen it in her beautiful eyes, so the gesture was a mere formality. And he was filled with even more regret than he'd been earlier over what he'd had to do. But it was too late to change things. And the tone of what was to follow between himself and Esme must be set now. Besides, if, as he expected, she would soon become a servant of the Empire, she needed to begin to learn that personal feelings, when in conflict with duty, always came second.

"Then," he said, very deliberately, "it is as well that I did not ask. Had I done so, your honor would no doubt have insisted that you comply fully with my wishes. As it is, you have no need to feel shame over the way you circumvented my orders."

Esme stiffened, and now it was her turn to search Raul's face for the truth and what she saw in his eyes made her gasp.

Raul sat up and leaned toward her, holding her gaze in the steady embrace of his own. "Now you will tell me how you did it, Esme," he said slowly, his voice implacable. "You will tell me the full extent of your powers. You will *show* them to me if I request it, and if they are as formidable as I believe they are, please do not labor under the delusion that you can blast my mind apart and escape retribution. At this moment, every man on this ship is under orders to shoot to kill if you step out of this room alone."

Esme shivered under the impetus of her own helplessness by the time Raul had finished speaking. She almost told him that if she desired, she could blast the entire Condor to fragments around the two of them. But by doing so, she would, of course, kill herself. And Esme was not nearly done with life as yet. Nor had she given up on her dreams.

"How did you know?" she whispered between lips that suddenly seemed frozen into rigid lines.

Raul's gaze was implacable. "I am asking the questions, Esme. You will answer them, and you will answer them now. We will start with why you withheld from me the fact that you have such powers."

Esme swallowed. Her tongue did not want to form the words she had so far withheld from everyone. But she recognized that she had no choice now.

"I was afraid," she said with all the simplicity of a child. "Never..." she added haltingly under the impetus of Raul's searching stare, "never have I shown anyone, other than the priest who sought my life and the one who helped him, the secrets of my mind. And I would not have done so then except that it was a question of life for life."

Raul nodded. He believed her. "So were you lying when you said the priest left you in the desert to die? Could you not have stopped him?"

Esme shook her head. "No, I could not," she said and then again, hesitated.

"Tell me everything, Esme," Raul ordered. "From the beginning."

And with difficulty and for the first time in her life, Esme was forced to lay bare the truth about her gifts. As Raul had requested, she started at the beginning, describing the unnatural awareness she had had as an infant. She revealed the story her mother had told her concerning her conception. She told of the suspicion she had endured from her People all of her days, and of the necessity to conceal her gifts lest the People learn of them and either stone her as a convicted sorceress or imprison her in a life of duty, subject to their unrelenting demands.

Throughout the first telling, the loneliness of the isolated child she had been came through, pinioning Raul's sympathy despite his best efforts to remain objective. Also was he now more than ever convinced that Esme was not going to appreciate having her life taken over and used in the service of the Empire. But those who were blessed as she was were seldom given choices in such matters. They were too valuable to be allowed the luxury of living their lives for themselves alone. However, Raul saw no reason why he should burden her for the moment with an explanation that she had escaped one life of service, only to face another.

When she told of the dreams that had haunted her sleep since early childhood, giving her the only pleasure in her otherwise barren life, Raul saw her face soften and heard her voice quicken with joy. She was suddenly as she had been when she was first brought to him, and he understood now why she had greeted the alien complexity of the ship, and the meeting with him as its captain, with such adaptable enthusiasm. They were not as new to her as he had thought. Though she admitted she could never remember the dreams upon waking, she had recognized the ship on some level.

Had she recognized him as well? he wondered

sadly. Had the two of them shared a special relationship in these dreams of hers, a relationship that could no longer come to be? He would have given much to question her on the matter. But there was no point to it now.

The one thing Esme left out of her recitation, due to her crushing disappointment over Raul's treatment of her, was the presence of a special man in her dreams. It would have been past bearing for her to confess her initial hope that he might be the one she sought for she was afraid he would laugh at such foolishness. And in any case, she was now certain that he could not possibly be that man. He would never have treated her as Captain Raul had.

Esme had lost track of time, as had Raul. But at the finish of her tale, her voice shook with weariness, her eyes drooped with fatigue, and her body swayed in the chair.

"If you wish," she said unsteadily, "I will now tell you how I made your men believe what they wished to believe today . . . but . . ."

"But you are so exhausted you are barely able to keep upright in that chair," Raul said drily, getting to his feet. "Come, Esme,' he said, extending a hand to her. "You will tell me and show me tomorrow. Tonight, it is time to rest."

Esme felt an odd reluctance to touch Raul. But she had not the strength to defy him, and so she rested her hand in his. Immediately, a slight shock, a tingling warmth, seemed to travel from his palm and fingers to hers, startling her.

She looked up at Raul to see if he had sensed anything, but he wore an impassive expression. Therefore, she said nothing and allowed him to pull her to her feet.

She stood swaying, and Raul, voicing a subdued curse, swept her up into his arms. And as he had feared it would, the contact with Esme aroused his desire for her, a desire he could not satisfy. Angry over the loss of such satisfaction, he grabbed the translator, and taking two long strides, placed her quickly down on his bed. He had no wish to torture himself by holding her any longer than strictly necessary.

Esme stared up at him, sensing turmoil in him, but unaware of what could have caused it.

"I must not," she said, pausing to swallow down the sudden nervousness that seized her, "deprive you of your couch."

Raul remained silent for a moment, staring down at her with a look in his clear blue eyes she could not interpret, but which somehow upset her equilibrium. Her breathing grew irregular and difficult, and her mind's powers were, for once, insufficient to steady her breathing.

"You will never," Raul finally said in a voice containing a note of momentary, and most likely useless determination to make his words true eventually, rather than embody the wishful thinking that provoked them now, "be able to deprive me of anything."

He then reached down and removed the plugs of the translator from her ears, and Esme felt both a sense of deprivation and a great relief at having their communication cease.

"Go to sleep, Esme," he said with a curtness that sprang from his efforts to control his body and his emotions. "I have things to do."

Since he had removed the plugs, Esme did not understand him. As her eyes blinked closed, she thought that if she was allowed to stay on the Condor, she must quickly learn his language. She wanted to be free of the plugs and the little black box, free of her own ignorance, free of her fear of the unknown. A moment later she was deep in the coils of a natural sleep.

After a call to his watch officer to reduce the extra guard and to put them back to work on repairs the following morning, Raul returned to the side of the bed. He stood staring at Esme, fighting the lust that raged through his loins, and the desire for her special regard that raged equally through his heart. Then, in an abrupt movement that spelled out his determination to conquer her effect on him, he went to the other side of the bed, flung himself down a good distance away from Esme's reclining body, and hit the button on the wall behind his head, dousing the lights in the cabin.

Expecting to lie awake all night, the victim of needs he had no intention of satisfying, Raul was surprised to find upon waking the next morning that he had slept the night through without interruption.

He was somehow not at all surprised, however, to learn that sometime during the night, his unconscious mind had sent his body across the protective gap between himself and Esme. He now lay with his arms around her sleeping form, and that part of his body most difficult to control during his waking hours, and that had complete autonomy when he slept, was as hard and eager for release as though it belonged to a youth in the throes of his first infatuation, rather than to an adult man with awesome responsibilities who knew when to indulge it.

Gritting his teeth in frustration, Raul forced himself to release Esme without waking her. Then he quickly rose from the bed and headed for the shower.

# CHAPTER TWELVE

Awaking to find herself alone, Esme showered, then stood in front of the reflecting surface Thorson called a "mirror," fascinated by her own image. She had never seen herself clearly before coming to the Condor, and she was rather shaken to find that her eyes resembled her mother's much more than she had ever realized. The similarity produced a loneliness within her. She had not missed her mother in a long while as much as she did at that moment.

Hearing the outer door open, and aware that either Captain Raul or Thorson had arrived, Esme hastily wrapped her robe around her, finishing just as Raul appeared in the doorway.

"Good. You're up," he said, then grimaced impatiently as he realized she couldn't understand him without the help of the translator. Abruptly, he turned to go fetch the tiresome contraption.

Esme followed him, feeling uncertain as to his mood. She sensed no hostility emanating from him, but his facial expression of a moment ago and his abrupt turning away from her made her uneasy.

The first thing he said to her after they'd both inserted the ear plugs of the translator, however, brightened her mood considerably, since it indicated that he was not thinking of sending her away, at least not yet. She had been afraid that the discovery of what she had done the day before, since it may have ended her usefulness to the captain, might make him decide there was no point in allowing her to stay on the Condor. But of course, she thought with distaste, he might still want her to use her mind to raise his men's morale.

"You are going to have to learn our language, Esme," he said gruffly. "I will not wear these things much longer."

He clenched his jaw as an eager smile lit Esme's face and a sparkle came into her eyes. She was lovely at all times, of course. But when she looked as she did now, her beauty made his guts twist inside him and his loins stir with restless impatience.

"I will be most glad to learn your language," Esme nodded happily. "I, too, am eager to dispense with these." She raised her hands to push back her damp hair and touch the plugs set in her delicate ears.

As Raul looked at the small, perfect lobes, he felt a sudden sinking sensation in his stomach as he involuntarily pictured himself nibbling them. It seemed everywhere he looked, there were parts of Esme that invited touching and tasting. But he was grimly impatient with such fantasies. What was the point of entertaining such thoughts when there was little likelihood of his ever having what he wanted? It was a waste of time and energy, and he had better ways of spending both.

"Let us eat," he said more loudly than he'd intended. As Esme winced, he sighed with resignation and lowered his voice. "I want to hear the rest of your story," he said more softly as he and Esme seated themselves and he punched the button to call Jaco. "And I want a demonstration or two of your gifts," he added drily. "Fairly tame ones, if you please."

Though Esme was not entirely at ease with Captain Raul's knowledge of her gifts, she discovered it was liberating not to have to hide them any longer, and a reckless feeling seized her. She pointed at the translator box. "Is this tame enough?" she asked, and as Raul watched, she lifted the box off the table and let it hover in the air, using only the power of her mind.

Raul watched the demonstration impassively. "That must be a handy talent to have," he said, "especially when your people have no mechanical or other type of power other than animal or human."

Esme was a little disappointed that he didn't seem more impressed, but she feigned unconcern as she set the box back on the table.

"Yes, but I only used it when I was alone on the high meadow," she explained. "Otherwise, I would have been in trouble."

Raul nodded. "Tell me, Esme, since you can inflict pain on another person with your mind, why did you not do so with my men yesterday instead of allowing them to believe you were fulfilling their sexual fantasies?"

Esme hesitated. But there was no point in lying to the captain anymore except about the special man on the ship which was to take her among the stars.

"Because I was afraid if I could not be of use to you in some way, you would not take me when you leave the Homeland," she answered quietly, without looking at him. "And I could not think of any other way to be useful. Besides, that was the way you desired me to be useful and if I had tried to change your mind, you would have become aware that I can read minds. Else how would I have known what was to take place, since neither you nor Thorson had told me."

Raul sighed and shook his head, wishing once again that Esme had felt free to be truthful with him. If she had, things could have been so much different between them.

"Esme," he said heavily, "I did not do what I did simply to get use out of you by raising my crew's morale."

Esme looked up in startlement. "But why then?"

Raul tried to keep his personal feelings out of his voice and his expression as he explained to her about trained seductresses and his fear that she might be one. "I had to know, Esme," he finished. "The safety of my ship and my crew was at stake. If you had only confessed your gifts to me, what happened yesterday would not have been necessary."

Esme had been horrified by his description of trained seductresses. Here was another instance where the sophistication of Raul and his people was untempered by a corresponding morality and wisdom. And she was also appalled that he had thought her to be such a woman. But at his last sentence, she was furious.

"But why did you not simply ask me if I was one of these terrible women?" she demanded indignantly. "I would have explained that I am not!"

"Because a trained seductress would have said the same thing, only she would have been lying. Therefore, your negative answer on that point would have meant little." Raul shrugged. "However, a trained seductress would have pretended to have no mind powers. So if you had confessed your own, I would have been fairly certain you were not a seductress."

Esme was not mollified. "But why did you suspect me of such a wicked thing in the first place? What reason did I give you to suspect me?"

But Raul was not prepared to answer her truthfully as he did not want to reveal how he reacted on a personal level to Esme. Not now. Therefore, he gave only a partially truthful reply. "Because I sensed you were holding something back," he said. "I am very good at sensing such things. And I was right, was I not? You *were* withholding information from me."

Guilty as charged, Esme looked away. She was dismayed by how much trouble she had caused herself by being less than truthful with Raul.

"Esme," Raul then said, "you will, if you please, practice discretion concerning your gifts here on the ship. Thorson and I are the only ones who know of your capabilities, and I want to keep it that way."

"Why?" Esme's look was curious, not disputatious.

"Because," Raul shrugged, "though my men have seen things and done things your people probably have never even dreamed of, the suspicious uneasiness people feel when around someone they know can invade the privacy of their minds is pretty well universal among humankind. People like to feel their thoughts are their own."

Esme blinked at him. "Is that why you and

Thorson—" She stopped abruptly, blushing as she realized what she'd just revealed.

"Why we close off our thoughts from you, Esme?" Raul finished what she had been about to say, his voice drily amused. "Yes," he nodded. "We like our personal privacy as well. But I also did not think it wise to give you access to all we knew before I learned of your intentions. For all I knew, you were the advance guard of an attack by the rest of your people."

Esme frowned, puzzled. "Advance guard?"

Raul sighed, and was, fortunately in his opinion since he didn't want to have to explain to Esme the ins and outs of warfare, saved from answering by the arrival of Jaco with their breakfast.

After Jaco had left and they were eating, Esme suddenly said, "I did not know such was possible."

"What?" Raul glanced up from his plate, enjoying the sight of Esme seated across from him.

"I did not know people could close off their minds so I cannot get in," she said simply. "No one ever has before." *And I wish you and Thorson had not done so in this case,* she added silently. *Otherwise, I would not have made the mistake of concealing my gifts from you.*

Raul smiled slightly. "There are a lot of things you do not know about your own gifts, Esme," he said calmly. "But when we get back home, you will be taught your own possibilities."

At that, Esme froze for an instant, her head down, her spoon poised over her bowl of mush. Then, slowly, cautiously, she looked up, and Raul thought she looked like a child who was afraid to believe she was being promised something wonderful.

## DREAMS OF DESTINY

She swallowed, and her voice shook as she spoke. "D–do you mean . . ."

Raul thought it cruel to keep her in suspense. "Yes, Esme," he said softly. "When we leave here, you are coming with us."

He was distressed when he saw her green eyes swim with tears. And then, before he knew it, she was out of her chair and kneeling by his side. Seizing his hand, she covered it with kisses.

"I thank you . . . oh, I thank you . . ." she said through her tears.

The kisses and her kneeling posture at his feet drove Raul past the point of controlling his body, and he jerked his hand out of her grip. "Get up, Esme!" he demanded, his voice loud and harsh.

His voice hurt her, and as Esme winced and raised her hands quickly to her ears, she looked up at him in dismayed surprise.

Raul regretted hurting her. "Get up," he repeated more quietly, with authority but no harshness this time.

Esme quickly rose, but didn't immediately go back to her chair. She stood, her eyes containing an eloquent expression of apology and gratitude.

"I am sorry," she gulped through her tears. "I forgot you do not wish me to touch you. But it is my dream, you see . . . I have waited so long. And now you are making it real."

Esme's mistaken belief that Raul no longer wished her to touch him made him clench his jaw against telling her differently. It would serve no purpose for her to know that now. And no matter that it was her own desire to be taken to Genesis, he felt guilty that he was taking her to serve the Empire, not to seek her

231

own happiness. In the interest of fairness, he decided it was time to make that clear to her.

"It is simply that your gifts can be useful to my people, Esme," he said gruffly. "That is mainly why I am taking you. And the other reason is that I do not feel it is safe for you to be returned to your people. They might try to harm you again, and I do not wish that to happen."

Raul's explanation provoked a sense of alarm inside Esme. She still had no desire to be at anyone's service other than the Master's. But his last statement, about his concern that she might be harmed and his wish that it not happen, softened her heart toward him and she could not protest his people's making use of her gifts. At least not at the moment. And perhaps, when the time came, the Master would rescue her from all but His own purposes.

"It does not matter why you are taking me," she said. "The important thing is that at least part of my dream is coming true." She hesitated over what she must say next, but her debt was clear, and she must at least offer to pay it, while hoping with all her heart that Raul would refuse.

Straightening her shoulders, she looked at Raul with firm seriousness. "And because you are the instrument of bringing my dreams to life, I am at your service, Captain Raul." As he looked at her, frowning and puzzled, she continued hastily, wanting to get the words out before her utter revulsion stole her courage. "So if you want me to continue to lift your crew's morale . . . if that is how I may best serve you, then I will do it . . . either with my mind only, or . . . or fully and honestly now, without tricking them into believing what is not . . ."

"No!" Raul thundered. The sudden, murderous jealousy that gripped him brought him to his feet so rapidly, he knocked his chair over.

Esme screamed and fell to her knees, snatching the plugs from her ears as she fell.

Instantly, Raul ripped his own plugs out and was beside her, and Esme felt herself being lifted into his arms. She huddled there, still shuddering against the pain he'd caused her, her eyes streaming tears, as he strode quickly to the bed and sat down, holding her on his lap.

"By all the comets, Esme, I am sorry," Raul whispered, shaken. "I did not mean to hurt you. Never . . . never do I want to hurt you . . ."

Then, realizing she couldn't understand him, he fell silent and simply held her, rocked her, stroked her, and hoped against hope he hadn't caused any permanent damage to her ears. While he touched her to give comfort, his own comfort flew away at the onslaught of desire that rose faster than he could stifle.

When Esme at last raised her tear-streaked eyes to look at the hard planes of Raul's face, she saw the obvious distress in his eyes, and got her first glimpse into his mind. In his concern for her, he had let his mental shield slip, and Esme, in her need to know why he had hurt her, slipped inside.

At seeing clearly the self-blame he was feeling and the worried concern for her welfare, she was satisfied that he had not really meant to hurt her, and she slipped out again before she also saw his rising desire. He had said he didn't want her in his mind, and Esme was prepared to honor his every wish in return for his giving her her dream.

"I . . . I am all right now," she whispered.

Her assurance did not decrease the concern on Raul's face, however, and at realizing that he hadn't understood her words, she endeavored to reassure him nonverbally. Looking directly into his eyes, she raised a hand to rest it against his cheek and nodded in an attempt to convey that she was all right.

Her direct look and the soft touch of her hand on his face tore at Raul's willpower. Though he silently cursed himself a fool for taking the risk, he couldn't help himself. Abruptly, he dipped his head and caught Esme's mouth with his own, intending to take just one chaste kiss to store in his memory.

But as he had feared would happen, the feel of Esme's mouth against his stoked the fire of desire inside him from a simmer to a flame, and he couldn't settle for just a taste of her. The next thing he knew, he was forcing her lips apart and hungrily thrusting his tongue deep inside her warm, sweet-scented cavity. And the more he tasted, the more he wanted.

Esme's lips had never felt the pressure of a man's kiss before, and certainly, she had never experienced the thrust of a tongue inside her mouth. So she was badly startled at first. But even before her instincts to pull away from the unexpected invasion registered, her mind remembered that she was in Captain Raul's debt. And with that came the resolution to submit to anything he might want or demand. Therefore, instead of resisting, she made her lips soften and yield and she slipped her hand to the back of Raul's neck to stroke his warm skin with soft encouragement.

Esme's willingness sent Raul's reason slipping further away on the wings of desire. He wanted this too badly to deny himself. Abruptly, he turned her and lay her on her back on the bed, then stretched his body on top of hers.

Esme found him heavy, but she merely adjusted her body to make breathing possible. As the kiss continued and Raul stroked with alternate roughness and gentleness the parts of her body Esme had learned the day before seemed to appeal to men, she concentrated, with intense curiosity and wonder, on the unfamiliar sensations she was experiencing.

The sensations were not unpleasurable, even at first, and as Raul continued, the pleasure grew. Esme was surprised to find that Captain Raul's weight had ceased to bother her, with a most puzzling result. Instead of her breathing becoming easier, it grew more constricted. And Raul, who shouldn't have had any trouble at all, was breathing so heavily and harshly, that she wondered if it was hurting him to breathe.

Esme's worry about whether Raul was in pain flew away on a gasp of surprise as he briefly broke his kiss to reach between them and open her robe. As he closed his hand over one of her bare breasts, Esme felt a lurching sensation of such intense pleasure cascade through her entire body, that she gasped again—this time in astonishment. And when Raul resumed his kiss, Esme automatically opened her mouth to receive his tongue, now wanting such contact as badly as he did. Esme's responsiveness almost depleted Raul's reason completely. He barely had enough left to remember not only that Esme was an inexperienced virgin, so that he must be gentle with her, but that there were compelling reasons why he must not take her completely no matter how desperately he wanted to.

Never had Esme suspected such exquisite pleasure was possible. And the pleasure was not restricted merely to her mouth and her breast. A tingle of warm, pulsating heat seemed to spread like wildfire through her whole body, especially between her legs, where Raul's hard, heated maleness pressed against her. When he moved his hips, the pleasure she felt at having that hot, hard part of him rub against the triangle between her thighs made her open her legs and move her hips in concert with his.

Then, to her further astonishment, Raul tore his mouth from hers and brought it down to the breast he held, to suckle it the way a lampkin nursed at its mother's breast. And a feeling Esme had no name for shuddered through her like lightning. She thought she was going to fly apart at any moment. Surely, no one could feel this much pleasure and stay sane!

Then Raul shifted his body off hers slightly, and even as she groaned in dismay over the loss of contact between them, he placed his hand over her femaleness, and the lost pleasure was replaced with another, more intense one when he stroked a finger against a place Esme had not known was made for her pleasure. She arched against Raul's touch and a cry of sheer joy escaped her lips over the exquisite sensation that resulted.

Raul raised his head from her breast to stare into her eyes, and from far away it seemed, Esme heard the rumble of his voice. He sounded pleased with her. And as his finger continued to stroke her, she stared up into his face, her eyes huge and drugged with the feelings consuming her, her mouth parted to draw in the air that seemed suddenly to be too thin to sustain life.

Dimly, she noted Raul's skin was suffused with color and his features seemed suddenly to be carved from stone. As her gaze went to his eyes, it seemed to her that a fire had somehow flared behind them, a fire that had the power to heat her body further without burning it. Becoming lost in that fire, as well as the fire consuming her body, she couldn't have looked away even if Raul had demanded it, though she thought she'd been prepared to do anything he asked.

"Come on, little Esme," Raul whispered hoarsely, holding her gaze, fighting with dogged will power his savage need to plunge himself into her and break the thin shield of her maidenhood. "Let it come . . ." he muttered, ". . . quickly . . . before my will breaks."

Esme did not understand Raul's words but she dimly understood that he seemed to be waiting for something to happen. But an instant later, she didn't care what he awaited. She didn't care about anything other than the ecstasy she felt within her own body, an ecstasy that built and built until she was suddenly shuddering convulsively against Raul's hand, lost in the grip of sensations that sent her mind reeling into a realm of joy so intense that it broke the barrier of remembrance between dream and reality. And even as her eyes rolled up, finally breaking the hold of Raul's powerful gaze, she knew this was not the first time she had experienced his lovemaking.

Though Raul had thought his will power had no limits, it was more than he could stand to keep himself from the same pleasure that wracked Esme's body. The most restraint he could manage, against his every instinct, was to withhold himself from taking her completely. Instead, he merely rolled further onto Esme and from the pressure of bodily contact alone, brought himself the release he desperately craved.

Esme, barely coming out of her dazed state, felt his body shuddering, and she automatically slipped her arms around his shoulders to hold him tight, waiting with her eyes closed for the wracking explosion that had seized him to be over.

When he at last lay still, he slumped against her, pinning her to the bed. Esme lay quietly under him, her lips curved in a smile as she accepted that another part of her dream had clicked into place.

"It *is* you," she whispered joyfully.

Her voice brought Raul back to reality. He propped himself on his elbows and looked down at Esme, whose returning gaze was filled with such radiant happiness that he had to smile. What had just happened had been no part of his plan where Esme was concerned, but he couldn't regret it. However, since he now knew he couldn't trust himself not to let it happen again, his smile faded as he considered how to keep the two of them apart in the future.

Esme's differing intention was made clear when she brought her hands around to cup his face and lifted her head to press her lips against his, her small tongue darting inside his mouth to explore.

Raul forced himself to draw back and shake his head. Though it tore his heart, he knew he must begin at once to dissuade her that what had happened between them would happen again and again.

## DREAMS OF DESTINY

Esme gazed at him in puzzlement.

Raul shook his head again, then rolled off her onto his back and stared up at the ceiling, grimly resolved to do what had to be done. The question was, now that he'd tasted Esme, how was he to keep from doing much more? And having shown Esme the delights of her own body, how could he expect her to understand that she could not have them again—at least not with him.

Esme rose up on her elbow and let her eyes roam his large frame with pleasure. Her gaze stopped when she spotted a wet stain on the front of his bodysuit. Her brow creased as she realized that there was also a wet feeling between her thighs where Raul had touched her.

Looking down, she lifted her leg and touched herself between her thighs. Withdrawing her fingers, she held them up and looked at the wetness there, then glanced again at the front of Raul's bodysuit.

Her actions caught Raul's attention, and despite his concern about what had just happened, he couldn't keep from chuckling over her innocent brazenness. She was a delight.

Hearing his brief spurt of laughter, Esme wanted to ask him what he found amusing, as well as a number of other questions but she needed the translator. She hopped off the bed, and as she went to fetch the hated device, she tied her robe around her.

Regretting that she had covered her beautiful body from his eyes, and regretting even more that he would likely never see her body again, Raul sat up, his gaze grimly wary. He had no illusions that the conversation to follow would be easy for either of them.

When Esme was seated cross-legged on the bed again, and both of them had donned the ear plugs, Raul forestalled the first question trembling on her lips with one of his own.

"Are your ears all right?" he asked softly. "Do they hurt?"

Esme shook her head impatiently. "I am all right," she said, and quickly asked, "The wetness. Is that how you and Thorson knew I had tricked the men?"

Raul hesitated about telling her everything, then thought better of hiding the truth from her. She needed to know what to expect when the time came for her to truly mate. But he quickly shut off that thought as he felt his jealousy rising. Since he couldn't be the one to introduce her fully to sex, some other man would necessarily have that pleasure. And Raul didn't even want to contemplate how badly he would react when that happened. The most he could hope for was that it would happen on Genesis, when he was away on battle duty, and he would not know first hand of his loss.

"That is not the way we knew for sure," he said gently, and then he proceeded to explain to her some things about her own body she'd never known.

When he was done, Esme looked down at the triangle between her thighs. "The barrier is inside there?" she asked interestedly, pointing at herself.

Despite his grim mood, Raul couldn't help but react with humor to her manner. Smiling, he nodded.

"And I will feel pain when it is broken?" she asked, staring directly into his eyes now, a thoughtful look in her own.

His smile fading, Raul nodded again. "And you will

most likely bleed," he said, his voice quiet.

After thinking about it a moment, Esme gave a firm, decisive nod. "Then let us break it now and get it over with," she said matter-of-factly. "You do it with . . ." she started to say, reaching to touch the drying spot on the front of Raul's coveralls. She broke off as she patted him, frowning as she discovered that that hard part of him had subsided.

"That happens to a man afterwards, Esme," Raul said on a sigh. But even as he spoke, he felt himself begin to stir as a result of her hand on him, and he added, drily, "But the hardness returns each time a man is ready to have sex with a woman again."

Esme was much relieved by that information, and her face showed it, provoking Raul into another spurt of laughter.

He sobered quickly, however, and removed Esme's stroking hand from his loins, keeping hold of her wrist. "I will not be the one to show you that part of sex, Esme," he said, aware that his voice, though quiet, had turned grim. It was beyond him to affect disconcern about a matter that tore him apart just to think about.

Esme looked at him, startled. "But why?" she asked, dismayed. "I want it to be you!"

Her words tore at Raul. He, too, wanted it to be him but it could not be. So he tightened his jaw and spoke with soft firmness. "That is only because I was the first man to show you the pleasure of sex. You can have those same feelings with another man." *But I hope I never have to know that it has happened!* he added silently, his jealousy tormenting him.

Esme stared at him, certain he was wrong. Though

it was true she was ignorant concerning these matters, he was the man in her dreams, she was certain of it. And surely, only the man in her dreams could bring her such pleasure. Surely, the man in her dreams was her life mate!

But might Raul's dreams be different than hers? she asked herself an instant later, alarmed.

"You . . . you have had sex with other women?" she asked with reluctant apprehension.

He nodded, then looked away. And his nod provoked an instant wave of some unfamiliar and thoroughly hateful emotion in Esme's mind and heart that made her feel sick. Unknowingly, her face and her voice expressed that emotion as she asked, "And did you feel the same pleasure with them as you just did with me?"

Raul hesitated. He did not want to hurt Esme. Furthermore, an affirmative answer would not be strictly true. There had definitely been something different and deeper about the sexual pleasure he had just experienced with Esme that he had never felt before. His emotions had been as deeply involved as had his body, and this was true even though he hadn't been able to take her completely. But an affirmative answer was the wisest one to give under the circumstances, though it made him feel sick to have to hurt Esme with such a lie.

"Yes, Esme, I felt the same pleasure," he said heavily. "And I will no doubt feel that pleasure with other women again," he added to his lie. But he could not look at her and see her pain as he spoke.

Esme felt as though a wolfhound had bitten through her chest and was chewing her heart. Her expression was so stricken that Raul, glancing at her too soon, had to look away again and clench his teeth to keep from erasing with the truth the pain he saw seething inside her.

Unbidden, the memory of what had happened the day before rose in her mind. Was what had happened then the reason Raul did not want her now?

"Is it because I am your men's whore . . . their 'leavings'?" she asked in a small, shaken voice that tore at Raul's will power. "Thorson said—"

"Aye!" The word was torn from Raul against his strong inclination to say the opposite. But the reason Esme had come up with for his rejection was, in some manner at least, the truth. It was not the only reason, of course, but it was the most immediate one. "The men do not know that nothing really happened," he forced himself to go on. "And I do not want them to know. As I told you before, you raised their morale. And right now, their morale is very important."

As Esme prepared to ask the next question, she felt herself grow remote from Raul. It was almost as though a physical force were sending them reeling apart from one another so that he seemed a long distance away, rather than seated beside her.

"Do you wish me to use my mind to keep their morale raised?" she asked so quietly that Raul barely heard her.

Raul didn't wish any such thing. Far from it. But he had already made enough mistakes which might alert her to his feelings for her, and it was best for her not to know of them. It was best for her to leave this cabin and begin to heal from the hurt he had already inflicted, rather than to ache, as he did, for things she could not have.

"Not at the present time," he said brusquely. "If it turns out I do wish it in the future, I will let you know."

Esme stared at him wordlessly, all hope that he was the man she sought dying with his statement.

Her look tore at Raul, and he took refuge from the feelings that overwhelmed him in curt instructions. "From now on, you and I will have very little contact, Esme," he said. "You will work with Thorson to learn our language and customs. In your spare time, I want you to write a personal history . . ." Raul paused and shook his head impatiently. "Never mind, I imagine you cannot read or write, and you will have enough on your hands just learning to speak Confed. So forget the history for the time being. You can do that back on Genesis."

Raul had other things to say, but though she gave the appearance of listening, Esme had tuned him out. His remark concerning her ability to read and write further emphasized the contempt she supposed he held her in, and she had to deal with her pain.

As Raul sat in front of her speaking, Esme erased her memories of what had happened between them. As she did so, her eyes went opaque, her expression remote, and Raul, at last noticing the change in her, abruptly stopped speaking.

"Esme, what are you doing?" he demanded. When she didn't answer, he seized her shoulders and shook her. "Esme! What are you doing?"

She was midway through the procedure, and she barely heard Raul. But the necessity to obey his wishes was already set strongly in her consciousness, and her lips opened and spoke automatically. "Erasing."

## DREAMS OF DESTINY

"Erasing what?" he grated, a sudden fear seizing his belly.

"I am erasing the memory of what happened here between us. The memory is painful. I do not wish to remember it."

She spoke like an automaton, and Raul, his face a mask of anguished astonishment, almost shouted at her to stop. He didn't want her forgetting anything that had happened between them here on this bed!

But then, realizing just in time that it would be kinder to Esme if she did forget, he closed his lips and watched in agony as Esme completed her task. At that moment, if he'd had the kind of talent Esme did, he would have used it himself. Physical pain he could stand. Emotional pain was entirely new to him, and he hated it with a savagery that made him want to lash out and strike something.

Esme blinked suddenly, and her eyes focused and cleared. She looked at Raul, who was staring at her in silence, and said, with polite formality, "You were saying you want me to work with Thorson to learn your language?"

Raul had to take a deep, shuddering breath before he could force himself to answer. "Yes, Esme," he then said, a note of bitter sadness coloring his voice. "You will work with Thorson. You and I have finished our dealings with one another."

He clenched his jaw against a violent protest as he saw that his last sentence left her unaffected.

"Very well, Captain Raul," Esme said with formal respect and nothing else in her clear voice. "I am at your service, and I will try hard to please you."

And Raul wished with an unnerving ferocity that she really could be at his service in the way he wanted her to be, and that he could be at her service as well. He wished his responsibilities and duty and Esme's more than likely future duty didn't have to get in the way of her "pleasing" him, nor in the way of his pleasing her. He nodded curtly, took out his ear plugs and crossed to the communications console to call Thorson and have him come and collect his pupil.

# CHAPTER THIRTEEN

As Esme's inner clock told her it was time to get ready for the day's lesson with Thorson, she finished writing, in the flowing script of her People's language, the last word of this particular morning's effort to transcribe her personal history, which necessarily included some of the history of the People themselves, in the thick ledger Thorson had given her.

Reaching behind her, she pressed the spot which would open the door of the small compartment in the elaborately carved headboard of the royal bed, popped the ledger and the ink pen into the space that also held the Sacred Pouch, and closed the door. Then, getting off the huge bed and walking barefooted across the thick carpet of the royal apartment, she went to the luxurious sanitation chamber, stripped off the silk robe in which she'd slept, and stepped naked into the shower.

Not long afterward, clad in a bodysuit she had patiently resewn to fit her, she sat breakfasting with Thorson, asking amiably in Confed what he had planned for her to learn that day.

"I am afraid you are on your own for a couple of days, Esme," Thorson said regretfully. "I am starting the first of the regular physicals I give the men this morning."

The regret Thorson felt over the hiatus in his teaching sessions with Esme was caused by the fact that, though he was, by now, used to Esme's startling capacity to absorb information and learn at a speed that was well-nigh miraculous, it was still a joy to watch her at it. In fact, it was a joy to be with Esme period, and though Thorson knew that his feelings for Esme were of a different nature and much stronger than were her feelings for him, he couldn't help loving her more each day.

Thorson suspected that part of the reason Esme learned so quickly was that she picked his mind—and that of every other man on the ship, save the captain's—clean regularly, but he had long since ceased to care that his thoughts and feelings were an open book to her. And though the men weren't aware that their every thought was at Esme's disposal, he doubted that they would care much either by now if they did know. Esme had won their hearts as easily as she had his and had not only taken on something of the nature of a beloved mascot to them, she was, just by her presence, in large part the reason for their excellent morale.

Since not one of the men ever behaved with the slightest lack of respect or circumspection toward Esme now, Thorson was of the opinion that she skillfully directed the men's minds in the direction she wanted them to go concerning her. But that was all to the good as far as Thorson was concerned. His love for her had grown to where, had the captain ordered him now to subject Esme to the sexual test, he would have risked court-martial and disobeyed the order.

In short, aside from Esme's almost nonexistent relationship with the captain—the captain went to extreme lengths to avoid Esme, and Thorson had his own ideas as to the reason for it—Esme had carved a place for herself on the Condor that would leave a very large gap when she was turned over to the psychic fellows back on Genesis.

"Then, if it is permitted," Esme responded amiably to the news that she would be free for a while, "I will spend my time outside with Jase. If we are to leave shortly, I want to savor the earth and air while I can."

Thorson smiled at her use of the words "if it is permitted." Esme knew well that just about anything she wanted would be permitted these days, but part of her charm was the way she never took advantage of her position.

"Of course you may spend your time with Jase," he said lightly. "And I am sure Jase will welcome your company. He says that on the days when you are near, his work goes twice as fast as usual. Could it be that you give him a little unobtrusive help?"

Esme glanced up at Thorson, a bland look on her lovely face. But there was also a slight mischievous twinkle sparkling in her clear green eyes. "Why, I know nothing of engineering, Thorson," she said innocently. "So how could I possibly be of help to Jase?"

"I do not know," Thorson replied with dry humor in his voice, "but if there is any way at all, I am sure you are employing it."

Esme merely smiled. In truth, by dent of exploring Jase's excellent mind, she knew quite a bit about engineering now. But Jase needed no help in his tasks, so Esme secretly helped the crew move heavy or cumbersome objects.

A short while later, as Esme strolled down the ramp that stretched to the sand, she inhaled deeply of the air untainted by the Condor's cycling machines. The day was not as yet scorched by the sun's heat, and the morning sunlight felt good on her face.

Esme had spent most of her life outdoors, and she enjoyed her few opportunities to venture outside the confines of the Condor. But she was also still in awe of the huge ship, and now, as she always did, she backed away from it, marveling that something so large could fly through the air like a hawkbird.

She knew now that the Condor was actually a very small ship when compared to the dimensions of those the Empire used to transport cargo, but it was the largest man-made thing Esme had ever seen, and she was filled with admiration for the builders of it.

After her ritual viewing of the Condor, she strolled to the oasis where Jase had set up a mini-foundry under the trees. Valo, the master craftsman, had already been at work for some time, and as Esme approached him, she automatically paused and stayed silent, since he was directing the pouring of molten ceramo-steel into large molds.

When he was done, he turned to her with a white smile stretching his mouth. His large, ham-fisted hands were on his hips, and there was sweat pouring down his broad brow into his squinting blue eyes.

"Greetings, Esme," he boomed in his large voice.

# DREAMS OF DESTINY

"So you will be helping us today?"

Esme grinned affectionately back at him. She knew he didn't really understand that she actually did help in concrete ways. He thought her presence merely inspired his men to work faster and harder in order to impress her with their strength.

"Aye, Valo," she said cheerfully. "And it is a glorious day to be outside, is it not?" She looked around her, savoring the sight of the blue water in the large pool, the green grass surrounding the water, and the tall palms surrounding the grass.

Valo snorted as he raised his hand to swipe the sweat from his brow, then wiped it on his filthy bodysuit.

"If you like to spend your time in furnaces, aye," he nodded, "it's a glorious day."

Esme wrinkled her nose at him. "Where is Jase?" she asked.

"Around the far side of the ship. They're closing up one of the holes."

Esme knew that when they bolted the huge heavy slabs of ceramo-steel onto the damaged sides of the ship, she could be useful in lessening the strain on the men of lifting and holding the slabs, so she started backing away, saying, "I will go greet him."

A few moments later, Esme came in sight of the work party laboring at their task, and she stopped short, reluctant now to approach further, because Captain Raul was watching the procedure.

In some manner Esme couldn't explain, she found it discomfitting to be around Captain Raul. Perhaps it was because he seemed to look through her rather than at her. Perhaps it was the rigid, utterly formal, chillingly polite civility with which he uttered the very

251

minimum of greetings on the rare occasions when it was necessary for him to acknowledge her presence on his ship.

Esme knew—she had plucked the information from Thorson's mind—that Captain Raul regularly required reports from her tutor on the nature of her progress. She also knew that Thorson had some vague idea that the captain held her in special regard. But, though she respected Thorson's knowledge and opinions on most matters, she utterly disregarded his opinion on this one. Indeed, it seemed to Esme that Captain Raul, if not actively hostile to her, harbored no regard for her at all. She thought that, to him, she was almost a nonperson, and though, on a level so deep within her consciousness that it was only a vague stirring, this lack of regard for her caused her pain, on another level it was quite natural. He still thought of her as his crew's leavings.

Though it had never been discussed between them —nothing had been discussed between them since that morning he had turned her over to Thorson—she imagined Captain Raul attributed the continuing high morale of his crew to her mental efforts to relieve their physical needs. And though she was, in fact, almost totally responsible for their high morale, only she knew that it had nothing to do with satisfying the men's physical needs and everything to do with the soothing of their natural disgruntlement because of their situation whenever she sensed such an attitude arising in anyone's mind.

Now, not wanting to impose her presence since she was certain it was not desired, Esme was about to turn away and go back and help Valo when Captain Raul, sensing her, looked up and spotted her.

## DREAMS OF DESTINY

Raul's sensitivity to Esme's presence was one of the reasons he had been able to avoid her as successfully as he had, for as long as he had, on a ship too small to prevent frequent contact. The other reason was that Esme herself helped him in his efforts to avoid her. It was as often she who, if the situation permitted, faded away rather than call his attention to her.

But the strain of denying himself the sight and touch of Esme was wearing increasingly on Raul's nerves and on his patience, so rather than look away and allow her to retreat as she normally would have, he continued to stare at her.

Esme hesitated. It would be a breach of the Service etiquette Thorson had taught her to turn her back on the captain of the ship without acknowledging his presence. But, oh, she did so want to spare herself the shriveling, humilating pain of having him look through her as though she didn't exist! Esme blinked, startled by that thought. Where had it come from? Normally, her own mind was as open to her as other minds were. But that thought had surfaced on its own, welling up from some secret depth in her consciousness she seldom acknowledged.

Swallowing, her steps reluctant, Esme did what she knew had to be done. She approached within greeting distance and waited for Captain Raul to hold his palm up in the acknowledging gesture Thorson had taught her.

It was always the captain's prerogative to give the first acknowledgment, but as Raul took his time about it, Esme had to control her increasing nervousness. As she was forced to stand waiting patiently under the flaming intensity of his clear gaze while he let his eyes make a leisurely journey from the top of her shining, fire-touched head to the peek of her toes through the straps of her sandals, she wondered why she had ever wanted him to look at her as a living, breathing person rather than as an inanimate object. Surely it was better to be looked through than to be examined as scrupulously as Thorson examined the little squirming bugs he placed under his electro microscope!

Finally, Raul took an unobtrusive deep breath and sketched the briefest of palm gestures.

"Greetings, Esme," he said, his voice dry with self-mockery over the lack of will power he was showing by allowing this meeting.

Esme returned the palm gesture more completely—she never wanted to show the slightest disrespect to the captain—and said, in a low, formal tone, "Greetings, Captain."

Raul noted that she called him "Captain" now, not "Captain Raul" as she had at first, and that annoyed him. He liked the sound of his name on her lips. By the comets, he liked the sound of Esme's voice, period! he thought with grim frustration.

"Thorson is conducting his physicals on the men?" he then asked.

"Yes, Captain," Esme said. As always, she was trying to keep from staring at him because when she did, she felt a strange combination of pleasure and discomfort. But, as always, she couldn't stay her eyes from making a surreptitious inspection.

She knew immediately that the captain had lost weight, a fact which caused an unwelcome feeling of gnawing anxiety and worry inside her. Though his large, well-muscled body was as powerfully threatening as ever, it was much trimmer than when she had last seen him.

## DREAMS OF DESTINY

His thick brownish-blond thatch of hair seemed to be suffering from a lack of attention that was worrisome to Esme also, since he usually kept it neatly trimmed. It lay long on his neck, slightly curling on the ends, and it cascaded in an untidy brush over his wide, tanned brow. The pleasing shape of his lips was set in its usual grim line, the rugged planes of his face seemed more sharply prominent than usual, and his ice-blue eyes, when Esme finally met them directly for the first time, contained an expression of suppressed hunger that almost brought a gasp from her lips. She wondered, once again, why she had ever wished to see him look at her more personally than he usually did.

"So you are free to play today, Esme," Raul said, noting with a certain black humor the reaction she was having to the way he was looking at her. If she only knew what was really in his mind, he wondered, not for the first time, how would she react then? The sort of wary dismay he saw in her eyes now? Or the kind of sensual, hot-blooded response he knew she was capable of feeling?

Esme smiled faintly. She wasn't sure if he was joking or not. It seemed unlikely given his usual manner with her, though he was not, in fact, acting as usual with her this day. And there had been something in his tone when he'd asked that question that hinted confusingly of a different meaning. But Esme had no idea what it could be.

"I came to watch Jase," she said, glancing to where Jase was directing his men in their task. "But I think instead I will—"

Raul interrupted her. Knowing she was about to bolt, he ignored his common sense for once, which was telling him to let her bolt if she wanted, that he should be helping her to do so.

"Ah, yes," he said, glancing in the same direction. "Jase has told me the work goes faster when you watch." Turning back to her, he said softly, so no one else could hear, "Why is that, Esme?"

Esme swallowed. She had felt perfectly free to avoid admitting her contribution to the work when Thorson had hinted at it that morning. But there was only one area where she ever felt able to hide the truth from the captain.

"I . . . I help . . . a little . . ." she faltered, her voice so low Raul could barely hear her.

"How?" His voice, though soft, contained the tone of command Esme would have had trouble resisting had he ordered her to drown herself in the oasis pool.

"Ummm . . . I . . . ah . . . lift things and . . . and . . . help place them."

Esme stared at her feet, and was startled when Raul's hand cupped her chin and made her look up at him. The warm, tingling sensation of his touch almost made her jerk away, but she didn't dare. She had all she could handle trying to keep her eyes from displaying the sudden panic that had inexplicably seized her.

"You sound as though you are reluctant to admit your gifts to me, Esme," Raul said, his eyes sharpening as he detected Esme's reaction to his touch despite her attempt to hide it from him. He wondered, with a sense of subdued excitement, if she was savoring his touch the way he was savoring the contact with her silken skin and he was noting, with a wry, resigned acceptance, the stirring of his manhood under his bodysuit.

Such a light touch shouldn't have caused such a strong reaction in him, he knew. He also knew that it wouldn't have, had this been any other woman than Esme he touched, a fact that he couldn't explain to himself, was ceasing to care to explain to himself the longer their acquaintance lasted and the higher his frustration at having to keep away from her grew.

"I know about your gifts, Esme, remember?" he almost whispered, softening his voice to a deep huskiness.

Esme blinked at him. The sound of his voice made her senses tingle. She didn't understand this new attitude toward her any more than she understood anything else about Captain Raul, which was perhaps not surprising when she barely allowed herself ever to think of him.

"I . . . I know," she whispered back. "I . . . I am just so used to concealing them from the men and I do not see you that much."

Raul nodded, his jealousy rising. He was aware that Esme must be using her gifts, despite his lack of an official order to do so, to keep his men's spirits up. Else why, while they were laboring under the sort of circumstances that would normally have made them as surly as groats and constantly at one another's throats, did they work in cheerful harmony in order to get them off this Hell planet and back home?

On an objective level, Raul was grateful for Esme's help. But on a subjective, purely personal level, he was not at all grateful for the manner he supposed she used to keep his men happy, and had it not meant a possible delay in lift-off should his men's good spirits deteriorate, he would have ordered Thorson to tell her to cease her efforts. He had been amazed to find himself contemplating doing it anyway on several occasions, usually when he had just failed to head off an accidental meeting with Esme in the corridors of the ship.

"Esme!" Jase called cheerfully at that moment, and Raul let his hand fall from Esme's chin and looked toward his chief engineer. Esme watched as Jase approached the two of them.

"You picked a great day to visit, little one," Jase said, displaying toward Esme the sort of affection he might have shown a favored daughter. "We can use some of the sort of boost your presence gives us because we cannot stop this process"—he gestured back at the work going on—"once it is started, and today we are going to have to work past the point where the sun usually forces us to stop."

"Then I am glad I was free to come," Esme replied with warm affection. As Esme and Jase spoke, Raul stared first at Jase in a puzzled manner, then looked at the men who stood smiling at Esme with the same affectionate respect with which Jase seemed to regard her. There was not even a hint of the casual, perhaps even slightly contemptuous, sexual interest in their behavior that Raul had expected—had dreaded if the truth be known—to see.

"Well then, sweetness," Jase said, "sit yourself down in your usual spot by the water bucket, and let us see if we cannot pick up a little speed and efficiency now that we have the pleasure of your company."

Esme hesitantly looked at Raul, unwilling to take her leave without his permission.

"Go on, Esme," he said, his tone absent.

Esme quickly hurried away.

Then Raul turned to Jase. "How much longer?" he asked. The question was merely perfunctory. He had something else on his mind.

"I think we can lift off in another week, Captain," Jase said confidently. "And though I cannot give an absolute guarantee, I think the ship will hold together whatever we put her through."

"Good," Raul nodded, placing his hand on Jase's shoulder in a gesture of affirmation he had been too preoccupied to use much lately.

"Aye, it is good, Captain," Jase replied. "I am as sick of this place as I have ever been of anywhere."

At that, Raul turned his gaze full on Jase and said, very quietly, "But your morale has stayed excellent, Jase, despite your distaste for this place. And while I might have expected that from an old hand like you, I find it surprising that the men's morale has held up so well under these trying conditions."

He hesitated, curiously reluctant to voice the question in his mind, but he needed to know. "Do you think it is because of what the men get from Esme that they are so cheerful?" Raul voiced the question differently than his mind had formed it, and he was cynically amused over his own reluctance to spell the truth out plainly.

Jase smiled. "Well, I cannot deny that when she comes around, we feel a lifting of our spirits and the work suddenly gets lighter," he said in a teasing way, "but just because the bunch of us, to a man, would lay down his life for her doesn't mean you can put too much credit on those sweet little shoulders of hers."

Raul held himself very still. He'd had the answer to his question, but he couldn't quite believe it. So he probed further. "To a man?" he asked doubtfully. "Are you saying that each and every one of my crew holds Esme in such regard that he would defend her as he would his mate or his daughter?"

Jase grinned. "A lot of them would be more willing to save her than their mates," he vowed. "Meaning no disrespect," he added hastily, when his remark drew a frown from Raul. "It is just that some of these men's mates can get a bit shrewish when their man's shore leave lasts overlong. But Esme . . ." He shook his head, smiling fondly at Esme where she sat ladling out a cup of water for one of the thirsty men. "There is not a shrewish bone in her body. She is like a sweet breeze and a cool cup of water on a hot day, and it was a lucky day for us when I found her out there by that pool."

Jase then looked up at the sun and wiped an arm over his sweating brow. "And speaking of hot and lucky days," he said, returning his gaze to Raul, an apologetic look on his face, "I think I had best make better use of this one than I am presently, with the captain's permission?"

Raul nodded, an absent look in his eyes, and raised his hand in a gesture of dismissal.

When Jase had hurried back to his work, Raul spared one long, thoughtful glance at Esme, before he turned on his heel and headed for the ramp leading into the ship. He wanted to let Thorson know his presence was requested for lunch at the captain's table.

"I do not know exactly how she does it, Captain," Thorson said with a shrug before he took a sip of the excellent wine Raul had opened to have with their lunch. "I suspect she simply manipulates the men's minds so they think of her the way she wants them to think of her, with affection and respect, just as she manipulated their minds when you . . . that is, we . . ." he quickly changed the pronoun, "put her to the test that time."

Raul regarded his medic with a sardonic expression on his face. "The first pronoun was the right one, Thorson. It was my responsibility, not yours."

Thorson stirred uncomfortably and made no comment.

"Tell me something, Thorson," Raul said, a brooding look of thoughtfulness in his eyes, "what do you think the men's reaction would be if Esme . . ." he hesitated, then found the right words. ". . . if Esme chose one of us for her special attention."

Thorson forgot himself enough to let his mouth hang open in amazed consternation for a full minute.

Raul finally glanced at him, growing impatient for an answer. "She is a woman, Thorson," he said, "not a saint. And she has a woman's needs. I am asking how the men, who apparently regard her very fondly, would react if she opted to bed someone. Will it threaten their morale?"

Thorson closed his mouth, but his eyes were filled with an emotion that Raul, unhappily, recognized.

"Well, I can tell you what I think, not what I know," Thorson said soberly. "And that is that the men would tolerate it only if Esme chose you to bed." He quickly lifted his glass to his lips and drained the rest of the contents in one gulp, obviously unhappy over such a prospect.

Raul stifled a sigh, thinking he should have expected Thorson to fall in love with Esme when they were in such close contact every day.

"Why me?" he asked.

Thorson glanced at him briefly before looking into space. But Raul had seen the jealous resentment

Thorson was feeling.

"Because you are the captain," Thorson said almost curtly. "Therefore, you are good enough for her." He hesitated, then added, somewhat grudgingly, "Although I doubt they would like it even then if you were some other captain instead of one they respect and admire."

Raul pretended not to notice how resentful Thorson sounded and looked.

"And what about you?" Raul asked in a level, uninflected tone.

Thorson's expression grew even unhappier, and he didn't answer immediately.

"I mean," Raul prompted, "how would they feel if *you* were the man Esme chose?" He knew how Esme reacted to him. But he wasn't certain how strong her feelings had grown toward Thorson during the time they'd spent together. This was the only way he could think of to probe the matter.

"Me?" Thorson said with surprise. And at Raul's nod, he gave a short, unamused laugh. "The saints know *I'd* be the happiest man—" He stopped short and clenched his jaw. Then he looked away and answered Raul's question in a tight voice. "The men would accept it better than they would anyone other than you because I have been working with her. But that is beside the point because Esme would not accept it. She does not feel that way about me."

Noting the bitter regret in Thorson's tone, Raul wondered if he was going to foster a one-man rebellion in his crew if he followed through with what he was thinking. But that he was going to was almost a foregone conclusion. Learning today that one of the good reasons he had had for keeping his distance from

## DREAMS OF DESTINY

Esme was no longer valid had practically settled the question.

True, there were still reasons why Raul knew it would be foolish to get involved with Esme. His career, which necessitated long absences from Genesis and encompassed a great deal of danger, and the duties she would likely have to take on after her training, would both make a satisfactory life-mating well-nigh impossible. And Raul's long habit of thinking that he would never take a mate made it hard for him to accept the idea of a *life*-mating despite the fact that he wanted Esme as he'd never wanted a woman before.

But the weeks of staying away from Esme had taken their toll. Raul's frustration and desire had grown to where he no longer cared about all the good reasons he still had for avoiding a relationship with her. Besides, the question of a life-mating could wait until later. All anyone ever had, especially one in his profession, and especially in view of the fact that the Condor might never make it home, was the moment. And at that realization, Raul abruptly made up his mind. He and Esme would take what they could have now, and leave the future to the future.

The only question remaining was how badly Thorson might react to losing Esme to another man. Raul did not want to see one danger to his crew's morale disposed of, only to have another threat erupt.

"And now answer the question you thought I was asking," he said to Thorson with quiet authority. "What would your reaction be if Esme chose me to bed?"

Thorson clenched his jaw and closed his eyes for a moment, before opening them and looking Raul straight in the eyes, a man-to-man look, not a subordinate-to-Captain look.

"If it is what she wants, I would have no choice but to accept it," he said grimly. "But if I thought you had taken her against her will . . ." he hesitated, then threw caution to the wind. "If you ever force her—" he started to say, his voice holding a quiet ferocity that alerted Raul that Thorson was about to say something Raul couldn't allow to be said for the sake of Thorson's career—and their future relationship.

"I will not force her!" he interrupted, his voice cutting across Thorson's like a whip. He held Thorson's gaze in a way that finally made the younger man look away to stare miserably down into his glass of wine.

Raul sat back and his voice was weary, but entirely convincing, as he went on. "You should know me better than that by now, Thorson. I am a hard man sometimes, yes. I have to be. But I'm not that hard. You know I had no choice other than to test Esme the way I did that time. Nor did you have any choice but to help. The regulations are clear, and we both did what we had to. But it was no easier for me than it was for you. And if I had not hoped very strongly that Esme would prevail—unless she truly was a trained seductress, in which case it would not have mattered—it would have been even harder to do than it was. So you can believe me or not, just as you choose, but Esme's wishes in the matter will be honored. I can assure you of that."

Thorson didn't answer for a moment, and then his resentment burst forth again. "But why does the matter have to come up at all? As far as I can tell, she does not have any interest in . . . such things. So why

## DREAMS OF DESTINY

not just let her go on as she has been?"

"Because I have strong feelings for her, Thorson," Raul said very quietly. When Thorson jerked his head up to stare at Raul, surprised, Raul realized his medic had thought he wanted Esme only physically, that his emotions were not as strongly involved as they were.

He went on, letting his voice and his gaze display the honesty of his feelings. "I have had such feelings, both physically and emotionally, for her from the beginning. In fact, that was the reason I first suspected her of being a trained seductress. Such a strong and immediate reaction to a woman has not happened to me before, and I thought it abnormal and looked for reasons other than the truth to explain it."

He hesitated, then added, "And another reason why the matter has come up is because she once had feelings for me as well, feelings I discouraged in her." A slight, rueful smile curved his mouth at the memory. "And I think she will recover those feelings when she realizes it is safe to. But if she does not . . ." He shrugged, his eyes unknowingly turning bleak. "As I said, the choice is hers."

"But if, as you say," Thorson asked, frowning, "she wanted you once, why did you discourage her? Why did you not take her then?"

"Because at that time the men believed they had had her." Raul shrugged. "And if I had taken her then, my effectiveness as their captain would have been at an end. And in the situation we are in now, Thorson, this ship needs an effective captain." He hesitated, and then, in the tone of a reminder and a warning, he added, "just as it needs a competent medic."

Thorson understood Raul's warning, and for a brief instant, his mouth thinned with angry resentment.

And then, at realizing that the captain had formerly put aside his desire for Esme for the sake of duty, Thorson realized he could do no less. Had Esme wanted him, of course, it might have been a different story. But then, she didn't want him, so doing his duty was really all there was left.

"How..." He stopped and cleared his throat. "How will you handle it?"

"Leave that to me," Raul said. "I believe she usually dines with you?"

Thorson nodded, not looking at Raul.

"Then please inform her you will be unavailable tonight," Raul said quietly. "And," he added after a moment's hesitation, "that I will join her in her cabin for last-meal. Since she has grown used to my disinterest, I imagine she will appreciate having a little time to adjust to the news that my disinterest is at an end before I arrive on her threshhold."

Thorson nodded stiffly, his face set in a rigid mold of impassivity.

Raul stifled an inner sigh, but he was not prepared to cater to the younger man's jealous resentment. He could sympathize, but he'd be damned if he'd discount his own needs, or Esme's, any longer.

Once Thorson was gone, Raul paced the floor, wondering if there really was a chance that Esme would reject him now. But as his eyes automatically went to his bed, and the memories of what had taken place there assailed him, as they had a thousand times, he knew she wouldn't.

Even though she had erased what had happened between them from her memories, the invisible bond he'd sensed pulling them together from almost the

## DREAMS OF DESTINY

first moment of their meeting was still there. He'd seen it in her eyes today, seen her fighting it, seen her refuse even to recognize it for what it was.

But before the night was over, Raul intended she would not only recognize that bond between them once more, she would revel in it.

# CHAPTER FOURTEEN

Esme prepared carefully for her dinner with the captain. She bathed and washed her hair, and for one of the few times in her life, to show respect, she twisted her hair in one long braid which fell down her back to her firm buttocks. She then donned the prettiest of the silk robes Raul had given her, and since it was still early, paced the floor of the royal cabin in an agitated manner.

Her mind was perplexed and her nerves were jangling with dread because she could not fathom why the captain had suddenly decided to acknowledge her existence. But as the time grew closer when the Condor would start on its journey among the stars, she distrusted anything that might get in the way of her being on the ship when it left the Homeland. And any contact with the one man who could deny her what she wanted was fraught with chances to displease him.

Esme suddenly paused in her pacing, cross with herself. What was she doing working herself up into a disastrous state where she might do or say something ill-advised out of sheer nervousness when she had the means to help herself inside her own thick skull?

An instant later, she sat cross-legged on the royal bed, her hands turned palms up, resting on her bare knees. Closing her eyes, she took deep breaths to calm her body, then worked on composing her mind.

By the time Raul knocked at the cabin door, she was calmer, but not completely relaxed by any means. Moving quickly, she pressed the button which would open the cabin door, then stepped back as the hatch slid open.

Raul, freshly bathed and clad in a midnight-blue silk robe Esme had never seen before and which suited his body and coloring superbly, stood casually leaning against the doorjamb. As the door thunked into its slot, he straightened in a leisurely manner and smiled at her.

"Greetings, Esme," he said in a low voice.

Esme felt no hint of disapproval or hostility in him, nor did she see anything threatening in his smile. Therefore, she relaxed somewhat. But her nod was still very formal, and her voice was extremely respectful as she returned his greeting.

"Greetings, Captain. Will . . . will you enter?" She stretched a hand out toward the inner room in a gesture of invitation.

Raul stepped across the threshhold, and pushed the button himself that closed the hatch behind him. And as Esme hesitated, not sure what to do next, he studied her with an unconsciously possessive look.

She was lovely as always but for some reason, she'd braided her hair. Raul preferred the long copper strands loose, and before he made love to her, he intended them to be a silken curtain to enclose two lovers in an intimate sanctuary.

Then he saw that her face was pale, her eyes huge with uncertainty, and he realized she was nervous. Her mood was understandable, and though for his own sake he regretted the time it might take to gentle her into accepting what he had in mind, he was not reluctant to spend it for hers. He had much to make up for where Esme's feelings were concerned, and he meant to make a thorough job of it.

"Shall we sit down, Esme?" he asked, smiling at her in a way he hoped would quiet her immediate nervousness. But he spoiled his own intention by stepping forward to take one of her hands in his own.

Esme, shaken as usual by the warm, tingling shock of physical contact with Raul, stammered a startled reply. "Oh! Oh, yes . . . of course!"

Though he was much encouraged by her reaction to his touch, Raul hid his satisfaction as he drew Esme to the table, and after seating her, punched the button that would call Jaco, whom he'd already alerted as to where dinner was to be served and the menu. He'd had an idea Thorson hadn't as yet instructed Esme in the art of entertaining guests.

"I hope you do not mind," he said with smooth courtesy, "but I have already told Jaco what to bring us to eat. I thought you might yet be unfamiliar with some of our foods."

Esme, much relieved by this information—it hadn't even occurred to her to worry about the menu!—gave him a look filled with gratitude.

"No, I do not mind." She shook her head, drawing Raul's attention again to the way she'd done her hair.

"Why have you changed your hairstyle, Esme?" he asked softly. "You have not worn it that way before, have you?"

Esme shook her head. "It is the way most women of the People wear their hair," she explained. "I have just never cared very much to have mine confined. But I thought because you were coming I wanted to show respect . . ." She stopped as it became clear to her that Raul preferred her hair unbraided. "You do not like it," she said disappointedly, thinking she'd just made her first mistake. She hoped it wasn't the first of many.

"It is not that I disapprove of it, Esme," Raul said gently. "It is a very practical style for day wear. It is just that your hair is beautiful and I prefer it down for a purely social occasion like this."

Esme's heart leapt in her breast. A purely social occasion? Then, he had not come to chastize her or to thwart her adventure!

Without a word, she reached behind her head and undid the braid, and as quickly as she could, tidied her hair with her hands and a little help from her mind so that it soon lay gently curling down her back.

"Is this better, Captain Raul?" she asked.

"Much better, Esme," he said huskily, pleased as much by the fact that she had added his proper name to his title and by her obvious desire to please him, as he was by the added beauty of her appearance.

There was something new in Captain Raul's voice that made Esme's pulse flutter erratically. But before she could decide what it was, Jaco knocked at the door.

## DREAMS OF DESTINY

Raul pushed the button by the table that controlled the door, and a moment later Jaco was deftly laying out tableware and food on the table.

"Thank you, Jaco," Raul said, and the silent steward bowed and quickly left the cabin.

Esme was much relieved to see that Jaco had left a carafe of water in front of her, but as she looked to Raul's side of the table and saw there was no wine there for him, she looked up at him curiously.

He got to his feet and went to a concealed cabinet on one wall, from which he withdrew a dark bottle. "I do not think the royal family will mind if I borrow one of their excellent vintages in honor of this occasion," he said, a light of sardonic amusement sparking from his blue eyes as he came back to the table, sat down, and opened the bottle.

"O-occasion?" Esme questioned, afraid he was going to insist she drink some of the wine if this were some special occasion. And what was special about the occasion? she wondered nervously.

"Do not worry, Esme," Raul said on a light, teasing note as he began to pour some of the rich red liquid into his glass. "I am not going to make you drink any of this. You may stick to your water."

Esme was relieved but she still wondered what occasion Raul was celebrating. He didn't enlighten her, however, so she had to be content with pouring water from the carafe Jaco had left into her glass. As she raised the glass to her lips, Raul held out his glass for one of the toasts he favored.

Esme detoured her hand and as she gently touched her glass to his, she looked up into his eyes. An instant later she was wondering whether her wits had somehow become scrambled. Was she imagining it or was

273

there a blaze of light behind the captain's clear blue eyes that seemed to reach out and warm her body? And why did he have the sort of expression on his face she'd seen before on Maza's face and seen once or twice on Thorson's? Surely, the captain had never looked at her like that before at least . . . Some vague memory struggled to surface in her mind, but the mental cap she'd placed on it wouldn't let it through.

Esme had the expression of one who was trying to remember something, and Raul was certain he knew what it was. Holding his body still, he willed that memory to surface completely. But when Esme shook her head at last, and no comprehension came into her eyes, he gave a resigned mental shrug, relaxed his muscles, and took a large drink of his wine.

"Thorson tells me you learn at an amazing pace," he said casually as he began to dish up the reconstituted meat and vegetables. "And I have noticed that your knowledge of Confed has grown quite proficient."

Esme smiled her pleasure. "Yes," she nodded. "I was anxious to dispense with those translator plugs, so I set myself to learning your language as rapidly as possible."

Raul smiled back. "I am glad," he said. "If you recall, I did not like the plugs any more than you did."

Again, a memory deep inside Esme's mind stirred. And again, Raul saw the expression on her face grow thoughtful and then disappear.

"Tell me something, Esme," he prompted. "If you want to, can you erase things from your memory?"

Esme was startled. She wondered how he knew. "Yes and no," she said. As Raul continued to look at her, obviously expecting more of an answer, she

## DREAMS OF DESTINY

explained, "It is not exactly a full erasure. But I can push things very far down and cap them. But I very seldom do that," she added, shaking her head. "Only when something hurts me very badly do I deprive myself of the knowledge which both good and bad experiences can impart."

Raul went very still for a moment before he set the spoon back into the dish he'd been serving from and sat back in his chair.

Esme noted that his eyes now seemed to be displaying a bleak regret, and she wondered why.

"Can you ever get the memories back?" he asked, his voice level.

Esme hesitated, not certain herself of the answer. "I do not know," she said at last. "But nothing is ever lost from one's mind. Perhaps if circumstances . . ." But then she shook her head and repeated, "I just do not know, Captain."

Raul nodded resignedly. Then he gestured at the food on her plate. "Eat, Esme," he said quietly. "You worked hard today."

Esme glanced up at him, startled again. "How did you know?"

Raul smiled. "By the amount of work Jase accomplished. It seems you are a very valuable addition to our crew, Esme. And I thank you for your help."

Part of Esme relaxed at that and she was relieved and pleased that Captain Raul seemed to appreciate her at last. But another part of her, the part that whispered he also meant another valuable service he thought she performed for him, was bleakly unhappy over his gratitude.

Raul saw the pleased reaction to his compliment fade from her eyes and knew immediately what was in her mind. He knew as well that until the matter that was bothering her was settled between them, the rest of the night would not go as well as he intended it should.

"I am curious, Esme," he said quietly, "as to how you erased from the minds of my men the memory of the day you supposedly fulfilled their sexual fantasies."

Esme abruptly froze and for a moment, she kept her head down, refusing to look at Raul. Then she cautiously raised her eyes to his, her heart pounding so hard, she could hear the beat in her ears, feel the movement in her chest.

"I only realized today," Raul said softly, "that my men regard you with the sort of affection and respect that is incompatible with what they would feel if they thought they had had you intimately. So how did you do it, Esme? And why did you do it?"

Esme was trembling now, afraid that her explanation might displease Raul enough to make him decide not to take her with him among the stars. But she forced herself to meet his steady gaze as she replied. "I merely imposed the truth of what I am over the fiction of what they thought I was," she said with a quiet composure she didn't really feel. "I did it because I thought it healthier for them and because I preferred their affection and respect to their contempt."

She paused, and now her voice grew slightly anxious. "I realize you gave me no instructions to do this. I did it on my own. But," she added, an unconscious plea in her tone, "I kept in mind your wish that their spirits be full of cheer, and I work to aid that condition when I sense anyone becoming downcast. So it is not really as though I disobeyed you, is it?"

## DREAMS OF DESTINY

Raul was startled by the turmoil inside her. Then he realized how afraid she was that he would leave her behind when the Condor departed this planet.

"No, Esme," he quickly reassured her. "You did not disobey me. If I had thought about it in the proper way, I would have known you could do such. But I did not think about it in the proper way."

Raul was frowning by the time he finished his statement. *Why* hadn't he thought about Esme's capacity to impart any sort of impression she wanted to in the minds of his men? And as uncomfortable and startling as the conclusion he reached was, he had to face it. He hadn't been avoiding Esme all this time simply because of all the good reasons he thought he had. He had also avoided her because he had been afraid of his feelings for her.

Was his emotional autonomy really so important that he had lied to himself? he wondered uneasily. And if it was, was it a mistake to go through with what he'd planned for tonight?

He realized that Esme still might turn him into the sort of besotted fool he'd seen other men become when infatuated unreasonably by a woman and whom he had always amusedly dismissed. He glanced up, the frown remaining on his lips, to see that Esme was looking at him with uncertain hope in her eyes. Quickly, he gave her the assurance she needed.

"I have not changed my mind about taking you with us, Esme," he said in the tone of a firm promise. "Relax. I am no threat to your dream."

Esme felt so limp with relief that she slumped back in her chair and closed her eyes.

Raul watched her with grim amusement. Would that he could solve his own problems so easily! He'd thought he'd made up his mind to take her and ease his frustration at last. But taking her was not as simple as he'd thought. It involved a risk he had hidden from himself, something he had never done before, and he still wasn't certain he was prepared to face that risk now.

But then Esme opened her eyes and sat up, and the eloquent look she gave him jarred his doubts into abeyance. By the comets, almost any risk would be worth it! he thought, as his need began to rise, and his control to slip.

"Thank you, Captain Raul," she said, her voice low and trembling. "My gratitude is beyond expression."

"I do not want your gratitude!" Raul said sternly. And when Esme drew back in startled reaction to his tone, he softened it. "And when we are alone like this, Esme," he said much more gently, "I am not the captain. I am a man. At such times, you will call me Raul."

Esme felt another infusion of heat in her body as a result of the flame in Raul's eyes, and as she started to tremble, she blinked in surprise at him. At last, an inkling of what this evening was all about came to her.

Seeing the knowledge in her expression, Raul smiled, glad that it wasn't going to be necessary to explain things to her.

"Eat, Esme," he said as he picked up his own spoon. "We have spent long enough over this meal already. And I have plans for the rest of the evening," he added in a softly meaningful tone, "that I want to get on with."

Esme obeyed, but for the rest of the meal, she didn't taste anything. She watched as Raul consumed more wine than food, and listened as he charmed her with light flirtatious conversation. But inwardly, she was trying to sort out how she felt about what was obviously going to happen later on.

There was no question of refusing to give the captain what he wanted, of course. That she would obey his wishes was a settled matter in her own mind. She would not hesitate to risk her life for him in return for his giving her the chance to live her dream, and his use of her body was a much smaller way to express her gratitude; in fact she considered such use of her on his part almost his right. But if he had rights over her body, her feelings were her own.

The problem was that her feelings wouldn't settle down. One moment, she was filled with a nameless dread of being hurt somehow by this new development, and not just physically. She knew about the barrier inside her that would be broken when a man penetrated her for the first time but she had no real fear of that sort of short-lived physical pain.

No, it was another sort of pain she wanted to avoid. But she could not define what that pain might be, nor why she expected that she might have to suffer it.

The next moment, an equally strong sense of anticipatory excitement that was both completely new to her, and yet strangely familiar, whirled through her mind and body, leaving her breathless and weak.

By the time Raul punched the button to call Jaco to come and clear the table, Esme was in a dreadful state of confusion, and she excused herself to go to the sanitation chamber to try to put some order back into her thoughts.

Closing the door of the chamber behind her, she

collapsed onto the sanitary receptacle and rested her head in her hands, wishing it were the time of her six-monthly cycle, so that she might have some time to get emotionally and mentally ready for what was to come. Thorson had said men didn't usually mate with women during their cycles. He had also been surprised her cycle came so seldom, and she had been surprised to learn that on other worlds, women's cycles came more often.

But her cycle wasn't due for two more months, and she had no time nor privacy other than here in the sanitation chamber to compose herself into a suitable state to fulfill the captain's wishes. She didn't want to anger or displease him by seeming to dislike his attentions. In truth, she had no idea whether she would like or dislike what was to come. Nor did she want to disgrace herself by behaving in a cowardly, unwomanly fashion as she was doing now.

On that thought, Esme raised her flushed face, her expression determined. There was little point to skulking here in this chamber and there was every chance that by doing so, she was incurring the captain's . . . Raul's, she amended quickly, disfavor. Therefore, she must meet her fate with dignity and courage.

Esme got up, cooled her face with some water, took a deep breath, straightened her shoulders, and rejoined Raul in the main cabin.

She was disconcerted when she found that Jaco had come and gone, and Raul lay naked on the big bed with her ledger in his hands. Somewhat embarrassed, she kept her eyes on his face rather than look at his body.

He glanced up at her, his expression puzzled. "What is this, Esme?" he asked, lifting the ledger toward her.

She crossed to the bed and stood at the foot of it with her hands tightly clasped. "It is my personal history," she said, proud to have him know that she had known how to read and write before Thorson's tutoring.

Raul glanced at the strange, flowing script, and raised his eyebrows. "I have never seen this language before," he commented.

Esme didn't know what to say to that, so instead, she said, "I am only just now learning to read and write Confed, and to use the computer. When I know how, I will transcribe what is there"—she gestured at the ledger—"onto the computer."

Raul nodded. "Good. I will look forward to reading it." Then his gaze softened and he added, with complete sincerity, "I apologize, Esme, for assuming that you were illiterate before you came to us. Forgive me."

His sincerity, as did the respect for her she saw in Raul's eyes, made Esme flush with pleasure.

Raul turned, put the ledger back in its space in the headboard, and closed it. When he faced Esme again, he stared at her silently, thoughtfully, for a long moment.

Esme was trying hard to keep from looking at his magnificent body, but it was difficult not to see it and not to react to its power and strength with a maiden's fear. But at the same time, the woman in her was reacting to Raul's muscled beauty with admiration and excitement.

At last he spoke, and his voice was husky, gentle, compelling. "I wish you to take off your robe, Esme," he said. "Will you do it for me?"

Esme was ready, and she didn't hesitate. Indeed, some instinct made her move slowly and with as much feminine grace as she could summon as she unwrapped herself from the folds of her borrowed robe.

When it lay in a puddle around her feet, she saw a small, leaping flame rise in Raul's eyes as they traveled the length of her nude body. There was another part of him rising as well, and as Esme stared at that powerful part of Raul's body, her breath caught in her throat each time she inhaled.

"Come here, Esme."

There was a throbbing, beckoning tone in Raul's voice that moved Esme more strongly than the actual words he spoke, and as she walked around the large bed, she had the sensation of experiencing a waking dream. She sat down on her knees facing Raul, her gaze mesmerized by a heated quality in his that made it even more difficult for her to breathe.

He reached up and placed his hand on the back of her head, and taking a fistful of her hair into his strong fingers, gently pulled her toward him until she could feel the touch of his breath on her mouth.

Her balance upset by the move, she moved her hands to his bare shoulders to steady herself, and immediately felt her palms tingle with the familiar shock she had experienced every time he'd ever touched her. His skin was warm to her touch, and she very much wanted to stroke it with her palms. But she was too shy to take such a liberty.

## DREAMS OF DESTINY

He held her gaze locked in his, and the flickering heat in his clear blue eyes enticed her and beguiled her until she could scarcely think.

"You know what I want?" he murmured.

She swallowed, then whispered shakily, "Yes."

"And you know it will hurt at first."

"Yes."

"Are you frightened?" His tone was gentle, empathetic.

"Yes. No. I mean . . . I do not know."

Her uncertainty brought a tender smile to his lips and a gleam of humor into his clear blue eyes.

"Thorson insists I am to ask your permission before I take you," he said, his voice a soft, sensuous rasp that made Esme's pulses flutter. "Do I have your permission to take you, Esme?"

The tone of his voice and the heated look in his eyes created a strange sensation in Esme's belly. A restless, not-at-all unpleasant ache was forming there. But his words made no sense to her. It was not for Thorson to give the captain orders.

She frowned, her puzzlement in her eyes, when Raul closed the distance between them and placed his open mouth over hers. His tongue slipped between her lips and though Esme was certain no man had ever kissed her thusly, she automatically opened her mouth. And as she did, a tiny jolt of recognition surged through her mind. But that sense of recognition only confused her more. She could not fathom why she should recognize something she had never experienced.

Then the confusion started to fade from her mind as she began to experience a warming pleasure in reaction to the lazy plunge of Raul's tongue in and out of her mouth. She touched his tongue with her own, tentatively at first, and then less uncertainly as she began to want to explore his mouth as he was exploring hers.

She felt a sinking sensation in her stomach as Raul coaxed her tongue into his mouth and suckled it. And after a while, he drew back slightly, searching her face, seeming pleased by what he saw there.

"Do you like my kisses, Esme?" he whispered.

"Yes . . ." she said, her breath catching in her throat. "Very much."

"Then do the same to me," he ordered gently against her mouth, and when he offered his tongue, Esme took it and did to it as he had done to hers.

But she had barely experienced the full pleasure of that activity when one of his large warm hands closed over her breast. As a groan of pleasure left Esme's mouth, he slid his slightly roughened thumb back and forth over her bare nipple. Esme drew back slightly, staring at him in heated delight.

"I like that as well," she whispered from deep in her throat.

Never ceasing the movement of his thumb, Raul held her eyes, a look of heavy-lidded satisfaction in his warm gaze.

"Shall I show you more, Esme?" he murmured. "Do you come to me willingly?"

Esme swallowed, nodded, and with complete submission in her eyes, folded limply into his arms, catching his mouth with her own as she stretched out on top of him.

Raul instantly removed his hand from her hair and moved his arm beneath her buttocks, turning her onto her back and following her, his mouth plundering hers as he moved.

Another jolt of recognition merged with the instantaneous pleasure of having his weight pressing upon her body, and Esme's eyes came half open to meet Raul's. He was staring down at her, and when he saw the look of muted comprehension in her gaze, he drew back very slightly and nodded.

"Aye, Esme," he muttered thickly against her mouth. "There has been this between us before. Only it will be different this time. This time, I will hurt you as well as pleasure you and then, when the hurt is gone, I will teach you to pleasure me."

As Raul's mouth descended onto hers again briefly, then moved on to her breast and from there to dispense more delight to other places on her body, Esme continued to have flashes of remembered pleasure which mingled with the pleasures of the moment. When Raul's mouth returned to her nipple and tugged at it, everything almost became clear.

But it was not until he placed his hand between her legs and his finger slipped inside the wet warmth of her, bringing her body arching upward in a spasm of ecstasy, that the whole memory burst into her brain like an explosion of lightning and her body stiffened against his searching fingers.

Raul's head came up and his face bore the same flushed, hard expression she remembered so well now that the cap enclosing her memory had departed.

"No!" she cried, her eyes wide with fear that she would experience the same emotional pain that had resulted from their last experience. She placed her hands against Raul's shoulders to push him away, but it was like trying to move a boulder set firmly in place without the help of her mind.

"Yes, Esme," he said hoarsely, his voice unyielding. "Oh, yes . . . I have waited for this too long to stop now." As his fingers brushed the wetness between her thighs, he added, "And you are more than ready for me. You cannot pretend otherwise."

An instant later, he lifted her hips and before she knew what he intended, he plunged forward. Esme felt the hard shaft of his manhood enter her with a swift inevitability that shattered her defenses, and as she felt the barrier inside her burst into a thousand splintering shards of pain, a muted scream left her lips.

She almost struck out with her mind to inflict the same sort of pain on Raul. But somehow, she caught the automatic reaction before it was too late and the next instant, she sent her mind flying back to the darkest corner of her head where almost all feeling was numbed.

As her mind huddled there, she was dimly aware on some level that Raul continued to plunge in and out of her and that there was a flood of her own warm, wet life's blood filling the cavity he plundered. But it was all at a distance, and the pain was blessedly fading, and gradually all awareness of him and everything else faded into the relief of complete insensate blackness.

After Raul had obtained his release and lain for a moment panting and recovering, he became aware that Esme was unconscious and bleeding.

Raising himself onto his elbows, he stared at her with incomprehension at first. Then, as understanding slowly dawned in his mind, he voiced a steady stream of violent, self-condemnatory curses as he got up, donned his robe, swathed Esme in her own, and lifted her into his arms to carry her limp body from the cabin to Thorson's sick bay.

Raul stood watching as Thorson, tense with jealous rage, conducted his examination of Esme's still unconscious body. Finally, Thorson stood back, and seeing that some of his anger had turned to puzzlement, Raul spoke, his voice as hard as stone. "Why is she still unconscious?"

Thorson turned his head and it was obvious that he was having a hard time letting go of his angry resentment. But it was equally obvious that he didn't feel nearly as justified in his feelings as he'd been before.

"I do not know," he said grudgingly. "There is no physical damage other than what I expected." He fixed Raul with a hard gaze then and asked, "Did you hurt her in some other way? Did you do or say something that . . ."

His voice died as Raul straightened and paced menacingly to within a foot of where Thorson stood. Thorson, his eyes widening at what he saw in Raul's face, involuntarily stepped back.

"Hear me, Thorson," Raul said in a dangerously quiet voice, his anger pulsating beneath the surface of his control. "I had no intention of hurting Esme any more than necessary. I have no *desire* to hurt her. And if you do not let go of your self-pitying disappointment because it was I who took her to bed instead of you and get started bringing her out of the state she is in and back to normal, you will be sorry you ever set eyes on either me or her!"

Raul was so quietly, dangerously convincing that when he fell silent, Thorson, without another word, turned with shaking hands to fetch a syringe filled with a powerful drug that was all he knew to use.

As he injected it into Esme's vein, he prayed with intensity that it would work, not only for Esme's sake but for everyone else's. Because if it didn't, he had a feeling the captain's rage would be so immense, that no man on the ship would be safe from it.

Esme stirred and moaned, and an instant later felt the powerful presence of someone leaning over her. Then a strong, familiar voice was ordering her to open her eyes.

Under the prodding of that relentless voice, she finally had no choice but to obey, and as she blinked her eyes open, Raul's face, looking haggard and grim and yet filled with relief, came wavering into view.

"Wh . . . what's wrong?" she asked through lips that didn't want to move.

"How do you feel?" Raul asked, his voice quiet and gentle.

"I am thirsty. I want water . . ." she managed to say.

She saw Raul look up at someone, then Thorson's voice echoed in her ears from her other side, sounding as though it were moving away.

"It is the drug. She is dehydrated," Thorson said, and a moment later he was back.

Raul slipped his arm behind Esme's shoulders and lifted her, and Thorson held the cup while she sipped gratefully until every drop was gone. She felt better then, though still groggy.

As Raul continued to hold her, she looked from his

## DREAMS OF DESTINY

face to Thorson's and back again. But she couldn't think, couldn't understand why they both looked so concerned. She wanted only to sleep. She sighed and leaned her head against Raul's chest.

"Take me to bed," she mumbled, before falling into a dozing state.

Raul looked at Thorson inquiringly. Thorson shrugged. "You might as well," he said. "The way she heals, she should be all right soon."

Raul immediately lifted Esme into his arms and carried her to the door, and then Thorson's voice stopped him.

"She may continue to bleed for a day or two," he said quietly.

Raul's temper rose for a moment. He thought Thorson was imparting the information because he was afraid Raul hadn't the sensitivity to keep his desires under control long enough to give Esme a chance to recover. But when he looked back at Thorson, he realized he'd been wrong. Thorson's expression contained no accusation, no hostility. It contained merely relief that Esme had recovered.

Raul nodded, then turned and carried Esme back to her cabin. His guilt over hurting her was such that though he had every intention of staying with her until she was fully awake, he would not lie on the bed with her. But when he'd put her down and started to straighten and move away, she unconsciously clung to him and pulled him down beside her. Then, she wrapped him tightly in her arms before falling into a deep natural sleep.

Grateful that she didn't seem to hate him, at least in her unconcious state, Raul folded her gently against his body and closed his eyes, expecting to lie awake all night trying to figure out exactly what it was he had done wrong and how to make up for his mistake.

But as had happened once before when he had slept beside Esme, instead of lying awake, he soon slept so peacefully that the night passed without either of them stirring.

# CHAPTER FIFTEEN

For the first time in many nights Esme dreamed of the Settlement and Bazil and a young man called Baldor. The dream was confusing. Bazil somehow threatened the People, but Esme knew not how. And Baldor, who had once harmed her, was somehow now her friend and Bazil's enemy.

Then that dream abruptly slipped away, to be replaced by a much more familiar and welcome one. She smiled in her sleep as she stood in the control cabin of the Condor and watched the large view screen display the shimmering luminosity of a nebula. And then the beloved warmth of familiar arms enclosed her body from behind and she turned joyfully to face her lover, lifting her mouth for his kiss.

But this kiss was somehow more real than any of the other kisses she'd received in this familiar dream, and gradually, as Esme started to come awake, the kiss, instead of ending, took on even more reality.

Her eyes opened, and as Esme found herself in Raul's arms with her mouth pressed to his, she abruptly drew back, gasping in surprise.

Raul's eyes came open, and his gaze quickly changed from one of sleepy haziness to alert inspection. And Esme, her eyes wide with recognition, whispered shakenly, "It *is* you! You *are* the man in my dream!"

Raul frowned, thinking she was hallucinating as a result of the drug Thorson had given her. "This is not a dream, Esme," he said with soft gentleness. "This is real. We are on the Condor, in your bed." He hesitated, then added, "And last night, you had a bad time of it."

But Esme paid no attention to his words. She merely continued to stare at him, her heart thudding in her breast, her mind struggling with the joy of recognition—and the fear of possible loss.

Raul saw only the fear, and he closed his eyes for a moment in self-disgust. Then a determination to erase that look on Esme's face filled him, and he opened his eyes and placed his hand on her smooth cheek.

"Do not fear me, Esme," he said gently. "I will not hurt you again the way I did last night. I vow it on my life."

Esme blinked, confused as to his meaning. Then remembrance came, and after sorting things out in her mind, she smiled hesitantly. "I know," she whispered. "The barrier is gone now."

He smiled back, but his smile was bleak. "I did not mean that," he said quietly. "I meant I will not force myself on you again."

## DREAMS OF DESTINY

Esme's smile immediately disappeared, and was replaced with a look of consternation. "But why?" she cried. "Did I not please you? Do you no longer want me?"

Raul frowned. "Of course I want you!" he said emphatically. Then he softened his tone and added, "But I do not want to hurt you, Esme. I never wanted to cause you the pain I have."

Esme felt a dart of hope lighten her heart. "But the barrier . . ." she said hesitantly. "Any man would have caused me the same pain you did."

Raul shook his head. "It was more than that and you know it," he said with dry self-blame. "The physical pain was the least of it."

Esme hesitated, holding his gaze, her own anxious. "Yes, that is true," she admitted. "It was your rejection of me, your sending me away from you, after the first time we were together that hurt me. And last night, I feared you were going to do it again. That is why I fled to the sanctuary of my own mind, to escape the pain I thought you were going to bring me again. But you are here with me now. And I dare to hope your being here means you are not going to hurt me that way again. Please do not send me away this time, Raul. You do not understand yet, but . . ."

She stopped speaking as Raul leaned on one elbow, and frowning, studied her expression, searching for the truth.

"You want me to stay?" he finally asked, speaking slowly and with a note of incredulous hope in his voice. "You want to continue to mate with me?"

Esme smiled, a light of eagerness in her eyes giving him his answer. But in case her look wasn't enough, she slid her fingers around the back of his neck and pulled his face down to hers. "More than anything," she whispered huskily, then opened her mouth over his and kissed him with a quickly learned expertise that had Raul's manhood stirring within seconds.

He drew back slightly, and stared into her eyes, noting with growing possessiveness the cloudiness of rising passion there, the sincerity of her feelings. "Then so be it," he muttered thickly.

His next kiss was heated, but a few minutes later, when in its roving, his hand came in contact with the surgical pad Thorson had placed between Esme's legs to catch her blood, he stopped what he did abruptly, then groaned in frustration, and rolled away.

Esme understood, and she was as disappointed and frustrated as was Raul. Then, as she looked over and saw that he was still aroused, she came up on her elbow and reached over to stroke his manhood with tender possessiveness.

Raul reached down and caught her wrist in his strong fingers, meaning to stop her from causing him such exquisite torture. But she resisted. Opening his eyes, he saw from her expression that she was fully absorbed in her own curiosity and wanted the chance to explore him for her own pleasure, as much as she wanted to pleasure him.

"Here," he said huskily, moving his hand over hers and forming her fingers to a position that suited him more. "Let me show you how."

As in everything, Esme was a quick student, but before long, having mastered one thing, she was ready to go on to another. She glanced up at Raul's face, and seeing the flushed hard look there that no longer frightened her, she smiled.

"Is there more?" she whispered.

## DREAMS OF DESTINY

Raul's eyes came open, and the look in them sent a shaft of pleasurable heat through Esme's body. "More?" he said, his voice thickened almost past recognition.

"Are there other ways I can pleasure you?" Esme murmured. "I want to learn to pleasure you, Raul. You said last night you would teach me to."

Raul, almost past thought already, wondered briefly if he could stand to deepen her education. But his body answered for him, and he raised a hand to place it on Esme's nape under her hair.

"Aye, Esme," he growled in a thick, passion-filled voice. "There is more . . . much more."

And for the next few moments, the only sounds to be heard in the cabin were his low-voiced, panting instructions.

And Esme, as she followed his instructions, learned something of the power of her own womanhood in the process.

Esme lay in the bed thinking, her mood impatient. Raul had risen, showered, and left to make his rounds, telling her he would be back later to breakfast with her.

Meanwhile, the same needs she'd satisfied for Raul, apparently to his complete satisfaction, she thought, with a pleased, womanly smile as she luxuriously stretched her body, were giving her much discomfort. Raul had refused even to attempt to ease her lust, fearing to hurt her. But if her body would only cooperate and stop the annoying bleeding that had worried him so.

A sudden thought brought a gleam of interested speculation to Esme's green eyes. Thorson had always said she healed quickly. What if she set her mind to healing even faster than she normally did? She'd never attempted to explore her own body, nor anyone else's other than their minds, but it was worth a try. Failure could certainly cause her no more frustration than she felt already.

Stifling a sudden giggling fit that seized her, Esme lay straight and relaxed and closed her eyes. And then, after a moment spent composing her mind, she sent it on a quest inside her body, to one particular area at least. Much to her delighted interest, she soon viewed the damaged area, pondering how best to go about repairing it.

First, she gently disposed of the remains of the barrier that had caused her such pain, and after the tiny fragments were sent floating away, she set her mind to repairing the damaged blood vessels. Little by little, the flow of blood trickled more slowly, and finally it ceased entirely.

Esme didn't stop with her successful endeavor, however. Her bottomless curiosity had been aroused by the amazing complexity of her own body. With increasing awe at the miracle the Master had wrought, she was soon lost in humbled contemplation of her own heart, lungs, muscles, skin, veins, and nerves.

When she finally blinked her eyes open, she lay quietly worshipful, thanking the Master for His skill in granting her the gift of such a superb vessel in which to carry her spirit.

Such thoughts led Esme to contemplating the destiny the Master had in mind for her. Why had He set her apart? What was the real purpose of the fulfillment of her dreams?

She was on this ship, which would soon sail among

## DREAMS OF DESTINY

the stars, and she had found the special man who had always inhabited her dreams. But sailing among the stars was as far as her dreams had ever gone. She had no idea what special task, or tasks, awaited her in the future. But there must be something she was to do for the Master.

Malthuzar had said not to speculate, that the Master would reveal her tasks as each one was upon her. But it was hard not to wonder, and part of her wondered whether Raul and his people were the other Remnant mentioned in the Sacred Scrolls who would someday be reunited with the People. Surely, if they were, they would know of the Master. But no one on this ship ever mentioned Him, and there was no reference to Him in any of the tapes in Thorson's library.

Suddenly, it was difficult for her to think. Her mind was clouding as if she was ready for sleep. And yet it was not the same. She was not tired. This lassitude seemed to be coming from a source outside herself.

An uneasy shiver quaked through her body as she abruptly sat up and looked around her in puzzlement. But there was no one and nothing to be seen other than the familiar objects of the royal suite. And after a moment, she thought her ignorance of the future might be for the best. If there was something to come that was unpleasant or dangerous or frightening, and if she knew of it beforehand, her steps might falter on the journey the Master had set her on.

Unwilling now to think anymore, she got up and took a shower. And by the time she had dried and neatened her hair and dressed in one of her silk robes, Raul was back, and she ran laughing to throw herself into his arms and kiss him with exultant welcome. He returned the kiss in full measure, thrilling her with his lusty response.

Afterwards, she lifted herself on tiptoe and whispered the news of her remarkable recovery in his ear. He drew back and looked at her questioningly, and when he was sure she spoke the truth, an anticipatory smile curved his lips. Without delay, he lifted her into his arms and took her to bed.

This time, Esme's participation in the foreplay was much more pronounced. With a growing lack of inhibition, her hands and mouth explored and dispensed pleasure every bit as much as Raul's did, and her voice joined his in heated whispers and murmurs of appreciation.

And yet, when it came time to take her completely, though Raul knew Esme was as wet and willing as any man could wish, he hesitated, afraid of hurting her.

Esme's eyes opened and she frowned in confusion. "Why have you stopped?" she whispered.

"I am afraid to hurt you, Esme," he whispered back. "Are you sure you're all right?"

A slow smile curved her mouth, and her hands were gentle as she pushed Raul to his back. Then she came to her knees and straddled his body.

He looked up at her in surprise.

"If you are afraid to hurt me, then I must take the matter upon myself," she said with loving humor. And an instant later, she had settled herself upon his manhood, wringing a satisfying groan of pleasure from his mouth in the process.

As Esme began to move, Raul studied her face. Her pleasure was there for him to read and there was not the slightest sign that she was in any pain.

"So be it," he muttered thickly, and an instant later,

it was Esme who was upon her back, and Raul who moved within her.

And then Esme marveled once again at the Master's skill in creation. How perfectly He had arranged things for His people's procreation! She and Raul fit together as though they were two halves of one whole.

But the Master, with typical generosity, had done more than construct the male and female body so that they would fit together neatly. He had given the ability to men and women to rouse within one another an intense physical pleasure so that the desire to come together made the joining easier. And when destined mates found one another, He had given of His own spirit of love so that the oneness of the mates' bodies was accompanied by a oneness of mind and emotion that turned the intensely pleasurable, procreative physical act into a joyous joining of heart and soul as well. Truly, Esme thought wonderingly, her eyes clouded with tears of gratitude, the Master had wrought a miracle.

Then, as her pleasure spiralled out of control, she could no longer think at all, but only feel. And before Esme and Raul ate the breakfast he had come back to share with her that morning, he had slaked one of her hungers to her complete, exhausted satisfaction before he took her hand and led her to the table to start feeding the next one.

At breakfast, Raul suggested Esme visit Thorson after the meal to reassure him she was all right.

Esme looked at him curiously. "But why should he think I am not?" she inquired.

Raul hesitated, then shrugged. "When you were unconscious last night and I took you to him, he was much concerned about your welfare. It is therefore only courteous that you allow him to see you are fully recovered."

Esme smiled at Raul lovingly. "I am more than recovered," she said with soft emphasis. "I am better than I have ever been."

Raul smiled back. "As am I," he admitted with equal softness.

Esme was pleased by his reply. But she had sensed something in his manner when he had spoken of Thorson that troubled her and she questioned him on the subject.

Raul was reluctant at first to speak plainly. But when Esme persisted, he finally decided that perhaps it was best if she were aware of Thorson's feelings, so that she might tread lightly.

"He holds you in special regard, Esme," he said quietly. "Surely, you must have suspected that."

Esme blinked, then slowly nodded. "I suppose I did," she agreed. "But he never made me uncomfortable about it, so . . ." She paused, then frowned thoughtfully. "Do you mean the relationship you and I now share causes him pain?"

Raul nodded. "Yes. And he is a good man, Esme. So we must be kind to him in his pain."

Esme agreed. "Then I will visit him as you suggested."

After they had eaten and had reluctantly kissed one another good-bye, Esme made her way to sick bay and Raul went to check on Jase's repairs.

As Thorson nodded his head to Esme's request for a moment of his time, she saw that he was studying her obvious state of happy well-being with mingled relief and sadness.

"I am well," she said softly, holding his gaze affectionately with her own. "I am happy and I wish that you could be happy for me."

Thorson's expression turned bleak, and he gave her a somewhat bitter smile. "Why do you not just come into my mind and make me happy for you, Esme," he said with weary mockery. "I have not used my shield for a long time with you. I am open to whatever you want me to feel. In fact, if you can turn me into a whole man again, I will welcome your invasion."

Esme stared at him for a moment, distressed. Despite the compliment he paid her of loving her, she took no pleasure in his unhappiness, nor in the idea of manipulating his mind. But the pain she felt within him required her to make the attempt against the advice of her instincts.

"I will try," she agreed.

As they stood face to face, Esme quickly slipped into Thorson's mind and flooded it with her own affection and respect and good wishes for him. Then, wincing a little as she saw the depth of his feeling for her, she slowly tried to turn those feelings into something less passionate. But after a moment or two, he started to resist, and she paused, puzzled.

*Do you not really want to stop hurting?* she asked him silently, mind to mind.

Thorson jerked a little. It was the first time Esme had ever spoken directly to his mind.

"I . . . yes . . . at least, I think so . . ." he responded aloud.

*You may think what you wish to say to me and I will hear it,* Esme said silently with patient gentleness. *But, Thorson, if you want to stop hurting, you must stop resisting me. I do not want to use the sort of pressure it would take to override your wishes completely.*

Thorson stared at her doubtfully. *Are you saying I can resist you if I like?* he asked. And at Esme's nod, he added, *Can anyone?*

*Up to a point.* Esme shrugged. *But if I care to, I can override the resistance and force my own will upon another's.*

Thorson remained silent for a moment and as Esme studied his thoughts, she realized the intimacy of engaging in this mind conversation with her, far from ameliorating his jealousy of Raul, had increased it. Thorson wanted more of such intimacy, but of a different sort and knew it was Raul's to have, not his.

His negative feelings toward Raul angered her and roused her protective instincts for her mate.

"If you do not wish it," she said aloud, "I will not take away the feelings you have for me, nor the pain those feelings cause you. But I hate the sort of thoughts you are having about Raul. I love him. And I will, if you do not relent voluntarily, wipe those feelings from your mind with a force you will find most unpleasant."

Thorson stiffened. Then, hurt pride in his tone, he said, "Have you appointed yourself his protector, then? If so, take care, Esme. He is a man, not a child, and I doubt he will appreciate it if you try to shield him from every problem that comes his way, especially one so negligible as my jealousy of him. He knows, even if you do not, that my feelings will not harm him in any tangible way." He paused, then added, "Unless you've been in his mind, turning it to your way of thinking instead of allowing him to be himself?"

It was Esme's turn to stiffen now. "I do not read Raul's thoughts, nor do I control them," she said with

## DREAMS OF DESTINY

prideful dignity. "He does not wish it, and I honor his wishes."

Thorson shrugged, but his jealousy rose another notch, and his male pride rose along with it. "Well, on second thought," he said harshly, "neither do I wish it. I am no more a child who needs to be coddled than Raul is, and I will handle my pain on my own."

And with that, he closed down the mental shield Raul had taught him and Esme was abruptly shut out of his mind unless she wanted to use the kind of pressure that would cause him a great deal of pain.

She hesitated, uncertain of Thorson's belief that Raul would not suffer from Thorson's jealousy of him, and that Raul would not appreciate her attempt to shield him from unpleasantness. But she wanted to shield Raul from anything that might hurt him!

Still, her affection for Thorson, though dented, remained, as did her gratitude for his patient instruction and she could not bring herself to hurt him either.

Abruptly, she turned on her heel and strode away from Thorson without another word. But she was filled with puzzlement, and a certain amount of anger toward him. She did not understand why he would cling to emotions that caused him to be so unhappy and caused her to feel slightly guilty, though there was no reason for her to feel such.

Esme was at first so caught up in the first true happiness she had ever known that she didn't realize the feelings of the crew echoed Thorson's in some particulars. It was impossible to keep many secrets on a ship the size of the Condor, and before the sun set on the day that Esme and Raul became lovers, the news spread through the men seemingly by osmosis.

Only one or two of the men's reluctance to accept

Esme's becoming the captain's mate rested in a muted sexual jealousy which her mind manipulations had not firmly dispelled. The rest of the men felt as if their innocent sister or daughter had been deflowered and turned from maidenhood to womanhood. They were anxious for her, wondering if she had given herself freely, or whether their captain had made her pawn to his power.

Raul, always sensitive to his men's attitudes, had expected some sort of negative reaction and, was aware immediately of the quality of the looks he was getting. They ranged from slightly troubled concern, as in Jase's kind eyes, to sullen resentment from the two men who were jealous.

Thinking on it, Raul rejected strongly the idea of asking Esme to use her gifts to soothe the situation. It would become altogether too easy, he realized, to start to depend on the powers she did not as yet fully understand herself. And that way led to a diminution of the strengths he had worked long and hard to develop in himself, and which he must depend upon again on the field of battle when he had turned Esme over to the care of those on Genesis, who would teach her her own possibilities.

Raul was not at all pleased to find growing in himself already a strong reluctance to do without Esme when the time came to give her up to her own destiny. But it took only the sight of her to make him forget to exercise a cautious hand over his own emotions. With her touch, he lost almost entirely the capacity to defend his heretofore invulnerable heart.

Esme became aware of the crew's feelings when, on the third day of her new relationship with Raul, after a night of fruitful instruction at his hands resulting in splendrous awakenings of her own burgeoning sensual nature, she walked with Raul to check on Jase's progress.

She found it hard to keep from clinging to Raul and to stop her eyes from disclosing her love for him each time she glanced his way. But Raul had cautioned her to maintain propriety when among others, and she therefore did her best to follow his lead.

"How goes it, Jase?" Raul asked, inspecting the progress so far made with his eyes narrowed and his expression thoughtful.

Esme didn't hear Jase's answer. She was suddenly aware of the quality of the atmosphere around her. First, there was the way the men failed to smile a greeting to her. Instead, they sent furtive looks her way containing everything from embarrassed tender concern to hostile jealousy. Then, alert that something was wrong, she explored the thoughts of the men who had formerly borne her only good will.

Her brow puckered as she failed to comprehend why her liaison with Raul should evoke such a strong reaction of concern for her. Among the People, there was only joy on the part of clan members when a man or a woman of the family met his or her destined mate and bonded. No parent would feel concern over such a happening. No sister or brother would feel protective. What protection did one need from love recognized and realized?

The fact that no man of the People had stepped forward to acknowledge responsibility for her own conception was, Esme knew, the beginning of her mother's real ostracism. Though the People had always been nervous of Esther, it was not until the unacknowledged seed began to grow in her belly that their fear of her had strengthened. It was unthinkable that any man of the People would fail to claim his child. Yet no man of the People would even admit to the coupling in Esther's case.

Because Esme had no blood kin, she had had no family to care for her after Esther's early death. And she had become a shepherdess on the high pasture from a strong desire to hide her gifts, and from the sad knowledge that her loneliness would be less in isolation than among people who failed to grant her the loving attention that was customary for them to extend to orphans.

Now, among these men she had counted as friends, she failed to find any happiness over her good fortune in finding the mate destined for her since birth, and never had she felt more the lack of any close family to share her joy.

"Esme?" Raul placed his large warm hand in a gesture of comfort on her shoulder, and his voice and eyes were filled with concern.

Even as her body reacted predictably to his touch, Esme was dismayed that she had let her inner sadness become outwardly visible. She forced a smile to her lips, and her eyes glowed with the love she felt for Raul as she answered. "Yes, beloved. How may I serve your needs?"

Raul's smile slanted, but his eyes were still searching for the reason behind her unhappy state. "You know very well how to serve my needs already and are adding to your knowledge at a speed I may one day have cause to regret," he murmured for her ears only, though Jase, standing nearby, heard, and a red flush of embarrassment colored his sun-browned skin before he looked away.

"What is wrong?" Raul then said in a tone demanding truth from her.

Esme hesitated, and because she thought she might cause him distress by answering truthfully, which she had no choice but to do, she raised her small hand to place it on his broad chest in a comforting gesture.

"It is just that I was regretting I have no family to share my happiness over our union," she said placatingly.

At that, Jase's head came up, and he stared at Esme as though seeing her for the first time as she continued to speak to Raul. "Among the People, when two people recognize one another as fated partners, there is cause for celebration among the family. I have no family there, but I had thought these"—she gestured at the men, who continued to work, but whose attention was obviously at least half on the couple who stood nearby talking softly—"because of the affection they seemed to harbor for me, and because of their fond respect for you, would count as family and be happy for us. Instead, our union seems to be causing them distress."

Esme stopped speaking, and looked into Raul's eyes with an unhappily confused expression in her own, asking for an explanation.

Raul hesitated, then shrugged. "Perhaps you did not do your work in manipu—" He paused, noticing that Jase was unabashedly listening, and changed what he'd been about to say. "The men feel strongly possessive of you, Esme," he said, speaking with dry self-recognition, since he was coming to feel quite possessive of Esme himself. "They regard you as belonging to all of them. It is hard for them to see you fall into the orbit of one man only."

Esme frowned. "But is not such an attitude unreasonable?" she said a little indignantly. "Thorson has told me that monogamy is the common practice in your society. It is generally the same in mine, though some few opt for polygamy if the numbers of males and females do not balance. But since polygamy is not practiced among your people, should it not be natural for these men to accept that, though my affection for them remains unchanged, I want to have a special bond with you whom I love?"

Esme had expressed her emotional love for him often and fervently during their physical lovemaking. And each time she had, Raul had felt a combination of exultant satisfaction and yet uneasy concern for the pain of loss Esme would someday feel when they parted. It was for the latter reason, as well as his own unresolved reluctance to accept the chains that expressed love would bind around him, that he had not, as yet, returned her affirmation. At least, not verbally.

"Men are not always as generous as you would have them be, Esme," Raul said. He had meant to speak with soft comfort. Instead, his tone contained an impatience that sprang from his own guilt at encouraging feelings in both of them that could not, in the end, be resolved to either of their satisfaction.

"And in this case," he added, glancing at Jase, who was looking shamefaced now, "you are the only female on the ship. Therefore, their possessiveness where you are concerned is not all that strange. You stand in the place of all the womenfolk they have left behind."

## DREAMS OF DESTINY

Jase stepped forward. "Aye, what the captain says is true," he admitted to Esme, taking one of her hands gently into his own rough, calloused fingers. "But here stands one man ready, if a little tardy about it, to wish you all the happiness your father might were he here in my place, Esme."

Jase's generosity brought tears to Esme's eyes, and a feeling of great release to her heart. Acting spontaneously, she slipped an arm around his neck and kissed his seamed cheek with affectionate enthusiasm.

"Thank you, my friend," she said shakily as she drew back.

Then, seized by a recklessness she had had too little chance of indulging in in her short life, she stepped back, turned to Raul, stood on tiptoe and drew his face down to hers.

Raul could have stopped her, but something he saw in her large green eyes touched his heart and argued against that choice. So instead, as her lips covered his, and she gave him a long, evocative kiss, he merely supported her back with one hand and tried to fight the instant arousal her kiss evoked in him.

When Esme finally loosened her hold on him, her face was as flushed as his, her body as tense with need as that part of him that bulged in his bodysuit. All eyes on them during that kiss and afterwards, recognized that Esme's desire for the captain was the equal or better of his for her, which did much to mitigate the feeling that he had exploited her innocence and helpless position.

Then Esme turned to face the men, all of whom were frozen in place and temporarily forgetful of the tasks that had previously occupied their hands and attention. Muting her mind probe so that they would not know how the impression originated, she sent them a message. No longer was she a childlike pet of theirs. Instead, she was a woman who belonged of her own free will to the captain. She needed not their concern nor their protection, but rather their friendship and good wishes. And if they wished to continue to have her fond regard, that regard would have to rest on the basis of an adult recognition of mutual autonomy where private matters were concerned.

Her message completed, Esme turned back to Raul, whose thoughtful gaze shifted from her, to his men, and back to her.

"With your permission, Captain Raul," she said loudly enough for everyone to hear, the formality of her words denied by the loving tone of her voice, "I will take up my duties at the water basin. The work here proceeds a pace, but I would have it go faster, for my eyes yearn to see the stars that have long haunted my dreams."

Raul stared at her for a long moment, then nodded. And Esme, with one last look he felt to his toes, stepped away, her back straight, her head up, to take her accustomed place at the water basin.

Jase and Raul then stood side by side and watched with identical expressions of relief, pride, and amusement, as the first of the men, his expression fondly tender, jumped down from the scaffold which had been placed against the side of the Condor and approached Esme.

The man was an old hand who had, on his last shore leave, reluctantly married off his eldest daughter to a man whose time and energy was spent piling up credits obtained from selling exotic off-world products, rather than helping to secure the safety of the Empire.

The man absently took the filled dipper Esme offered him, and only she heard his words.

"I wish you the happiness I would like to believe will come to my own daughter," he said softly. "But she is joined to a man whose honor rests in possessions, while you have had the good fortune to win the heart of a real man. May you and the captain take such joy in one another as is ever granted to mortals while the saints permit life and feeling to continue to fill your bodies."

Esme blinked away renewed moisture in her eyes and nodded. "I thank you for your good wishes," she said gratefully. "And may your own life and happiness rest in the Master's gentle hands," she added a standard phrase of the People, one she meant wholeheartedly.

The man smiled, and then, though it was obvious his thirst was not the reason he had come to her, drained the cup she'd filled for him, returned it to her, and rejoined his fellows.

By the time the third man had gone to Esme for a drink and a word of good wishes, Raul knew his crew's resentment had changed to acceptance. And exchanging a look of amusement with Jase, he then turned to go check with his navigator.

As he walked, Raul was not sure if Esme had used her mind powers to ease the men's resentment. And he wasn't going to ask. But he reminded himself never to underestimate Esme under any circumstances and never to release to her at least that part of himself that he would need to continue his life with relative contentment when he had to give her up. Otherwise, the Empire might lose a telepath of extraordinary potential, as well as its most seasoned battle commander.

And while, without any undue modesty, Raul was aware that his absence would be sorely felt, he did not as yet suspect that Esme's absence could make an even greater difference to the lives of the people who lived upon the worlds that made up the Empire.

# CHAPTER SIXTEEN

THE NIGHT BEFORE THE CONDOR WAS TO LAUNCH, ESME'S every nerve was awake and jumping and her mind couldn't settle on anything for more than a few seconds. She wished Raul would join her and give her an outlet for her excess energy with his lovemaking, but he was prowling the ship, giving everything and everyone a last-minute check.

At last, she tired of pacing and flung herself on the big bed where she retrieved her journal and sat cross-legged scanning what she'd already written. Her history was now complete, up to and including her new relationship with Raul, and since she wrote with complete frankness, her own words brought a smile to her lips and a shiver of remembered ecstasy down her back.

Briefly, she considered sending her beloved a silent message to hurry back to her so that she might have more of the exquisite pleasure he dispensed with such generosity. But then she grimaced and shrugged, as she realized that on this particular night, he would not appreciate having his duties interrupted. Raul, as she was learning even without benefit of access to his mind, was a man so bound by duty that everything else, including herself, took second place.

She had included part of the history of the People as an adjunct to her own story. Now, however, she took up her pen to expand on the subject by recreating the words of the Sacred Scrolls which had bound her People from ancient times. She wrote how the Master had created the People and gave His laws to them through His prophets. But He did not force His love nor His laws on the People.

Esme would have had no trouble remembering each and every word even had she not had the ability to go to that place in her mind where she stored such precious material and retrieve them. For the schooling of every child of the People before they went on to learn whatever skills they would use in their adult lives was very simple. After first being taught to read and write and count, each child was given a set of copies of the scrolls and set the task of transcribing a personal set of their own which they were to study throughout their lives.

Esme's set still rested in a cave near the high meadow where she kept the few items of personal import she owned. She had not had the opportunity to retrieve them before her life had taken its present course. But she had never needed to look at her set once her childhood transcription was finished. Each word had found its place in her heart and mind and had long since been melded so thoroughly into her

## DREAMS OF DESTINY

consciousness that she needed no overt thought to recall the history, the rules of conduct, and the precious Prophecy that governed her own life and the lives of her People.

Though she had never penned in her copies the historical portion of the scrolls that was added by the seekers, she was aware of the history that had unfolded during her own time. Her mind, after plucking the knowledge she required from the minds of the seekers, had done its own recording.

Her pen was flying across the pages of her journal when the door to the royal cabin slid open and Raul crossed the threshold, looking physically weary but mentally satisfied.

Esme immediately popped her journal and pen into its compartment and flew into his arms.

When her clinging mouth was finally momentarily satisfied, Raul smiled down at her and stroked her hair.

"I thought you would be asleep," he said, his voice tired.

"I could not," Esme shook her head. "I am too excited about tomorrow."

"Excited or frightened?" Raul asked, his eyes searching hers even as he gently pushed her away and stripped off his bodysuit.

"Both," Esme sighed. She folded her hands and watched his body emerge from its covering, taking absent pleasure in the magnificence of its structure. "My mind knows what to expect and is prepared. But my body is proving unexpectedly reluctant to leave the solid earth."

Raul grinned as he straightened and, nude, stretched the kinks from his weary muscles.

"That is to be expected," he shrugged as he turned and headed for the shower. "Everyone feels the same on their first lift-off."

"Do they?" Esme said curiously, sliding around him to reach the shower chamber first and provide him the small service of adjusting the water to the temperature she knew he liked.

"They do," Raul said drily.

He stood with his hands on his naked hips, watching her with ambivalent feelings. It was not so much that he was unused to having such services performed for him, or that he found such help displeasing. It was that he was unused to having a woman of Esme's obvious superiority perform such personal tasks for him out of a simple desire to please the man she loved. Such an act would never occur to a highborn Genesian woman. She would feel it was beneath her dignity.

But as Esme, having adjusted the water to her satisfaction, turned to him, and her eyes clouded with a look he was beginning to know well, he forgot what a highborn Genesian woman might or might not do, and blessed his good fortune in finding another kind of woman where he had never expected to.

Reaching a hand to her cloud of copper hair, he twisted his hand in it and pulled her close. She came willingly and leaned against his body in contentment, her green eyes, as she looked up at him, half concealed behind her long dark lashes.

"If you are so eager to ease my burdens," Raul murmured thickly, "perhaps you will consent to shower with me and wash my back?"

"I will consent," she smiled languidly, "to do anything you wish."

"Such power may corrupt me yet," he muttered

## DREAMS OF DESTINY

against her mouth, and he kissed her long and deeply. Then he stripped her silk robe from her and pushed her with gentle force into the shower cubicle, where he proceeded to make her live up to her incautious offer.

Later, as they lay entwined upon the royal bed, he stroked her with gentle hands and whispered reassurances about what the morrow held. And when she slept at last, she knew not that he continued to hold her close while he stared into the darkness and wondered bleakly what the future held for the two of them.

What would happen the next day, and for many days afterward, troubled him far less than what would happen when the Condor once again touched down on Genesis, and he and Esme were faced with the separation that would likely last most of the rest of their days.

Raul's sensing, though different than Esme's, worked well enough when he cared to use it, and he knew she would not be happy at lift-off anywhere other than by his side. Therefore, when the Condor hummed into life the next morning, Esme felt the sensation in her strapped down limbs from a couch in the control cabin and not in the windowless crew's launch quarters where she had feared she would be placed.

But in truth, as the great ship vibrated ever more powerfully, and Esme's heart raced at a pace to match it, she wasn't so sure she really wanted to see the earth slip away and the darkness of space rise to take its place.

Raul was always the last to strap down. And as he received the nod from his pilot that told him it was time, he paused on the way to the couch beside Esme's and placed a comforting hand on her shoulder.

Despite her best efforts, the gaze she lifted to his was filled with fear, and even his reassuring smile didn't quieten her heartbeat appreciably. Then his hand was gone and he strapped himself down in the couch beside her, and Esme's mind wailed a litany of loss over the absence of his reassuring touch.

So she was very glad when Raul reached his arm across the space between them and offered her his hand, his palm outstretched. Esme seized it gratefully, and her fingers clung so tightly that Raul's mouth twitched with tender humor. He would have spoken more words of reassurance had he thought they would do any good. But he thought Esme past hearing, so he remained silent, and merely held her hand as the ship shuddered under the first thrust of lift-off.

A small gasp left Esme's lips as she felt the ship lift, and then she clenched her teeth together and tightly closed her eyes as her stomach lurched in reaction to the ship's movement.

Sometime during the ascent through the Homeland's atmosphere, Esme opened her eyes and forced them to stay that way, staring with fascinated apprehension at one large view screen which now showed the Homeland diminishing rapidly beneath the ship. Another view screen showed the space above them darkening, and as they approached that darkenss with a speed that terrified Esme, she automatically slipped down into the more familiar darkness of her own mind where there was peaceful release from the panic threatening to overwhelm her.

As she was slipping away, however, she felt Raul's fingers tighten painfully on her hand, and she winced

## DREAMS OF DESTINY

and turned her head to stare at him in reproach through the cloud that was fogging her mind.

"Do not!" he ordered, his voice commanding, his eyes holding her in a fierce vise of intense will that made her blink away the protection she had sought.

When she was fully aware, Raul ignored the sullen pout of her lips and the glaring glow in her green eyes. "Good!" he nodded curtly, and turned away to watch his pilot bring the ship through the last wisp of atmosphere and up into the airless calm of space.

"Gravity control on," the pilot announced, and Raul immediately unstrapped himself and stood up.

Esme continued to glare at the black width of the bodysuit covering his shoulders as he paced to the controls and began a rapid check of conditions with his men. She was still glaring when he finally deigned to remember her presence again and turned to seek her with his eyes.

Her expression brought an unrepentant grin to his lips. "Come, Esme," he said, holding out his hand. "Come have your first look at your home from a different perspective than you have ever seen before, and at the space between the stars you have dreamed of seeing for so long."

His words erased the glare from Esme's eyes and the scowl from her lips, replacing them with an eagerness that still contained an element of anxiety. It was too late to have second thoughts now, however, and she had begun to get over her fright in any case, so after fumbling her straps loose, she moved rapidly to Raul's side.

Along with the large view screens, there was also a see-through strip of material stretched around the curving half of the control cabin, and Raul took her to an area where she wouldn't be in the way of his men and pointed.

Esme's breath froze as she saw the vast emptiness surrounding the ship. Suddenly she had a floating sensation, as though there was no longer any solid support for her feet. Looking down, she saw the gray plasti-steel of the deck stretched firmly beneath her. But in her mind's eye, she saw also the miles of empty space between the ship and the solid earth of the Homeland, and a trembling took hold of her limbs she feared would never end.

Raul's arms came around her from behind and his low, calm voice spoke in her ear. "You will get used to it," he assured her. "I think you will even get to like it. You do in your dreams, do you not?"

And suddenly, Esme knew this moment was a reliving of moments she'd experienced in the dreams Raul had mentioned, and her mind abruptly ceased its whirling turmoil. She took a deep breath and the trembling in her limbs calmed.

"Aye," she said, wonder slowly dawning in her tone. "I have been here before in my dreams. And as you say, I have liked it. Nay, I have loved it. And I think also I will again."

She felt Raul's cheek against hers moving in a smile. Then he gave her one last squeeze before bidding her to sit and stay out of the way and look to her heart's content.

"I have things to do," he said and left her to go about his duties.

Esme obeyed and sat for what seemed like hours, her attention shifting from the view screens to the see-through strip, and watched the globe of the Homeland spin beneath her, alternately darkening and

## DREAMS OF DESTINY

glowing with sunlight. For the first time in her life, she saw what was beyond the valley that had sheltered her almost all of her days and the People for untold centuries.

The mountains enclosing the valley were located a little above the central thickening of the globe and the desert stretched not only all the way westward, but southward to a small icecap as well. North of the valley containing the Settlement was empty barren land which turned gradually white, ending in a second polar icecap. And east of the valley was a vast body of water that stretched all the way around the globe until it met the western desert and lapped its shores.

As Esme stared, she realized once again that the Master had directed her steps when she had begun walking in the desert. Had she gone in any other direction, she would have walked to her death. For just as the scrolls said, there was no other place on the Homeland other than the Settlement where life was possible, and therefore there must be no other people than the Remnant.

A shudder of relief traced her back and a great feeling of gratitude filled her heart that the Master had taken care of her. The sandstorms which had cut off her sensing had not been accidental. Nothing had been accidental. She had ended where she was intended to end. And she had no doubt that Malthuzar had been right when he had told her that she would one day return to the Settlement for whatever purpose the Master had in mind.

Her thoughts turned to the Sacred Pouch, which rested in the compartment beside her journal. It, too, she felt certain, would one day play a part in her destiny. But what that destiny was, she had no clearer idea than she had ever had.

"Come," Raul's voice broke her concentration as his hand rested on her shoulder. "Let us eat while the navigator decides when and where we will make our first jump. There may not be time for a meal for a long while if we end up where I hope we will."

Esme followed him to the royal cabin, where Jaco had already laid a meal, and she was quietly thoughtful, as was Raul, while they dined.

Finally, she dragged her thoughts away from what her destiny might entail, and looked at Raul across the table. His thoughts also, had obviously been far away.

"What are you thinking?" she asked softly.

Raul looked up, and though his expression was impassive, she thought she detected a trace of grimness about him. "Esme, when we have made our first jump, if it is the right one, we may encounter enemy ships. If we do, there will be fighting, and I do not want you in the control cabin should that be the case."

Thorson had explained to Esme about the war between the central government of the Empire and the Rebel planets who, feeling they were being mistreated and abused in the alliance between the worlds, fought to impose their own government over the Empire.

Esme felt a niggling of fear begin inside her. "Should I fear for you?" she asked shakily.

Raul shrugged, and a sardonic smile appeared on his lips. "No more than I should fear for you. If the Condor is hit hard enough to be destroyed, we will enter the spirit world, if it truly exists, together."

Esme felt relieved. She hadn't wanted to hear that Raul might die without taking her with him.

"That is acceptable," she nodded firmly.

Raul raised an eyebrow. "Not to me, little one," he

## DREAMS OF DESTINY

said drily. "I have a great deal more living I want to accomplish before I take the journey to the afterlife."

"As do I," Esme said simply. "But I think we will not be sent on that route any time soon. I meant that should it come to be that I am wrong, I would not wish to survive if you do not. That would not be acceptable."

Raul took a deep breath. It was time to remind her of what the future held for them when they arrived on Genesis and he was positive Esme was not going to want to hear it.

"And if we both survive and make it home," he said with quiet firmness, "you realize, Esme, that we cannot remain together."

Esme froze. A part of her had known. She hadn't forgotten the plan to turn her over to tutors of the mind skills. But once joined with Raul, she had refused to think about it. And she wanted even less to think about it now since his voice had made it sound as though their separation would not be a short one.

"For a while," she spoke through dry lips, refusing to meet his glance.

But Raul could not allow her to hide from reality, any more than he could allow himself to. He reached across the table and took her chin in his large hand, forcing her to look at him.

Esme shivered at the implacable look in his eyes.

"Possibly it will be only for a while." He nodded, his voice firm. "And possibly it will be for much longer than that. It is even possible it might be forever. I am a warrior, remember?"

Stricken, Esme violently shook her head and tried to release herself from his grip. But Raul would not let her go. He continued to hold her eyes. Though there was compassion and regret for her pain in his expression, as well as a bleakness that spelled out that he was no happier than she was at what was to come, there was also no hint that he intended to try to change it.

"Yes, Esme," he said heavily. "You, as I, will do as the Empire requires us to do. Our lives do not belong to us alone."

Esme went still, her green gaze rebellious. Her thoughts were clear to Raul, though he had no mind-reading skills to aid his understanding.

"You cannot rebel alone, Esme," he said softly. "And I will not aid you. I have lived too long at duty's mercy to try to change my nature now."

At that, Esme's eyes swam with moisture, and Raul was on his feet in an instant, to gather her up into his arms.

A moment later, they lay together on the bed and Raul held Esme with tender compassion as she cried the tears that seized her at the thought of losing that which she would keep above all else.

When her sobs diminished, Raul kissed her gently, and looked into her eyes. "No one has guarantee of any more than the present moment, Esme," he said, his voice gentle. "And thus, only a fool wastes what moments he has."

She took his meaning from the nature of his kiss and the way his hands touched her. And though a small corner of her mind refused to release the terror of loss his words had burdened her with, the rest of her followed his lead, taking each moment for everything it was worth and giving to Raul all that he might require to make his own moments more than satisfactory.

\* \* \*

## DREAMS OF DESTINY

Esme, once again strapped down, while less tense than she had been upon lift-off, was nevertheless again anxious. For while it was true that she had traveled among the stars in her dreams, her body had been always earthbound until now. And though it had been explained to her, she did not truly understand how the Condor, which had seemed so large to her at one time and now seemed dwarfed among the immensity surrounding it, could skip across such vast distances which her mind could not yet comprehend truly existed.

As she waited for what Raul called the "jump", she closed her eyes and used her skills to calm herself. And with the calm, the sterile knowledge—sterile because she hadn't as yet comprehended its true meaning—she had been given of how the Condor worked, suddenly joined with her limited knowledge of how her own powers worked, and she felt a glimmer of understanding at last.

Perhaps, Esme thought with a great sense of relief, it was somewhat the same as when she sent her mind soaring away from her body. On such noncorporal forays, the speed of her mind's journeys, while not instantaneous when the distance was great, was greatly increased. She had often wished her body could move so fast. She had wished, in fact, that she did not have to leave her body behind on such journeys, and her instincts told her that such was possible, if she could find the key to unlock that ability within herself.

Raul's people's abilities were apparently the reverse of hers. While they did not have the ability to send their minds soaring—she discounted the mechanical means which sent their words from place to place, since their minds stayed within their own heads during the process—they could send their bodies. As long as they were encased in a protective shell such as the Condor, they could soar over vaster distances than Esme had ever known existed, much less had contemplated taking her body.

Still with her eyes closed, Esme smiled happily. She considered it fortunate indeed that the Master had seen fit to negate the deficiencies in her skills by joining her with those whose skills in the one area she needed were more than sufficient.

"I am glad to see your nervousness decreased, but what has you smiling so smugly, little one?" Raul asked from his couch as he pulled his straps across his broad chest.

Esme opened her eyes, turned her head, and bathed him in the loving glow of her green eyes. "I was seeing the Master's hand in my life," she said simply. And added to herself. *Not only in placing me where I am supposed to be, but in placing me with you, who bring me such joy.*

Raul glanced at her absently. "Who is this Master?" he asked. Then he didn't wait for her answer because the pilot spoke at that moment.

"Ready for the jump, Captain."

"Then let us be on our way," Raul responded calmly. And he was calm, despite any reason to be so in this case, but he was always calm when the die was cast and a choice no longer remained to be sought.

Without coordinates to guide them, the possibilities of where the Condor, and the human cargo it contained, might end up were well-nigh endless. Within a few seconds of real time, they might crash on the surface of some planet, or be torched into a puff of smoke in the center of some blazing sun, or drift directionless beyond recognizable galaxies.

Under such circumstances, the thought of remaining on Esme's planet, returning her to her people and living out the rest of their lives in relative safety, had crossed Raul's mind more than once, especially as the bonds of his feelings for her had tightened about him. But he had never considered such a course seriously, nor did he now that the moment of choice had reached the point of no return. What would be, would be.

"Jumping," the pilot called out.

Esme, who worried over Raul's question concerning the identity of the Master—how could it be possible he did not know of the Master's existence?—automatically extended her hand, and Raul took it. Then, her eyes on the large view screen directly in front of her, she felt at first, a sinking sensation, followed by a wrench of her whole body. She almost panicked when it seemed as though the very cells of her body were trying to drift apart from one another, but even in her frantic effort to hold herself together, her eyes noted the speeding blur of irridescent colors reflected on the view screen.

It was as though the Condor punched its way at blinding speed through a narrow shaft it forced for itself through a solid core of blending colors encompassing every shade Esme had ever seen or imagined and others she'd never dreamed existed.

Then there was an abrupt cessation of movement and the Condor drifted free in the black eternity of limitless space, a blackness that Esme at first thought was total.

Raul's hand moved on hers, in an attempt to gain release, and she became aware that her palm was slick with sweat. Glancing down, however, she sucked in her breath. For the wetness was not sweat, but blood. Her nails had pierced Raul's skin! Quickly, she drew her hand from his and looked up at his face, her expression eloquent with apology.

"I am all right, Esme," he said with a grimacing smile as he flexed his fingers. "I will heal."

"I am sorry," she said.

"Forget it." He wiped the blood from his hand onto his black-covered thigh, then released himself from the straps of the couch.

As he rose, the navigator let out a whoop of relieved joy. "We made it!" he yelled. He quickly adjusted a knob, whereupon the view screen flickered. An instant later, its surface reflected a spiral galaxy spinning in lonely majestic splendor against the blackness.

Raul grunted with satisfaction as he stood, his hands on his hips, staring at the screen. "How long to Genesis?" he asked.

"A matter of days," the navigator said joyfully. "I am plotting the jumps now."

Raul nodded, then went and clapped his left hand on the pilot's shoulder, his right hand on the navigator's. "Well done," he said, grinning, before turning to Esme, his expression resembling a small boy's who has just received a special treat.

And as he did, another chunk of Esme's teachings found recognition inside her, and she understood for the first time the danger they had faced and conquered.

Quickly, she unstrapped herself and ran to him, leaning trembling against his body. He took her under his arm and dropped a kiss on the top of her head.

## DREAMS OF DESTINY

"Relax, little one," he said jovially. "The hard part is over."

But even as he said the words, he realized they encompassed only part of the truth, and his grin faded. When Esme tilted her head back to look up at him, he was smiling still, but she sensed the change in him, and a chill of premonition surged through her briefly before she impatiently shook it away. Raul's words about taking the moment for all it was worth had found a sound place in her heart, and she meant to abide by them.

On that thought, she raised herself on tiptoe and whispered in his ear, and when she was done, his grin had returned.

"In a while, I promise," he whispered back, and his eyes caressed her in a way that made the blood surge through her veins. "Go to the cabin and await me while I check with Jase as to how the ship fared during the jump."

Unmindful of the crew, Esme placed her lips lingeringly against Raul's cheek before she turned away, her eyes already clouding with anticipation, to do his bidding.

As Raul watched her go, his face settled into a bleakly hard expression.

*For this little while*, he thought, one of the few flares of rebellion against duty he had ever experienced flaring through his mind, *as the time of famine approaches hard on our heels, I will free myself of extraneous chores and feed Esme's hunger as long and as fully as she needs. For myself as well will I do this. And if it makes the separation harder, so be it. At least the store of our memories will be full and running over.*

And a short while later, his checks made, his instructions given, he sealed himself and Esme behind the doors of the royal cabin.

She came into his arms and lifted her mouth for his kiss. And afterwards, she murmured, "How long before you must return to duty?"

Raul picked her up in his arms and held her gaze as he carried her to bed.

"This once," he said huskily as he put her upon the coverlet and lay down beside her, "we will forget duty for a while and we will forget time. Until we arrive on Genesis, there will be only the two of us. We have memories of one another to create."

Then he began at once, by the process of melding the two of them into one flesh, the process of also embedding the two of them inseparably in one another's hearts, minds, and memories.

# CHAPTER SEVENTEEN

As Esme felt the Condor jump across yet another boundary of space, she swam partially up from the wild tangle of her senses and was momentarily diverted from her pleasure.

And as he had done twice before, Raul murmured, "It's all right, Esme. Forget the ship. Concentrate on us."

His teeth grazed her over-sensitized engorged nipple, and though she felt a stab of pain, Esme stifled the involuntary cry of protest that welled in her throat. She knew Raul would stop what he did if he became aware he was hurting her, and she did not want him to stop because experience had taught her that the pain would not last. Soon, it would turn to exquisite pleasure.

In truth, even had her expectation not been borne out shortly thereafter, she would not have asked Raul to stop his lovemaking. For had he not shown her, again and again over the past few days, that her body was now as much his to command as it was hers? And had not her voluntary submission to such joint ownership brought emotional rewards that were as compelling as the ecstasy rising now within her?

This time, however, among the many times that Raul had wrung from her a total release of her inhibitions and control by his gentle or forceful use, Esme's body abruptly froze midway along the ever-spiraling road toward the inevitable explosion that marked the end of each such journey with her beloved.

In the space of an instant, and without premeditation, her mind was soaring outside the Condor, into the black void surrounding the ship, and she desperately sought the source of the danger she knew, without knowing how she knew, to be there.

Inside the ship, Esme's body lay stiff and unresponsive. Her eyes stared blankly at nothing. Raul, baffled and terrified by the sudden change in her, shook her shoulders trying to bring her out of her sudden frozen, almost lifeless, immobility. When her condition remained unchanged, he sped to the communications panel to call Thorson.

Outside the ship, Esme's mind was unaware of Raul's terror or of his actions. She had found the danger now. It was cloaked somehow, visible to her mind's eye only as a limned dark bulk that had the shape of another, smaller, starship, and it was still a great distance away, positioned directly behind the Condor. But it was coming fast.

As Esme watched, she saw long, slender lights leave the enemy ship's belly and speed toward her. And though she had never seen missiles before, she somehow knew these approaching emissaries meant death for the Condor and the humans sheltered within its bulk.

There were six of the shapes, strung out in a line two by two. Judging their speed, Esme knew instantly that there was no time to take them one by one, and that controlling two at once would test her strength to the limit. And indeed, it took tremendous energy to break the strong guidance that controlled the first two and to edge their speeding hulks in tandem away from the Condor and into a circling arc.

When the first two were at last turned and were speeding back toward the belly of their mother, she immediately tackled the next two, and felt her strength draining further as she did the same with them. Turning the last two took almost everything she had to give.

As she struggled to return to her body, lest she be separated from it forever, Esme was dimly aware of the terrified consternation rising in the minds of those who had launched the missiles as they watched their deadly toys return to them. But she had no strength to spare pity for the would-be murderers. Rather did she feel only a deep sense of relief that they had failed in their intention.

Then her mind slid back into her body and she fell instantly into a deep, natural sleep.

When Esme finally opened her eyes, Thorson's anxious face filled her gaze. She frowned, wondering why he was there.

"She is awake," Thorson said, his voice trembling with joyful relief, and then, Raul hovered above her.

She smiled as he bent to place his lips against her temple. But when he raised his head, the smile faded. He looked red-eyed and haggard, as though he hadn't slept for days.

"What ails you, my heart?" she asked anxiously, struggling to sit up. Raul's large hands on her shoulders pushed her back upon the bed, and at discovering that her body was weak and unwilling to struggle, she stopped trying to. Raul sat down beside her.

"I am fine now," he said gently. "And you? How do you feel?"

Esme looked at him in surprise. "I? Why, I am only a little weak." She smiled, waveringly. "Which is perhaps not surprising after the hard use you have been making of . . ."

But then her memory returned with stunning force, and she struggled against Raul's restraining hands as her eyes shifted in horror around the royal cabin.

"What is it, Esme?" Raul spoke urgently as he contained her struggles. "Tell me."

"The other ship!" Esme gasped, subsiding again as her strength reached its limits. "Did I truly kill it, or does it stalk us even now?"

She saw Raul and Thorson exchange a grim look. Then Raul's gaze was again upon her, and she quailed a little at what she saw in his considering blue eyes.

"If you mean," he said, his words coolly precise, "that the explosion we recorded on our rear yesterday was a ship that you somehow attempted to destroy, we cannot be certain that you succeeded. Since our sensors did not detect its approach, it means little that we did not detect its retreat, and it may still be out there somewhere."

As he saw that his last words had evoked Esme's

fear again, Raul softened his voice and added, "However, from the violence of the explosion which we did detect, I think it unlikely that is the case. I think you did, indeed, kill it."

Esme's frantic heartbeat subsided a little. Closing her eyes, she relaxed against the bed for a moment to regain her strength. However, when she opened her eyes and saw again that considering, almost cold look in Raul's eyes, she lost some of her composure.

"What is wrong?" she asked, softly anxious. "What have I done that makes you . . ." Her words faltered as she realized at last, even without trying to probe his mind, which she knew would be closed to her in any case, what was behind Raul's look. She sighed and shook her head, her gaze pleading.

"I did not tell you I had to leave you because I did not know myself what was happening. Suddenly, in the midst of our lovemaking, my mind was outside the ship dealing with the situation," she explained. "I do not know how I knew the threat existed. Such has never happened to me before. But there was no time to hesitate nor to spare in seeking consultation with you."

Her last words brought a smile to Raul's lips but it was not a pleasant smile nor was it one of complete understanding.

"Perhaps then," he said softly, "if we can only find out how to duplicate your talent, there will be no further need for warriors. We can simply transport you and those like you to the battle scene and take our ease as you perform our duties."

Raul fell silent then, staring at her in an objectively thoughtful way that finished the substitution of ice for warm blood in Esme's veins. A sense of impending

335

loss was heavy upon her.

"Raul," she said, softly pleading. "Please . . ."

"Do not think I am not grateful," he broke in, though to Esme's ears, he sounded not the least grateful. "I suppose we would all be dead had you not acted. And when you have rested, I will have from you an account of exactly what transpired. But now," he concluded, getting to his feet and standing over her with his hands twisted in the weapons belt he wore which Esme had not seen on him often, "you will rest while I oversee our approach to Genesis. I will speak to you again before we set down."

Another moment and he was gone, leaving Esme with Thorson, who was staring at her in a way that brought her almost as much discomfort as had Raul's stare.

"We are there then?" she asked dully.

"Aye," Thorson nodded. He came closer and stood over the bed.

"Sit down!" Esme snapped, her temper fraying. "It makes my head ache to look up at you!"

As he sat, Esme saw in his mind that he had obeyed quickly because he feared she would force him, and she closed her eyes and shook her head in disbelief.

"Am I a monster now in your eyes as well as Raul's?" she asked, and, opening her eyes, her gaze upon Thorson contained bitterness.

Thorson hesitated, then smiled. He shook his head. "Not to me, Esme. Never to me."

Esme read into his words the unspoken statement that Thorson might be the only one who now viewed her so generously. She looked away, her heart torn with distress.

At seeing her distress, Thorson's love for her dispelled his jealousy of Raul temporarily. "The captain will, perhaps, have reconsidered his present mood when he returns," he suggested consolingly. "It frightened him badly when your mind departed your body, Esme. You were as one dead. It always frightens him when you do something like that. And in this case," he added, at seeing that Esme's expression didn't lighten, "I think he was afraid he was responsible for your mental retreat."

At that, Esme turned her head, her gaze puzzled. "What do you mean?" she asked.

Thorson clenched his jaw, and his eyes grew cooler. "The two of you had been in here for four days before whatever happened, happened. He did not spare you physically during those days. You said so yourself. I imagine he thought he had taken from you more than you had the strength to give."

He shrugged and looked away from the incredulous expression in Esme's eyes.

"And then," he continued, "after all that misdirected anger, fear, and self-disgust, you come awake and tell him you saved his ship, his crew, and himself." He shrugged again. "How do you expect him to feel?"

Esme hesitated, then shook her head. "No differently than he does, I suppose," she said with soft regret. And then her voice tightened with hurt anger. "But it is a hard thing to bear knowing you have done the only thing you could—the right thing!" she interposed with a defiant glance that lasted only for a moment. Then her face crumpled, and she finished as tearfully as a punished child, "And have only the resentment of one you love as a reward."

Thorson almost laughed at Esme's expression. But

he thought better of such a reaction and reached to pat her hand. "As I said," he reminded her, "he has been half-frightened out of his mind and filled with self-blame and now he feels useless as well. It is the captain's habit to be in charge, to be a protector of others. It is not his habit to think of himself as needing protection, especially the protection of a woman. And in your case, you are not just any woman. You are *his* woman, and therefore he feels doubly protective of you. So it will require a great deal of mental adjustment on his part, Esme. Try to understand."

He hesitated, then added, "He is also tired, Esme. He slept not at all while you were under."

At that, Esme's face softened, as did her heart. Then, with a sigh of resigned acceptance, she carefully sat up, motioned Thorson to get out of her way, swung her bare legs over the side of the bed, and motioned Thorson to help her up.

When she was on her feet and had stopped wavering, she pointed. "Help me to the sanitation chamber, Thorson," she said wearily. "It seems even a monster's body has functions that cannot be ignored. I also would like to wash and tidy myself before Raul returns."

And shutting her mind firmly to the jealousy she felt rise in Thorson's mind at having to help her get ready to receive his perceived rival, she concentrated on the simple demands of her body, not on the complicated emotions of men.

Had there been any choice in the matter, Raul would have denied to himself and to everyone else the extent of Esme's talents. But even if Thorson had not heard her words, and even if Raul had been able to pretend he hadn't heard them himself, and even if the telepaths he would turn Esme over to had not been able to discover the true extent of her abilities, Raul could not, in all good conscience, conceal her gifts from those who controlled the Empire. His government was at war and Esme had just proved she might be of valuable use in that war.

As he prowled the control cabin, however, he delayed returning to her to hear the story of her experience, even though his ship was safely in a crowded orbit over his home planet. His mind and heart were in turmoil and it was not only the thought of his and Esme's impending separation which rode him hard. The realization of his own inadequacy as compared to Esme's talents upset his very sense of self-worth. And the fact that he would shortly have no control over what was to happen to either of them did nothing to repair the damage to his self-respect.

His men gave him a wide berth. The scowl on his face was ferociously intimidating; the tension in his coiled body was palpable and dangerous. And when he finally, with a muttered, violent curse that rang throughout the control cabin, left them, they breathed a collective sigh of relief.

Esme was alone, bathed, dressed and rested, by the time Raul rejoined her. And despite the tense aura he exuded from every pore, she left the bed and went to him, to stand silently with her arms around his large body, her head on his chest, willing him to acknowledge that her welcome was the same as ever, as was her love for him.

At last, Raul gave a great, shuddering sigh and enfolded her in his arms. Esme melted into him. The knot of apprehension in her stomach relaxed, and the ache of fear in her chest was swallowed by the abundance of her relief.

For a long time, they stood. Esme lifted her head, her eyes pleading, and Raul gave her, without reluctance, what he saw in her gaze she badly needed. Then he picked her up in his arms and carried her to the two-cushioned couch where he sat with her on his lap.

Esme had seldom used the couch, and she did not want its use now. She would much have preferred Raul to take her to bed. But she said nothing yet, merely waited, her gaze solemn on his stern face, for him to speak.

"Tell me," he finally ordered.

Esme hesitated. "If you would allow it," she said softly, "your purpose might be better served if I showed you instead."

Raul frowned and stiffened. "Let you in my mind you mean?" he asked.

Esme nodded. "I would not abuse the privilege," she whispered. "I have never done so. You have my word on it."

Raul knew she spoke the truth, but he remained reluctant to have his inner privacy so invaded. Only once before, during his evaluation for command, had he allowed such a thing. He had loathed the crawling about in his mind that had taken place then, and he expected to like it no better now, even though the invader wore Esme's lovely face.

Nevertheless, his experience of the value of firsthand knowledge in battle at last caused him to agree. Reluctantly, he let down his shield and sat stiffly, his expression redolent with distaste, as Esme began.

Taking a chance she feared might prove unworth the risk, Esme went slowly, starting by bathing Raul's mind with the soothing warmth of her love for him. Her heart leapt with joy as she felt him relax and saw in his clear gaze a lessening of his distaste for what was happening.

Taking another chance, she re-created in his mind the lovemaking they had been sharing when the danger had appeared. She let him see with absolute clarity the feelings and sensations that had consumed her during their lovemaking. She did her task so well, that she felt the heat of his maleness begin to rise in his mind and in his body, and her own began to take fire from his.

"Esme, stop," he said thickly, gripping her arms and giving her a small warning shake. "Get on with it."

Sighing, Esme reluctantly obeyed and in a few swift seconds of clear re-creation, she showed him exactly what had happened. When she was done, she was amused to find that though his mind had been diverted from what she'd shared with him earlier, his body was still hard and pulsing.

At seeing her expression, Raul was firm with her. "Get out of my mind, Esme," he said quietly, and at the same moment, he raised his shield again.

Hurt, Esme withdrew from him, both mentally and physically. She would have risen from his lap, but he held her where she was. Absently, he began to run one hand over her silk-clad thigh, creating a breathlessness inside her that while predictable, in this instance annoyed her. Briefly, she allowed herself to resent his power over her emotions. But her resentment died when he spoke, his voice both worried and resigned.

"They have something new, then. I heard that one of our scientists working on an anti-sensing stealth project defected to the Rebels. It seems that he took with him more than we knew."

Esme sat silent, watching him and when his eyes pinned her, she felt a sudden dart of apprehension.

"You will have to show others what you have just shown me, Esme," he said. "And once you have . . ." His voice trailed off.

"Once I have?" she prodded him out of his silence.

Raul shrugged, and the expression in his eyes was bleak. "Once you have, your life will no longer be your own. Nor will it be mine."

Esme swallowed, then started to shake her head. Raul threaded his hand through her thick hair and stopped the motion.

"Aye, Esme," he said.

There was no arguing with that tone in his voice, and the words of rebellion died on Esme's lips. In any case, it would have done her little good to try to speak, because Raul's mouth was abruptly on hers, draining all rebellion from her with a passion that left her weak and trembling.

He stood up with her in his arms and carried her to the bed. They lay entwined, naked, on the coverlet and Raul's mouth was again plundering hers with an urgency that had a hint of desperation in it.

Esme, unable this time to dispel the silent wail of loss within her, gave her cooperation as best she could, but without the wholeheartedness of former times.

Dissatisfied with this departure from her normal manner, Raul raised himself on his elbows and stared into her eyes. At seeing the extent of her pain, he abandoned his last defense against her.

"Mayhap," he said, his voice thickened and gentle, "if I open my shield again as I just did, you will be able to abandon this withholding of yourself that plagues me so severely?"

Esme's wide green eyes opened to their limits. She could not believe, at first, that he was offering what she thought he was. But when she tested the matter, hesitantly at first, and saw the same raging sense of loss that was within her own mind in Raul's, coupled with a need for her that made her shudder with longing, she at last believed.

She could do no other than match Raul's gift. And so, with much tenderness, and with Raul's cooperation, she pushed their twin griefs out of the way, until only their mutual need and love for one another stood dominant in both their minds.

The coupling that followed began, in a way, like the mating of two virgins, hesitantly exploring. But as their mutual trust and confidence grew, they leapt, with a speed that left them both dazed, across the bridge of previously unimagined possibilities to the platform of full-blown realization, and seized, without compunction, that which was now much desired.

# CHAPTER EIGHTEEN

Esme concluded her tearful good-byes to the crew of the Condor, then stepped with Raul for the first time upon Genesis.

Esme had looked forward to again touching soil and grass with her feet and smelling flowers and breathing fresh air. But she stepped from the ship onto concrete, while the smell in the air bore no sweetness of natural vegetation. In fact, there was nothing of the Master's creation in sight anywhere other than the blue sky overhead.

Thorson had taught Esme a great deal about Raul's home, but her studies had not truly prepared her for the shocking reality of it. The holographs Thorson had shown her of the huge buildings crowded together had not really indicated their intimidating size and intricate construction. Her journey in the Condor had not been as frightening as being whisked at blurring speed in a small mechanical vehicle to Raul's luxurious quarters. Her book knowledge of the vast numbers of people who inhabited Genesis had not told her that she would feel suffocated by their overwhelming presence.

Raul was aware of her bewildered state, and he held her hand and stayed close by her side as she clung to him tightly.

When she and Raul were at last alone in his quarters, she felt a little better. Her surroundings were still strange, but the accommodations on the Condor had better prepared her for this environment than what lay outside of Raul's quarters.

Because he knew how much she was suffering from culture shock, Raul was reluctant to leave Esme as soon as he had to, but after changing into a formal uniform, he prepared to leave.

Holding her trembling body tightly in his arms at the door of his apartment, he said, "I'm sorry, Esme. But I must report to my superiors. It is required. But I will be back in time for last-meal with you. Meantime, explore your new home here. Get comfortable. Try to relax. You will get used to all this, believe me."

At the moment, Esme believed no such thing, but she did not wish to distress Raul by crying like a child, so she pasted a wavering smile on her lips, kissed him good-bye, and allowed him to take his leave without protest.

Alone, she thoroughly explored her new abode. Since she had prepared no meals on the Condor, she recognized none of the equipment in the eating area and knew she would have to ask Raul to explain it to her before she could prepare his meals. The living area

## DREAMS OF DESTINY

was comfortably furnished with a couch large enough even for Raul to sleep on, two chairs, some scattered tables, and a large view screen she feared to touch lest she damage it.

The bedroom contained a large bed, two tables, a chair and an enclosed area wherein she found many of the silk robes Raul favored, shoes and some of his uniforms.

After exploring the bathroom and experimenting with controls that were different than the ones on the Condor, she wandered back to the living area and sat in a chair in front of a large clear window, gazing with mingled dread and fascination at the small corner of Genesian life visible to her.

After a while, she sadly realized that she felt a thousand times more lonely here, on Raul's world, than she had ever felt upon the high meadow, or even within the confines of the Settlement where people shunned her.

When Raul returned to his quarters for last-meal, she greeted him with a fervor unusual even for her, and he, understanding her state of mind, first eased her tension with his lovemaking, then showed her how to prepare a meal in his kitchen.

As they ate, and later in bed when they had retired for the night, he told her in detail of the benefits to be had from living on a civilized world, hoping to make her more comfortable with her situation.

But though Esme listened intently and asked many questions, she still considered that the only benefit to be had on Genesis as far as she was concerned, was Raul's presence here with her.

And even that benefit was withdrawn only three days after their arrival at Raul's home.

\* \* \*

Raul paused inside the door the green-uniformed guard had opened for them, and Esme tightened her fingers on his forearm. The room was white-walled, gray-carpeted and almost wholly taken up by a huge gray plasti-steel table surrounded by matching chairs.

Milling behind the chairs and around the table, talking in whispers, stood a number of men variously garbed, some in the uniforms of the various Genesian military services. Also there were four women, all more plainly dressed than Esme. Everyone grew quiet and stared as Raul drew Esme forward to greet the high counselor, who stood in a simple white silk robe at the head of the table.

Esme tried to divert her mind from the crawling sensation induced by being the object of so many eyes. She wondered if she had been wrong to wear the prettiest of the flowing, irridescent, diaphanous gowns Raul had ordered sent to his private apartments in his Service's complex immediately after they had arrived there. Surely, the expressions of the plainly dressed women in this room were disapproving of her? True, she wore no skin paint as they did. Raul had not known what to order for her and had said she had no need of such adornment in any case. But. . . .

Her attention was diverted as they arrived at the head of the table and Raul spoke to the high counselor.

"Sir, I present to you Esme," he said, his voice quiet and respectful.

"Indeed, Captain," the white-haired, white-robed man responded, his tone, and the look in his amused, sparkling blue eyes, kind. "Welcome to Genesis, Esme."

He extended a hand that seemed much more aged

than his unlined face. Upon the middle finger was a ring mounted with a large black stone, and on the stone was carved the image of a bird Esme had never seen, but which Raul had explained was a sesphawk, symbol of the Empire.

As Raul had instructed her to do, Esme bent one knee in a graceful curtsy, took the extended hand in her right one, and pressed her unpainted lips lightly to the surface of the black stone. Straightening, she would have released the high counselor's hand, but he surprised her by sliding his fingers around hers and keeping hold of her. Then he pulled her close and bending from his great height, kissed her unrouged cheek.

Flustered, Esme glanced away from the twinkling look in the high counselor's blue eyes to Raul. His expression was impassive, but she sensed that he was as surprised as she was by the high counselor's unusual greeting.

"Thank you, Raul," the high counselor then said in a tone of dismissal, before he returned his attention to Esme. Pointing her toward a chair next to his, he said, "Come, Esme. Sit. I have a few words to say before you give us your demonstration."

Esme sat, reluctantly, for Raul now stood with his back to the wall behind her, where she would be unable to see his face without craning around conspicuously as she was doing now. He had an absolutely impassive expression on his face and his arms were folded across his broad chest in what Esme knew was the "at rest" position in the Service when one was in the company of one's superiors.

She gave him a pleading look with her eyes but he stared back without expression. Esme sighed with inward resignation. He had told her that he would be unable to help her at this gathering of the highest governors and militarists and scientists of the Empire who were based on Genesis, but she had hoped at least to be able to see his face and perhaps take comfort, if not cues to guide her, from him.

The high counselor rapped his knuckles lightly on the surface of the table in front of him, and the rest of the company, who had seated themselves around the table, fell silent immediately.

"Gentlemen, . . . gentlewomen," he began speaking in a quiet, but attention-holding voice, "this is Esme, to whom we owe a great debt and may owe still a greater one in the future. Greet her with the respect she is due, please."

At that, Esme was again the focus of all eyes, and everyone at the table spoke in unison. "Greetings, High Lady," they said.

Esme blinked. "High Lady" was a term Thorson had explained was reserved for those women who, by dint of birth or accomplishment, rested on the upper tier of Empire society. She was astonished to be so regarded and just in time, remembered the proper response.

"My greetings in return, Gentlemen, gentlewomen," she said, her voice low and hesitant. Darting her eyes to those of the high counselor, she saw that he was smiling at her approvingly. She swallowed, and aware that her former nervousness was on the rise due to her bewilderment over the way she had been addressed, she quickly used her mind to calm her nerves as best she could.

"Esme will, in a few moments, show us the answer

## DREAMS OF DESTINY

to a question that has been greatly troubling us in recent weeks," the high counselor resumed speaking. "As you know, we have had scattered reports of unusual attacks upon our cargo and battle craft, attacks where there apparently was no enemy ship in the area. In fact,"—he nodded at Raul, whom Esme automatically turned to see, and whose stance had changed not at all, not even when he became the object of all eyes in the room—"it is because of one such attack that we have added a new ally to our ranks, Esme."

Esme, after one last lingering, longing look at Raul, turned back around as the high counselor went on.

"The Condor, which Captain Raul commanded on its journey to carry my son to visit his mother, and its escort, were engaged in battle upon their return. But after apparently routing the enemy, the Condor was attacked mysteriously and sustained major damage. She jumped into unknown space. Fortunately, after landing on an unidentified planet after the jump, in order to make repairs, Esme appeared on the Condor's threshhold, so to speak. And it is to her we owe the explanation of what new weapon the Rebels have been using against us."

He turned to Esme then and reaching for her hand, drew her to her feet. "Esme, as you have been told," he resumed addressing the group, who were silently hanging on every word, "is a telepath of extraordinary, if untutored, abilities. When she has finished her task here with us today, she will receive the tutoring she so richly deserves, and since I am told she learns at a pace as extraordinary as her abilities, the Empire will soon, I am confident, be blessed with a new weapon of its own against our ungrateful brothers."

He turned to Esme then, and his eyes were warm and kindly upon her. In a low voice, for her ears only, he said, "Esme, I presume Captain Raul has told you that most of us here are possessed of mind shields, which we will lower now so that you might show us what happened seven days ago while you were aboard the Condor. I assume he has also told you that those with your abilities do not, without invitation, invade unnecessarily the minds of those unblessed with shields. So once you have finished your demonstration, please be so good as to withdraw immediately from the minds of those who have no protection from your gifts. Those of us who do will, of course, immediately shield again when you are finished."

Without waiting for her assent, he turned back to the group.

"Gentlemen, gentlewomen," he said in the tones of an order, "those of you who have them, please let down your mind shields now. Esme." He then nodded at her, and resumed his seat.

Esme, who remained standing, twisted her fingers together in front of her waist to still their shaking, and one by one, looked at the people circling the table, lightly probing each mind to test its openness. Most of the thoughts there were predictable. Intense curiosity was in the forefront of all of these minds.

In some of the men, however, she found another sort of curiosity that brought a flush to her cheeks. She discovered they were all aware of her relationship with Raul, and almost all were speculating rather lewdly about the private details of it. Esme quickly went on to the minds of the women around the table.

All but one of the women were offhandedly jealous of her beauty and her place in the spotlight in equal proportions. The remaining woman, much to Esme's distress, was jealous only on one count—Esme's relationship with Raul. Not only did the woman have feelings for Raul that Esme would much have preferred to remain unaware of, it was clear that she had once, briefly, shared with him the same sort of relationship that Esme did now. The image, sharp and clear, of the two of them in bed brought a knifelike pain into Esme's heart that was only partly eased by the fact that it had been Raul who had broken off the relationship.

By force of will, Esme tore her mind from that of her would-be rival's, and moved on to the man's who sat next to her. And there she paused again, puzzled and wary. For the man had put only part of his shield down, the rest of what he thought and felt was mostly hidden from her. But Esme was sure she felt a hint of antipathy connected with those thoughts and feelings he hid.

Then she was startled as she felt his voice, drawling and amused, in her mind. *Come now, Esme. You know it is impolite to linger. You and I will deal with one another later. For now, get on with it.*

Shaken by the knowledge that this particular man had obviously read her thoughts, and not knowing how to respond to his comment, she did as she was bid and, perfunctorily now, finished rounding the table. But there was a lingering disquiet inside her that she had to push aside in order to perform the demonstration she was not even sure how to handle.

Experimenting, she flashed, on a broad wave, an

## Jackie Casto

image of the Condor hanging in deep space.

"Is there anyone who does not see what I am projecting?" she asked politely.

There was no response, and much relieved, she began the demonstration. She saw no reason to share with this group what she had been doing at the moment of her apprehension of danger.

Swiftly, she visualized the sequence of events, and just as swiftly, withdrew from their minds.

At feeling her departure from his mind, the high counselor spoke to the group. "Any questions?"

One of the scientists nodded. "Please, Esme," he said politely. "You were so fast. I would like to see it again, very slowly."

Obligingly, Esme projected her mind's images again, much more slowly this time. At the moment where she was breaking the control of the first two missiles, the scientist spoke. "Stop! Hold it there. Try to show how you did this."

Esme complied as best she could. But it was very difficult to explain to herself, much less anyone else, an operation of her mind that had been so automatic as to be almost beyond definition.

The scientist was obviously not satisfied, but when Esme informed him that she had done the best she could, he shrugged and bade her go on. He stopped her again, however, time and again during each stage of the visualization. And when she was done, the scientist looked, frowning, at the man who had greeted Esme mentally and told her not to linger in his mind.

"Laon, can you explain what she did better than she has been able to?"

## DREAMS OF DESTINY

Laon shrugged. "Not at this point," he said in a lazy, drawling voice that matched the mental one he had used in speaking to Esme mind to mind earlier. "Perhaps, after working with her for a while . . ." His words trailed off and he smiled directly at Esme with a smile that made her uneasy. "It may be, however," he drawled, "that Esme has more to teach us than we have to teach her. And mayhap, what she does is unteachable."

Esme was not at all pleased to discover that this Laon was obviously going to be one of her tutors. Already she had no desire to spend much, if any, time in his company. Nor did she wish, for reasons she was unsure of, to teach him, in turn, what she did or how she did it even if it were possible.

She determined, then and there, that whether such an exchange was possible, when it came her turn to impart knowledge, she would remain deliberately obtuse until she had a firmer sense of what lay behind Laon's shields. She felt a strong sense of danger where this Laon was concerned.

"Well, Gentlemen, gentlewomen" the high counselor asked, "any further questions?"

When there were none, the high counselor nodded and turned to Esme.

"You will be glad to know, my dear, that since your timely destruction of that enemy ship, there have been no further attacks of that sort on our fleet. We can only assume that they have few of these stealth ships to use at present, and are now afraid that we have the means to destroy those few they do have. Therefore, as you embark upon your studies with Laon and his people, you will say nothing to anyone other than

Laon about what you did. Though our people will no doubt discover the truth sooner or later, it will be much to our advantage if the Rebels continue to think we have found the means to foil their secret weapon. We need time to speed our own work on the technology they already have, as well as to learn if you can teach our telepaths to do what you have done. If we cannot do either of these things, Esme," he said gravely, "the Empire is in dire jeopardy. Therefore, you will, if you please, begin your studies and your instruction at once."

Even as the high counselor stood politely and raised her from her seat, then gestured at Raul to take her, Esme was filled with despair. Raul had warned her that she might have to leave him after this meeting but she had not wanted to believe him.

"With your permission, High Counselor?"

The lazy, drawling voice Esme was coming already to dislike intensely spoke, and as she turned to look at its owner, she found that he also was on his feet.

"Yes, yes, Laon," the high counselor nodded. "Go with them. There is no time to waste."

Esme's bitter dismay was acute. She wanted time with Raul alone, time to say a proper good-bye, though she intended, with all her will, that their separation be only temporary.

She said nothing, however, as she placed her hand on Raul's arm and allowed him to walk her down the length of the table, where Laon, with a lazy, slanting smile, joined them.

Once the large wooden doors had closed behind them and the three of them were outside in the gray-carpeted hallway, however, Esme turned to Raul,

## DREAMS OF DESTINY

whose eyes gave nothing away, and started to speak. "Raul, I—"

Laon interrupted. "I will take her now, Captain," he said, placing his hand on Esme's arm, his grip firm. "You may return to your duties."

Esme froze, and suddenly, she was no longer the nervous, frightened little barbarian that she knew Laon considered her to be. She turned, her expression set and cold, and with the merest flick of her mind, flung his hand from her arm.

Laon was startled momentarily then hostile. He took hold of her arm again, and this time, Esme had more difficulty releasing herself. When she finally managed it, she had the feeling that Laon had allowed it for the sake of propriety, rather than continue to struggle with her there in the hallway under the eyes of the curious guards.

"Leave us!" she hissed at him, both mentally and verbally.

Laon's face whitened under the strength of her attack for a second but he did not back down. "I cannot!" he said, his voice clipped and cold. He then looked at Raul in a meaningful way.

Raul's jaw was clenched, and his eyes were as coldly blue as Laon's were coldly black. He was holding onto his temper by a thread.

"Captain," Laon said, his voice a grating command, "if you cannot convince Esme to leave you, I shall be forced to use means to enforce your separation that neither she nor you will like."

Esme, shaking now, looked from one to the other. Their mutual hostility was like a wall of hot ice shimmering between them, and it finally occurred to her she must take care on Raul's behalf. Laon's power on this world, at least concerning her own disposition, obviously outweighed Raul's.

"If," she quickly said to Laon before Raul could speak, "you will allow us a few moments of privacy in which to say my farewell, I will go with you willingly. Otherwise, you will have to force me, and I do not mean that force will be required only to get me where it is you want me to go. My continuing cooperation must also then be forced, that is, if you have the power to do such."

She did not know the extent of Laon's mental powers, but judging from the difficulty she had had in removing his hand from her arm, they were most likely considerable. Still, if they extended as far as hers did, the need for her help would be nonexistent, so she felt safe in challenging him. She thought he might find it very difficult to explain to the High Counselor and the High Council why she had suddenly become uncooperative.

He regarded her from those now flatly cold black eyes, and for a moment, she felt him in her mind, digging at her thoughts, a process she had never undergone involuntarily. Esme was appalled by the feeling of violation his inspection produced within her. She felt helpless, vulnerable, enraged. For the first time in her life, she understood what it was like to have one's inner privacy stripped bare.

Since Esme had never in her life needed a mental shield, she had never constructed one. Therefore, her only defense was to cloud her thoughts, obscuring them with visions of the High Counselor, the others in the room they'd just left, anything she could think of that would conceal whatever it was this Laon sought within her.

He smiled and withdrew from her mind. Esme shivered, for the smile had been one of lazy triumph. She had never felt so vulnerable, not even in the desert when the sun and sand had sought her life.

"Certainly, High Lady," he drawled with amused contempt. "I will visit the sanitation chamber, thereby giving you and your captain a few moments to say your farewells."

He was barely out of earshot before Raul turned her roughly to him, his hands hard on her upper arms. "You should not have challenged him, Esme," he said low-voiced through clenched teeth. His eyes were fairly blazing. Esme had never seen him so angry. "That one"—he tossed his head contemptuously at where Laon was disappearing behind a door—"can make your life hell, and there is nothing I can do to stop it!"

Esme knew then, the source of Raul's anger. Used to command, he found it exceedingly galling to be in a situation he was helpless to change, especially a situation involving her where he thought she was being treated shabbily by a man he despised but could not challenge.

"Raul, listen to me!" she said quickly, holding his eyes with her own. "I do not trust him!"

Raul looked impatient. "I have no love for him myself, Esme," he grated, "but he and his people are the only ones who can teach you what you do not yet know about your own skills, and you are going to have to deal with him!"

Esme shook her head. A great stubbornness, a great

**Jackie Casto**

fear rose inside her. Raul didn't understand, and she had no time to explain.

"Raul, teach me the mind shield!" she begged. "Now! This minute!"

Raul's anger drained as he looked at her in astonishment. "But you already know it," he said slowly. "You must know it."

Esme shook her head, growing desperate. "No, I do not!" she said fiercely. "I have never needed it before but I need it now, Raul! I need it desperately."

"But there is no time!" he responded, frowning.

"There is if you will open your mind to me," Esme whispered, all her fear in her voice. "Please, Raul. I know now why you do not like to . . . I would not ask it of you if I had a choice, but—"

Raul interrupted. "Esme, they will teach you that at—"

"No!" she broke in. "I need it now!" Tears choked her voice and fell from her eyes, and Raul immediately took her into his arms.

"All right, Esme," he said soothingly.

Esme sensed Laon returning and rising on her toes, she brought her mouth a breath away from Raul's. "Now," she said, begging him with her eyes and her voice. "While I kiss you good-bye, open your mind to me and give me what I need."

"Esme—"

But Esme cut off whatever he'd been about to say with her lips on his, and after a second of hesitancy, she felt Raul's mind open to her. Quickly, deftly, she took the instruction she needed and afterward bathed his mind in turn with her love and her agonizing sense of loss over their impending separation.

## DREAMS OF DESTINY

Raul, whose sense of propriety was much offended by having to conduct their farewell in an open hallway with the eyes of half a dozen guards witnessing their kiss, forgot propriety under the strength of Esme's emotions. As his arms tightened around her and his mouth took command of hers, he sent her a mental message. *It is only for a while, Esme. Somehow, we will be reunited. I will not live my life without you indefinitely. That I vow.*

*And I echo your vow,* Esme responded mentally, with fervent purpose in her tone.

"Please, Captain," Laon drawled coldly from behind Esme, "have you forgotten the demands of propriety entirely?"

Raul deliberately paid Laon no mind. When Esme's arms around his neck would have loosened, he merely held her more firmly, his kiss as invasive and intimate and leisurely as though they shared a private bed rather than a public hallway.

Esme, delighted by Raul's defiance of Laon, took his lead and responded in kind. And for her part, she made no effort to construct the shield Raul had taught her. If Laon wanted to eavesdrop on what she felt for the man who made him, with all his mental powers, seem sorely inadequate by comparison, let him.

Slowly, Raul broke the kiss but he held her eyes for a long moment afterwards, his gaze loving. "My heart goes with you, Esme," he murmured almost beneath his breath. "Keep it safe until we meet again."

"If you will do the same with mine," she whispered back, her voice breaking at the end.

"Be assured of it."

Then Raul reluctantly let her go, took a step back,

turned, and strode away, his carriage powerful and straight.

Esme watched him until he turned a corner and disappeared from her sight. Then, very slowly, constructing her shield as she did so, she turned to face Laon.

His smile was cold. "Is that the best you can do?" he said, his voice lazily contemptuous.

Esme knew he spoke of her as yet inadequate shield. He had penetrated it and was rambling in her mind but not so easily and thoroughly as he had before. And she took care that he learned nothing from her thoughts that she did not want him to know.

She returned his smile, her own as cold as his. "For the moment," she agreed. "But now that I have the fundamentals, Laon, I will build upon them. Before this day is ended, you will no longer trample uninvited where you do not belong."

For a long moment, green eyes met black in a silent, hostile duel. Then Laon began to smile more naturally and finally to chuckle.

Turning from Laon, she faced forward and gazed sightlessly down the hallway. As they walked toward a waiting craft, she worked hard at improving the mental shield Raul had taught her. For she was now convinced that she must use every means available to protect herself, and possibly Raul, from the manipulations of a man she suspected could make poor Bazil seem seriously deficient in the practice of evil.

Laon was obviously revered and trusted by the High Council. And Raul, too, though he liked Laon not at all, seemed not to feel that there was anything seriously untrustworthy about him.

But Esme felt differently. At that moment, Laon seemed to her to be the personification of the Master's enemy, which meant he was her enemy as well. Of that one thing, among a wealth of uncertainty on other matters, was she sure. Therefore, she prepared.

BE SURE TO READ . . .

*DAUGHTER OF DESTINY*
by
Jackie Casto

The stunning sequel to
*DREAMS OF DESTINY*

Coming in December 1990
from
LEISURE BOOKS